One Flew over the
Banyan Tree

One Flew over the Banyan Tree

A Novel

ALAN JANSEN

ONE FLEW OVER THE BANYAN TREE

iUniverse books may be ordered through booksellers or by contacting:

iUniverse
1663 Liberty Drive
Bloomington, IN 47403
www.iuniverse.com
1-800-Authors (1-800-288-4677)

ISBN: 978-1-4917-6896-9 (sc)
ISBN: 978-1-4917-6897-6 (e)

Library of Congress Control Number: 2015909635

Print information available on the last page.

iUniverse rev. date: 09/21/2015

To Mummy – in another dimension, you will smile...

CHAPTER 1

The Dragon's Den, Bellakay, and the Nameless

There was an old lady who lived in a shoe.
She had so many children she didn't know what to do.
She gave them some broth without any bread
Then whipped them all soundly and put them to bed.

DAWN HAD BROKEN OUT AT Jellicoe Junction – the jostling, palpitating, microcosm in Portopo, the capital city of the island of Victoria. Although it was somewhat dark, a golden aureole bathed the edge of the distant horizon, signalling oncoming daylight, rising and expanding as the clock ticked on and a new working day beckoned.

Jellicoe Junction was not by any means the most prosperous of the city's urban settlements – not by a far cry. Vicious tongues from the more prestigious parts of the city referred to its inhabitants as 'those morons', considering the community gormless – beyond self-betterment. It was a hub of bustling, steaming, vibrating life – a genuine working-class haven – dotted with small industries, a few government offices, and strangely enough in comparison, one of the island's most prestigious boys' schools.

The Junction's name puzzled many, prompting long and hefty

1

discussions at the dilapidated illegal restaurant situated beside the great banyan tree (*Ficus benghalensis*) that grew near the outskirts of the marketplace, which for want of a signboard, was affectionately called the Nameless. The impoverished customers at the Nameless were quite frequently represented at breakfast, most grateful for the cheap prices charged by the establishment's popular and colourful owner, Sonny. Additionally, the breakfast sessions proved an excellent tonic for and escape from the grinding ennui of life, which the majority of the clientele – the 'breakfast-eaters', as they were sometimes popularly called – found unbearable. Cheerful banter and humorous anecdotes were the order of the day – before, during, and after the breakfast meal, although, on occasions, well-meant discussions would spill over into thunderous arguments and tempers would become more than a touch frayed. Sometimes the breakfast-eaters' palavers became so intense that arguments turned into fist fights or wrestling bouts, resulting in an odd injured limb or, at the worst, a blackened eye, but never anything beyond. Sonny would often intervene and break up the combatants if things went too far, using the threat of expulsion to drive his point home. Of all of Sonny's known threats, expulsion was the one most dreaded by the breakfast-eaters. To a man, they all loved the banter, atmosphere, and camaraderie prevailing within 'their' own little microcosm – expulsion spelling out a major catastrophe. In any event, they had, in fact, nowhere else to go, as they were unable to pay double and treble for breakfasts at the more orthodox restaurants in the city. The simple breakfasts at the Nameless, in addition to being *the* cheapest alternative, were quite tasty – unpretentious food always served together with piping-hot Victorian tea, the most famous in the world.

Despite his popularity, Sonny was famous – or rather, to be more accurate, infamous – for two things. He had a short fuse reminiscent of Captain Haddock's in *The Adventures of Tintin,* even possessing a full black beard and moustache exactly like the explosive sea captain's, and was also the most promiscuous man at Jellicoe Junction. His female conquests were as many as they were legendary. He would often appear to be quite exhausted in the mornings, a trademark quizzical look of shame stamped upon his bearded face that betrayed just what he had been up to the night before.

At the onset of one particular morning's discussion which touched upon the origin of the Junction's name, Bellakay, the impoverished incumbent sage and acknowledged intellectual at the Nameless, told the others in no uncertain terms that their former British lords and masters had named the Junction in memory of their famous admiral and commander, Lord Jellicoe. Bellakay's nous was beyond question. He, a walking encyclopaedia, was full of facts, although disinclined to relating anecdotes, as humour was never his strong side. The breakfast-eaters, to a man, believed in most things Bellakay said, except for grumpy old Benjy, who didn't, and Catnips – a mischievous troublemaker prone to frivolity who loved nothing better than heckling Bellakay at the slightest given opportunity.

Benjy did temporary work for the municipal council, beachcombing the city's coastal esplanade during the monsoons, when the sea washed ashore a potpourri of debris on almost a daily basis. He was noted for being somewhat of an overzealous patriot in addition to being quite rumbustious at times. He was openly displeased that the Junction wasn't named after one of the inhabitants' past colonial heroes. The current name sounded an out-and-out misnomer – at least to him – and he was having none of it. Disagreeing with Bellakay about the origin of the name, he put forward his own theory, boldly proclaiming instead that the Junction was named after the pesky jellyfish occasionally found in the coastal seas around the island, especially around Portopo's warm waters. Bellakay remained unfazed right throughout Benjy's subversive tirade, listening patiently to the latter without interrupting. As soon as the firebrand had finished, the sage spoke out, pooh-poohing Benjy's jellyfish theory with sharp and stinging disdain.

'Why the devil did them British chaps want to go and name an important junction after a dang-blasted blooming jellyfish? Tell me that, eh? And besides, our jellyfish are those "moon" jellyfish creatures that only swim about during full-moon time and are sometimes seen when they are washed ashore. Nobody cares, and everybody knows how to avoid them! It's just some tourist fellow or two who gets stung – and even when they do, any damn fool knows how to treat the poison's effects with some good old vinegar fomentations! Why should our Junction be called after these insignificant, blithering jellyfish, eh? It's that Lord Jellicoe fellow them British chaps had in mind when they named the Junction, I'm telling you. No doubt about that! No doubt at all.' His defence complete, Bellakay wiped his mouth with a napkin of cut-out old newspaper in a grand gesture of finality.

'Don't talk so wretchedly about them jellyfish, Bellakay! They are all in the Almighty's circle of life, you know! Perhaps they were once kings and queens in another life! All creatures great and small are a part of our karmic life, you know! Evildoers and troublemakers will be born again as lesser creatures, whilst the good will be given another chance again as humans. Why, I am quite certain some of you fellows who are always fighting like cockerels and behaving so violently in this eating house might jolly well go on and be punished by being born again as a jellyfish or, heaven forbid, perhaps even a cockroach!'

The rebuff came from the octogenarian Sadhu – a much-respected, silver-haired holy man often attired in a saffron-coloured robe wrapped around his body with white markings of an unknown substance smeared in thick stripes on his forehead. Sadhu spent the early part of the morning at the Nameless before going on his rounds through the winding city streets. On his wandering through the metropolis, he would, from a little pot nestling inside a sachet slung over his shoulder, smear 'holy ash' on the foreheads of those who so desired it. His smearing of the ash would inevitably be rewarded by the grateful receiver, who would press a coin or two into Sadhu's free hand. Another distinctive feature of Sadhu's appearance were the two puncture marks on both his cheeks into which he inserted a thin shaft of metal that went through his mouth. Once the arrow shaft was in place, he would screw detachable little arrowheads on both sides, rendering speech impossible. At the breakfast sessions, however, he was sans his 'double-headed arrow', which enabled him to eat and talk freely. Piercing was a kind of penance holy men endured from time to time in that part of the world, although nobody quite knew why Sadhu suffered the arrow. As far as everyone could recollect, he had always led an ascetic kind of life, some even revering him as the living embodiment of a saint.

The breakfast-eaters squirmed uncomfortably at the thought of being reborn as jellyfish or, worse still, a cockroach. Even old Bellakay stared uncomfortably at Sadhu, not because he thought for one minute that he would be reborn as a jellyfish or anything else, but because he hated any sort of religious intervention in a discussion. A diehard agnostic, he didn't believe in karma, heaven, hell, or any form of afterlife. He longed to tell Sadhu to sod off but was far too polite and refined to use such crude language.

Benjy wasn't quite finished though – reluctant to give in to Bellakay's version of things. 'Bah, who cares about that damn-blasted popinjay Jellicoe? I say it's the jellyfish what gave us the Junction's name. Anyway, what do we Victorians care about some British lord chap, eh, fellows? Our poor old jellyfish are not good enough, are they? It's the jellyfish what must get the honour, not a blooming dead and long-forgotten damn English lord!'

Here, the rough-and-tough clientele at the Nameless went silent, not knowing with whom they should throw in their lot. The idea of Jellicoe Junction's being named after a famous lord of their former colonial masters didn't augur too well. They were all very fond of everything British, but on the other hand, Benjy's jellyfish theory strongly appealed to their spirit of adventure and seemed definitely preferable to some long-deceased English lord of whom they hadn't the foggiest notion. They would have loved to shout out their support for rough old Benjy, but their great respect for the resident sage made them temporarily mute. Where Bellakay got *his* information, none of his cronies really knew – and nobody bothered to ask, either. He was respected and renowned amongst the breakfast-eaters for his profound knowledge on almost any subject and for seemingly possessing a scripted panacea for any problem. Everyone knew he was a walking, talking, breathing encyclopaedia.

It had been a very eventful day, mused Rohan, a young boy of eleven living on the charity and mercy of his maternal grandmother together with his mother, Rebecca, and three siblings, as he lay awake before falling asleep that night – eventful but surreal, as nearly all days were at his strange old grandmother's house. Today's events though had infused into him a feeling that perhaps there was another postern of reality in the adult world. Lots of matters in the adult world were a mystery to young Rohan, and a conversation he had recently overheard between Baking Jane and Bellakay was no different. All verbal interactions between adults were tremendous Gordian knots of a sort that would take him future years and his inevitable ascension to puberty to unravel...

Baking Jane, a moniker given to a handsome woman of around forty, prepared and sold breakfast to more-than-eager customers at Jellicoe Junction. It was convenient for people to buy cheap breakfasts from enterprising entrepreneurs like Baking Jane rather than labouring over preparing their own, especially as time was of the essence in the mornings in this working-class haven. Baking Jane's breakfasts consisted solely of 'hoppers' – local pancakes of sorts with crisp outsides and soft centres – a national breakfast immensely popular in the country. A woman of great beauty in the past, Baking Jane still had a commanding hauteur and figure, although age was taking its toll – rotundness slowly replacing her disappearing figure-eight splendidness. She usually did her baking bare-breasted, clad only in a long skirt reaching down to her ankles, although she took good care to cover herself with a shawl whenever she spotted a younger client coming in through the front door or when she saw dubious persons whom she knew, from past experience, were only interested in making advances with the intent of bedding her. Her little house was one long corridor really, with small rooms on either side, enabling her to have a bird's-eye view of anyone coming in. That 'normal' adult customers viewed her breasts, she gave a tinker's curse about, even secretly enjoying her unintentional flashing at times. Her ovens did emit a great deal of heat, and her breasts enclosed in a brassiere were a terrible discomfort. This particular morning, her forehead and temples were covered in small beads of sweat, causing her to loosen the clasp of her sarong-like skirt and lift it up high to wipe off the moistness, momentarily forgetting the clean cloth she kept by her side for that very purpose. Whilst she was tying the slippery skirt back in place, the garment evaded her grabbing hands for a moment and fell low below her knees, falling right down to her feet. She retrieved it unhurriedly – serenely at ease – giving Bellakay, her sole customer present, a more-than-fleeting glance of her beautifully formed frontal nudity. Tying it back again, the skirt evaded her grasp once more, showing off her splendid assets a second time around. She bent to pick up the skirt yet again, uttering a small oath under her breath, this time managing to tie it firmly back in place.

Bellakay was stunned, bowled over by the magnificent sight – especially Baking Jane's somewhat bald vulva, which actually seemed to glisten with mysterious moisture. He was thunderstruck to note that his dear friend didn't wear knickers, additionally surprised at his own arousal – surprised because he had trained himself over the years to purge women and coitus from his mind. He had been tremendously successful in both endeavours, although right now, captivated by Baking Jane's raw nudity, he wasn't quite sure that he had fully mastered those difficult urges. The bulge in his trousers severely betrayed his supposed immunity.

An unperturbed Baking Jane remarked coyly, 'Blasted material these skirts are made of! I buy them ready-made from those useless blooming shops at the bazaar, you know! It's all imported from Japan and other outlandish places, and the material is slippery like butter. Why the devil our local chaps don't produce skirts and dresses using our wonderful home-grown cotton, God in heaven knows.'

Baking Jane didn't seem overly upset about her little faux pas, and except for the little oath she uttered when the skirt slipped down a second time, displayed no emotion. She hadn't done it intentionally, but she was overjoyed inwardly, experiencing a flush of sexual pleasure. She wasn't too concerned about her absent knickers, either. It wasn't just the heat or carelessness that prompted her to do her baking without wearing knickers. The truth of it all was that it gave her immense erotic satisfaction to know that she was naked under her thin skirt, a feeling that compensated somewhat for her not having a husband or regular coitus in the past decade. Her upper nakedness, though, had no erotic overtures whatsoever. The baking ovens *did* emit a great deal of heat which, together with the humid dryness of the morning, made her large breasts most uncomfortable when contained within a brassiere or a blouse. She had done her baking bare-breasted the very first day she embarked on her business five years ago, a habit that had become almost ritualised. As for her recent faux pas, she was glad it was just Bellakay and not anybody else who had seen her total nakedness in that brief instant. Other grown-ups would have had a good laugh about it all or even tried to make erotic advances, but she knew that Bellakay was a safe bet. Everyone knew the man was an out-and-out neuter well known for his total abstinence from sex.

Despite his 'sexless' reputation – a fallacious reputation really – Bellakay was as sexually alert as any other adult. It was just that he took great pains to hide his true feelings, shutting out mental images of coitus and its peripheral rituals in his mind. At the old abandoned railway station at the edge of the city where he lived together with other homeless people, privacy was almost non-existent. Often, he would witness his closest neighbours having coitus, also seeing women change their clothes openly, stripping down naked, almost every day. Bellakay had trained himself to ignore the nudity and erotic acts performed almost before his very eyes and had fast earned a misguided reputation amongst his fellow squatters as well as his circle of acquaintances at the Nameless for being an out-and-out neuter. Baking Jane's indiscretions bored a hole in his head despite his best efforts to ignore them. He had put on a mask of complete indifference when Baking Jane's naked body stared him in the face, but he couldn't for the life of him forget her magnificent vulva, which even overshadowed her bulging, naked breasts. Secretly, Bellakay vowed to himself that he would someday rid himself of his poverty and ask Baking Jane to marry him. Right now, he was painfully aware that no woman would take him on; his dishevelled state, his hand-me-down clothes, and the perpetual three-day stubble on his face, an instant repellent. Even if women looked beyond all that, they knew he was destitute, barely able to support himself, let alone a partner.

Bellakay, who had a good many acquaintances, had just two real friends – Sonny, the proprietor of the Nameless, and Uncle Pongo, a dapper elderly man whom he met up with regularly. He shared his sensational experience with Sonny the very next day.

'You know, Sonny, when that skirt of hers fell down, her thighs and thingie were slightly wet sort off – as though she had come out of the shower or done a pee on herself!'

'Wet thighs and thingie, eh! Maybe Baking Jane's secretly lusting after a good romp. She's been a widow for some time now, you know! Some women get that way when they want *it*, you see!' volunteered Sonny, a well-known rake and philanderer often likened to as a local Cassonova of sorts. 'Maybe it was *you* who put her into that state,' he concluded mischievously, looking up at Bellakay obliquely from his spot behind his rough cashier's desk.

'Bah! Rubbish, man! You know damn well I'm not interested in women, and Baking Jane knows that only too well too. Naaah! It's not me; maybe she just has a wet vulva all the time.'

The day's events for young Rohan began that morning with his grandmother's clarion-like shouts at him to hurry along and complete his morning chore of buying breakfasts for the ménage – a chore young Rohan took turns in doing every alternate day with his older brother, Mahan. The breakfast-buying expeditions were conceived and commandeered by his grandmother, who absolutely brooked no refusal. Rohan's grandmother was an enigma – probably the queen of all enigmatical beings. She was beyond all known axioms of human behaviour. No one knew from one day to the next what really went on in the old lady's head.

Rohan, who didn't really need anyone to remind him of the breakfast-buying chores, had only just awoken from his night's slumber, which he had spent on the thin mobile mattress he used for sleeping. He had heard his grandmother's yelling, of course, but wasn't too overly concerned about it. Grandmother had yelled at him ever since he could remember, her voice always high-pitched and querulous. It was expected – a ceaseless daily mantra – harmless yet disconcerting at the same time.

A bit over twelve years old, Rohan was slightly small in stature, but he more than compensated for his lack of height by possessing exquisite facial features, a mop of unruly curly black hair, and a disarming smile that lit up his whole face whenever it was on display. There wasn't much going on, however, in young Rohan's life these days to bring about a smile – nothing, really – ever since his father's fortunes had so dramatically taken a turn for the worse, plunging the boy and his family into instant tribulation and near destitution. Rubbing his still-sleepy and half-closed eyes, Rohan stood up and tried his best to smooth the wrinkled-up day clothes he had slept in – a pair of shorts and a T-shirt. Turning his attention to his hair, he ran his hands over his head, putting in order the natural curls that otherwise ran amok by patting and pressing them into place. Satisfied he was somewhat 'presentable', he couldn't help reflecting on the sponge-like mattress he had slept upon spread out on the cold cement floor. It was a far cry from the comfortable bed he had slept in two years before, when his family lived in splendid circumstances – almost epicurean in some people's books. Every single room in his parents' house was air-conditioned then, something only the wealthy could afford. It was difficult adapting to the change initially, but with time he had gotten used to his new sleeping mode, and sometimes, when the monsoons had passed and the tropical heat at night was at its unbearable zenith, he actually found the mattress spread on the cool cement floor to be much more suitable and comfortable to sleep on than a conventional bed. At times, he would discard the mattress completely and just sleep on the cold, bare floor – it was so wonderfully cooling!

Rohan placed his rolled-up mattress in the corner of the room he and his elder brother slept in. The mattress was difficult to roll, but young Rohan had gotten used to it by now – the original stiffness of the foam becoming quite flexible with time. The blanket and his slightly dirty and smothered pillow he put into a large, lidless wooden chest specially placed in a corner of his mother's bedroom, into which the children were ordered to store their sleeping gear. His older siblings had already awoken and had dumped their sheets and pillows into the chest in a haphazard fashion, causing it to overflow in a wild shemozzle. 'Mother won't be pleased,' he thought, gazing ruefully at the disarray, dismayed at his siblings' callous carelessness.

Rohan's grandmother, or Grandmummy, as the children called her, was already awake and bustling about in her scrupulously clean little kitchen, as was her wont at this time of the day. A framed portrait print in colour of the young British royal couple hung high up on the wall above the kitchen worktable in a corner of the room, the pair seemingly looking down upon the proceedings below. A young, radiant Elizabeth, splendid in her famous wedding dress of richly embroidered white satin interwoven with garlands of pearl orange blossom, syringe, jasmine, and white rose of York, smiled down benevolently at Grandmummy. Beside Elizabeth, a stern-looking Prince Philip in full naval uniform seemed to look on disapprovingly at his current surroundings, probably wishing he hung in a more grandiose establishment instead.

Looking around herself inquiringly, Grandmummy tilted her head obliquely in the direction of the second bedroom and yelled at her young grandson for the second time that morning, this time in a more perplexed and irritable fashion. Her domineering, puissant voice carried well and could be heard all over the entire house.

'Rohan. Rohan! How many blooming times must I remind you that it's your turn to buy the breakfast this morning? It's nearly six o'clock soon. You better look sharp, boy! Aunty Primrose and Aunty Celeste will be getting late for work if you don't hurry up!'

Out of earshot of anyone within hearing distance, she muttered fiercely to herself, 'Damn-blasted dratted boy! Always late for everything, the good-for-nothing brat! Just like that blooming ne'er-do-well father of his! Deserves a good bloody smacking, the lazy young sod!'

Grandmummy would often chunter thus, conducting a running commentary on all sorts of issues, the actual words she mumbled audible only to her. Her incoherent gobbledygook mutterings often made those meeting her for the first time consider her harum-scarum or even senile, but the truth was far from what people purported. Widowed at a comparatively young age when still a stately woman and a reputed beauty, Grandmummy was now in her late sixties, very much overweight because of a sedentary lifestyle, but still in full command of her mental facilities. The matriach had passed on her famed beauty to her four daughters: Rebecca, Daisy, Celeste, and Primrose in varying degrees, although Daisy hadn't much facial beauty to talk about – compensating somewhat by having an alluring figure eight body. As with an old wine, but against all axioms of known human nature, Grandmummy's mental powers seemed to mature and grow to an even more astute level the older she became.

The loss of her husband had a profound effect on Grandmummy. Although not going to extremities like a disconsolate Miss Havisham, she became definitely hermit-like. She wasn't the most gregarious of persons, either, and was well known for her idiosyncratic ways – rarely ever leaving the confinement of her somewhat modest home, preferring to live in a state of permanent self-imposed seclusion. When she did waver from this strictly practised rule, it was often to attend Sunday Mass on occasion or to visit one of her only two friends: the local parish priest, a charming elderly Frenchman from Bordeaux, or Mr Macmillan, a former first secretary at the British embassy, now retired. Through the parish priest, she had also made the acquaintance of Dr Nader, a medical practitioner whom she would now and then consult whenever she felt ill or out of sorts, although, strictly speaking, the good doctor didn't actually count as a friend, seeing that she only consulted him professionally.

The aftermaths of her visits to Mr Macmillan, a close yet very much younger friend of her late father, always found Grandmummy in a 'joie de vivre' frame of mind. She perked up something extra-special immediately afterwards, forgetting her usual morose ways for a few days, at least. Together with the Christmas season, these were the only times Grandmummy deviated from her isolation, putting her otherwise idiosyncratic ways on hold. Mr Macmillan was over seventy. He had decided long ago to live out his retirement in his adored adopted country rather than go back home to relatives in England whom he hadn't being in touch with for several decades. He had been a tower of strength to Grandmummy in the days immediately after she was widowed, and it was rumoured that he *had* comforted, and still *did* comfort her in more ways than one. Grandmummy still possessed some remnants of her former beauty in spite of her large bulk, and what went on during her visits to Mr Macmillan was anybody's guess.

Despite her somewhat unpleasant ways, no one could say that Grandmummy was really tetchy, either. She would often chuckle profusely whilst listening to the BBC comedy broadcasts she loved to hear over the radio or at something amusing she read in the newspapers, but the general consensus was that she was difficult to deal with, aloof, and almost unapproachable. She swore by the British colonial system, had unwavering aristocratic ways, and considered herself to the manor born. Perhaps her aloof manner had something to do with her ancestry. Grandmummy was English – almost. Her father, an Englishman from the south of England, had settled down in Victoria as a very young man in the days when the Island was a fully fledged colony within the British Commonwealth. He quickly learned and made a career in the tea-cultivation trade, an area of work exclusively reserved for, and diligently run by, the British diaspora. The maternal side of Grandmummy's family was all clouded in obscurity. Her mother was supposed to have been Eurasian, part English and part Victorian...

The reference Grandmummy had earlier made touching on Rohan's 'criminal father', as she so smugly put it, stemmed from an alleged financial wrongdoing the unfortunate man had supposedly perpetrated at his place of employment. The aftermath of a court case resulted in her son-in-law's getting the sack from his well-paid job – one which had hitherto enabled his family to live a life of considerable bliss. Contretemps following the sacking – mainly a disastrous financial collapse – completely ostracised him and his family from the kind of society and lifestyle they had hitherto been accustomed to. Up to the events leading to the calamity, the family had rubbed shoulders with the *jeunesse dorée* of the land, living an epicurean lifestyle and proudly taking their place on the glamorous upper rungs of the local social ladder, but everything changed almost overnight. Unable to face up to mounting financial commitments and the seemingly harrowing prospect of supporting a young family with no income whatsoever, the poor man decided the only available option was to quietly 'disappear' for a while until such time he could redeem himself, become solvent, and get his life on track again. He did just that – leaving suddenly and quietly one day without so much as a word of farewell to anyone. Rohan's mother and siblings, having no place to live, were forced to move in with Grandmummy – the only other option being a life on the streets.

Rohan showed remarkable sangfroid at his grandmother's repeated shouts at him to hurry up with the breakfast-buying chores, not out of disrespect – God forbid! He was as obsequious towards her as was the rest of the family, but Grandmummy's stentorian cries to get the breakfast chores done didn't really require an answer. Her puissant 'breakfast shouts' in the morning at him and his brother, Mahan, were more or less a daily mantra they were all well accustomed to. She barked out churlish comments and commands at them throughout the day, especially at young Rohan, except of course during the long interlude when the children were away at school. It was not only the boys – or to be more exact, just Rohan – whom Grandmummy constantly nagged and generally bossed around. Everyone in the household had to endure her sharp tongue and general crotchetiness. Her unequivocal dominance over everyone in the family was as total as it was discerning.

Opening the bathroom door to do his morning wash and brush his teeth, Rohan was flabbergasted to find his sister Laura standing by the washbasin mirror dressed only in her underwear. Laura screeched out loudly in shock and anger, grabbing a nearby towel to cover herself better.

'You young scallywag! How dare you barge in on me like this! Wait till I tell Mother!'

'Who blooming well barged in? Why don't you lock the door like everybody else? And as if I want to see you in your silly old knickers and brassiere! They look a bit dirty to me! Hasn't Mummy told you to change your underwear every day? Mahan and I do!' retorted Rohan, angry at being called a 'young scallywag' and throwing in the 'dirty' underwear jibe just to get even. Laura's knickers and brassiere were, as always, spotlessly clean.

Laura glared at him threateningly, equally angry about the insulting jibe about the state of her underwear, although immensely relieved she hadn't been fully naked when Rohan walked into the unlocked bathroom.

Seeing Laura in her underwear, Rohan's thoughts automatically drifted into a black hole he couldn't quite comprehend – a regular happening these days. Although his sexual awareness was still very embryonic, there were some distant bells ringing and clanging in his head, hinting at something dark and wonderful to come. He didn't quite know *what* the bells were signalling, but they always seemed to come whenever he saw women half-naked as was the case when he saw Laura just recently. Right now, all he knew about the opposite sex was what he had learned at the Scripture classes at school taken with ancient Father Ambrose, a Catholic priest with strict Rhadamanthine views on Christianity. The Ten Commandments said that one had to marry just *one* wife, an easy enough task and a silly commandment, in his opinion. After all, why on earth should one want to marry *two* or more? And then there was this business of 'coveting' a neighbour's wife, which he couldn't quite fathom out. Old Father Ambrose was unusually silent about that commandment, not ranting on as much as he did when discussing the other commandments. All he said was that it was a sin to want a neighbour's wife, a conundrum young Rohan was very much puzzled over. Want a neighbour's wife for what? A few of the other commandments were a bit puzzling too, but most were straightforward enough – although to hear old Father Ambrose rambling on and on about it all in his pontifical manner gave Rohan and his fellow scholars at school quite a headache.

Religious repercussions always filled young Rohan with malaise. He was in a constant state of worry about going to hell – a worry brought upon courtesy of the strict religious leanings his fine Christian school advocated. Old Father Ambrose, especially, was most insistent that breaking the commandments and committing other sins would lead to a rendezvous with the Devil and the fires of hell unless they were addressed and dealt with at the confessionals. Rohan liked Father Ambrose a good deal in spite of the old priest's narrow-minded views on sin, but he was wary of having to confess to him at the confessionals, given the latter's well-known over-diligence, where in some instances, he would roundly abuse the horrified confessor kneeling in front of him after listening to a more 'juicer' confession. The worst part of it all was that Father Ambrose's voice carried so much that every single person in the confessional queue overheard the abuse. Rohan couldn't recollect anything in the Ten Commandments or his Scripture book about the mysterious bells ringing and clanging in his head that gave him the strange uplifting feeling he felt, but he was rather wary of the whole business anyway, in case his euphoria was a sin that risked the fires of hell. It was a harrowing thought to burn in hell, one which young Rohan tried hard to obliterate whenever it flashed through his mind. Visions of being pierced on a fork and being tossed into a raging fire by a grinning, black-horned Devil, complete with hoofs and a tail, made him shudder in fear and apprehension.

There were quite a lot of things about religion that Rohan didn't quite understand. For instance, Mr Odd Bull, his history teacher at school, had told his class only last week about a great big rocket that had sent a man into space in a small cone-shaped capsule and then circled around and around the world. The newspapers were full of it. Pictures of the spaceman and his capsule were splashed all over the front pages, and everyone was in a fever of excitement, talking about it in rapturous wonder at every opportunity. Could the rocket reach the kingdom of heaven, where the good Lord lived with all his angels and saints and all the good people who had died? Upon deeper introspection, Rohan wasn't too sure about the kingdom of heaven floating in the sky either, which added to his general confusion about things. He was a deeply religious boy and tried hard to believe in it all, but Mr Foxley, his science master at school, had told him and the boys in his class that there was nothing in the sky except empty space, the sun, the moon, the planets, stars, and something he called 'meetors'.

Rohan's immediate family, apart from his absconding father, Rainier, and his mother, Rebecca, consisted of Laura, Mahan, and a three-year-old baby sister, Sussie, whom he loved more than anyone – even more than his mother. Laura, a scholarly type, was the eldest at fifteen, whilst Mahan, the older brother, was twelve, soon to be thirteen in a few months. Rainier's hasty departure from their lives – which they all fervently hoped and prayed would be only temporary – was attributed to an alleged financial swindle he was supposed to have perpetrated at his place of work. He had, according to his employers, purloined a vast sum of money from a position of trust, but had escaped punishment as the charges brought against him could not be substantiated in a court of law. When the case was tried at the Portopo assizes, he was unanimously acquitted. His employers, disappointed and enraged at his acquittal, sacked him (he had been only suspended at that time) and, in an additional fit of vengeful spite, colluded with other leading commercial establishments to make it almost impossible for the poor man to find any work at Jellicoe Junction – or in the rest of Portopo, for that matter.

Grandmummy summarised it all rather viciously – as one would expect coming from her –whenever Rainier's fate came up in any discussion. 'That bloody fine-feathered fellow was sure as guilty like hell! Why on earth did he go and do a bolt like that after the trial, otherwise? Maybe he was afraid the truth would come out! God in heaven knows what the damn brute did with all that money he stole. Maybe he's gone abroad and started a new family with some fancy woman! Always was a shifty bugger – the dirty, rotten scoundrel!'

Rohan made his way to the rear section of the house, where Laura was busy making the morning coffee. Mahan too was present, watching and waiting patiently for his cup of coffee. Laura glared disapprovingly at Rohan as he came in, still fuming over the little fax pas in the bathroom.

A rather plump but pretty girl in her early teens, Laura was gradually carving a name for herself as an assiduous scholar, often finishing at the top of her class in the monthly and end-of-term exams. She was a brilliant student revered by the entire teaching staff at the school she attended.

Young Laura's coffee-making effort was entirely in line with Grandmummy's explicit command, which necessitated Rebecca's making tea and coffee separately for herself and her small family. Even the rest of the culinary tasks, like preparing lunch and dinner, were done in the same apartheid-like manner, conceived and commandeered by the old Dragon. Grandmummy and Rohan's aunts Celeste and Primrose cooked for themselves whilst Rebecca cooked her young family's meals separately. Rebecca's home-cooked meals were quite simple affairs, usually just cooked rice or boiled potatoes, a meat or fish concoction, and a rough salad. The children had no other nourishment of any sort, although Grandmummy secretly indulged Mahan, often giving him a share of the better sort of food she and the aunts ate – often featuring Marmite, fresh butter, cheese, smoked bacon, quality jams, Ovaltine, creamy biscuits, or powdered milk – all locked up in a large wooden cupboard. The aunts, who could hardly boil an egg, didn't do much of the actual cooking. They just helped their old mother with the gutting and cleaning of fish, cutting meat and vegetables, and sometimes even reluctantly doing the dishes and scrubbing pots and pans glisteningly clean.

Grandmummy's house was much revered and was often referred to by her rather mundane neighbours as the 'big house', although it did look kind of small – even crooked – when seen from the front. The house faced the street and had no front garden, just a few steps leading from the pavement up to the front door. The impression of smallness was deceiving, although the 'crooked' label was a tad justified. Well inside, one wandered into a twisting, winding construction stretching on from room to room and finally ending at a doorway leading to a partially abandoned garden surrounded by a wall that had crumbled away in small sections. It was the kind of house Dickens would have loved to write about, an ideal setting for one of his more morose novels. It reminded one of gargoyles and turrets despite the absence of any. The house was old, well over hundred years, possessing all the ailments of an aged construction. The tiled roof leaked to high heaven in several places when the monsoon rains came cascading down, making it necessary to have several buckets in store to catch the unwanted rainwater. In the dry season, the roof was patched up by well-meaning, but blundering local builders, only to result in newer spots where the rain managed to seep through the next time it poured down.

Apart from the leaking roof, there was nothing much wrong with the old construction. Although the plaster on the walls chipped off regularly and, together with the cracks in the floor, needed yearly repairing, the bearing walls were solid – built entirely of strong bricks and mortar. Like a few houses that still stood firm from the old days, it was fashioned in a hybrid Dutch–English architectural style. Most of the garden was covered in a wild shemozzle of thick bushy vegetation, tall grass, and a few stunted trees bearing red berries uneatable for both humans and birds. The immediate area outside the kitchen, though, was neatly cleared up – a sort of mini-garden within the rest of the overrun garden. A solid but small shed stood under the shade of a large wild-pear tree in the middle of the cleared section. In the mini-garden, Grandmummy, who had a great panache for gardening, took considerable pains to plant and maintain a few rose bushes and a bed of geraniums in small furrows lined by a dainty wooden palisade.

On rare occasions, a mynah bird with its distinctive yellow beak and feet would fly over and sit on a branch of the pear tree to peck at the ripe fruit when in season or, alternatively, on the many insects and grubs living in the cracks in the bark, but otherwise there was a complete absence of the colourful parrots, kingfishers, bulbuls, cockatoos, hummingbirds, and the like found in abundance in the villages and countryside.

Plenty of rats, centipedes, cockroaches, and other insects lived side by side in the old house, sometimes boldly showing themselves to the human occupants. The rats could be seen scuttling up and down the old roof beams at night – a favourite time of the day, one in which they were most active. They often left the house in the evenings immediately after it grew dark to venture out into the streets and rummage through the numerous dustbins and rubbish dumps in the area to search for food.

The cockroaches were another matter. They were always making a nuisance of themselves, making it necessary for food to be safely stored away at all times. Grandmummy tried 'Jeyes Fluid' at first with little success – afterwards regularly resorting to spraying the house with all sorts of other insecticides – alas, to very little effect. The cockroaches just refused to go away. Defeat of any sort did not come easily to Grandmummy. She was quite disconsolate over the fact that she could not find an effective way to defeat this age-old pesky enemy of humankind. The various other, smaller insects were all quite harmless except for the finger-length roof centipedes, whose tiny pincers injected a painful sting. Nearly every person in Grandmummy's household had been stung by them at some time or other.

Grandmummy's stepmotherly treatment of Rebecca was a conundrum. In the grand old days prior to her husband's downfall, Rebecca showered her mother with large sums of money, in addition to regularly inviting the Dragon over for short stays. The money was gladly accepted, but staying away even one night was out of the question. Grandmummy's rigid self-imposed exile didn't permit this frivolity. The truth of the matter was that she hadn't stayed overnight at anyone's house for the past two decades and would probably continue thus until the day she died. She did condescend, however, to have lunch and spend a day at Rebecca's now and then, but always made it a rule to return home in the evenings before nightfall, Rainier graciously volunteering to drive her home. What prompted the Dragon to insist on spending every single night under her own roof, nobody knew – it puzzled everyone.

Celeste, Grandmummy's raven-haired third daughter, had been married to a local engineer who had callously abandoned her a few years back. Their union had resulted in the little girl, Maria, now four years of age. The engineer was known to have secretly sneaked out of the island on a P&O steamer to England, causing Celeste to subsequently take out a divorce on the grounds of abandonment. Divorce was a rare occurrence in Victoria, and Celeste found herself, for a while at least, a much talked of person at Jellicoe Junction for going through her pioneering deed. Celeste was not over-distressed by her husband's seemingly lowly actions. Her marriage to the engineer wasn't the most perfect of unions – petty arguments and various differences always in the forefront of their stormy relationship. At the end, when the divorce was finalised, both parties were equally relieved and very, very thankful to get away from each other.

Grandmummy heartily disapproved of Celeste's divorce mainly on religious grounds and never missed an opportunity to chide her headstrong, rebellious daughter for it. 'It was your bloody big mouth that drove that man away,' she would often say. 'You don't know how to talk properly to people, that's what! You think any man is going to put up with your foul temper and tantrums? You think men *like* being talked to like that, eh? If you had only treated that man decently, he would still be with you and the girl!'

Celeste brimmed with indignation over the allegations that she didn't treat her former husband as a woman ought to. She would counter-attack Grandmummy in a most disrespectful way, often using choice expletives. Grandmummy would reply using even harsher language than Celeste's, making it all sound like a vulgar barroom brawl. They would squabble back and forth like two fighting cocks until one of them retired to fume in private, unable to take any more. More often than not, it was Celeste who was forced to show constraint, retire, and bite the dust.

Grandmummy's only son, Robert, was married and lived on the other side of the city with his wife and two young daughters, whilst her eldest daughter, Daisy – a large, well-set woman who had married a few years back – lived with her husband and in-laws in a more affluent part of Portopo. Daisy was a tower of moral strength, at least in Grandmummy's eyes. The Dragon would often use her eldest daughter as a shining example of success and righteousness in her frequent squabbling sessions with Celeste. She took a morbid delight in lecturing poor Celeste about Daisy's successful marriage, which irked the latter no end.

'Just look at Daisy,' Grandmummy would often exclaim. 'See what a good marriage she has made and how she lives independently with her husband, respecting our religion and ways. If only you take after her, you might still make something of your bloody useless life as well. It's not too late to change, you know. You are still quite young!'

Celeste, who cared a fig for her elder sister and everyone else, would always have a scripted answer ready whenever thus compared to Daisy. 'Bah! Who the devil cares? And why do you want me to take after her, eh? The bloody woman's been married for four years now and still hasn't left her damn mother-in-law's house. Nor has she produced any children. That blooming namby-pamby husband of hers doesn't know how to impregnate a woman and make children. Probably has a dingle the size of a peanut! Or maybe he doesn't know what end to stick it into, the damn mama's boy! At least my husband was a real man who knew how to give me a child.'

Grandmummy would scream out a few choice expletives after hearing these somewhat crude and vulgar comments, but she never took matters any further. In truth, Celeste's words worried her a great deal. She often wondered why Daisy didn't rent a house and move out of her in-laws' and would further ponder deeply over the former's childless state too. Maybe Celeste was right in insinuating there was something physically wrong with that haughty damn husband of Daisy's, Grandmummy would often reflect – one never knew with those murky old Portopo families. Rumours and mumblings of the 'old families' having sordid sexual preferences and that kind of thing always surfaced within Portopo society – kinky sexual orgies an often hinted vice. Grandmummy hoped to high heaven that Oswald wasn't involved in any such nastiness or that he was consorting with, and preferred men – or, even worse still, young boys. She shuddered whenever thinking thus, often making the sign of the cross for good measure to absolve herself from the sin of entertaining such indecent thoughts.

Daisy visited Grandmummy once a week together with Oswald, who absolutely abhorred these visits, considering them a perfect nuisance – but there was no way out. He had long since deemed his wife's family unfit to mingle with, roundly detesting them all, with the exception of Robert and, in the past even Rainier, when the latter was an absolute society lion. He did try in the beginning of their married life to persuade Daisy that the weekly visits weren't really necessary, but Daisy put her foot down firmly and squarely; the visits had to take place whether he liked it or not, she informed him curtly.

Grandmummy never warmed up to Oswald. As the years went by, she developed an intense dislike for her son-in-law, often calling him unflattering names behind his back. Her dislike stemmed primarily from his haughty upper-class manner, his fastidious family, and – oddly enough – his skin colour, which was very dark. It was even odder considering that the Dragon wasn't really a racist and that *her* late husband had been a very dark-skinned man. Grandmummy herself was a perfect facsimile of a Caucasian European and could have easily passed for one, which she very often did. It was only when she spoke that people realised she was local. There was a slight soupçon of her late father's English accent in her speech, but most of the time it sounded quite indigenous and a far cry from that of the British diaspora's.

Daisy had rather horse-like facial features, although she stopped short of whinnying like one. The 'horsey' features notwithstanding, she had a wonderful, voluptuous body that turned many a head. She usually wore short narrow skirts and form-hugging blouses, showing great legs and an ample bosom pointing out from beneath her tight brassiere. At times, the skirt and blouse were discarded for full dresses cut well above the knee. The blouses were always deep-necked, highlighting her centre cleavage, whilst the short skirts and dresses more than amply showed off her shapely bottom and legs to advantage. Whenever visiting with Oswald, she sat in such a way that her knickers kept showing. On occasions, her flimsy knickers barely covered her privates, clearly showing parts of her hairy vulva. The somewhat prim and prudish Oswald would always snort out his disapproval when this happened, much to Daisy's amusement, although it was probably the very sight of her alluring short skirts, scanty knickers, and protruding vulva that had initially mesmerised the man – and then captured his imagination to such an extent that he just simply had to have her.

'Can't you sit properly, woman?' he would often protest in his high-pitched, stentorian voice. 'Every blooming person in the room can see those ridiculous knickers you are wearing under that dress of yours.'

'Pshaw!' Daisy would reply coyly, ignoring Oswald's bleating protests. 'I don't wear trousers like you men, and anyway, it's Mummy's chairs that are too high for anyone to sit properly on them. It's not my fault,' she would conclude, blaming a lack of trousers and the old-fashioned, Dutch-style hall chairs Grandmummy absolutely refused to do away with. The chairs had long legs, often causing one's own to dangle a bit above the floor unless one was exceptionally tall. Celeste and Rebecca, who observed the knicker-showing interludes with more than keen interest, summarised rightly or wrongly that the knicker-flashing was done on purpose. Celeste often teased Daisy relentlessly about it, whilst Rebecca just shrugged her shoulders resignedly, laughing it off as 'just one of those things'. As for the Dragon, she hardly noticed the flashing but would on and off rebuke Daisy in a mild manner for wearing her skirts and dresses too short at the hem.

Grandmummy was easily able to pay the maintenance costs the old house demanded and still have quite a lot left over after other expenses were met. She had a widow's pension and very generous allowances from Robert and Daisy. Primrose gave her almost the whole of her small salary, whilst Celeste contrastingly gave her a frugal amount despite the fact that she earned much more. To top it all, the Dragon boosted her 'earnings' by running a modest winery inside the confines of her home – a business venture that yielded a handsome yearly profit.

Rebecca and the children were given a breakfast allowance of ten cents each morning by grandmummy – a trifling sum – hardly enough to buy an adequate breakfast. The combined fifty cents hardly dented the old Dragon's finances and, in fact, made only microscopic inroads into her handsome combined income. Grandmummy's miserly breakfast contribution left Rebecca with the task of providing the children with lunch and dinner from the meagre earnings she made as a door-to-door saleswoman for a large mercantile company dealing in cosmetics and hygiene products – a job she had somehow managed to secure despite having no previous experience. In all probability, she had received the billing on account of her great beauty and shapely body – looks considered a great asset when propagating consumer products door-to-door. It was also a job quite easy to obtain. A good many job-seekers didn't really relish the work because of the hours and hours of seemingly endless walking one had to put in, a tedious task on very hot days – a regular climatic feature in the country. The job wasn't in the least bit glamorous or sought after, but Rebecca had to do *something* to get *any* sort of income after her husband had left her high and dry. Rebecca abhorred the work intensely. It was most difficult sometimes to make people buy anything and quite often she had to grovel shamelessly, almost to the point of begging, to make a single sale. She even learned to flaunt her body shamelessly, often crossing and recrossing her legs on a chair when talking to men. Her sales pitch and strategy could become quite erotic at times...

'This product for men is the best aftershave in the market today. Just smell the wonderful aroma from my sample bottle, sir!'

Saying thus, she would lean forward to put the bottle under a male customer's nose, parting her legs very widely, showing her slightly transparent tight knickers. Captivated by the 'accidental' sight, the customer would be most solicitous to keep a conversation going, hastily buying the aftershave on the spot and then asking to see what else Rebecca had in her canvassing suitcase. Rebecca would oblige, shamelessly showing off her knickers again and again, sometimes even succeeding in making an additional sale. She swallowed the ignominy of it all as long as she sold something, often feeling quite small and cheap when she got back home in the evening after fulfilling the quota preset for the day by her strict supervisor. Missing the cut too many times would put her position in jeopardy and risk an outright sacking on grounds of incompetence. She was expected to be able to sell – and sell well…

Going back to the day's proceedings, the morning coffee done with, the young aunts and Rebecca dressed for work whilst Rohan and Mahan put on their school uniforms of blue shorts and white shirts to get ready for school. Laura did likewise, looking all neat and tidy in her white pleated school skirt and maroon blazer.

The aunts, or 'ladyships', as Rohan called them sarcastically behind their backs, often chewed peppermint-flavoured gum before leaving in order to give them a fresh-as-possible breath after their breakfast meal. Rebecca didn't, often brushing her teeth once again without toothpaste, this time around to save toothpaste costs. It was almost surreal to find herself trying to save on toothpaste – an item she gave scant thought to in the days before her and her children's sudden plunge into poverty.

Dental hygiene, or cleaning one's teeth, was a subject often discussed by the breakfast-eaters at the Nameless. Catnips, who had a perfect set of pearly white teeth, wasn't a fan of toothpaste. He wasn't in the same 'super-patriot' bracket as Benjy, but was more a genuine believer in the 'old' ways, or rather how things were done before the three European usurpations his forefathers had experienced the past three hundred years or so.

'You fellows are a lot of ignorant jackasses,' Catnips ranted on one instance when the subject of dental care came up. 'Why the devil do you chaps want to go and use that poisonous bloody toothpaste, God in heaven knows! Them dentist fellows always say sugar is bad for the teeth, but what do you find in toothpaste, eh? Why is it so sweet, eh? Any damn fool knows them factories use tons and tons of sugar to make toothpaste, that's what! And that blooming toothpowder! Why, that foul stuff is even worse! Not only is it sweet, but it also has so much soft sand in it that it grinds down your teeth, leaving you with a few stumps!' (A blatant lie) 'Now, if you use our good old local methods of cleaning teeth, using powdered charcoal, which even our ancient king chaps used, you're never going to harm your teeth! Why, in them olden days, before them damn foreign rascals came and conquered us and all that, our Victorian people had all their *thirty-two* in shipshape condition right until they kicked the bucket from old age! Nowadays, you chaps just give business to them fancy-pantsy dentist fellows at Coronation Park or to those grinning Chinese devils at Sir Francis Drake Street who fix you up with those bloody awful false teeth that break regularly and make you look like blooming Frankenstein.'

Catnips's talk on the evils of toothpaste and toothpowder didn't cause any undue ripples of worry amongst his colleagues, but his surprising mention of one's *thirty-two* teeth caused a major stir. Most of the breakfast-eaters didn't know of the 'thirty-two' standard. After Catnips had spoken, they latently rolled their tongues over their teeth to count the exact number they possessed, anxious to see if they had somehow, by some mishap or anything else, missed the cut. Sonny, who always listened very alertly to everything being said, often even contributing to the daily palavers himself, discreetly left his place behind the tea counter and went to the garden behind the Nameless to count his teeth in solitude. He discovered, to his great joy, that not only did he have thirty-two, but also had an extra one growing on the side of his left fang tooth!

'By jingo,' he mused, 'I sure do have one hell of a set of teeth.' He wanted to rush back inside immediately and shout out the joyous news to his friends at the breakfast table, but, thinking a bit deeper, he decided to keep his discovery to himself. 'Better to keep quiet about the extra one. God only knows what that damn Bellakay or that blasted popinjay Catnips might make of it all if I open my mouth and say anything. You can never tell with those two – especially that blasted Catnips. He might well say it's the work of the Devil, the damn bugger, always rousing the others with his mischievous wild talk!'

Back at Grandmummy's and after cleaning their teeth, washing, and grooming, everybody was looking forward to breakfast.

Except for brewing tea, nobody actually ever prepared any solid breakfasts at home. Everything was bought at nearby small restaurants, unanimously dubbed 'eating houses' or 'hotels' by all and sundry, and from enterprising neighbourhood women who sold varying breakfasts for a reasonable sum of money.

Prearranged by Grandmummy, Rohan and Mahan took turns buying breakfast for the clan. Today, it was Rohan's turn to do the breakfast round. He went around to everyone and made a small list of what they wanted to have for breakfast. The choice of breakfasts made by the household were never the same, ranging from traditional Victorian food to the growingly popular Western substitutes increasingly sold at most eating houses.

The young aunts were always the fussiest, often wanting special breakfasts like crispy bread rolls with bacon, meat, or fish fillings inside, or pancakes sealed with cane-sugar syrup inside.

'Here, Rohan! You get me one of them egg-and-bacon rolls from the New Modern Café – and ask them to put a sliced tomato and a lettuce leaf in it. Bring me back the exact change, too! I'm sure you gave me less change last time!' said Rohan's aunt Primrose sternly, giving him fifty cents for the expected purchase.

Rohan took the money, but not before giving his aunt a withering (or so he hoped) look of disdain. The 'exact change' comment was highly unnecessary, as Rohan never, ever purloined a single cent – but then Primrose was like that, a terribly parsimonious young woman.

The other aunt, Celeste, was in one of her patriotic moods and was, at present, consuming only local food in an effort to go native in everything she did. She narrowed down her selection accordingly, her purchase intended for herself and her little daughter, Maria.

'Buy five *rotis* from Red's and ten cents worth of onion relish from the *corner boutique*,' she said curtly, giving Rohan thirty cents for her purchase. Rotis were a small wheat- or rice-flour cake of sorts, and the onion relish was a fiery mix of fried onions, red chilli, and spices, slightly sweetened to dull the effect of chilli.

The 'corner boutique' onion relish was very popular – the old amma [mother] who made it a reputed neighbourhood cook specialising in traditional Victorian dishes.

Rebecca was usually the last to place her breakfast order. She asked Rohan to buy her and her little girl Sussie five hoppers and a small portion of coconut relish. The coconut relish was not unlike the onion relish, the difference being that the chief ingredient used was grated fresh coconut kernel instead of onions. Of her modest purchase, she would eat three hoppers and give the remaining to Sussie.

Rebecca and her family's pathetic ten cents was just adequate to buy a small breakfast – a meal that hardly ever stifled anybody's morning peckishness, especially the boys'. In comparison, the 'ladyships' – Rohan's aunts Celeste and Primrose – ate sound breakfasts, which normally cost between fifteen to twenty five cents – much more than the miserly ten cents Rebecca's young family had to do with.

Grandmummy didn't contribute anything more by way of food to Rebecca and her young family other than tiffin, in which she indulged daily. Tiffin was holy – a relic of a long-forgotten era when her father was alive and had maintained a perfect facsimile of an English home. Grandmummy always made tiffin at home; nothing was bought from the eating houses. A small fruit cake, finger sandwiches, or varied sorts of sweet porridge was usually on the menu. Importantly, and quite out of character, she shared this with everyone in equal portions, including Rebecca and the children. There wasn't much tiffin to go around, but at least it was some additional food for Rebecca's small family.

Laura took her breakfast money with her to school, where she would buy two small buns from a food vendor who had his hand-drawn mobile wagon permanently positioned at the school gate. Rohan and Mahan bought whatever was available and possible with the ten cents Grandmummy gave them. Mahan was now and then given an extra five cents by Grandmummy, but young Rohan had to do with the doleful ten cents every single day.

Grandmummy always ate a breakfast of white bread and butter, sometimes coated with an application of Marmite and sometimes with a liberal coating of jam. She had ample stocks of all she needed in her food safe and did not place orders with Rohan or Mahan for any sort of purchase in the mornings. The white bread she would replenish twice a week, buying it directly from Alphons, the mobile bread and pastry vendor who did a daily morning round at Jellicoe Junction. She liked eating white bread, preferring it over rice and potatoes – the main staple food of nearly everybody in Victoria. The rich white bread, the pure butter, and a craving sweet tooth may have had something to do with Grandmummy's general portliness, although, to her credit, she never did surfeit. Except for mangoes, which she dearly loved and consumed insatiably, Grandmummy always ate in moderation.

Rohan's modest breakfast never satisfied his hunger. There were times when he would have loved a larger breakfast, but his ten-cent limit just did not permit it. Ten cents would have gone down well at the Nameless, but it was too far away from Grandmummy's house, and speed was of the essence in the mornings when everyone had limited time on their hands to get ready for work or school. On the weekends, however, Rohan always made a beeline to the Nameless for his breakfast where he was more than welcomed by Sonny, who knew him quite well. Sonny was aware of Rohan's circumstances through Grandmummy's disinherited brother, Uncle Pongo, who ate his breakfast at the Nameless every single day. Sonny personally supervised young Rohan's breakfast, frying two eggs and serving them along with a large meat or fish bun, followed by a steaming cup of tea – often even making a small parcel of food to be taken away for Rebecca and young Sussie.

'That dratted chronic old woman's treating you all right, boy? She gives you all enough to eat?' Sonny would ask in genuine concern. Rohan, despite being ill-treated by Grandmummy and the aunts, was reluctant to criticise the Dragon out of a misguided sense of loyalty.

He would nearly always reply, 'Ah! She's all right, Uncle Sonny. I think it's just her piles that make her angry all the time. She can be quite nice too, you know!'

Rohan hadn't the foggiest notion what 'piles' were, but he had often enough heard Celeste admonish Grandmummy thus when she well out of reach of the Dragon's hearing…

'Bloody wretched old woman! Got her damn piles out again!' Celeste would say frequently in deep vexation after a particularly severe altercation with her mother that had gone badly. What piles were, and how they could be *in* or *out* of a person, sounded mind-boggling to young Rohan, who discussed the matter a few times with his best friend, Salgado, at school, but the latter couldn't shed any light either. Salgado, a rotund giant of a boy who was two years older than Rohan, often possessed a great deal of knowledge on many things, but the subject of piles stumped him as much as it did Rohan.

Sonny wouldn't probe the boy further but often offered to take in Rohan under his wing. He had rather taken a shine to the boy and, being the direct and outspoken man he was, never hesitated to show it openly. 'You let me know if you people need anything, you hear! If that crazy old bird can't keep you all, at least *you* can come and stay with me. I lead a rough life, but I'll feed and clothe you properly. At least it will be one less person for that damn grandmother of yours to push around.'

'Oh! Thank you, Uncle Sonny. But I can't leave Mummy and the rest, you know! And besides, Mummy told us only last week that Daddy will be coming back to us very soon now to take us all away from Grandmummy's.'

Sonny would sigh and say nothing, not wanting to upset Rohan unduly. Both he and Uncle Pongo weren't expecting Rainier to return for a long, long time … if he ever returned at all! 'Poor boy,' Sonny would murmur softly to himself. 'Poor little chap's going to grow up without a father.'

Rohan skipped along on his breakfast-buying expedition, pockets jingling with money, the breakfast list clutched tightly in his hand. He was joined by Poppsy, the family dog, who propelled himself into action as soon as he saw Rohan leaving, prancing around gaily in anticipation of joining the young master on his breakfast-buying expedition. Poppsy was quite a small, but sturdily built, dog, possessing a healthy coat of tan frizzed fur and a very friendly face. Originally, he was not allowed the run of the house because Grandmummy and the aunts did not like him sniffing about and shedding his fur all over the place, which happened more often than not. Subsequently, he was chained most of the day in the back garden. On one of these occasions, he had somehow broken the short chain from its attachment and escaped through one of the gaping holes in the back garden's wall. Poppsy made his excursions a regular habit, coming back by way of the same route but sometimes even having the audacity to arrive through the front door if it was open, pleased as Punch with his self-imposed wanderings. In time, he was more or less given a free run of the house to do whatever he wanted, although the aunts made an almighty fuss whenever they found signs of fur on their possessions. Chaining him was useless. An escape artist in the best Houdini tradition, Poppsy only devised more and more cunning ways to break loose and bolt. Besides, everyone in the household reasoned, if he could find his way about the heavily trafficked streets and even come back through the front door, he might as well be spared the confinement of being chained. Their reasoning had selfish undertones, as none in the household were keen on – or more honestly speaking – too downright lazy to take him for a walk on a leash. It was only Rohan who really cared for the dog, giving him a portion of the midday meal and evening dinner in addition to bathing him on weekends. Rebecca, whenever she had the time and energy, helped out too, but it wasn't very often.

Poppsy feared Grandmummy, behaving in a fawning, cringing manner in her presence, always keeping a wary eye upon the Dragon. Grandmummy was not too keen on pets and barely tolerated Poppsy, but she grudgingly allowed him to stay, as he regularly barked if strangers knocked on the front door, but mainly because he caught and killed a rat or two at times, which pleased the Dragon no end. It was she who made the final decision to allow the dog a free run of the house, largely on account of his rodent-killing skills.

Rohan was very fond of Poppsy. He always took the small mongrel along to the Nameless on the weekends, where he had an agreement with Sonny to give Strangefellow – Sonny's dog – a weekly bath in return for some much needed pocket money. Taking Poppsy along served Rohan in good stead, as he was able to bathe the 'home' dog too, knowing fully well that nobody else at Grandmummy's would. Rohan would often complain to Salgado at school about how the others treated Poppsy.

'Blooming lazy lubbers, the whole lot! All of them are at home on Saturdays and Sundays, but not one of them ever wants to bathe the dog! The only time they show any interest in the fellow is when he kills one of them no-good rats or barks at strangers. But bathe the dog? Never! For that, they don't have the time and always make excuses. I know Mummy would. Mummy loves dogs, but she gets so tired when the weekend comes that she just wants to rest her feet after all that blooming useless walking she does.'

Salgado, who had a dog of his own whom his family took turns in bathing and grooming, sympathised. 'Pah! That stinky old grandmother of yours and them horrible aunts are just a bunch of dirty old rotten eggs! And that proud damn jackass of a brother of yours is no better! Why can't he help out? I can have a little chat with that sneaky fellow, you know, if you like. You want me to talk to him, Rohan?'

Here, Rohan hastily intervened. He knew what Salgado's 'chats and talks' were all about. They usually ended in total furore and a sound thrashing applied to the unfortunate recipient of the talk or chat. 'No, no. That's not necessary, Salgado,' he said hurriedly. 'Mahan doesn't need any talking to. If you go and talk to the fellow, it will only end up badly for me. He's sure to tell old Grandmummy and find a way to put the blame on me. It's only going to make matters worse! You know how Grandmummy is ...'

'Bah!' Salgado would often expostulate, reiterating his earlier insults – even adding some more. 'A useless bunch of scumbags, that's what your grandmother and them blooming aunts of yours are. Scumbags and pigs, I'm telling you! The sooner you people get out of that old woman's house, the better.'

At the dog-bathing sessions under the shade of the great banyan tree a few yards away from the Nameless, the two canines got on admirably well together. Strangefellow was always happy to see another dog at the Nameless, which wasn't often, as Sonny uncharitably drove off stray dogs who ventured into 'his' premises with a fierce zeal. A few, however, did manage to slip through Sonny's guard now and then and bond with Strangefellow. The bonding became quite intimate at times if the visitor was female – the bitch copulating with a more-than-willing Strangefellow right under Sonny's horrified nose. The dogs would get stuck immediately after mating, bringing howls of laughter and lewd jeers from the rough-and-tough clientele, with the exception of Sonny, who, notorious rake that he was, sympathised deeply with his trapped dog. Bawdy comments would fill the air...

'Got stuck again, eh, Strangefellow? Can't get the old dingle out of the well, eh?'

'It's true love, Strangefellow! The missus dragging you about everywhere she wants to go, eh? You better get used to it, you old boy! That's married life, you know!'

More terribly lewd comments would follow in a stream. Sonny would frown upon the lewd jeering, but there was nothing he could do about it except sympathise with his dog in silent solidarity. Strangefellow, always a dignified dog, could do little about the heckling, either. He would look on obliquely at his detractors with a fatuous expression upon his face, completely unable to get unstuck from his lover. Secretly, though, he would make a mental note of the most vociferous of the jeering mob so he could avenge his shame by snapping at their ankles at some suitable unguarded moment in the future, or by urinating on their bicycles (many came on bicycles to the Nameless) or other possessions.

Strangefellow was strange in a true sense of the word, seeing that he was the only tree-climbing dog in the whole country, probably even in the whole world. He would often ruminate in wonder over his human companions at the Nameless, bemused by what he considered to be their very odd and strange behaviour.

'What a strange species the *two-legs* are. I wonder why God ever created them!' he would often philosophise, reposing high up on a trifurcate branch on the immense banyan tree, keeping one eye cocked on the breakfast-eaters below. 'Eating with their paws, no fur on their bodies, not a tail amongst the lot to hide their nakedness, and fighting all the while like wretched cockerels, not to mention their constant jabbering! God, how the two-legs love to jabber! Gives me a bloody headache to listen to all their blooming talk and talk and talk! At least we dogs have the good manners to just bark occasionally! And what odd fellows one sees around here! That oddly dressed fellow they call Bellakay, that old white-haired, half-naked holy man with that strange-smelling powder in his pot. And then there's that sleazy Catnips creature! Surely he couldn't be a real two-leg? A sort of a cat, I think! He doesn't smell like a cat, though, but one could never be sure! I'm sure like hell going to keep a good eye cocked on that fine fellow! If I ever catch a whiff of cat smell on him, I'm going to take a good bite off his bloody backside! The fellow could be a gigantic cat in disguise, waiting to pounce on the master and gobble him up. Can't understand why the master tolerates the slimy creature around here – but then, Master never did have any good taste in picking his friends! Just look at all that weird-looking lot gobbling up all his good food! What a waste!'

On other occasions, when heckled by the breakfast-eaters whilst copulating, Strangefellow would ruminate on the falseness and shallowness of the two-legs. 'Look at that useless rabble pack!

Jeering and hooting at me and my lady! At least we dogs don't hide in bedrooms at night and copulate in the darkness! Copulating seems a shameful act to the wretched two-legs – so shameful that they have to do it in secret! What's so shameful about it, anyway? Doesn't it bring young ones into this world? It's a gift from God, isn't it? Are the useless two-legs even ashamed of God? Even Master [Sonny] does it in secret, chasing me away from his bedroom when he wants to get *stuck* with a female. And the scores of females that man brings home! How the devil he runs through so many is a bloody marvel. Why, the poor man's dingle must be black and blue after getting *stuck* so many times and being dragged about all over the blooming place!'

Strangefellow was, as with most other dogs at Jellicoe Junction, of mixed lineage. Portuguese, Dutch, and English invaders had all brought along their unique breeds of dogs during their ruling stints in the country, and after generations of copulating with local breeds, the resulting canine hotchpotch was of a rather startling mix. Strangefellow seemed to have several strains of dogs in him. He had a rather large torso and paws, a pink nose (which was very unusual), black furry circles around both eyes, and half an ear – not genetic, but a proud relic of one of the many battles he had fought with the competition at the marketplace over a responsive female. He had a shaggy grey-white coat of fur and always looked at people sideways, with an inquiring sort of look on his face – his remaining good ear cocked at 'alert'. His posture was comical yet somehow unnerving at the same time, especially when meeting the canine for the very first time.

In spite of his reservations about the two-legs, Strangefellow was on fairly good terms with most of Sonny's regular clients, apprehensive only of Catnips or any newcomer who showed up. He would bark madly at any new face and then stop and snarl, showing off his strong white teeth in a gesture of defiance, which seemed to give a clear message of warning. 'You'd better tread carefully here, stranger! If the master doesn't want you, I'm going to take a jolly good piece off your backside!'

Strangefellow's apprehensive treatment of strangers, in particular his loud barking, served as an excellent early warning system for Sonny, who was instantly put on guard against any probability.

Still, it was not for his unusual looks that Strangefellow was appropriately named, but for his strange and un-canine-like habit of climbing trees. He would regularly and with consummate ease climb the large banyan tree whose enormous umbrella-like leaves sheltered the Nameless from harsh winds and rain that the frequent tropical storms brought in their wake during the monsoons. Strangefellow was often seen perched high up on a favourite trifurcate branch, where he would lazily curl up, always keeping a watchful eye on the proceedings below – coming down only to eat food, which Sonny lovingly provided twice a day, when strangers showed up, at some unusual event, or when he wanted to roam the market bazaar to meet up with his pals. Reposing on his vantage point, he was like a true monarch of all he surveyed – a canine monarch – but a monarch nonetheless.

When the heat of the mating season was in full swing, Strangefellow would descend from the tree more often, roaming and stalking the marketplace bazaar, where he would fight it out with numerous stray males for the attentions of a responsive female. It was here, in one of his more intense battles, that he had lost half his ear.

Rohan's breakfast-buying expedition didn't cover any prodigious distances, requiring only a swift walk around the neighbourhood block. He went to Baking Jane's first.

As usual, he had to walk right through the entire house to arrive at Baking Jane's kitchen – the rear entrance door always bolted for some strange reason. It was still early morning. Baking Jane's family members were lethargically going through the motions of getting up – slouching in half-sleepy repose on their thin mattresses spread out on the floor, and wishing to high heaven they could sleep some more. Baking Jane, a widower since her husband passed away a decade ago, had three children, all daughters, ranging from a girl of six to the eldest, a strapping Amazon of eighteen who had inherited her mother's voluptuous curves. The young Amazon was married and, together with her husband and two toddlers, also lived in the small house. Rohan's presence did not warrant any undue surprise, nor did it bother the sleepyheads the least bit. They were quite used to seeing their mother's customers walking through the house in the mornings and into the kitchen, where business was conducted.

The young Amazon was prone to having coitus early in the morning with a more-than-willing spouse but was careful that they copulate long before her mother's customers started to stream in. She had left it a bit too late this morning though, copulating a short while before young Rohan walked in and moaning slightly as her rather puny husband rode her, his blanket firmly wrapped over his back all the way down to his feet. One of the Amazon's huge breasts could be clearly seen, protruding out from under her husband and the blanket over him. Baking Jane's stern voice reverberated from the kitchen. She had heard the moans and realised what was going on.

'I know what you two are doing! Wasn't last night enough, with all your bloody shouting and screaming? I'm doing business in the mornings, for God's sake! Cut that out at once, you hear me, or find your own damn place to live, where you can have as many romps as you like all day long. It's almost time for my customers to walk in. Nice state of affairs, this. If they find you two going about it like wild beasts, they will think we are a household of sex maniacs!'

A mundane yet much loved woman, Baking Jane always perked up a bit special when she saw Rohan. Although she loved her daughters dearly, she had always wanted a son – disappointed she didn't have a male child. She liked Rohan a great deal and showed it openly, greeting the boy affably with a warm, welcoming smile; her slightly parted lips revealed a set of well-formed but slightly discoloured teeth – a condition brought about through excessive chewing of betel leaf mixtures.

Rohan, in his turn, was somewhat infatuated with Baking Jane and was fast determined to ask her to marry him once he was grown up and had a splendid job. (He never doubted for a single moment that

ALAN JANSEN

he would have a splendid job!) He was quite sure Baking Jane would say yes, seeing how happy she seemed whenever he came along to buy breakfasts. In any event, he felt sorry for Baking Jane, seeing how hard she worked and slaved over her hot ovens. He felt quite chivalrous in the knowledge that he would be taking her away from a hard and harsh life if she agreed to marry him sometime in the future.

Bellakay, who was Baking Jane's only other customer that morning, and who had just recently seen Baking Jane's voluptuous nude body, wasn't overjoyed to see Rohan but condescended to acknowledge him with a wry nod of welcome. Rohan knew Bellakay, of course (as did several others at Jellicoe Junction), taking in instantly the latter's ruffled hair and three-day beard stubble, the baggy flannel trousers patched at the seat, the much stained coat bursting at the shoulder seams, and the greasy blue and white striped tie, dirty and worn loose at the knot. Rohan wondered why Bellakay bothered to wear a tie. The clothes, he could understand; they were, in all likelihood, obtained from the Salvation Army's stock of second-hand clothing donated from donors in Europe and distributed free to the needy and destitute. But why wear a tie? Only important men wore ties; Rohan's father always did and so did the masters at school, but why on earth did Bellakay wear one?

Bellakay had no say over his choice of clothes, as Rohan rightly purported. He accepted gratefully whatever the mother-hen-like old ladies at the Salvation Army stores gave him, his only other option to go about naked. A familiar sight for a lot of people at Jellicoe Junction, and although well known for his absolute nous amongst the breakfast-eaters at the Nameless, others considered the man to be a crackpot, something of an enigma. The 'crackpot' label was a misconception – 'a beggar of sorts' probably a more accurate description. Bellakay would wander around the city dishing out a good deal of Shakespeare and citing famous Greek philosophers to anyone who came his way, expecting a few coins in return for his erudite knowledge. Additionally, he was a brother-in-arms to the riotous school gangs at school cricket

40

matches, where the impish boys contracted him for a small sum of money to stand in front of the VIP pavilion and blast off speeches very few understood. The boys would pretend (prearranged by the contracting parties) to heckle him, creating a devilish ruckus in the process, jeering and hooting and often turning the cricket matches into an orgy of puerile rioting to the chagrin and dismay of the school authorities and genuine cricket lovers.

Baking Jane, who always baked just hoppers, generously gave Bellakay a few free of charge – those not coming out the right way in her pans. These discards had broken or imperfect centres and could not be sold, although they were perfectly all right to eat and tasted as good as the aesthetic ones. She usually kept the discards for her own family's breakfast, but she very graciously conceded to give Bellakay a decent portion of them as well. Bellakay never ate the hoppers for breakfast, making a parcel of it instead and taking them away to be eaten for lunch. Breakfast he always ate at the Nameless, where Sonny sold the cheapest breakfasts available at Jellicoe Junction, perhaps in the entire city. Sonny sympathised deeply over Bellakay's fate, often adding a larger portion of whatever breakfast Bellakay ordered and very often 'forgetting' to make out a bill, feigning absent-mindedness. Bellakay was aware of Sonny's kindness but didn't refuse the charity. It was an unspoken rule that both men never speak of it.

Charity from Baking Jane was completely different from Sonny's act of altruism. It was almost as though Bellakay paid for the discarded hoppers. He entertained Baking Jane with all sorts of gossip currently making the rounds at Jellicoe Junction, his accounts often featuring juicy local scandals which Baking Jane was immensely fond of hearing. Of course, Bellakay spiced things up a great deal, and his version of matters often bordered on the truth, but he did so only to keep his benefactor interested. Baking Jane lapped it all up like a contented cat, never tiring of hearing the endless soap-opera-like episodes. An excellent raconteur and like little Tommy Tucker, Bellakay literally 'sang' for his supper.

Baking Jane's greeting upon seeing Rohan was no different from other occasions. 'Ah, if it isn't our young Rohan again, eh! Good morning to you, young sir! Come to buy hoppers from old Jane, eh? You're getting to be a big fellow now, child. What class are you in now, my boy?'

Rohan knew that Baking Jane liked him, and the feeling was mutual. He dutifully replied, 'Aunty Jane, I'm now in the third standard.'

'What! The third standard, you say, eh! Goodness gracious me! Already in the third standard! How clever you must be! Soon you will finish your fine education at that great big school of yours and get one of them big-shot jobs, what? Don't forget old Jane then,' she would add with a chuckle.

Rohan rattled off his order, gazing at Baking Jane in adoration. It would be wonderful, he mused, to take her away from the hard life she led. He was quite sure in his mind that Baking Jane would drop everything and marry him. Even the religious aspects of such a union were no impediment. True, she had been another man's wife once, but the Ten Commandments didn't say one couldn't marry a widow, did they?

Bellakay gazed on at Jane too, although his thoughts weren't innocent like young Rohan's. Baking Jane had covered herself with a lengthy shawl before Rohan had stepped into her kitchen, but Bellakay couldn't quite get the image of her firmly rounded breasts and thick brown nipples he had seen earlier that morning out of his head, not to mention the magnificent vulva when her skirt had slipped to her ankles. His mind on her delicious breasts, Bellakay wondered why on earth women covered their breasts with brassieres – a useless contraption, in his opinion.

'What on earth do them women need brassieres for? It's such a stupid garment, like a blooming catapult or something,' he lamented to his bosom friend Sonny, on one occasion when the two men were chatting amiably under the banyan tree.

Sonny wholeheartedly agreed although he couldn't quite resist a pun, 'Asch! Didn't you know? It's to stop them boobs from growing to the ground! You remember what old Pongo [another breakfast-eater of no mean repute] told us about them Chinese women who tie up their feet with cloth to fit them into funny-looking wooden shoes and stop them growing? It's the same with boobs. If women don't wear brassieres, their boobs keep on growing!'

Bellakay, who never laughed and rarely smiled, lit up a bit at the pun, adding mischievously, quite out of character, 'Yikes! What a sight it would be to see them boobs dangling all the way to the ground and women dragging them around like a ball and chain! Do you think that if we men didn't wear underwear, our dingles would also grow all the way down to the ground too?'

'Naaah! Dingles know when to stop. Dingles have a mind of their own, you know,' concluded Sonny knowingly, thinking primarily of his own giant penis that had grown to a vast length when he was a teenager and had mercifully stopped growing since. Even today, quite a few women complained of his lengthy penis, which caused Sonny to penetrate with extreme caution.

Rohan's arrival at Baking Jane's kitchen interrupted Bellakay, who had been chattering away with the former in a servile sort of voice. The tending of her hopper ovens needed constant assiduous care, but in spite of it all, Baking Jane still managed to chat with nearly all her customers in between operations. Bellakay was using his God-given raconteur skills very smoothly today, hoping to keep his patron in a relaxed and, most importantly, a generous mood – thinking primarily of the free hoppers he would receive for his endeavours.

'You know, our government chaps are getting down more and more of them students from abroad to stay at the youth hostel at Sea Street these days. Some kind of international agreement, I've been told. One can hardly pass that damn place without bumping into them. It's also very good business for them small shops around the place, you know! Those chaps always seem to need to buy some thing or another. Them foreign fellows have a lot of newfangled ideas and things, you know. And the gadgets they have! I saw one of them using a battery-driven razor to shave, all the while walking cool as a cucumber down the street! One never knows what they are up to next! Old Appu at the junction boutique was telling me the other day he's now stocking romping rubbers for them student chaps to buy. Very expensive these rubbers are too, I hear.'

Baking Jane, nonplussed, looked at him. 'Romping rubbers? Whatever for? What the devil are romping rubbers used for?'

Bellakay gleefully enlightened her. He loved playing the role of educator and wise man, seeing himself as some kind of local oracle who knew almost anything (which, in fairness to him, he was) and a cut above other Jellicoe Junction types (which he also was) whom he considered to be an out-and-out ignorant lot.

Condoms had only recently made their way into the Victorian market, and the usage of this particular type of contraceptive hadn't as yet become as widespread as what it would become in later years. Historically, Victorians had their own methods of contraception that worked well enough for them, their present modest population a living proof of this. Very few families had more than two or three children and had maintained the same level of posterity even during ancient times, when overpopulation worries were of no concern.

'Romping rubbers? Romping rubbers? Why, my dear, dear woman, don't you know?' exclaimed Bellakay, looking around himself warily. He stooped low to whisper in Baking Jane's ear, to prevent Rohan from hearing. 'That's what these foreign chaps use to put on their dingles, you know.' He lowered his voice even more, throwing a cautious look at young Rohan before continuing. 'That is to say, when the fellows want to have a romp with a woman and not make her get a baby! It's a long rubber thing that covers a chap's dingle and snaps tight on the top. No using our natural methods for these fine fellows! It's only them blooming rubbers that count!'

'Yikes! Exclaimed Baking Jane loudly in horror and disgust, which was exactly the kind of response Bellakay was expecting. Unlike Bellakay, she didn't care tuppence if Rohan was present or if he was listening or not. 'A long rubber thing, you say? You're telling me them fellows put this rubber thing on their dingle before a romp? What if the blooming rubber gets stuck inside the damn woman and never comes out, eh? Why, the poor woman will have a deuce of a time to get it out! How the devil do these foreign rascals come up with these things? Whatever will they think of next?'

Rohan, who had been listening earnestly, was puzzled about it all. What rubber thing was put into women? For what? And why put it on one's dingle? And why did old Bellakay whisper into Baking Jane's ear to try and prevent him from listening? He was determined to discuss the rubber thing with Salgado at school the next day. Perhaps his great friend could shed some light. The fat one usually knew quite a lot about worldly matters!

Baking Jane made out Rohan's order, wrapped it up in a piece of used newspaper, and handed over the parcel to her friend, who paid up promptly. Rohan was a tad reluctant to leave, envying Bellakay for staying on to enjoy Baking Jane's company. His parcel under one arm, he skipped along hurriedly to his next stop, the New Modern Café, Poppsy faithfully following behind at his heels. It was from here he would buy the egg-and-bacon roll his aunt Primrose had asked for.

Bellakay watched on eagerly as Rohan departed, glad to be alone with Baking Jane and expand his little discourse on condoms. He was an old-world conformist and disliked discussing sexual matters in the presence of children, preferring a tête-à-tête between adults. Supremely pleased with his sensational news and the ruckus it had created, he continued airily, befitting a man of his worldly wisdom and knowledge. He was back to using his normal voice again, considering whispering no longer necessary now that Rohan had left.

'Ah, my dear Jane, my dear, dear Jane, it's no use trying to fathom out these foreign chaps, you know. They are a different breed, you see, what with all their newfangled ideas and ways of living. Why, even their prime ministers and other big shots also use them romping rubbers.' (He didn't know this for sure but decided to take a wild stab at it anyway, to increase the severity of his case and keep his audience enthralled.)

Baking Jane envisioned this scenario in silence for a moment, revolted as it slowly sunk in. Thank God, she thought, that her own country's prime minister had the good sense not to have gone over to this awful habit ... or had he? Alarm bells rang in her head. It was hard to envision the prime minister wearing a romping rubber around his dingle; he looked so distinguished otherwise in person and in photographs. She shuddered at the thought that perchance the great man, their very own leader, had switched over to that disgusting habit Bellakay spoke of! After all, if those foreign fellows, prime ministers, and important people wrapped that rubber thing around their dingle before a romp, then maybe *he* had succumbed to this wretched new habit too.

She broke off her train of thoughts momentarily and addressed the gloating Bellakay, who was absolutely delighted by the reception his piece of news had evoked. He was assured of a good haul of discarded hoppers today – of that he was certain.

'I say, Bellakay! You think our prime minister has started using them disgusting rubbers too and abandoned our methods?' adding with some firmness, 'If he's gone and done that, then I'm jolly well not going to vote for that fine fellow and his blooming party at the next election, I promise you that! How can we decent people vote for a bugger that has them rubbers stuck up his blasted dingle? Old Appu selling dingle-rubbers, indeed! A fine state of affairs, I'm telling you. What this country is turning into, God in heaven knows! Everything's going to the dogs – that's what!'

She continued to ponder over the offending condoms, unable, for the life of her, to fathom how anyone could actually pay good money to buy them, let alone wear the offending abominations on their penises!

'How much do these rubbers cost? How much is old Appu selling them for?' she asked Bellakay with a true businesswoman's acumen, turning the conversation from safe sex to worldly finance.

Bellakay replied – slightly untruthfully, as it turned out – that he didn't really know. The all-knowing oracle was momentarily stumped. 'I heard old Appu saying three rupees, or something like that, for one packet of three,' he said a bit hesitantly, recalling a conversation he had overheard between Appu and one of the youth hostel tourists. He had a faint recollection that something like three rupees was mentioned.

Bellakay continued, a venomous tone creeping up in his voice as he recalled the many unsuccessful attempts he had made to purchase a few modest articles on credit from Appu. 'Knowing that shrewd damn bugger, he's sure to have bought them for one rupee less.'

'Whaaat?! Three rupees!' screeched Baking Jane. 'Why, I can buy the best takeaway steaks or even a plucked chicken at the marketplace for that kind of money. These foreign chaps are a blooming bunch of nincompoops, I'm telling you. Three rupees, my foot! And just to mess up their blooming dingles with the disgusting things! Romping rubbers, indeed!'

Bellakay, not really sure the offending condoms cost the three rupees he had tentatively mentioned, used a pacifying tone just to be on the safe side, in case Baking Jane questioned Appu about the actual cost of the romping rubbers. He didn't quite like the notion of being exposed as a liar. 'I *think* he said three rupees, my dear. I *think* he said that, but I know the shrewd rascal just puts up the prices when it suits him, especially when it comes to these foreign chaps, whom he can easily fool. He sells them rubbers to us local people for much less. Can't fool us local chaps, you know!'

Baking Jane beamed at him in amusement upon hearing this answer, a twinkle in her eye. She was quite fond of Bellakay. He was one of few people within her circle of friends she could confide in about her innermost affairs and share any genre of joke. Additionally, she really appreciated the platonic relationship they had together. He had never made a pass at her – not even once – unlike a good many neighbourhood men who lusted after and troubled her with their ceaseless advances and lustful looks, a few even attempting to fondle her forcibly at times. She always felt utterly at ease in Bellakay's company – almost like a queen.

'How do you know all this, eh? How do you know he's selling them rubbers cheaper to us local people? You starting to use those romping rubbers too, then, are you? How about showing me, eh? Bring one of them rubbers along next time you come and show me how it snaps onto your blooming dingle like you said! Maybe you can allow me to try and fit it on your blooming dingle while I hold it!'

Startled at first by this lewd comment, Bellakay was bemused, but then realising it was meant to be a pun, forced a hearty laugh. Secretly though, he would have given his right arm for Baking Jane to hold his penis and fit him on with a rubber.

The forced laugh at Baking Jane's jest literally hurt Bellakay's throat, the physical function being rather unusual for him. Privately and even when in the company of his cronies at the Nameless, he was seldom known to laugh. He had, however, not entirely forgotten this otherwise common human function, although it was hidden deep within his repertoire of professional emotions. On rare occasions, he did allow himself the luxury of a laugh, albeit a very hollow-sounding one, like that of a man without a soul.

The 'New Modern Café', Rohan's next stop, had opened a few a few months earlier, specialising in Western food like sirloin steaks, bread rolls with meat and fish fillings, assorted sandwiches, pastries, frosty cakes, and thick, meaty soups. Delicious frothy milkshakes and ice cream were available all day long too – a small luxury for many impoverished families at Jellicoe Junction who could barely afford them. He bought the egg-and-bacon roll which Primrose wanted and, putting it into the satchel over his shoulder, continued on his breakfast-buying expedition, Poppsy dancing merrily at his heels.

From the New Modern Café, Rohan made his way to a small eating house, Red's. The little eating house was aptly named. The owner, a portly, heavy-bellied Moor man, regularly dyed his hair bright red with a certain type of henna – a sort of tradition within his ethnic community. Red employed a staff of two: an elderly tea-maker and a young man who functioned as waiter-cum-dogsbody, doing all the various odd jobs that regularly needed tending to.

Red somehow managed to squeeze two tables and a tea-maker section within the small space he had at his disposal, putting benches beside the tables instead of chairs to ensure maximum seating capacity. Red's wife pre-cooked all the food available at the little eating house in the confines of her kitchen at home, whereupon Red's son would deliver it on the pillion of his bicycle two or three times a day – the food then stored on hotplates inside the eating house. Many of Red's customers ate their simple meals on unbreakable enamel plates as they stood or squatted on the pavement outside the eating house, for want of adequate sitting space inside. At breakfast and the lunch hour, a row of squatters could be seen outside, sitting cross-legged in Gandhi fashion, eating their meals on plates gingerly balanced on their laps. Nobody seemed to mind…

At Red's, Rohan purchased the last of his orders, the rotis Celeste had asked for. He bought the onion relish from Red too, deliberately ignoring Celeste's command to buy it from the 'corner boutique.' He knew fully well that Celeste wouldn't be the least bit wiser, as old Red did a jolly good onion relish too, although a somewhat nagging rumour purported that Red's onion relish caused stomach problems for his customers. A wide school of thought staunchly maintained that Red kept his onion relish too long in the tropical heat, whilst others firmly and squarely insisted it was the man himself who was the culprit. Red's appearance wasn't particularly confidence-boosting or inspiring. He didn't look clean, often clad in a cotton vest that had many food stains on it, as had the apron covering his rather dirty white trousers. Almost a chain-smoker besides, Red had a lighted cigarette between his lips most of the time, the ash falling quite anywhere he happened to be. Rohan, who devoured the comic strips in the Sunday newspaper with keen enthusiasm, always thought Red was reminiscent of the grumpy cook at the diner where the cartoon character Dagwood Bumstead usually ate his lunch whilst away at work.

Rohan deliberately and gleefully disobeyed Celeste about the onion relish, as she had been quite nasty to him after a recent incident when he had been caught red-handed purloining some of her face cream. Celeste had made an almightily big fuss about it all and even complained to Grandmummy, who had smacked Rohan on the head for his daring. Hell-bent on vengeance of some sort, he was rather disinclined to do anything special for his aunt right now.

'I'll give her "corner boutique" onion relish, indeed! Hope old Red's onion relish gives her a real nasty blooming stomach ache today,' he muttered to himself, recalling Grandmummy's rather painful smack.

He was further encouraged in his vindictive thoughts by the fact that Red was looking even worse for wear today. The burly proprietor's once white vest was stained brown and yellow in more than the usual places, and he appeared to be in dire need of a clean shave, a scrubby two-day stubble increasingly prominent on his chin, cheeks, and upper lip. He hadn't bothered to comb his red hair either and repeatedly ran his hands through his dishevelled locks, only to handle food with them seconds later. At times he would scratch his flaming hair in a way reminiscent of the enormous red orangutan Rohan had seen when the entire junior school had gone on an excursion to the local zoo a few weeks back.

Red was a fanatical dog-lover, and Poppsy was an established favourite. It was fortunate for the dog that Celeste had wanted rotis today, as Red generously broke up and threw a large roti at Poppsy, which the mongrel wolfed down ravenously within seconds, wagging his little tail in glee and sniffing around the ground afterwards to see if he had missed out on any minute bits that might still be lying about. Poppsy had got nothing from Baking Jane earlier on and was most grateful for Red's kindness.

Rohan returned to Grandmummy's with his purchases and distributed them accordingly, the young aunts harrying him, wanting their purchases before anyone else got theirs. The 'ladyships' and Rebecca had already prepared steaming-hot tea to wash down their respective breakfasts; Rebecca making tea for herself and the children whilst Primrose and Celeste made their own, sharing it with Grandmummy.

Rohan watched as the rest ate, a saturnine look on his face. He kept a keen eye trained on Celeste as she partook of Red's onion relish. Like some infamous poisoner at a decadent Roman emperor's banquet, he was hoping the food would turn in her stomach and cause his aunt a severe stomach ailment. She seemed to be enjoying it though, blissfully unaware it was bought from the dangerous Red.

'You should try this onion relish, Mother. I'm telling you, nobody makes better relish than that old amma at the "corner boutique"', mumbled Celeste in between mouthfuls, serenely unaware she was eating onion relish bought from Red, the bacteria mogul of Jellicoe Junction.

'Bah! I can make much better relish. And anyway, I don't know how you children can eat that blooming muck from those dirty eating houses! Why can't you and Primrose eat some cheese and buttered bread like me – or fry an egg? We are, after all, English, aren't we? We're not damn natives or riff-raff like our bloody neighbours!'

Celeste, who was in one of her fighting moods this morning, fired off a resounding salvo at Grandmummy, ready to nip away nimbly if Grandmummy struck out at her with her chubby hands. She was still recovering from a steamy argument she had had with Grandmummy the previous evening, seething with vexation at having come out a poor second in their altercation.

'English, eh? We? How the devil can we be English? It's only your father who was English! We others are all mixed from God knows what. And as for that cheese and bread you keep harping about, fat lot of good it has done you, hasn't it? Look at your damn size? We'd soon be needing a blooming crane to lift you anywhere!'

Grandmummy flushed a deep purple at this outrageous reference to her bulk and her precious family lineage amidst the giggles of the others present. She assessed the possibility of giving Celeste a severe smack on her head from where she was sitting but, finding the distance to be too far for any such action, resorted to roundly ticking off her daughter instead. She made a mental note to sit next to Celeste the next time they ate breakfast.

Celeste was over the moon at the success of her insults. She didn't give a tinker's curse for Grandmummy's scolding, having weathered hundreds of similar tirades before. Instead, she was highly elated over having scored off her impossible mother, at least this time around, additionally pleased that the rest at the breakfast table had giggled loudly at the Dragon's expense – another rare occurrence to savour.

Much to Rohan's great disappointment, nothing happened to Celeste. She showed no symptoms of acute poisoning or even of being remotely ill, to all appearances hale and hearty after finishing her breakfast. Rohan lingered around hopefully till she departed into her bedroom to put on her make-up and office clothes before leaving for work, but nothing happened still. His aunt didn't show the slightest signs of a violent stomach ache or anything similar. Red's more than usual dirty and dishevelled physical appearance this morning appeared to have been very much fallacious. He hadn't contaminated his precious onion relish in the least bit.

CHAPTER 2
School and an Eating Champ

Frogs and snails and puppy dogs' tails.
That's what little boys are made of...

IT WAS MONDAY AT JELLICOE Junction, the start of a brand-new working week. Schoolchildren lugubriously trudged on to school, whilst adults, equally mournful, put on brave faces, wishing to high heaven that it was Friday instead, and that the weekend beckoned. Rohan and Mahan had packed their schoolbooks into their small suitcases – a popular method for carrying books in Victoria – and had departed for school. Primrose and Celeste had already left for work, and so had Rebecca. Grandmummy was still bustling about in her kitchen, mumbling incoherent gobbledygook all the while – the kind only she understood – whilst the two little girls, Sussie and Maria, were playing house on the kitchen floor. They were still far too young to attend school – Montessori or day-care centres for very young children still a distant concept in the country's future.

Rohan and Mahan attended one of the island's finest and most prestigious boys' schools, which conveniently for them happened to be situated only a stone's throw away from Grandmummy's somewhat queer-looking house. One wondered how on earth they could afford to attend such a grand school in their present circumstances, but the truth of the matter was they had enrolled in that magnificent place of learning a long time before their unfortunate father's cock-up, a time when the offending parent, Rainier, had ample means and was a bigwig in society. The grand school happily welcomed the boys, and Rainier kept the school happy – his substantial cash donations made to the school's coffers much appreciated by a delighted school bursar. Things had changed, of course, since then… Rebecca couldn't even pay the boys' monthly school fees these days, let alone volunteer a cash donation. Rohan and Mahan would regularly bring in notes written by the bursar's office demanding Rebecca pay the boys' current school fees, and the arrears accumulated. Matters reached fever pitch when the bursar, tired of sending notes to Rebecca, informed the school rector, who in turn asked, or rather demanded, that Rebecca meet with him immediately.

The school rector, an out-and-out raunchy type, was living under a cloud, albeit a cloud known only to two other persons besides himself: the local bishop and old Father Ambrose. A year ago, he had been caught in the sanctum of his study, sans his school gown and with his trousers down, in the act of ravishing a fully naked young female teacher who wasn't averse to his attentions – far from it. To make matters worse, there were two other women in the room with him, clad only in their brassieres and stark naked from waist below.

When hauled up before his superior, the bishop of Portopo, who also served as head of the school board, he pleaded clemency on religious grounds, claiming that even the good Lord forgave his worst persecutors and enemies.

'My lord bishop,' he began, a look of false repentance on his rat-like face. 'My lord bishop, forgive my lapses, please. It was a moment of weakness. Even our great Lord Jesus was tempted by the Evil One in the desert – wasn't he?'

'Yes, yes, Rector, but our Lord didn't succumb to temptation, did he? All those women in your room without a stitch of clothing on! What utter wantonness! It was lucky for us that it was our faithful

Father Ambrose who caught you all in this vile act, not anyone else. He is under my strict command to keep quiet about this and will do so. I know Father Ambrose well, and his lips are sealed. If word of this gets out to the public and press, the school will be finished! Finished, I tell you! I have no option but to sack you!'

The rector wasn't going to fold up all too easily. He knew he had a trump card, and decided to play it. 'All right, my dear lord bishop. Like you, I am glad only the church knows of my trespass. It would be a disaster *if* the press got to know about this – a huge disaster. My good friend Charles, who is chief editor of the *Jellicoe Journal,* was telling me only the other day that they were so desperate for a story they would even pay a small fortune for something big. Things have been very quiet in the city these days, he said.'... It was a veiled threat to have the school lampooned – a silky and subtle one.

'You keep out of that sly fellow's way, you hear me! I forbid you to see the chap. I have heard only wicked things about him. Only last month, he wrote in his filthy communist newspaper that our school was run by misogynists – wanted girls to be enrolled too.'

'My lord bishop. You have just sacked me from my post. I *have* to find some other employment. I have a family, you know! Charles is sure to give me some sort of job to start with. But don't worry, Bishop; I'll try my best not to divulge a thing! I don't want the school to be ruined, you know! Imagine what a disaster that would be!'

It was a precarious situation, and the bishop knew he was beaten.

'Oh, all right, you damn rascal! I'll let you stay on, but if I ever get to know anything like this has happened again, I'll sack you on the spot, school or no school, newspapers or no newspapers! And you're not getting away scot-free, either! Your salary for this month is revoked, and there won't be any pay increments for you for the next two years!'

A few weeks later whilst the boys were at school, Rebecca took time off from work to meet with the school rector and sort out matters. She had made a prior appointment and was anxious to keep it. Explaining her situation to the great man, she pleaded with him to keep the boys on at the famed school on a sort of credit arrangement. She implored, or rather – more closer to the truth – begged, the school rector to waive aside the boy's expensive school fees until such time her husband recovered from his financial demise, promising to pay up all areas accumulated in due course. The rector, who had never seen Rebecca before, was bowled over by her alluring charms, stricken silly by her sex appeal. Rebecca was a beautiful woman, quite in league with her two younger sisters, though her looks were more sensual and mysterious in some sort of way. She had worn a short tartan skirt and a thin jumper on her visit, showing off her shapely legs and generous bosom to advantage, although she hadn't done it intentionally.

Rebecca was ushered into the rector's private study and, in a rare moment of leniency brought about more by lusting after her body than anything else, the promiscuous school head succumbed to her pleas to keep the boys on until such time as her situation improved and the payment of school fees was possible again.

'All right, Mrs Wendt, all right! I'll let the boys stay on for some time, but I want you to come and see me at the start of each term so that we can review the situation. Let us take it from there and see what can be done.'

The rector cunningly dropped his pen after he spoke and bent down on all fours under his desk, ostensibly to look for it, but boldly to have a view of Rebecca's knickers, which he hoped would be visible in her sitting position in front of the empty foot space of his large desk – a deed completely vilifying the sacrosanct office he held. He was not disappointed. Rebecca's short skirt didn't hide much in her sitting position. Her knickers were visible – very much so. She had carelessly worn a rather flimsy pair today, one which left little to the imagination. The voyeur enjoyed his view so much so that he had visions of soliciting private meetings with Rebecca in the near future, hoping, through gentle and subtle persuasion, perhaps even a little blackmail, to induce her into having a clandestine affair with him. He was besides aware of Rohan's father's criminal case, as it had been splashed all over the local newspapers at Jellicoe Junction, and was hoping that a mention would be made in the press of his, and the school's, generous offer of waiving aside the school fees. His close connection with his friend Charles and a few well-placed hints here and there would do the trick, he mused. It would do the school some good too, he further deduced, and his personal show of empathy might even improve his relations with the bishop. He was well aware that he was immensely disliked in Jellicoe Junction circles for the rather draconian and dictator-like tenancy of the office he held and was always ready and willing, through some cheap act or other, to redeem himself in the eyes of his many critics.

The rector, shortly after having dropped his pen, even 'carelessly' dropped a few important-looking papers under his desk to facilitate another close look at his victim's scantily covered privates.

'Here, let me help you,' said Rebecca, supremely unaware of what was taking place. 'Don't bend down so much, Mr Roland. It's not good for your spine, you know. I can reach those papers easily.'

'No, no, Mrs Wendt. Please, sit down! I can't have my guests crawling around on all fours! Sit, sit. I'll retrieve the papers in no time. Don't get up, please!' Saying thus, he bent down once more to savour his treat, pretending to gather the offending papers in the process.

That whole day, the sight of Rebecca's scantily covered womanhood and the hope of possible coitus preyed on his mind, giving him immense pleasure. Waiving aside the school fees was a small price to pay for the eventual benefits he could reap, he reflected. As for the woman's husband, surely he deserved to be made a cuckold of? After all, hadn't he gone and abandoned her and all that? A man who abandoned such a beautiful woman should only blame himself for whatever consequences his actions brought in their wake, he concluded.

The famous school Rohan and Mahan attended was recognised as a sort of local adaptation of Eton College in England. Conceived by European missionaries leaning heavily on the dogma of the Anglican

Church of England and built by a reputed foreign construction company, the school's imposing buildings stood out majestically, as did a vast chapel built later on in the late eighteenth century. An impressive sports ground for cricket, rugby, hockey, football, and athletics was also constructed, and a swimming pool of Olympian standards added later on. There were about a thousand boys attending the current school – as in Eton – consisting of both boarders and oppidan scholars. A school uniform was mandatory, although the pupils here were spared Eton's heavy pinstriped trousers, being required to wear trousers of light-blue flannel and white shirts with an open collar – a sensible combination more suited for Victoria's climatic conditions. Chapel attendance, where Latin-chanting Mass, complete with incense burning and all the other rites and trimmings of Christian nomenclature, was inevitable and mandatory. Unfortunately, at least where the boys were concerned, corporal punishment like caning was allowed and was frequently administered exactly like at Eton, although students weren't asked to pull down their trousers before a caning was administered.

The school motto, 'In scientia et virtute', was much admired, although many left school with a somewhat tricky knowledge of the sciences in their baggage and with rather suspicious virtues imprinted on their characters.

The bell rang for the English class – the last period before the lunch interval. The boys, including Rohan, quite ravenous now, looked patiently forward to their approaching lunch. Breakfast seemed like an eternity ago, and they all longed for the lesson to be over and done with. As usual, Rohan had done well with the essay which the boys had been ordered to write last week. The selected topics for the essay were 'my father's occupation' and, alternatively, 'my family'.

The corrected essays were in the process of being publicly dissected, as was the custom practised by their somewhat weary-looking but very erudite English teacher, old Mr Withers. He had spent the previous evening at home in the onerous task of reading and correcting the boys' work. Over the years, Mr Withers, barring a small handful, had become gravely disappointed by his young charges' academic performance, or rather, to be brutally honest, their lack of any...

Unlike most of the other masters – a gravely sententious lot – Mr Withers did not moralise, nor did he inflict corporal punishment. He didn't even vent out his anger by ranting out his displeasure at erring students. Instead, he maintained an innocuous front, developing through the passing years a sublime talent for the best kind of cynical mordacity, which he practised profusely on his young charges. The biting, caustic comments he constantly subjected the students to pleased old Mr Withers no end, although it was utterly wasted on the boys, who never quite got his drift. Even on the few occasions when his subtle barbs *did* go home, the boys just didn't care. They accepted corporal punishment as a necessary evil and weathered a direct admonishing without flinching, but sarcasm – *that* was lost on them!

Mr Withers's non-violent approach notwithstanding, the boys treated him cautiously, as, besides the sarcasm, he was quite famous for sending alarming notes to their parents for the minutest of scholarly or disciplinary lapses – a regular happening. Worse still, Mr Withers demanded his notes be signed by both parents and additionally would scrutinise the signatures most carefully to see if they were forged – another talent he had acquired and perfected over the years. He was no fool and knew what his young charges were capable of.

Mr Withers was Eurasian, a tall, thin, somewhat dried-up-looking man. He was quite old, completely white-haired, and had served the school loyally for nearly four decades. At the onslaught, when he had first arrived at the school as a freshly examined teacher, he was the spirit of buoyancy itself, never doubting that he would, and could, make a profound impact by contributing positively towards his charges' proficiency in English. As the years rolled by, his embryonic exhilaration slowly diminished as the hopelessness of his task became more and more apparent. His steady comedown stemmed from the gradual realisation over the years that nothing he taught really sunk in to the minds of his students. Where exhilaration reigned initially, apathy took root subsequently. Mr Withers's initial buoyancy grinded to a complete halt. These days, he taught more in a state of automation than anything else. The earlier ranting, cajoling, and pleading had long since disappeared, and in their place sarcasm and subtle comments reigned supreme.

Mr Withers had often hoped at least one of his pupils would have gone on to become a great international lawyer arguing his cases in prolific English, or a famous writer of English novels, or someone who distinguished himself in debates at the great universities of England – even anything remotely close, but sadly for him this had hitherto never happened. Judging from the present lot he taught, it wasn't likely to happen, either, although he did wonder a bit about young Rohan…

As the years accumulated and new batches of students came and went, Mr Withers gradually lost all hope. The drudgery of teaching year in and year out to what he considered was a perpetual hopeless lot finally took its toll. There was a veneer of resignation imprinted on his countenance these days whenever he took a class. His teaching had lost its soul, and his daily lessons had cumulated into a regular mantra.

Right now, he was admonishing William, whose prowess in English, written, spoken, and otherwise, was abysmal, to say the least. William was being chided for his poor submission of an essay the boys had collectively been required to compose the previous day. Mr Withers had admonished hundreds of 'Williams' in the past. He was just following procedure – business as usual.

'William, your effort was quite preposterous, to say the least. Hasn't anything I taught sunk into that head of yours? I'm sure if one looked close enough through one of your ears, one might be able see right through the other!'

He continued amidst the boys' laughter over his insinuation that young William had no brain or, to be strictly anatomically correct, any actual brain matter from ear to ear.

'When you ask a friend what his father's occupation is, you don't say, "Job father's is what?", you silly boy! You have to ask the question, "What is your father's profession!" Why, for God's sake, didn't you use the word *profession*? How many times did we go through this word and its meaning last week when we discussed the various professions a person could have? Doesn't anything get into that airbag you call a head?' Mr Withers demanded scornfully of the young scholar, a sardonic grimace making his wrinkled countenance look more like a witch from Macbeth than a respectable schoolmaster.

William listened glumly; his body slunk deep into his chair. Mr Withers continued, the sardonic grimace metamorphosing into a weird, clown-like grin. The grin was intended to show that he was about to say something amusing. Mr Withers always thought he looked amusing when he put on his infamous grin, although no one else did. His face resembled a very dried-up old apple with patches of discolouration, which no grin or touching up could ever change for the better. He continued without showing the slightest remorse for William's feelings. 'And your father's profession is not a lawman.' (William's father was a lawyer.) 'We are, after all, not living as in the Wild West of America! I'm quite sure your father would resent being titled a lawman! He is a professional lawyer and not a blooming gun-toting sheriff, you stupid boy! I will be sending a note to your parents about your horrendous work. See that it's signed, and bring it back tomorrow. And don't even think of forging the signatures or *accidentally* spilling any ink on my written comments like you did last time. One more forgery and off to the rector you go, you rascal!' (He accentuated *accidentally* in a most sarcastic manner. William, of course, had spilled the ink deliberately.)

The boys guffawed loudly. The expression *gun-toting* was new to them, nor did they know the meaning of the word *horrendous*, but they certainly sensed and knew that Mr Withers had a good thing going against William. Wicked to the core, they were also delighted to learn that the latter's earlier attempts at forgery had been detected, something they hadn't known before.

William slunk a little more deeply into his chair. He looked around fiercely at the other boys, daring them to make any uncomplimentary remark, which he would deal with later, all the while deeply resenting their loud peals of laughter. Like Emperor Caligula of old, whose reign was discussed in detail at their last history class, he longed for them all to have just one neck so he could swipe it off with a single blow of his sword.

William wasn't the only boy who had problems with English grammar. Victoria, although a former British colony and traditionally very British in law, infrastructure, culture, and most everything else, did not possess a great many citizens who were fluent in writing the Queen's English, although they could and did speak English somewhat satisfactorily after a fashion. Dialects were distinctly local and quite different from any of the archetypical English accents one would expect to hear. Certainly nobody spoke the kind of English dialects heard on BBC programs aired over the radio, in English films, or in international Pathé newsreels shown at local cinema halls in the run-up to main feature films.

Turning his attention from the squirming William, Mr Withers hailed Salgado, the largest boy in the class and another well-known 'connoisseur' of English-grammar violations. Salgado was well over fourteen years of age, whereas the others in the class were all around twelve. He had spent an additional year in the second form – kept back by the school authorities not because he was lacking in intelligence or learning qualities, but because of his sheer laziness and complete indifference in applying himself to academic work of any sort.

Salgado possessed two attributes of fame. He was the official class clown and could eat more than anybody else in the whole school. Fat as a well-rounded pig and with a suspicion of a moustache and beard already appearing on his chubby face, he could at times pass for a young adult. He even looked more mature than some of the senior boys in the upper sixth. He was the dominant boy in the class, well liked by his fellow classmates, especially Rohan, who was his absolute best friend. He looked up indifferently when addressed thus by Mr

Withers. He knew what to expect, what was coming, and wasn't overly concerned.

'Harrumph! Salgado, your inept essay on the subject of your family was preposterous, to say the least, full of mistakes and just one page. Rather thin, I would say, wouldn't you? Not quite as bulky and rotund as your own elephantine frame, eh, boy?' said Mr Withers, adding insult to injury.

Mr Withers's little dig was not lost on the boys. Peals of laughter burst forth from the appreciative audience at this obvious reference to Salgado's massive corpulence, even though the words *inept, preposterous,* and *rotund* were way beyond their grasp. *Bulky* they knew well enough, and they assumed that *elephantine* had something to do with an elephant. The laughter had no effect on Salgado. Unlike William, he was unperturbed by his schoolmates' mobbing. He didn't care a fig for Mr Withers's insults and didn't mind in the least bit being the butt of his classmates' jokes – even laughing along with his comrades at his own chastisement.

Mr Withers held out the offending essay paper in front of himself for the whole class to see. Although just barely filling the single foolscap sheet and cunningly double-spaced by the author, the correction marks in bright red ink were so numerous, they dominated the budding essayist's blue-inked effort. Mr Withers continued. 'Hardly a sentence correct, as usual, and who the devil asked you to write double-spaced?' Here, Mr Withers stopped and looked sharply at Salgado, expecting some sort of explanation about the double-spacing. Getting none from a mute Salgado, Mr Withers continued anyway.

'Besides, you say your father is six yards tall.' (More laughter from the boys) 'I'd like to see this father of yours, my boy. Don't you know anything of the measurement tables? I really must have a word with Mr Strool.' (Mr Strool was the boys' arithmetic master, whom they callously and gleefully nicknamed Mr Fool.) 'Stay in after class is over and correct you mistakes before you go for lunch. And yes, you will get a note from me, to be signed by your parents too.'

Salgado's hitherto grinning face fell abruptly at the news of this most disturbing punishment. Mr Withers's note to his parents he cared tuppence for. He was a past master at forging *both* his parents' signatures – forgeries so perfect that even the old warhorse Mr Withers couldn't detect his felonies. It was his delayed lunch that bothered him. He was quite ravenous, looking forward eagerly to his lunch like everyone else and positively hated anything coming between him and his meals. Corporal punishment he could take in his stride; insults he could bear; Mr Withers's sarcasm an enigma he didn't understand – but belated or missed meals was an abomination. He had a permanent love affair with eating, one that needed constant nurturing and, of course, a great deal of food – most importantly, served on time. Missing lunch or any meal even by a few minutes wasn't very appealing to the colossus.

Mr Withers concluded his public autopsy of the boy's work, sublimely dissecting two other unfortunates' efforts as well. He would have loved to dissect a few more and continue practising his subtle sarcasm and acid wit, but time was of the essence. The lunch-hour break loomed ahead. He looked at his wristwatch and said conclusively, 'As for the rest of you, don't imagine for a second that you are any better. Most of you have written absolute rubbish – except for Rohan and even De Merl, who have excelled, as usual.'

The boys, upon hearing this last statement, looked up respectfully at Rohan and De Merl, wishing they could emulate the duo's scholarly feats. Rohan, who was quite used to similar praise from *all* his schoolmasters, said nothing and just waited anxiously for the bell to ring for lunch. A naturally gifted scholar, he didn't need to put in too much of an effort to get top marks, although he diligently did all his required homework. The kudos and compliments which often came his way, he accepted as a matter of course, often shrugging them off without much ado. De Merl, on the other hand, an out-and-out swot, swelled up with pride each and every time he was singled out for praise. He really enjoyed the accolades, gloating whenever he outshone his classmates. The only thing marring his pleasure was the fact that Rohan too had featured in Mr Withers's kudos.

De Merl was Rohan's great scholarly rival. Hailing from one of the most wealthy families in the island, he was a proud and arrogant boy. He had all the social advantages that Rohan did not possess and was a very good student besides, matching his lowly rival's proficiency in all the class subjects, although never quite exceeding them. His family spent a great deal of money on private tutors and the likes, and the results showed. De Merl excelled in sports too and was the current year's captain of the under-thirteen cricket team – an excellent compliment to his academic prowess. It all cumulated, like the proverbial icing on the cake, in making him an ideal candidate for future head prefect, an honour reserved for the school's most prominent student, one with the right family background and 'connections'.

Rohan would have made an ideal candidate for future head prefect too, but his father's recent disgrace and subsequent fall in Victorian society had all but ruined whatever chances he may have had. The entire school, the boys' parents, and even supporters, would have dreaded the prospect of having a son of a prominent local criminal as their head prefect! It just simply wouldn't do.

The English class, after some further scholarly activity by the boys, supervised by Mr Withers, slowly drew to a close. Salgado, who abhorred the looming prospect of a delayed lunch, politely asked Rohan to help him out with his unfortunate essay.

Rohan liked Salgado a great deal, and his feelings were reiterated. He agreed to help. They were the best of friends – an odd couple – but loyal and very fond of one other, each in his own way. There were about ten minutes left before the lunch interval bell rang, which time Mr Withers used to correct a few papers from another class he taught, leaving Salgado and the others largely to their own devices. Rohan took full advantage of the temporary lack of supervision to correct Salgado's unfortunate essay, finishing it very quickly and with a minimum of effort. Salgado was grateful. All he had to do now was to pretend to correct his essay a few minutes after the bell went off and then hand it over to Mr Withers, shortening his incarceration considerably – all thanks to Rohan's help. He patted Rohan's back in appreciation.

'I'll buy you your ticket next time we go to the matinee on Friday,' he said, much relieved after Rohan had handed the corrected essay back to him.

'Oh! That's not necessary, Salgado. I have money,' replied Rohan airily – never one to take advantage of his scholarly ability, especially with regard to Salgado, whom he considered his best friend.

'Bah! You save your money for next time, Rohan. Pa asked me to take his Sunday trousers to Salim's to be dry-cleaned, and you know what I found in them stinky old pockets of his?'

'No. What did you find there, eh?' asked Rohan.

'The old man forgot to clean out his pockets, Rohan, and in one of them I pulled out a five-rupee note!' exclaimed Salgado in triumph.

'What! Five rupees! Why, that's a fortune! What are you going to do with it?' asked Rohan excitedly. (There was absolutely no question in the minds of the two friends that the money ought to be returned! 'Finders, keepers' was their unholy motto!)

'Oh!' sighed Salgado, reminiscing on what had been and how he had spent the proceeds of his paternal heist. 'That happened last Saturday, you know! I've eaten at the New Modern Café three times since then, and only yesterday I bought a whole packet of them tasty dog biscuits from Mungo at the school gate. The money's all finished now, except for one rupee and fifty cents, which I saved for the matinee at the Empire. My cousin Barney wanted me to see that *World by Night No. 3* film at the Elphinstone that all them adults are talking about, but you know they won't admit us. The Elphinstone manager had put an "adults only" tag on the film, and there is nothing we can do about it. One and fifty is enough for two tickets to see the new Dracula film at the Empire.'

The 'dog biscuits' Salgado touched upon were a large local biscuit about four times the size of a normal biscuit. They were very popular with the good people of Jellicoe Junction, especially with children, who absolutely adored them. Nobody quite knew why they were called 'dog biscuits'. In all probability, it was a pun caused by some frivolous person – a pun which nevertheless had caught on and spread like wildfire. They were dark brown in colour, sugary on top, and tasted wonderfully sweet, with fluffy insides simply melting in one's mouth. There were sinister allegations freely flouted as to the ingredients that went into their making, but nobody could ever prove anything to substantiate the rumours.

Rohan nodded his head knowingly at the mention of the *World by Night No. 3* film. Whilst the school gang clamoured to see any half-decent adventure film featuring cowboys, Tarzan, and the likes – even faithfully attending a frightening *Dracula* reel – the promiscuous *World by Night* films, an absolute aesthetic delight for adults, had gradually piqued their juvenile curiosity, although they could do nothing about it. The films, shown in sequences dubbed 1, 2, and 3, with a fourth scheduled for production in a Hollywood studio, were classed as 'adults only', beyond the boys' viewing possibilities. Still, whenever they viewed the usual type of films they hankered after, trailers of forthcoming films, whether 'adults only' or not, were freely shown. Rohan, Salgado, and the gang gazed in amazement at the very short interludes on display, gasping over the glimpses of partial nudity that flashed on the screen. The *World by Night* films had taken the whole country by storm, capturing audience interest like no other film ever had. All they showed in the films was a potpourri of nightclub cabarets cleverly stringed together and featuring naked and seminaked women in all manner of song scenes, dance sequences, and poses. Such brazen nudity was never, ever before seen in films in the Victoria cinema circuit, people flocking to cinema halls to lap it all up – often waiting hours on end in queues for a prized ticket.

The school gang were on the verge of pubescence – every one of them – and the worst-affected was Salgado, who often even got an erection at home and at school and didn't know quite what to do with it. He had considered speaking to his father about it, but whenever a suitable moment arose, he just couldn't bring himself to open the subject, feeling far too embarrassed by it all. At times, he even thought of soliciting the help of old Father Ambrose, the school's catechism teacher, but he discarded the idea as perilous, seeing how much the old priest raved and ranted at the boys at the chapel confessionals for even the most trivial of sins – a trait frowned upon by Father Ambrose's boss, the bishop of Portopo, who had warned his octogenarian colleague for remonstrating excessive zeal at the confessionals on many occasions. Salgado did, however, discuss his dilemma with his cousin Barney, a strapping young man of eighteen who was studying at the University of Portopo's medical faculty.

'I say, Barmy. (Salgado mischievously addressed his cousin as Barmy after having learnt the true meaning of the word in a Laurel and Hardy reel.) You know, I've been thinking of asking you, er, does your dingle ever become very hard and big-like?'

Barney, whose 'dingle' had long since entered that particular phase, listened solemnly, but he didn't quite know quite how to explain it all to his young cousin. He tried a rather soft explanation, hoping Salgado would forget the matter and not bring it up again until the latter had fathomed it all out himself.

'I think it's your size, Salgado! A chap as big as you should have a big dingle. I think your dingle has realised that and has decided to grow along with you. It must be that huge people get huge dingles and smaller people get smaller dingles. You are getting so big; your blooming dingle wants to get big too. It's all human anatomy, you know!'

'Yes, yes, I've thought of that, Barmy,' said the fat one testily, 'But mine's not only getting bigger. It gets hard as rock too! It keeps pointing out from my underwear.'

'You know, Salgado, I think you should ask Uncle Bertram [Salgado's father] about it. I'm not very sure about your condition. Uncle Bertram will throw some light into the matter. Everyone knows he's so very clever.'

'Bah! Blast it all. Barney, you are studying medicine and all that, aren't you? You got cow dung in that blooming brain of yours? Why the devil don't you know? You should know! Bloody fine doctor you'll turn out to be! Might kill half your blasted patients, if you ever pass out, that is!' expostulated Salgado, irritated by his cousin's scandalously poor medical acumen.

Barney stood his ground, repeating his sagacious advice. 'Ask Uncle Bertram, Salgado. I've only just begun my term at uni. I hardly know anything about that blooming medical stuff as yet. I think your large size has something to do with it.'

Salgado wasn't too sure about Barney's instant diagnosis. He just had to have that talk with his father, he mused dejectedly, throwing a withering glance of disdain at his cousin for being unable to unravel the mystery of his condition.

The school bell rang for the lunch break after Mr Withers's English class, the boys departing on their separate ways. Some of them ate at the school lunch hall, the cost of which was charged to their monthly school fees. Others either brought their own lunch packed in neat little lunch boxes or ate at the many nearby eating houses, which, conveniently for them, were scattered around the vicinity of the school – never more than five minutes away. A favourite amongst the boys was Simon's Vegetarian Lodge, where they ate scrumptious vegetarian dosas, the cheapest food available anywhere in the whole country and pivotally for them, resulted in having money left over to buy candy, bubble gum, or fruit.

Both Rohan and Mahan went 'home' for lunch. Rebecca, who had pre-cooked the little family's modest meal before she went to work, kept the cooking pots suitably elevated over the dying embers of her firewood oven so the children had a fairly warm meal to eat. Her own lunch she would pack and take it with her to work, eating it cold. Little Sussie would wait patiently for Rohan and Mahan to come home before she ate, the boys dutifully dishing out a portion for her before they began. The brothers were quite fond of their little sister and supervised

that she ate all her food – a most difficult task, for the little girl was a
chatterbox and loved nothing better than to jabber away on all sorts
of topics in between mouthfuls of food. Grandmummy, faithful to
her apartheid policy, didn't eat any of Rebecca's prepared food. She
had a much superior lunch delivered from one of the nearby eating
houses and shared it with Celeste's little girl, Maria. Grandmummy
wasn't exactly over-fond of eating traditional Victorian food, often
calling it 'native muck', but she hadn't much say in the matter, as
little Maria absolutely refused to eat anything else. Besides, preparing
lunch for just herself and the girl was tiresome and not very practical.
The boys ate quickly, although Rohan was the last to finish, not
because he couldn't keep up with Mahan, but because he always
patiently paused in his trenching to answer his garrulous little sister's
questions. Sussie especially loved chatting with Rohan – a favourite
victim – much more than with Mahan or anyone else. Today's topic
was no different from the many previous ones.

'Rohan, is it true that giants can eat people? Maria said that
giant fellow in the *Jack and the Beanstalk* picture book we saw in the
morning had got fat and big by eating people. Is it true, Rohan? Is it?
Is it? Is it? Is it true he ate people?'

Rohan sighed before answering. He would have dearly loved
to contradict young Maria – the notion of anybody eating people
not quite appealing to him, but he kept his riposte affirmative, not
wanting to draw out the conversation. 'Yes, yes, it's true, Sussie. He
was an evil fellow, that giant, eating all those poor people.'

'What a lot you know, Rohan. I'll tell Maria that *you* said it's true.
Can you *tell* the picture book again, Rohan? After we eat? Please,
please, please?'

'I don't have time, Sussie. I have to get back to school in time for
my lessons. I'll tell you what, though. We can read the book in the
evening or after dinner, all three of us, you and Maria and me.'

'I'm going to school too when I get big, Rohan. Mummy said I will
need iniforms.' (She was referring to uniforms.)

'Yes, Sussie. Now eat your lunch like a good girl.'

'You tell the picture book in the evening after you come home then, and don't you get late playing "clicket" or anything like that!' said Sussie sharply, a stern look of warning creeping up upon her young countenance.

'All right, Sussie. I won't play cricket after school. Eat your food now. It's getting cold.'

After saying goodbye to young Sussie, Rohan hurried back to school, where the school gang usually played fiercely contested cricket matches the rest of the long lunch interval. The game had been fondly introduced by the British at the turn of the century and had caught on like wildfire during the long period of British usurpation. It was now elevated to the national sport of Victoria – Victorians proving to be surprisingly good at it, even beating their old colonial masters at international games, much to the latter's embarrassment and chagrin.

When Rohan arrived at the sports ground, it was literally covered with small gangs of schoolboys playing out their own little 'battles' on different segments of the playing field. Although cricket was the favourite sport and dominated most of the proceedings, a few teams playing football were also sweeping back and forth over the ground in rippling waves, without being stymied by one anothers' activities – not to mention keeping their eyes focused on just *their* own playing ball and game.

Rohan's schoolmates had already divided themselves into two teams. Rohan found himself on the side of Ranjeeth, the best cricketer in the class and a reputed batsman.

Boniface, the youngest member of the school gang, looked on resignedly, clutching a much battered suitcase with both hands. He was hoping a miracle would happen and his suitcase would be spared from cricketing service this time around, but his intimidating colleague William dashed his hopes. 'Didn't we tell you last week to ask your pa to buy you a new suitcase? It's a blooming disgrace, your damn suitcase. The useless thing is almost falling apart!'

'I asked Pa, but he said no! Said he had bought this one only two months ago. Maybe we can use some other boy's suitcase, eh, William, please? I mean, mine's all half broken and all that, like you said!'

Boniface, a faint glimmer of hope in his heart, looked on at William, but the latter just glared back threateningly. Both boys knew in their heart of hearts that it was Boniface's suitcase – and none other – that would be used.

The boys in Rohan's gang marked the ends of their cricket-playing pitch. On one end, behind the batter's crease marked out by a rough line in the grass, they placed Boniface's suitcase in an upright position to serve as their wicket. The other end – the bowling crease end – was marked by Boniface's shoes, which he was sternly and forcibly ordered to remove.

Boniface was the timidest boy in the gang. He was utterly innocuous and passive, constantly subjected to all sorts of tomfoolery and bullying by the rest. Like a weak puppy in a strong litter, he found himself a regular and favourite butt for pranks and jokes. Whenever they played cricket, it was always *his* suitcase that was used as the wicket, and it was always *his* shoes that marked the bowling crease. The boys hardly bothered to ask his permission. It was taken for granted that they would use young Boniface's possessions. On the instances he plucked enough courage to bleat a feeble protest (which happened quite seldom), he was vociferously shouted down into submission by the others, who brooked no argument.

Young Boniface, a decent enough scholar, was useless in any sport. Needless to say, he was an absolute prosaic cricketer, hardly able to hold a bat, never mind wield it. Nobody wanted him on their team, which was all very convenient, as the teams needed an umpire for their matches and Boniface fitted the bill perfectly. In his bare socks and unable to get away because his suitcase and shoes were in absolute indispensable cricketing service, he was automatically (reluctantly for him) elevated to the post of umpire, a position hardly requiring any cricketing acumen, at least where the boys were concerned.

Boniface's umpiring duties were a mere formality. He rarely had to make any decision, the boys judging themselves whether a batsman was 'out' or not. Sometimes when a batsman was judged 'out', fierce disputes arose between the two teams, resulting in utter chaos and huge embroilment amongst the factions. On several occasions, cricket matches ended in a free-for-all and the termination of the match until one or more of the warring parties gave in.

Boniface's usefulness as an umpire was confined to his arithmetical prowess only. He was expected to count the number of balls delivered by a bowler and to shout 'over' in a loud voice when the full six were delivered. It wasn't much of a life for young Boniface, but on the bright side, he found himself in the thick of all the gang's activities and wasn't isolated in any way. He was the gang's very own buffoon – albeit a well-loved buffoon – and he knew it.

After the lunch interval was over, the boys reluctantly marched on to their classroom for the rest of the school session, Boniface clutching his battered suitcase with both arms, the handle having come off long ago, courtesy of regular and intensive cricketing service…

There were no difficult subjects that particular afternoon. The first subject was geography, taken by the very mild and very ancient Mr Veron.

Mr Veron had a terribly scarred throat, a result of some major surgery done many years ago in his younger days, which prompted the boys – so cruel and slick in handing out nicknames – to wickedly dub him 'Cutthroat'. The sobriquet was a terrible injustice, as a more mild-mannered man could not be found in the entire school.

As with animals' ability to sense fear, the boys had developed an uncanny sense of discovering just what mettle a teacher was made of – a talent vital for their existence. Apart from Rohan, De Merl, and a very few others, they were not a very sedulous lot, more interested in sports and tomfoolery than in their expected scholarly pursuits. They had long since discovered that Mr Veron, or Cutthroat, as they unanimously called him behind his back, was a harmless old fogey and paid scant attention to him, using his class to engage in all sorts of nefarious activities. They even dared to take the mickey out of the old master with outrageous comments and insults over the state of his scarred throat and other scandalous matters.

'Sir, sir,' one of them would say, 'my dingle wants to do a pee. Can I be excused, please? Otherwise, Mr Dingle might pee in the class,' or, 'Sir, sir, an ant has run up my trousers into my underwear sir, can you pull them down and have a look, sir? I don't want to be bitten, sir,' or 'Sir, sir, is it true that cutthroats are very bad people, sir? The word is in our *Treasure Island* reader, sir. Bad men are called "cutthroats" there.'

The last comment especially stung deeply. Mr Veron, like the other masters, was painfully aware of his soubriquet and hated it immensely.

Cutthroat kept mum at the barbed comments he was constantly bombarded with. He was old, very old, and did not seem to care, or perhaps pretended not to. He was a harmless, dreamy sort of man, living in a long-lost, forgotten world. Often, when he rambled on about the qualities of the river Po or the Yangtze, he seemed to be far, far away in Italy or China rather than in the classroom he presided over. His academic lectures these days were sing-song affairs, addressed to nobody in particular and full of hard facts, but totally wasted on the unresponsive young scholars, who hardly ever listened.

Still, in spite of the disrespect the boys showed, things weren't all too bad. Cutthroat had a secret understanding that was amiable and worked superbly for both parties. Apart from their occasional vulgar heckling, the boys didn't riot or cause too much noise during his class, whilst Cutthroat – infinitely grateful for their quiet behaviour – left them pretty much to their own devices. An obstreperous class would only draw attention from the school rector and jeopardise his continued employment at the school, a fact Cutthroat was only too well aware of. He had been cautioned by the school authorities a few times in the past for presiding over noisy classes, and was most anxious these days that the boys under his charge keep quiet. He had put in his long-overdue retirement papers and was just a year away from saying his final goodbyes to the school he both loved and hated. He wanted, and was most careful, to see the year through without incident so as not to blot his service record by getting the sack so close to his impending retirement.

Cutthroat's special 'understanding' served him in good stead with most of the boys at school but best with the boys in Rohan's class. The only occasion he insisted they pay attention was when the monthly and midterm exams came around where the boys were duty-bound to participate. Rohan, who was very good in geography, usually finished the test paper in record time and generously helped most of the others, who slyly copied as many of his answers as possible before the end-of-period bell rang. The outrageous yet empathic deed was not forced upon Rohan, but was done more in a spirit of genuine altruism than anything else. Cutthroat may have been ancient and dreamy, but he was no fool. He was aware of the mass cheating, but he shrewdly decided to let things go. In addition to a noisy class, which had the potential to endanger his job, a majority of the boys failing geography would also reflect negatively on his prowess as a teacher. He knew the school office kept immaculate records of student results – a potential two-edged sword. The records, besides being used for preparing the boys' report cards, were also subtly used as a barometer by the school rector to assess the abilities of individual teachers or, rather, their lack of them.

Salgado's eating habits were as phenomenal as they were famous. Only last school term, he had taken a bet with the boys that he would eat twenty dosas at one sitting at Simon's Vegetarian Lodge, and had successfully completed the feat – much to the astonishment of those privileged enough to witness the stupendous and mind-boggling effort.

Dosas, a type of flapjack first introduced by South Indian immigrants, was made from wheat or rice flour, broken down with a vegetable broth before eating by using ones fingers. Spicy sambal made of grated fresh coconut, in addition to a mulligatawny-like curry soup served in small brass tumblers, enhanced the main dish which was served on a cured banana leaf. Dosas were popular in the cities being both tasty and extremely cheap, each dosa costing just five cents.

The vegetarian eating houses serving Indian food at Jellicoe Junction were an attraction in themselves, especially to the wondering eyes of tourists. They had a great many pictures of Indian gods strung up in a haphazard fashion on the wall behind the cashier's desk, garlanded in tiny electric lights that blinked on an off. Images of the elephant god Ganesha, the remover of obstacles, Shiva, the cosmic dancing destroyer, and other well-known deities looked down benevolently upon the clientele from their lofty perches, lighted joss sticks sticking out between cracks in their picture frames. The air smelled perpetually of spicy food blended with the scented aroma released from the joss sticks. There was the usual cigarette smoke too, as most customers usually lit up after a satisfying meal, but the tobacco odour was snuffed out, drowned in the much heavier aroma of the joss sticks and spicy food. Radios, another inevitable hallmark, blared out popular local songs with hourly interruptions for news broadcasts. Nobody seemed to mind the gods, the smells, or the noise from the radios. Customers were immune, wormed and weaned from many decades of fraternising.

Salgado was given sixty cents – a more than satisfactory sum – by his parents to buy lunch, although to hear him grumble about its inadequacy, one would have thought his parents were parsimonious and held tight onto their purse strings. He was an only child and the apple of his parents' eyes, especially his mother, who absolutely doted on him. She would have gladly parted with much more money for her darling boy, but Salgado's father put his foot firmly down. *He* wasn't easily fooled.

'Sixty cents is far more than what most schoolboys get, Mabel,' he would protest whenever his wife brought up the subject of increasing Salgado's lunch allowance. 'It's not healthy for the boy to eat too much, and, besides, I know he spends just forty cents on those dosas and other food he eats, while the rest goes for that rubbish he buys from that Mungo chap at the school gate. At our office, the lunch allowance for the staff is only forty-five cents, you know! Ample for any grown-up!'

'But Bertram, my dear, the dear boy's *soooo* very big! He maybe needs more nourishment than what other children do!'

'Nonsense, Mabel! He's all right! And besides, he eats well enough at home, doesn't he? Wasn't it only yesterday he finished off everything at dinner when you were hoping to save some of that roast beef for lunch today?'

Salgado's mother sighed. She loved to see her boy eat, the walloping of the offending roast beef not bothering her the teensiest bit. On the contrary, she had looked on lovingly until he had finished the last piece. She would bring up the matter of increasing Salgado's lunch allowance again after some time and repeat it a few times until her husband gave in. She knew how to grind her man down.

Most of the other boys in Rohan's class did as Salgado, often frequenting Simon's Vegetarian Lodge, as they both liked the food and appreciated its very low cost. All of them could eat three or four dosas at a sitting, which cost just fifteen or twenty cents. It filled their stomachs to satisfaction, but more importantly, they had about twenty cents left over for candy and other tempting stuff to buy from Mungo at the school gate. Mungo did a brisk trade and never had to shout out his wares, as did most of the other street vendors. He was a tough character and never one to back down from physical combat, often guarding his little plot beside the school gate with fierce zeal. The undisputed king of the gate, he tolerated no other vendor doing business within reasonable vicinity, often chasing away competitors by using physical force when sheer intimidation or a resounding ticking off failed. It was only Catnips, the mercurial breakfast-eater from the Nameless, who had the uncrowned regent's regal blessing to peddle his wares beside Mungo. Catnips did not sell edibles like Mungo did, confining himself to all sorts of strange paraphernalia like cheap penknives having many blades inside the casing, fountain pens that looked beautiful but leaked to high heaven after a week or two, small harmonicas, unused but outdated diaries, and brand-new comic books with the front cover page missing for some strange reason. He sold many other odd things too, keeping the impressionable schoolboys in suspense wondering what unusual items he would have for sale the next time around. Catnips didn't sell his wares every day like Mungo did, often going 'missing' for many weeks, sometimes even months, only to turn up some day as though he had never been away. They got along well – Mungo and Catnips – which was all well and good for the king of the gate. For all his roughneck manner and toughness, Mungo was quite lonely at the school gate, sorely missing having an adult to talk to. At times, he would loudly lament Catnips's frequent absences.

'Where the devil has the blooming chap gone off to this time? I can't understand how he can make any profit from his business when he stays away so often. Maybe it's true what people say about them damn ganga joints he smokes. How the devil he gets the money to buy the damn stuff, God only knows! Can't be from that awful junk he sells here! Those damn ganga joints are bloody expensive, I'm told. Maybe the man has some secret business elsewhere. You can never tell with that blasted chap. He's such a bloody mystery! I hope he comes back soon, though!'

Nobody quite knew why Catnips was a street vendor or where he got his strange merchandise from. It was widely rumoured that he had made a pile of money some years ago through an infamous underworld heist and didn't have to work at all if he really didn't want to. A wide school of thought purported that he masqueraded as a street vendor from time to time only when he couldn't bear to put up with life's grinding ennui any longer. Others, though, wicked tongues for the most, explained his long absences from his spot at the gate to a periodical addiction to smoking ganga joints – a mind-blowing Victorian psychotropic drug made from the cannabis plant's leaf and other unknown ingredients.

Salgado usually ate about eight dosas for forty cents, leaving him a healthy twenty cents to buy anything else he fancied from Mungo later on. One day, egged on by the boys, Salgado spent his entire sixty cents eating ten dosas and then indulged in a large helping of sweet sago pudding, which the management had only recently included in their menu, polishing it all off with a steaming cup of sweetened cocoa. This was no mean feat, and the boys, to a man, cheered him. Drunk with valour, Salgado boasted he could eat an additional ten dosas and even more pudding if only he had the money. He was not afraid of his boast, knowing jolly well that none of the gang would willingly volunteer to give him the extra money for an additional ten dosas – or anything else, for that matter. The gang laughed and ridiculed him.

'You do that and you'll burst, you damn fat fool,' said Lizard, a regular dosa eater of no mean repute.

'Whom are you calling fat, you stinky old *lizard*!' retorted Salgado hotly, more in automation than any real anger. Gang insults always demanded an instant and cutting riposte. Salgado was just following procedure...

Salgado knew he was overweight, grossly so, but unlike most fat persons, he was proud of his size and didn't have the slightest desire to change any part of his portly anatomy.

Lizard had a skin affliction on his lower legs which caused them to look ugly and scaly, not completely unlike the scales of Victoria's large local monitor lizard, *Varanus salvator*, hence the sobriquet. He was well used to being addressed as 'Lizard,' but he winced all the same every single time anyone addressed him thus. He ignored Salgado's insult in silent pain, deciding wisely that a retort would be useless. Besides, they had both cancelled out each other's insults – and the gang's sacrosanct code of honour had been maintained.

Obadiah, another dosa regular and the established pessimist in the gang, decided to put Salgado to the test. 'All right, Salgado! We'll all chip in with our balance money. I think we have enough for them ten dosas you say you can eat.' He paused to smirk disbelievingly and then continued. 'You order them ten now, and we'll see if you can eat them or not. If you can't, you will refund our money tomorrow and double it.' (There were five boys eating lunch at Simon's Vegetarian Lodge that day, and they could just about cover the costs of the additional dosas.)

Salgado was rather taken aback by this sudden and unexpected Samaritan offer. He wasn't afraid of failing to consume ten new dosas, but the truth of the matter was that he had just that very day eaten five large ripe mangoes an hour or so before lunch during Cutthroat's geography class, courtesy of some extra money his mother had given him the previous evening for ironing a few of her blouses. The lunch he had just consumed on top of it all had filled him completely. Obadiah's surprising offer didn't augur too well for any eventual success – not just now – not how he felt. He would fall flat on his face and fail if he accepted the bet and made the attempt. He knew this instinctively.

'All right, all right, I'll accept your blasted money and the bet, but another day. Not today,' replied Salgado firmly.

'Why another day? What's wrong with today?' inquired Lizard with a caution befitting his reptile status.

Salgado stuck to his guns. The gang often enough teased him about his phenomenal eating habits, even calling him a glutton at times, and although he didn't mind the teasing in the least bit, he drew the line at being accused of gluttony – a sin that even goofy old Father Ambrose had warned them about at catechism class. Right now, he didn't want to reveal his pre-lunch mango-eating feat, which, in retrospect – even to him – did *indeed* sound quite a lot like gluttony. The bet was to be held another day or not at all, Salgado insisted sententiously, firm in his resolution, brooking no refusal.

The gang, seeing he was adamant on this, point didn't argue any further. After some heated discussion, they unanimously agreed that the proposed feat should be performed the coming Monday. It was already Thursday, and Friday somehow didn't quite appeal, as most of them usually cut school, disappearing after the lunch break to get home early for the much longed for weekend break, or alternatively to attend a Friday afternoon matinee at the nearby Elphinstone or Empire cinema hall.

Down at the Nameless, news of the oncoming dosa-eating challenge had already reached the ears of the always nosy breakfast-eaters. They were, to a man, itching to talk about it. Uncle Pongo, Rohan's impoverished great uncle and a regular breakfast-eater, was highly sceptical that young Salgado would succeed in his record-breaking effort.

'What a bloody fool that fat Salgado boy is! Nobody in his right mind can eat so much. The fellow's surely going to burst his stomach if he tries to eat so many of them blooming dosas. Why, I myself – a grown man – can't eat more than three! They fill you up like hell, you know! And then there are those Indian fellows' soups and thingies they serve on the side too!'

'Poppycock!' exclaimed Bellakay from his usual seat in the corner. 'Stomachs can't burst, my dear, dear Pongo. It's a medical fact that a stomach can't burst. It's all old wives' tales – pure balderdash!'

'Huh! Sometimes you think you know everything, don't you, Bellakay?' quipped Catnips acidly amidst his trenching. 'Of course, a stomach can burst. Don't you chaps remember that glutton, the huge fat old minister fellow who got sick and died while eating like a damn pig at that election dinner? The newspapers were full of it. They definitely did say his stomach burst, and he died because of it. I think the word they used was *riptured* or something like that.'

Bellakay listened patiently. He was used to Catnips's constant contradiction of anything he proclaimed. As soon as Catnips had finished, the resident sage's riposte came flashing through. 'Tchah! What a lot of damn rot those newspaper chaps print sometimes! And it's *ruptured*, not *riptured*! That's the word you're looking for, Catnips. That glutton of a minister fellow's appendix ruptured, and he died because of the infection afterwards. *Ruptured* means "burst", sort of. His stomach did not burst like those damn foolish newspaper journalists wrote. His appendix did.'

'Bah, riptured, raptured, ruptured – who the hell cares! I'm not a bloody walking dictionary like you! Something did burst in that glutton's stomach while he was eating all that food, and that's good enough for me. Anyway, I'm going to Simon's Vegetarian Lodge tomorrow to see the fat boy eat. It's not every day you get to see a fellow kick the bucket from a good old stomach bursting, eh, chaps? Any one of you fellows want to come along and see him die? You better not miss it, lads. These kinds of things don't happen every day, you know! It's an once-in-a-lifetime opportunity to see all the twisted *tubes* and *thingies* inside a fellow's stomach!'

Catnips's remarks were deadly intentional and not meant as a joke. He looked around the breakfast table inquiringly and in earnest, but the others, not as morbid or bloodthirsty, politely declined. In any event, they weren't too keen on seeing a young gladiator die in the arena, especially one as young as Salgado. They all muttered excuses of a sort and backed off. Catnips was clearly put off – very much disappointed by this shocking lack of interest for such an excellent case of potential stomach bursting.

'Huh! All right, then, all right! I'll go alone if none of you lazy buggers can't lift your damn arses and come along. If anything interesting happens and the fat boy's stomach bursts, you fellows are only going to blame yourselves for not coming and missing out on such a big happening. Don't blame me afterwards. Remember, I did ask you all to come and you said no!'

Uncle Pongo, who heartily disapproved of Catnips, shouted out disparagingly, 'You're a damn bloodthirsty villain, Catnips, that's what you are. Are you so happy to see someone die or get sick? If there is any devilment going on, you're always in the thick of it! You're going to end up badly, you know! Won't be surprised if it's going to be the gallows for you at the end, you damn rascal! You're going to meet the hangman one day. Just wait and see! You want us to come and watch, eh? We'll come, all right. We'll all come to watch *you* the day *you* hang!'

Catnips grinned devilishly at Uncle Pongo, not in the least bit taken back or shaken over the latter's macabre prophecy. He loved upsetting and baiting Uncle Pongo or, for that matter, anyone else at the Nameless. It was not as though he *disliked* any of them – far from it – but mischief was like second nature to him. He had a dark sense of humour, a quality regularly popping up amidst his other mercurial and sometimes downright Machiavellian qualities.

'Bah! Fiddle-diddle! Pish-posh! Just sod off, Pongo! No blooming damn gallows will ever get me! Don't worry about that! It's not the gallows that's waiting for me, Pongo – it's fame and glory. I'm going to be the most famous fellow in Victoria one day. You fellows are going to be surprised like hell! One day soon, you, Pongo, and all you others, will come begging and creeping to me for favours. You'll be crawling and kissing my hands and feet. Just wait and see! Just wait and see!'

Uncle Pongo declined to answer. Catnips nearly always countered any criticism of his errant ways by forecasting a brilliant future for himself, as he did now. The 'most famous quip' of his was as legendary as it was tedious to hear, at least for the breakfast-eaters. They had heard it all before, a million, zillion times before!

The following Monday, Simon's Vegetarian Lodge was much more crowded than usual. Word had got around, not only in Rohan's class, but also even to most of the junior school, that Salgado would be attempting a new eating record and would consume twenty dosas in one sitting. Rohan too was present, abandoning his usual lunch at Grandmummy's in order to witness the forthcoming spectacle. Sonny had paid him the day before for bathing Strangefellow, so he had money for a modest lunch. He told Sussie she would have to eat lunch with only Mahan for company, as there was a function at school he had to attend and would not be eating at home. Little Sussie didn't quite like what she heard, but went along well enough after Rohan promised to bring her a small bag of sweets that afternoon after school was over.

The lunch hour grew nearer at Simon's Vegetarian Lodge. The waiters at the eating house went about their business as usual, but one could tell they were buoyant and in a special state of expectation, often looking at the entrance, expecting Salgado and the rest to troop in at any moment. They were quite fond of the boys, even enjoying the impish comments they made and the constant acts of tomfoolery they enacted on each other whilst eating. Besides, they were quite flattered that these scions of Victorian high society patronised their humble little eating house.

The waiters, of course, had their information sources and were aware of the bet between the boys and Salgado. Gambling addicts to a man (they bet on local horse racing like madmen), they had subtly organised an internal betting syndicate amongst the staff – even the proprietor joining in. The odds were severely stacked against young Salgado. As long as they could remember, nobody had ever eaten more than seven or eight dosas in a single sitting, and it seemed just nigh on impossible to consume twenty! Still, one or two brave hearts did bet against the run of play, sagaciously reasoning they were in for a minor windfall if the fat boy, against all odds, succeeded.

Catnips, faithful to his declaration during yesterday's breakfast palaver at the Nameless, was seen at a smaller table for one, eating a lunch of dosas and eagerly awaiting a good old stomach bursting or anything else remotely macabre – even mass murder, if it came to that. Catnips didn't really like dosas – a rare exception for Victorian trenchers. He almost always had rice and curry for lunch at the best eating houses at Jellicoe Junction – a dish he dearly loved – but had decided to forgo it today in lieu of what might be, elated by this heaven-sent opportunity to break the humdrums of day-to-day life he found so excruciating.

The eating game started in earnest… The boys kept Salgado company until their modest lunches of three dosas were consumed. Relaxed and content after their meal, they sat back to watch their fat friend succeed or fail in his monumental feat.

Salgado went on. He maintained a dignified countenance and passed the ninth dosa with seemingly no trouble at all – already a new record at the eating house! Apparently unperturbed, he then proceeded to calmly order another six. He ate slowly, his fat cheeks and lips moving about sideways, like a cow chewing grass. There was some difficulty in putting down the fifteenth dosa, but he overcame that hurdle by swallowing a gulp of water to help it along his throat, his Adam's apple faintly visible in his fat throat, wobbling up and down in rhythmic accompaniment.

The waiters and the boys looked on with bated breath, tensely following the drama enfolding before their very eyes, fascinated to the core. The other guests in the eating house had stopped their trenching too, watching on in muted, yet keen, interest. Salgado ordered another five dosas in a hoarse voice, his eating hand trembling like an old man's as the eating recommenced. He ate as if in a trance, little beads of sweat forming on his forehead and upper lip. His fat fingers trembled and he shifted his weight several times uncomfortably on his chair, yet he kept on going, his eyes glassy and fixed directly on his banana leaf. There was a veneer of impregnability around him that didn't bode well for the betting odds. How the boys cheered and jeered – even the previously mute guests joining in – sensing an unlikely triumph. Catcalls and whistles filled the air, drowning the songs on the eating house's radio, which was hardly audible for all the shouting going on.

Finally, with the greatest of efforts, Salgado finished off the last dosa and pushed his empty and soiled banana leaf away. He had won the bet but had temporarily lost his power of speech; additionally, for the life of him, unable to find his legs and balance to stand up. The beads of sweat on his forehead and temples had become small rivers, whilst his face took on a shade of grey ambergris. An obliging waiter, a broad grin on his face, came along and took away Salgado's empty banana leaf whilst his colleagues were seen in the background settling betting scores.

Catnips, who had been eagerly following the proceedings, was crestfallen, thoroughly disappointed by the outcome. He yearned to poke or prod Salgado in the stomach to sort of kick-start a good old stomach explosion – or what was it that old goat Bellakay had said? 'Appendix burst', wasn't it? Or was it a 'raptor burst'? But thought the

better of it. Looking around him, he realised that most of the crowd
seemed happy over the fat boy's success. If he prodded the fellow's
stomach and it went and burst and all that, it might upset their 'joie
de vivre' frame of mind. They could turn dangerously against him. He
had experienced situations before where mobs had threatened, and
sometimes did give him, a sound thrashing for interfering in matters
that didn't concern him. The outcome of the foregoing events meant
he wouldn't have a flamboyant story to tell the others at the Nameless
the next day during the morning's breakfast session. Still, all things
considered, he could at least contradict prim-and-proper old Pongo,
and inform him that the fat boy *did* indeed eat all those twenty dosas
he had said he would. Wouldn't the old sod be flabbergasted! The
thought of vindicating his worst critic comforted him somewhat as
he quietly and discreetly exited the lodge.

Salgado's immobility caused a new and unexpected problem for
Rohan and the school gang. Their position was precarious, the state of
affairs alarming, to say the least. If they left their all-conquering hero
back in the eating house, the proprietor would certainly telephone the
school rector and inform him of the situation. Once the betting story
got out, it would surely end badly for them. Their parents would be
informed, and if *that* wasn't bad enough, they would all be subjected
to the rector's personal disciplinary action, which, in all likelihood,
would be corporal, courtesy of his stinging rattan cane. Parental wrath
and a severe caning from the much-hated rector loomed ominously
ahead. It was then that Rohan, the often successful resuscitator of
hazardous situations, spoke up.

'I say, chaps! Look here now! I think we'll have to transport the
fellow. He can't walk or talk, it seems, and we can't just leave him here,
can we? We'll all fall into trouble if we do.'

The boys listened to Rohan attentively knowing he always had
clever ideas and respecting him for it, but his current suggestion
seemed downright far-fetched.

'What dang-blasted cock-and-bull transport are you talking
about? How the devil are we going to transport him? Do we have

money for taxis? Or maybe you have a car of your own, eh? You're talking rot, Rohan!' said Obadiah vehemently.

Rohan countered Obadiah's assault disdainfully, giving the latter what he hoped was a withering look of scorn while thinking at the same time what a damn annoying fellow his classmate was, with his constant disapproval of every single thing.

'Who's speaking of taxis, you grumbling fool? Are we blooming millionaires? And you blasted well know I don't have a car at my disposal, you silly jackass! We can hail a cart from here and ask the driver chap if he's taking the school road. Plenty of bullock-carts pass by the school all the time. The waiters are sure to help us lift Salgado and dump him in the cart. We can give the carter fellow twenty cents for his trouble. He's sure to agree. We have twenty cents amongst us, surely?'

The boys' countenances brightened up considerably at this suggestion. They could easily manage the twenty cents between them. Besides, the very thought of Salgado being transported like a sack of coal in a rickety old bullock cart appealed greatly to their wicked sense of humour. Their temporary jitters seemingly over, they were firmly back in the saddle.

And so it was. Salgado, partly immobile and too exhausted to protest (he was able to stand up now with some help, but he still couldn't walk or talk), was unceremoniously dumped in a passing bullock cart, with clear instructions to the obliging carter to stop at the school gate. Rohan and the rest of the gang followed the slow-moving, rickety contraption on foot. The particular cart they had successfully hailed was transporting a manure mix of semidried cow dung and straw. Salgado was lifted by the hands and feet and roughly heaved onto the cart by the combined efforts of the obliging waiters and the boys. He lay there sprawled on the foul-smelling manure, face upwards and quite helpless. The cart rattled and shook a great deal on its wobbly wooden wheels during the short journey, ensuring that Salgado was well and truly immersed in the muck by the time the cart and the motley crew trouping behind arrived at the school gates.

The stench emitted from the cart and Salgado wasn't pleasing. Well forward at their destination, the boys, together with the carter, reluctantly helped to unload their human cargo. Salgado had recovered his ability to walk somewhat by now and was able to wobble along unsteadily without any help. He managed the short walk to the classroom amidst the cheers and jeers of his classmates. The boys helped Salgado brush away most of the straw and dung particles hanging onto his clothing and person, but, for the rest of the afternoon, the somewhat unpleasant stench of cow dung hung over his person and the immediate vicinity around him. The boys warily kept their distance. Well inside the classroom, those usually sitting immediately around their hero scrambled for sitting accommodation at vacant desks well away from the unpleasant smell.

Salgado had fully rediscovered his speech by now and was as cheerful and chirpy as ever. He boasted incessantly of his eating feat. Not even the humiliation of the cart transport or the stench of dung clinging to his rotund person could rob him of his triumph.

The first lesson after the lunch break was history, and the boys braced themselves nervously, awaiting the history master, Mr Odd Bull. Mr Bull, a well-built man in his late thirties, wasn't really 'odd', as his name suggested, but was definitely avant-garde. Nobody really knew his ethnic background, nor did his surname give anyone a clue either. He was of an extremely fair complexion – almost pure white – and had long, pale-blond hair, unusual for a Victorian. Some maintained he was Scandinavian, others a European Caucasian, whilst there was a growing school of thought who swore he was a local man inflicted with vitiligo, an albino-like skin condition known to afflict a few Victorians. He was neither liked nor disliked, but was definitely very much respected. The boys paid Mr Bull the utmost attention, as they knew he tolerated no nonsense and wasn't slow to administer corporal punishment if he felt it was required. Alongside Mr Cedric, the boys' Latin and civics master (a nefarious, sadistic man of slight build and the most hated man in the entire school), the duo were considered impossible to fool in any way. The boys paid more attention to both Mr Cedric and Mr Bull than to anyone else on the teaching staff, more from actual fear than anything else.

Mr Bull sniffed the air with some distaste as he entered the classroom. He paced the classroom curiously, searching for the epicentre of the stench, and wasn't slow to find it. It was obvious that the bad smell generated from that fat boy, Salgado, and no other. Mr Bull was well aware of Salgado's many idiosyncrasies and escapades, but this was something groundbreakingly new.

'You're adding bad hygiene to your other villainous ways, boy?' he inquired, a distasteful look crossing his waxen face. 'We can't have that here. You're supposed to shower and clean yourself thoroughly before coming to school. How dare you come here smelling like this?'

The boys giggled in mirth, knowing very well why Salgado smelt badly, but stopped short of sharing that bit of information with their formidable history master.

Mr Bull, realising he would get nowhere probing further into why the fat boy smelled so badly, proceeded to act on matters at hand. 'Bend over, you dithering young whale, and take out that stuff from your back pocket.'

Salgado, always in trouble with the school authorities, had a permanent rolled-up newspaper in his hind pocket – an ingenious and inventive precaution to soften the cane blows to his vast behind he was so often the recipient of.

Mr Bull, however, was made of sterner stuff and had a sharp eye. Not much of the boy's tricks or scheming escaped his watchful alertness. He had long since being aware of Salgado's cute little ploy with the rolled-up newspaper. Salgado reluctantly did as requested, resenting the fact Mr Bull was aware of his small precautions. 'Blast him,' he thought resignedly. 'The blooming albino jackass seems to know every dang-blasted thing! How the devil did he know of the newspaper?'

Bending over as ordered, Salgado received three stiff cuts from the determined Mr Bull's formidable cane. It wasn't much of a caning as canings went, and Salgado was immensely relieved it wasn't the hated Mr Cedric he had to square up with. He returned glumly to his desk, glaring in defiance at nobody in particular. He disliked being hit, irrespective if it hurt or not, and was secretly planning to come back after he had finished his schooling and thrash the living daylights of all those who had caned him, especially mean old Mr Cedric. He would often fantasise about it all whilst sitting with his parents on the front porch at home after a particularly good dinner, smiling contentedly to himself. His thoughts drifted to how he would pin the somewhat scraggy Mr Cedric against a wall and twist off one of his arms, snapping it like a dried twig. He had seen it being done in the last *Tarzan* matinee the boys attended at the Empire Talkies and was pretty sure he knew how to master that particular technique. Or maybe he would just tear off one of the evil master's ears after first wrestling him down to the ground and sitting on him with his huge torso. Both deeds filled him with immense pleasure, and his smile would widen even broader the longer he dwelt upon them. The frequent smiling didn't go entirely unnoticed by his adoring mother, who – poor woman – hadn't the faintest clue about the horrible deeds her beloved young son was planning.

'Look at the dear, sweet boy, Bertram,' she would whisper to her husband. 'Isn't he a happy and contented little man? Just look at the way he smiles at the world. What sweet thoughts the darling boy must be thinking! Just like a little angel, isn't he?'

Her husband, Bertram, however wasn't quite convinced of his son's alleged angelic qualities, although he couldn't help being intrigued by the frequent smiling. He had experienced far too many of his offspring's hazardous escapades in the past, which his good wife conveniently chose to forgive and forget. He loved his son very much too, but he wasn't as trustful as his wife and absolutely wouldn't go so far as to term Salgado 'angelic'. Not by a mile…

Passing the school's cricket ground on his way home that afternoon, Rohan paused awhile to watch – somewhat wistfully – the senior cricket team hard at practice. All along, and in spite of his wonderful prowess in scholarly activities, his real fervent desire was to someday be able to play for the school's cricket team. Everything else paled in comparison. Looking on now as the players went through their motions, he sighed in utter hopelessness.

Sports were expensive. Cricket, especially, needed imported studded boots, white shorts, jockstraps, groin guards, and other such expensive paraphernalia. Rebecca had refused him outright when he had asked her to buy him the gear he needed, not that she disliked sports, but there simply wasn't enough money. Asking Grandmummy or the aunts was futile, as the cruel family nepotism Rohan was subjected to placed him at the very bottom rung of their affection ladder. It seemed so unattainable, he ruminated, like howling for the moon, and would probably remain impossibly so unless his family could by some great stroke of luck repair their dilapidated fortunes, re-establish themselves in society, and revert back to the glory days when his father had been such a bigwig in society. What a magnificent turnaround it would be, Rohan concluded, his ruminations complete.

One day shortly afterwards, a stroke of great good fortune came by Rohan's way. Mahan had received a pair of used, but perfectly good, cricket boots from one of the wealthy Moor boys whose patronage and company he so often solicited. He was definitely not as interested in cricket as Rohan was and had no intention of using the boots, but kept them anyway – adding them to his private collection of hoarded treasures he jealously guarded day in and day out. He was a possessive sort of boy, Mahan, carefully keeping all his odds and ends in an old wooden chest. Old bicycle bells, foreign postage stamps in albums, discarded catapults, broken alarm clocks, rusty penknives, old toys, and many other odds and ends went into the chest, hardly ever to see the light of day again. He liked to hang onto his many treasures although he rarely had any earthly use for them. Rohan knew this only too well and knowing the destiny the boots would in all likelihood suffer, suggested to Mahan he be given the pair of cricket boots, in exchange for which Rohan would do both the morning breakfast and the evening grocery chores for a period of two months. The suggestion delighted Mahan, who hated these shameful duties from the bottom of his heart and who, in any case, had no earthly use for the boots. He agreed airily, but not without first hemming and hawing a trifle, not wanting to show his bursting delight all too openly.

'Harrumph! I don't know, Rohan, them boots are worth a lot of money, you know! Besides, I may want to play myself someday. I really don't know if I can give you the boots just like that, you know!'

Mahan was rather keen to keep Rohan on tender hooks, seeing how eager his brother was to get the deal done and get his hands on the boots – enjoying the sight of his sibling's anxious and hopeful face in his own little twisted sort of way.

'Please, please, Mahan. Please let me have the boots. Think of all the shame you will avoid doing all that awful marketing. And if you want to play one day, why, Daddy's sure to come back someday soon, you know. Mummy always says so! He will be able to buy you several pair of boots if you want then.'

After what seemed an eternity to Rohan, but in reality only took a few seconds, Mahan finally said 'yes.' The boots deal rowed home, Rohan was able to report for junior school cricket practices the very same week.

There were about twenty boys or so who had turned up for cricket practice. The sports master, Mr Pontybum ('Ponty' to the boys) served as the school's official junior cricket coach. Mr Pontybum was a past national cricketer and rugby player of some repute. Plump and elderly, he was quite immobile, standing motionless for the most by the bowler's end only to suddenly burst into action and bawl out coaching advice whenever he thought his protégés needed it. De Merl steered much of the practice sessions with the help of his close cronies, and although Mr Pontybum was officially responsible for selecting the final team, De Merl's influence and recommendations were total and binding.

De Merl sneered when he saw Rohan on the practice ground, wondering how on earth his arch-rival had managed to get his hands on a pair of perfectly good cricket boots. Hadn't the damn fellow gone and gotten poor and all that? Pulling himself from his initial surprise, De Merl went through the motions of the practice session on hand, a hundred schemes going through his fertile mind – schemes to sabotage Rohan's best efforts to play himself into the team. Rohan had to be kept out of the side by any means possible, and De Merl knew just how to get about the nasty whole business. He was damned if his 'enemy' would outshine him in sports as well. Coming second in his academic pursuits was bad enough…

The practice session commenced. Each boy was given a chance to bowl and bat, whilst special fielding practices were also on the agenda. At the bowling sessions, De Merl cunningly steered things his way, following a Machiavellian plan for sabotage he had already worked out in his twisted mind. Rohan wasn't given a chance to bowl at all. All the boys were given a small try-out except for Rohan, whom De Merl conveniently seemed to have forgotten.

Rohan fumed in silence. After being overlooked several times, he signalled frantically to De Merl to be given a chance to show off his skills to the head coach, Mr Pontybum, but his desperate signals fell on deaf ears. De Merl pretended not to see Rohan's frantic signalling or even hear his shrill verbal requests to be given a chance to perform.

When it was time for batting practice, De Merl let all the others bat first and when there was just five minutes left, he signalled for Rohan to put on his leg pads and have a go. Rohan had time to just face a few balls. De Merl had also very cruelly arranged for him to face the team's fastest and deadliest bowler…

Perhaps rage and disappointment had an invigorating effect on Rohan, for he brandished the next few balls to all parts of the ground with ruthless relish. It was a masterful, truculent display of cricketing skill, all his pent-up feelings seemingly guiding his bat as he clouted the fearsome bowler to all parts of the playing field.

Alas for young Rohan, this magnificent display of batsmanship did not affect anything at all. By the time Rohan had come on to perform, the ageing Mr Pontybum, longing for his evening tea, had already left the ground to go home. Rohan's short stay at the batting crease and its efficient occupancy had sadly gone unnoticed by the great man – a wasted effort. It was exactly what the aberrant De Merl had intended and schemed would happen.

All the subsequent cricket practices that Rohan attended followed the same pattern, De Merl intentionally keeping Rohan out of the limelight and ruthlessly overseeing that Mr Pontybum was either occupied elsewhere or wasn't present at all whenever Rohan was called on to perform. Rohan's good friend Ranjeeth, who also attended the practice sessions, quickly figured out what was happening and tried to get De Merl to stop his unfair bullying tactics. Ranjeeth was the best junior cricketer in the school – an indispensable regular in the team – admired by the entire cricketing fraternity for his sublime acumen with both bat and ball.

'Hey! De Merl!' Ranjeeth shouted irritably. 'Rohan's a damn good batsman. Why the devil don't you let him bat when old Ponty's around, eh? What are you hiding the fellow away for? Let old Ponty see what he can do, blast it!'

De Merl snarled back at Ranjeeth, spitting out his riposte in no uncertain terms. 'Who's the bloody captain of the team, eh, Ranjeeth – you or me? I decide when that fellow performs and when he doesn't! Can't you see there are many other boys wanting in line to bat and bowl? We have to give everyone a chance to perform, haven't we?' De Merl lied through his teeth, ostensibly pretending solidarity with the rest of the hopefuls waiting to get into the team.

Ranjeeth wasn't easily fooled. He knew that De Merl's self-proclaimed kindred empathy was just a well-executed ruse to restrain Rohan from performing when Mr Pontybum was present. Fed up with it all, he tried to put things right by playing the part of resuscitator – a finger-pointing resuscitator.

'You're just jealous of Rohan, you old rotten stinker,' said Ranjeeth in disgust. 'If we have Rohan in the team, we can have one really good side that will help us win many matches. You know that, but you're keeping the fellow out anyway because you just hate him. Isn't that so? You awful blooming bully!'

De Merl squirmed upon hearing Ranjeeth's telling words. He disliked Ranjeeth – had done so for a long time – and longed to remove him from the team, but dared not, as the latter was their acknowledged best player. Besides, he was well aware of Ranjeeth's popularity with the school's cricket fans, knowing instinctively that any attempt to exclude the star player would meet with massive and total hostility. It might even be the start signal for his own downfall, his influential family and connections notwithstanding.

Despite his squirming, De Merl hadn't any bad conscience over his actions. Ranjeeth was untouchable and would in all likelihood remain a thorn in his side all his schooldays, but he was fast determined to at least keep Rohan out of the team.

The days that followed found De Merl pressing on even harder with his furtive plan, using cunning and stealth not to give Rohan the remotest chance of showing his cricketing prowess in front of old Mr Pontybum. When the others in the pool besides Ranjeeth also questioned his foul tactics, he dismissed them scathingly. 'You lot who are not satisfied with my management can leave the practice pool immediately. Nobody's *forcing* you to be here, you know! Like Ponty often says, we must have *unity* in the team. Follow me as your captain, or leave now.'

Of course, none of the protestors wanted to leave – a most disagreeable option. Each and every boy was hoping for a place in the final team selection.

At the end of the month, the names of the selected players were printed and posted on the school's main notice board. Fifteen players were selected, including three reserves. Rohan's name was not amongst them. He stopped going for practices and stored his cricket boots safely under his mother's bed.

A week later at school, Rohan went through the motions of

the morning session before the bell clanged for the lunch break, whereupon he went home for his modest lunch pre-cooked by Rebecca. After first seeing to little Sussie's lunch, he ate ravenously – his only previous meal a paltry breakfast he was able to buy with the meagre ten cents he had received from Grandmummy that morning.

Returning to school, Rohan noticed his schoolmates talking in hushed tones and whispers in small groups. Most active and agitated were De Merl's small group of ardent followers, who seemed greatly perturbed over something. Approaching his good friend Salgado, who was in earnest conversation with some of the boys, Rohan inquired curiously, 'Why are you fellows all in groups and whispering like old women, eh? Why are you all standing here like this? What about our cricket match? Didn't Bonny [Boniface] bring his suitcase today, or have we lost the tennis ball – or what?'

Salgado looked up at Rohan in surprise. 'Why? You're asking why? And what blooming cricket match? Haven't you heard the news, Rohan? That fellow De Merl is in hospital – serious case, it seems. Fellow might die soon, they say. Serve the dirty rotten bugger right.'

Rohan was blown away by this extraordinary bit of news – flabbergasted and definitely surprised. 'De Merl's in hospital? Serious? What are you're saying? Why is he in hospital? What happened, Salgado? The fellow caught some dangerous fever or something?'

Salgado supplied the wanted information gleefully. He usually disliked dwelling on negative matters like sickness and accidents, but he definitely revelled in being the harbinger of bad news this time around. 'Bah! Sick? *Him*? No, he's not sick. That fellow never gets sick! He's gone and met with a blooming car accident. Broke his two legs and nose and things. Them doctor chaps say he may never walk again. Some say the fellow might even kick the bucket.' (Salgado was most articulate when accentuating the 'kick the bucket' bit, wanting it to be firmly drilled into Rohan's head.)

Rohan was struck dumb. His body trembled somewhat as he

inquired further in a voice that was hardly coherent. 'How did this happen, Salgado?'

Salgado continued, savouring every word, even accentuating a few of them very strongly. 'Bloody Mr Know-all De Merl thought he could do *anything*. He took his father's new Morris Oxford and somehow or other forced the driver fellow to allow *him* to drive. De Merl had only driven their old car a couple of times before – just to learn sort of. He could not control that big, new car. Near Coronation Park, the blasted car skidded on the pools of water from last night's rain and crashed into the Brighton building. De Merl's hurt badly. Fellow's bones are all *broken* and all that. His head's not right too. Some "conkissing" thing or something, they say. The driver fellow escaped with small injuries, but the new car's all smashed up.'

Rohan digested Salgado's narrative in amazement. As a humanitarian, he felt instantly sorry for De Merl's horrible injuries and life-threatening condition, but his conscience pricked him. He had on many occasions wished great ill will on De Merl and often hoped his nemesis would just disappear from the face of the earth, but he hadn't expected *this*. His feelings were ambivalent. He didn't want De Merl to suffer, but in the midst of the reality of what had transpired and the probable consequences of things to come, a nagging ray of hope lifted his spirits. His heart skipped a few beats as he considered the opportunities that lay ahead. It was a terrible thing to be elated over his classmate's fate, but he couldn't stop his treacherous soul from singing silent hosannas of joy. Wobbling on unsteady feet into the classroom, he took his place at his desk and awaited the arrival of Mr Strool, the arithmetic master, who was to take the next class.

Later on that afternoon, Mr Bull, who, in addition to taking history, was also the school's headmaster, made a formal announcement. Addressing the boys, he spoke in his forthright, bellowing fashion. 'My dear boys! My dear boys! I have some unfortunate news to convey to you all. Terribly unfortunate news! Some of you are already aware of what has happened, but it is my painful duty to officially inform you anyway.'

He cleared his throat and waited for the class to fall completely silent.

'Your dear classmate De Merl is in the general hospital, having met with an automobile accident last evening. His condition is very serious, although the doctors have informed his family there is no real danger to his life. The poor lad has, to my knowledge, fractures in both legs, a broken nose, and a severe concussion. He will not be attending school for some time. I will keep you informed of his progress, and I hope a delegation from this class would be able to visit him sometime later, once his doctors permit visiting. We hope and pray for De Merl's safe return to us.'

'Good if he doesn't return at all,' muttered Salgado under his breath, his remarks within earshot of those closest to him, who openly sniggered.

The always alert Mr Bull was too far away to hear what Salgado said but was quick to inquire anyway. He was, as always, deeply suspicious of the fat boy. 'What's that you said, Salgado? Stand up and speak up, boy! Speak up! I didn't hear you from over here.'

Salgado stood up to answer, but not before first turning his face away from Mr Bull to grin devilishly at the boys behind him. Turning around to face the master, he answered with great hypocritical aplomb, the devilish grin turning into a look of profound pretended sadness. It was not only his large bulk that made him a popular choice to play adult roles at most of the school plays. Mr Johns, the drama master, had even praised his acting talent, often talking about it to anyone who cared to listen.

'I only said, sir, that we're all very sorry to hear them very bad news about De Merl, sir.'

Mr Bull, who was often furious with Salgado for his various scholarly lapses and disciplinary offences, did not quite believe the lie, but unable to find any immediate fault this time around, took the opportunity to correct Salgado's failing English instead – a mild comfort. '*The* bad news, boy. *The* bad news. Not 'them' bad news,' he said admonishingly, wagging a corrective finger at Salgado.

'Yes, sir. *The* bad news, sir. Thank you very much for correcting my poor English, sir,' said Salgado, feigning great humbleness and sobriety, not wanting to get into a new skirmish with Mr Bull. He had experienced many skirmishes with Mr Bull before, a great many resulting in corporal punishment of some sort. He definitely did not want to aggravate the cantankerous headmaster, not today, anyway. Today was special, a day to celebrate!

The very next day, Rohan rejoined the cricket pool and soundly impressed old Mr Pontybum with a truculent display of cricketing acumen. The old coach was flabbergasted that this 'new boy' hadn't shown up for practices before and promptly included him in the junior team to play the rest of the school fixtures that year.

That night before going to bed, Rohan spent a longer time at prayers to his beloved Deity – the good Lord Jesus. 'Dear Lord', he opened after saying his customary three Hail Marys, 'I know *you* didn't cause stinky old De Merl's injuries, Lord, but I thank you very much for getting me into the school team. Mr Pontybum said I would be included in the junior school team for the rest of our matches. Dear Lord, I also ask for another thing. I want to marry Baking Jane when I am older. She's so wonderful, and her boobs are so big, Lord, but she may not be so pretty when I am grown up. She might be quite old then. Dear sweet Jesus, please stop her from getting old – please, please, please. You *can*, dear Lord. Father Ambrose said at catechism class that you can do *anything*.' (He hadn't really intended to plead for Baking Jane's eternal youth in his statement of thanks but thought it a good time now, in his hour of cricketing triumph.)

Saying thus, Rohan concluded his night prayers by making the sign of the cross, and then went to sleep, immensely relieved that the Lord Jesus would grant his request and make Baking Jane immune from ageing.

CHAPTER 3
Lodgings Available

Come, fill the Cup, and in the fire of Spring
Your Winter-garment of Repentance fling.
—Omar Khayyám, from Rubáiyát

CELESTE, ROHAN'S TEMPESTUOUS YOUNG AUNT, was in the act of performing coitus with her new lover, Don, who had only just recently rented a room at Grandmummy's strange-looking large house. A casual peeping Tom gazing discreetly through the keyhole of the fourth bedroom could easily see Don's well-endowed member dipping in and out of a seemingly endless cavity between Celeste's legs and might wonder, at the same time, if it hurt the young woman. She moaned now and then, as though in pain, right through the entire performance.

Celeste and Don never removed their clothes entirely during their lovemaking, naked only from the waist below, their underwear partly hanging over their ankles or completely discarded, lying on the bare floor. They would latch the door but never did get fully naked, half expecting a knock on the door anytime, completely overlooking the little keyhole on the front lock – forgetting it could provide a generous view of their antics. The adults in the ménage knew that Celeste was inside the room with Don, but they didn't give much thought to exactly what was going on therein – coitus sounding incredibly daring – an almost implausible happening at the Dragon's lair. Nobody ever dared to copulate at Grandmummy's for decades, the last one to do so probably the Dragon herself many years ago when her husband was alive. At the most, the household imagined kissing and fondling on the cards, but nothing more. After the couple finished copulating, Don would fondle Celeste's bare buttocks with one hand, his other wrapped around her upper waist. It was a splendidly erotic sight for any half-decent voyeur, had there been one. But there were none…

It had all started about a month ago. Grandmummy had just concluded a bargaining session with Bongo, the fruit seller, and was very much elated over the outcome. The Dragon bullied all the door-to-door vendors who did the rounds on the street where she lived, but none as shockingly as she did old Bongo. She would always offer the most scandalous of price reductions during a haggling session, nearly always emerging the victor. Poor Bongo was mesmerised by Grandmummy's cobra-like gaze and manner, folding up quite easily. He had several times tried to bypass Grandmummy's house as silently and discreetly as he could, with his hand-drawn cart, but the Dragon was not to be fooled. Sitting in her favourite vantage point in the veranda, she would loudly hail Bongo when he sneaked by and then once he had come back, would rebuke him soundly for not shouting out his wares.

After Bongo had left, Grandmummy turned her attention to solving the weekend crossword puzzle in the Sunday newspaper. Five across and twelve down, 'A bolt from the blue', was the intricate and appropriate crossword clue which had stumped her for some time now. Grandmummy, her brain whirling around at express speed, pondered intensely to try to find the right word to match the crossword teaser. Her attempts proving futile, she put down her newspaper in vexation, removed her reading glasses, and after wiping them with the folds of her dress, let them dangle from the chain she wore around her neck. She had been working hard on the crossword puzzle since Sunday morning, when it first appeared in the magazine section of her favourite newspaper, the *Jellicoe Sunday Journal*. A keen adept at solving crossword puzzles, Grandmummy always had her final solution ready well before the newspaper's deadline – partially worked out by her and partially through the efforts of her eldest son, Robert, who came to visit once or twice a week. A couple of years ago, she had actually won the newspaper's handsome prize of three hundred rupees for the first correctly sent solution – an effort that spurred her on enthusiastically in pursuit of a new win. She quickly became a fanatical crossword fan – even an adept – faithfully sending in her entry week after week, greatly encouraged by Robert, whose contribution was by no means modest. Right now, temporarily stumped by the crossword puzzle's resilient clue, Grandmummy turned her thoughts to her other favourite 'hobby', or, if one was to put it in more sober and realistic terms, her semiprofessional business venture – wine production.

Wine was not completely unknown to the people of Victoria. When Portuguese invaders first appeared on the scene in the fifteenth century, watching spies from the Victorian court observed the Portuguese drinking 'blood', as was recorded in their ancient chronicles written exquisitely on papyrus-like Ola leaves – as good as any parchment the Western world used for writing at that particular period in history. Of course, the 'blood'-drinking notion quickly disappeared as the locals quickly discovered just what the red drink really was. Wine drinking, however, never really caught on with the locals, primarily because obtaining the stuff meant being in cahoots with the Portuguese usurpers, and secondly because drinking the highly potent local 'wine', or toddy (as it was lovingly called by the locals), made from coconut-flower juice was deeply rooted and preferred. Even after British settlers had introduced beer and whisky production in the early nineteenth century, toddy still remained a widely drunk alcoholic beverage.

At the Nameless, the clientele boasted many regulars who made a steady beeline to Ali Baba's tavern after the sun set in the evenings. The tavern's real name was a simple 'Jellicoe City Pub' but for some unknown reason it had always been called Ali Baba's. The majority of Ali Baba's guzzlers drank just toddy, although the tavern did sell local whisky and beer assortments of a surprisingly excellent quality. At the outset of the British usurpation in the seventeenth century, pioneering English settlers had duplicated British whisky, and beer-making methods in breweries started with help from experts specially brought down from England – breweries that still existed and flourished in modern Victoria. Wine, however, stubbornly remained an alien sort of alcohol to most Victorians. It wasn't drunk by ordinary citizens, being instead a sort of luxury vice for opulent locals and a modest necessity for the European diaspora. Certainly none of the breakfast-eaters at the Nameless had actually ever drunk any genuine wine at all in their entire lives. Everyone *imagined* it to be a sweet, wonderfully cooling, exotic drink. Catnips, whose imagination was the most vivid of them all and who frequently told countless lies to back up his cockeyed fantasies, spoke out in a knowing fashion when the subject came up one day at one of the usual breakfast palavers. He had overindulged at Ali Baba's the previous evening and was a bit worse for wear.

'Harrumph! A good bottle of that European red wine is what us Victorian chaps need to drink every day instead of our beastly toddy, which gives us such a splitting headache the day after and makes our stomachs all rumble like hell.'

'How do you know that? You ever drunk any of that foreign red wine?' asked Sonny, the proprietor of the Nameless, in a tone of disbelief mixed with unconcealed sarcasm. Sonny frequently challenged Catnips. He was mischievous in his own right and knew that challenging anything Catnips said would nearly always result in some sort of entertainment for himself and his roughneck clientele.

'*Me*? Drunk red wine? You're asking *me*? Of course I've drunk plenty of red wine! Especially the French sort. Why, only last week

I drank a chilled bottle which I bought from Barnabas Wine and Spirits down at the bazaar, and very good wine it was too. Didn't get no blooming headache at all, and my stomach was as silent as a mouse the next day!'

'I don't know why the devil you want to go and lie about these dang-blasted things,' protested Karolis, the fishmonger. 'Everyone at Jellicoe Junction knows old Barnabas stocks imported wine and whiskies and stuff only for them rich European people and our local toffs to buy. How'd you gone and afforded to buy a bottle of red wine, eh? That dang-blasted foreign wine costs a bloody fortune! Where the devil did you get the money, eh?'

'Bah,' retorted Catnips in disdain. (He hated when people questioned the state of his finances, which *he* considered was rock solid.) 'Are you insinuating I have money problems, Karolis? I'm not like you fellows, pinching and scraping and going about without a damn extra cent to scratch your damn arses! I have plenty, plenty of money to buy imported wine if I want to! Even a dozen bottles! Anyway, why the devil are *you* worrying about what I can afford and what I can't afford? Do I come and borrow money from you, eh? Do I inquire about *your* finances, eh? Do I?'

Karolis shrugged his shoulders and declined to answer.

'What did the red wine taste like?' inquired Uncle Pongo curiously, an undertone of disbelief creeping into his voice.

Catnips, who had never once set his foot inside the Barnabas Wine and Spirits store, let alone ever tasted imported wine, lied through his teeth as only he could. He replied airily, like a true connoisseur dissecting a famous wine, seemingly lost in an imaginary world of nuances, esters, and whatnot. 'Ah! I'm telling you fellows, it was heavenly. It tasted like very sweet, ice-cool *sherbet* [a popular local fruit drink]. The only difference is that wine makes you feel strong and brave because it's so powerful-like, even stronger than our damn toddy. And you know what, chaps? One never gets any damn headache the day after, either! That's why them Portuguese rascals always drank wine in them olden days. It made them all brave and fearless, you know! While our own kingie chap's soldiers drank our blooming toddy and got thundering headaches, which made them quite useless in battle, them Portuguese fellows were all shipshape and ready to fight at any time without any damn headache at all! *That's* the main reason why those chaps won all their battles. It was their wine that did it!' He rounded off with a smirk, wonderfully satiated by his terribly flawed hypothesis.

As soon as Catnips concluded his conjecture, Bellakay, the widely acknowledged sage at the Nameless, intervened and put an end to Catnips's blatant lies. Without sounding superior or condescending in any way, he spoke out in a calm and collected manner. 'Red wine is not sweet, and it is not strong like toddy. It has lower alcohol content than our toddy, and nobody in his right mind ever drinks red wine chilled. The clarets of Bordeaux or the chiantis of Tuscany or any other red wine aren't drunk chilled. You open a bottle and allow it to breathe awhile before drinking it at room temperature. And oh! You drink too much of it, you'll jolly well end up with right royal headache, all right – just like with any other alcohol!'

Nobody quite grasped the bit about clarets or chiantis, nor did they know where the devil Bordeaux or Tuscany were or how the deuce a bottle of wine could 'breathe' – although they were familiar with room temperatures. (Toddy had to be stored in a dry, ventilated place.) Still, they knew that clever old Bellakay never lied. What he had just said had to be true. Catnips had been exposed for the terrible liar he was – yet again! The air went electric for a moment.

Catnips glared dangerously at Bellakay for a full minute, thoughts racing through his head. He had not expected to be shown up by the incumbent sage, at least not in the matter of alcohol. 'How the devil did the meddling old goat know anything about imported wine or alcohol? The blasted fellow never makes any visits to Ali Baba's and never indulges in other spirits, either – everybody knows that! Bloody know-all! Just has to poke his damn nose into everything – the damn interfering busybody! Why the devil can't the damn sod find some other place to hang about and leave us all in peace here?'

His ruminations complete, Catnips stormed out, his head held high like the drama queen he was, in the direction of his favourite spot beneath the banyan tree to calm himself and digest his shame.

Grandmummy's famous wine had its roots in a treasured recipe for making wine from dried raisins – a recipe handed down from generation to generation. She guarded the recipe carefully, not even sharing it with her immediate family members, despite both Rebecca and Daisy regularly clamouring for it. A month or so after the start of each New Year, she would buy large quantities of raisins from local vendors who imported the stuff from the Middle East. Raisins were quite cheap to buy and freely available in all grocery shops. Some bought them to be used in cakes, buns, puddings, pastries, or fruit salads, but most did so just for the pleasure of eating them outright.

Grandmummy placed the raisins in batches into a huge metal cauldron together with large quantities of water, an exact-measured portion of sugar, and other ingredients from her secret recipe. She mixed everything together with a paddle-shaped wooden ladle and, when satisfied the mixture was well churned, added yeast seeds to speed up the fermentation process. The resulting mixture was then transferred carefully into large clay pots, which were then covered and left to ferment for a month or so.

After the fermenting process was over, Grandmummy strained the rather opaque-looking young wine several times in a large home-made canvas strainer inside which additional layers of soft cloth were sewn in to maximise the straining effect and eliminate every single solid particle. She had several strainers. The one she started with – a rather crude affair – effectively took out the raisin skins, raisin seeds, and remnants of her secret ingredients, whilst two additional strainers, extra-padded with minute linings, took out every remaining solid particle. She reciprocated the straining process over several days to make the liquid as clear and transparent as possible.

The resulting young virgin wine had a sherry-like taste and smell, and even at an early stage, compared very favourably to the very best imported sherries modestly stocked at some of the more renowned grocery shops in the city. How the wine attained this quality after fermenting just a short while, nobody knew. The dried raisins alone could never have done it. In all likelihood, it was the Dragon's secret ingredients that did the trick.

After the straining process was over and done with, Grandmummy would meticulously bottle and seal the young wine. The bottles would then be placed horizontally upon tall wooden racks inside the empty fourth bedroom of the house to mature till early December – the start of the Christmas and New Year season – before sales began.

A confirmation of the superb quality of her indigenous wine, or rather sherry, as it could closely be compared with, came from a rather unexpected source. Grandmummy's monthly visits to the local parish priest with whom she was on very cordial terms turned out to be a trump card in the advancement of her wine business. Father Clement was probably the only person Grandmummy treated on an equal footing, perhaps because of the fact that she confessed her discrepancies to him, the strict laws of her Christian religion demanding it.

On occasions Grandmummy presented the genial and well-liked priest with a bottle of her wine when visiting, which the latter politely accepted as a matter of course, not really bothering to sample it. Father Clement was a wine connoisseur of no mean repute. He was fond of the red clarets of Bordeaux, but sherry was his absolute favourite. He narrowed his own choice to amontillado, although he did find mazanillas pleasing to his palette as well. He loved the dryness of fortified fino in the amontillado together with its delicate sweetness and scent of hazelnuts and honey, which probably gave it the edge in his preference over the mazanillas. Besides, drinking manzanilla wasn't quite practical. The somewhat craving sherry required the entire bottle to be drunk within two days of opening, something he couldn't quite manage because of his priestly duties. A tipsy priest would only give rise to much talk and whispering that would eventually lead to a rendezvous with the local bishop – a man whom Father Clement didn't always see eye-to-eye with.

Father Clement was used to receiving small presents from members of his congregation and didn't think too much of Grandmummy's wine gesture, casually putting away the bottles in a dusty corner of his large storeroom together with other expandable gifts he sporadically received from members of his congregation. One day, for want of having nothing better to do, he decided to sample a bottle.

'Let's see what *this* abomination tastes like,' he mused to himself. 'If it's as bad as that other awful stuff they produce in this country and have the gall to call wine, then at least I know what to do with the next bottle she gives me. Can't be collecting this stuff anymore. Just look at the state of my storeroom! Hardly any space longer.'

Opening a bottle and pouring a small quantity into a wine glass, he found himself very much surprised, to say the least, his jaw dropping several notches after the very first smell and sip. The aroma and taste of the contents were very much compatible to the best sherry he had tasted. In fact, it *did* taste like his favourite brand of amontillado he secretly imported along with several bottles of claret for his own private consumption – a luxury kept well hidden from his perpetually disapproving and prudish superior, the bishop. He knew jolly well for sure that the latter, a notoriously draconian type and a teetotaller to boot, would never quite understand a Frenchman's needs and would, in all probability, roundly admonish him for leading an epicurean life – which, of course, he didn't.

Father Clement spoke out in ecstatic terms when praising Grandmummy's wine to his fellow countrymen living in Victoria and to his large circle of friends, sometimes even to casual acquaintances he occasionally met up with and struck a longer conversation. He dubbed Grandmummy's product a sherry, although the Dragon stubbornly insisted it was a *special* sort of red wine. 'A very special sort,' she was known to say smugly.

Of course, Grandmummy was terribly wrong to call her product a red wine. She didn't use fresh grapes, and she did add quite a lot of sugar into her fermenting product, not to mention her pivotal secret-ingredient mix. Still, she stuck to her guns and stubbornly dubbed her product a red wine, even having impressive labels printed to that effect.

The young wine was stored in the empty fourth bedroom adjoining the open patio that separated the kitchen and the back garden. It was the driest room in the whole house, caused by some freak of architecture no one really understood. Nobody wanted to sleep in the room, as it was too far detached from the other bedrooms and the house. Although its distance away from the other rooms was the main reason for its unoccupied status, Rohan's young aunts spiced up the whole situation by making up frightening stories of it being haunted. They had a vivid imagination, the aunts, and professed quite vehemently that they had on several occasions heard strange ghostly noises and singing coming from within the room. This was, of course, a blatant lie. There wasn't the semblance of truth or substance in their stories, but they shamelessly persisted the room was haunted with unwavering vigour. True, faint noises were sometimes heard from within the room, but Grandmummy's entire household knew that the innocuous sounds were caused by rats scurrying to and fro across the roof beams – and nothing else. As for the purported singing, it was no more than the faint sound of the next-door neighbour's radio – the aperture between the two houses being very narrow, allowing sound to easily travel between them.

The children were originally quite frightened by their young aunts' insinuations, but they gradually got tired of it all as they slowly but surely came to the conclusion there was no truth in the matter whatsoever.

During the fermenting process of the wine, the rather sweet, raw mixture proved to be a constant source of temptation for Rohan and Mahan. The sight of bloated fermenting raisins floating in sweet brine appealed to their young palates. It didn't take too long before they were secretly sampling the young wine. It was wonderful to the taste.

The fermenting concoction's young alcohol content, potent as it was, made them feel all strange and tipsy, a sensation they had hitherto never experienced. True, they had seen their father drink his whiskies and other spirits during the good old days, but they were never quite interested in purloining any of the stuff during *that* wonderful period when life was fabulously splendid and when proverbial milk and honey spilled over the cup of plenty.

On their very first attempt at 'sampling' the wine, they drank more than half a cup each and were very close to exposure, becoming quite woozy a few minutes after drinking the potent stuff and then turning quite sick shortly afterwards. Rebecca, their trusting mother, thought it all due to something entirely different.

'You can sleep on my bed, the both of you! Just look at all the damn trouble you have brought upon yourselves! It's lucky today's Saturday or you might have missed school, too! Haven't I told you never to eat anything from that blooming Mungo chap at the school gate? What did you eat this time? Unripe mangoes peeled and left to gather all sorts of germs in the hot sun, wasn't it? Or what?'

Rohan and Mahan, relieved that Rebecca had assumed it was Mungo's alleged bad fruit that had caused their condition, went along well enough with this wonderful escape route.

'Er, yes, Mummy, we did buy some special sort of mango he was selling for half price. A lot of boys were buying it, so Mahan and I also bought some,' lied Rohan, Mahan nodding his head vigorously in agreement.

'Well, I hope this teaches you both a jolly good lesson! Don't ever let me hear you two have bought anything from that filthy fellow again. You hear me?'

'Yes, Mummy,' chorused the boys, feigning absolute contrition.

Never in her wildest dreams could Rebecca have imagined that her sons' condition had anything to do with their very first negative experience with drinking alcohol. Although sick as dogs, Rohan and Mahan held their nerve and managed to see through the worst. Though very afraid of their condition, they remained unflinching, holding out a whole day despite the discomfort they felt. The siblings were greatly relieved when they awoke the next morning feeling very much better after their horrendous ordeal, although they did have a slight headache.

There was the religious aspect of things too as the boys discovered to their horror, the main impediment being that their strict Christian religion demanded frequent visits to the confessionals for any minor or major sin they committed. Rohan and Mahan fervently discussed the purloining of the wine in a joint soul-searching effort, hoping their combined palavers would find a possible loophole, a way out of confessing the grave sin of robbing Grandmummy. It was horrifying to confess they had stolen and consumed alcohol, a deed tailor-made to send steam whistling through old Father Ambrose's ears. The old priest was known to openly vent out his anger at times upon hearing a particularly juicy confession from an unfortunate wrongdoer. He would rant from his confessional box, denouncing the poor confessor – his voice audible for many in the confessional queue to hear, much to the embarrassment of the kneeling victim in front of him. The very moderate Father Clement was often heard to say with a chuckle and a twinkle in his eye that his octogenarian colleague would have made a great career in the Dark Ages of the Spanish Inquisition.

On their last discussion about whether it was a sin or not to steal Grandmummy's wine, Rohan and Mahan came to a joint conclusion that ended the matter once and for all – pleasing the brothers no end and effectively putting it to rest.

'Huh! Even Jesus drank wine,' opened Mahan astutely, reasoning that if the good Lord drank the stuff, then surely it was all right for them to do so too. After all, he was God!

'Yes, yes, he drank, all right, but he did not *rob* the wine, did he?' countered Rohan, shaking his head in an undecided sort of way.

'Oh! Pish-posh! How are we supposed to know that, eh? How *can* we know that? You think those blooming bearded prophet fellows went and wrote things about the Lord robbing wine in them gospel books? Them holy books only describe the *good* things the Lord did, not about any robberies he might have done! You think Jesus didn't rob a little of Joseph's wine now and then when he was a boy, eh? Surely he must have been tempted like us? And besides blooming wine, why didn't them gospel chaps write if he liked roast beef instead of stinky old smoked fish? Or if he liked milkshakes instead of orange soda? Beef sausages instead of pork sausages? Why didn't they write if the Lord liked cricket or football or swimming in them gospels and epistles and whatnot? Surely our Lord played sports when he was our age?'

Rohan was troubled by Mahan's telling logic. He did so very much *like* the Lord Jesus and was averse to associate the Holy One with robbery. Mahan's quip about the roast beef and milkshakes and other things didn't go to well either; surely it wasn't respectful to ask God what he liked or disliked to eat and drink? As for sports, maybe it was swimming the good Lord liked best. After all, he was often out at sea with that ear-cutting chap, Peter, and those other fishermen. Ruminating thus on these grave theological matters, Rohan experienced a sudden epiphany flashing through his young mind, sparking off a minor brainwave. He recollected Father Ambrose's vivid version of the wedding feast at Cana at their previous week's catechism class where the good Lord, it seemed, dominated wine proceedings. Rohan spoke out enthusiastically with a newfound conviction.

'Jesus did not *need* to rob wine. Why, Father Ambrose told us in the last catechism class that the Lord went and changed water into wine at that wedding feast. Very good wine it was too, said Father Ambrose – the best at that old wedding reception! So why should he want to go and *rob* wine when he knew how to *change* water into wine?'

Mahan was stumped by this answer. One side of him, the side of sibling rivalry, longed to demolish Rohan's impeccable defence of the good Lord, but common sense prevailed. The counsellor for the prosecution, his charge sheet empty, chose to capitulate, but not without first admiring the great Lord's wonderful feat, which the young defence counsellor had so winningly presented.

'That's a whole heap of wine Jesus must have made when he went and changed all that blooming tap water into wine. There are hundreds of people at weddings!'

Here, Rohan swiftly interrupted his brother, saying in a rather superior voice with a smug, all-knowing look upon his face, 'Tap water? What tap water? Them fellows had no tap water in them olden days. There were no taps and pipes and thingies then. They all drew water from wells. It was only well water them Bible chaps had, not any pish-posh tap water!'

Mahan wasn't pleased by Rohan's superior knowledge of biblical plumbing or, rather, the lack of it. More often than not, he was always on the losing side of most discussions he had with his younger brother, and it irked him no end each time it happened. Making an effort, he put aside his feelings of animosity to concentrate deeper on matters in hand. A flash of inspiration suddenly hit him. 'If Jesus made all those huge big amounts of wine, I don't think he'd mind us sampling just a little bit of old Grandmummy's wine, surely? After all, it's not *really* robbing, you know. It's good that we take a sip now and then just to see if the wine is coming along all right. If it tastes bad, we can always make old Grandmummy know some way and save her a lot of trouble!'

Rohan pondered over his brother's novel statement, buoyed by its resounding logic. It was seldom the two siblings hit it off, had the same views, or agreed upon anything, but in this instance Rohan fully concurred with his brother's reasoning. 'Yes, yes, you're quite right, you know, Mahan. What's a *tiny* cup of wine to the Lord when he went and made all those large barrels and barrels of wine for all them hundreds of chaps to drink at that wedding, eh? Jesus is sure to say it's *all right* for us to drink a bit of Grandmummy's wine. Father Ambrose and them other priests always say the Lord is very kind and understanding. The Lord *was* a wine man, and he's sure to understand that we just like to drink a little bit too. And then there is that *testing* thing you said. We are doing Grandmummy a favour, really. Why, we don't need to confess this to old Father Ambrose at all! Lord Jesus can see that it's all right and not a sin.'

Mahan agreed wholeheartedly, pleased as Punch over their joint reasoning. As matters stood, neither of them needed to make any special confession to cantankerous old Father Ambrose, the phantom of the confessionals.

The immediate days following the boys' brush with their very first hangover, Grandmummy's wine business received a severe setback, bringing the whole year's venture to a premature standstill. Perhaps the crossword puzzle clue 'A bolt from the blue', which Grandmummy had earlier on struggled with, was an ominous sign of warning. A large wooden beam supporting a section of the roof gave way suddenly one night and fell plumb over all the large wine pots, crushing them into pieces, the young fermenting wine spilling out all over the floor. Nobody knew what caused the beam to cave in the way it did or, even stranger, how it fell exactly over the spot where the pots were. The dryness of the room could have caused termite attacks, but on closer inspection of the fallen beam, no evidence of termite infection was ever found. When Grandmummy and her husband purchased the house many years ago, the seller fervently declared that all the roofing beams in the house had been repeatedly kyanised and would last for generations to come. The mystery deepened and only served to support the young aunts' theory that the room was haunted, although the others still remained sceptical, pooh-poohing the notion of supernatural interference. Rohan and Mahan, especially, were quite dismissive of the ghost theory, as they had, on their wine-purloining expeditions, spent quite a few pleasant moments in the wine room without ever having seen any spirit, goblin, or ghost. Even harrowing Count Dracula, whom the boys feared most after seeing the evil Rumanian nobleman's exploits during a spate of horror films recently screened at the Empire Talkies, didn't show up. But then again, the Count was reputed never to drink … *wine*.

Grandmummy was devastated. Months of solid hard work had gone down the drain in a single cruel blow of fate. Besides, the calamity came at a most inopportune moment – a very, very inopportune moment. Christmas and New Year season was fast approaching and there was absolutely no time to start afresh and get a new batch of wine ready for sale. An air of uncertainty and sadness hovered over the crooked old house and its inhabitants like an immense and invisible grey cloud of gloom.

The Dragon bemoaned her loss every single day, a gloomy look on her face, her manner distant and foreboding. Tears running down her heavy jowls, she wandered around the house like a ghostly apparition, frequently muttering incoherent gobbledygook. Everybody, afraid of her soliloquising and behaviour, kept out of her way, not wanting to say anything that might unintentionally aggravate her moroseness to a degree far worse than what it had already descended to.

'Oh, God,' she moaned. 'Why did you do this thing to me, Lord? Why did you send me this terrible burden? How am I to support the family now when you have taken away my wine? What am I to do? Tell me, what I'm supposed to do? What's to become of us all now? And Rebecca and the children here with me, too! How will I manage? However will I manage? Where's the money going to come from?'

It was a ceaseless mantra, her chunter echoing and re-echoing the whole day till she waddled off to bed at night. She continued in this fashion the next few days, hardly eating or drinking or talking to anyone.

In retrospect, it wasn't a major crisis. It wasn't even a crisis, let alone a major one. True, the wine business for that year was obliterated beyond repair, but she would survive financially, as there was still money coming in from her pension and the ample contributions from her son and daughters to 'support' the family, as she fallaciously called the action. Apart from giving Rebecca and the children a miserable ten cents for breakfast and offering them a roof over their heads, she did not 'support' anyone. Besides, she had hitherto hardly ever spent any of the profits she made from the winery the previous years. It was all hoarded in her special almirah year in and year out, hardly ever seeing the light of day.

The business of the spilt wine and Grandmummy's reaction had a profound effect on young Rohan. Although not a favourite of Grandmummy, and not over-fond of the Dragon, he couldn't help feeling sorry for his old grandmother over the whole matter. He had never seen this tough, fierce woman cry before, and her tears moved him deeply. When the wine pots broke, leaving Grandmummy a sobbing wreck, he tried to make things right his own way by asking the powers above to intervene. He wasn't especially religious, but he had a genuine love for the good Lord Jesus, firmly believing all that was told him at catechism class by old Father Ambrose. The octogenarian priest took great liberties when narrating events in his young charges' Bible study book, often spicing up things in a preposterous fashion and completely twisting events to suit his own fantasies.

Supremely confident he could solve the whole matter, Rohan went about filling a few empty wine bottles with water from the bathroom tap. These he placed in the now deserted wine room and kneeling before them, proceeded to address his beloved Deity, the good Lord Jesus. He spoke out in a most humble and respectful tone. 'Dear Lord Jesus. You know how old Grandmummy got them wine pots all broken to pieces and all the wine spilt out and all that. Please, dear Lord, I have now filled these bottles with tap water, so I'm asking you most kindly to make them into wine tomorrow morning – you know, like you did at that wedding feast Father Ambrose told us about, where you went and changed all those Bible chaps' water into very good wine!'

He concluded his request by solemnly reciting three 'Hail Marys' just for good measure, made the sign of the cross several times over for even better measure, and then rose up from his kneeling position. Taking a final look at the filled bottles of water, he skipped on his way with relief in his heart and a lighter spring in his step.

Rohan had no doubt that the great Lord Jesus would accede – grant his request on the spot. After all, wasn't he a good Christian always trying to do the right thing? And didn't he make his confession regularly to old Father Ambrose like he was supposed to? The only hinder he saw to the good Lord's granting his request was his previous wine-purloining raids along with Mahan. True, both he and Mahan had logically come to a joint conclusion that their deeds weren't a sin, but one never knew for sure how things operated in the kingdom of heaven, Rohan mused in slight consternation. He thought long and hard about it before finally giving himself the benefit of the doubt. Lord Jesus *was* a wine man and wouldn't punish a fellow wine connoisseur, he reasoned yet again. Besides, the Holy One had the whole world to run, and with such important matters under his belt, a little boy's discretions, whatever they might be, paled in comparison.

That evening when the whole family had gathered around the radio (except for Grandmummy, who had gone to bed, too depressed to do anything else) after dinner, Rohan looked upon them benevolently like a gracious king contemplating distributing the entire royal treasury to his poor subjects. How pleasing it was going to be for everyone when they discovered that *he* – a scarce twelve-year-old – had, through *his* grand request to the Lord, put everything right again. He envisioned Grandmummy fawning over him in an immense show of gratitude upon seeing the new bottles of wine the good Lord would have miraculously provided. Jesus wouldn't refuse *him*. He *was* sure about that! Extremely pleased by his ruminations, he went to bed, falling asleep almost instantly. He dreamt of the wedding feast at Cana where the Lord was drinking wine from a huge glass, chatting away amiably with Peter and Paul and the rest of the disciples, who were also guzzling merrily away. Old Father Ambrose was in the dream too, raving and ranting ferociously at the wedding guests to make their confessions to him until the good Lord got tired of his ramblings and turned him into a large pot of wine! How the wedding guests cheered and clapped to be rid of the old nuisance!

The next morning Rohan got up earlier than usual and made a swift beeline to the wine room, quivering with excitement. Rushing over to the bottles, he examined their contents, but to his great consternation found them still containing tap water! The following three days, he repeated the experiment over and over again just in case the good Lord hadn't heard him the first time around, pleading much *louder* in these instances. After all, he mused, the Holy One must be quite old now and perhaps a little bit deaf too, having lived and done all those miracles and things so many hundreds of years ago. The tap water, however, obstinately refused to change into wine, not even after several more fervent pleading sessions with the good Lord. Rohan was bitterly, bitterly disappointed. In his prayers at Mass the next Sunday, he maintained a stoic countenance, reciting from his Mass book in a sing-song, uncaring sort of voice to mark his displeasure and disappointment with the Great One – highly upset over his blunt rejection. In hindsight, it just had to be the wine-purloining raids that had come between him and the good Lord's help. Lord Jesus must have indeed witnessed his surreptitious drinking sessions and roundly disapproved of them. There just couldn't be any other explanation...

Now that divine help was definitely not forthcoming, Rohan considered a more pragmatic approach. Unlike most others in the household, he wasn't afraid to speak his mind when addressing Grandmummy, or anybody else, for that matter – a trait that brought him no favours, only frequent tongue-lashings from the Dragon and sometimes even from his mother, Rebecca. He waited until Grandmummy was alone, sitting in her favourite chair in the front veranda, to put forth his suggestion. Never one to dawdle or dither, he came straight to the point.

'You know, Grandmummy, now that them wine pots are broken and all that, why don't you start some other business?' he suggested boldly, keeping a safe distance away from his grandmother in case she clapped him over the head for his insolence.

The Dragon looked at him apathetically. In her current state of mind, she had no desire to impinge or bandy words with her rather saucy young grandson. She replied more in automation than anything else, expecting nothing. 'What other business, *boy*? What are you talking about? What is there to do?'

Grandmummy's reply startled and stumped Rohan somewhat. He hadn't expected his grandmother to ask *him* what sort of alternative business options there were, taking for granted that the Dragon might have plenty up her sleeve …

Rohan thought this one over swiftly. Luckily for him (and his grandmother, as it turned out later), his young mind conjured up an alternative income source right then and there – on the spot – on the spur of the moment. It was a spontaneous brainwave, a sudden flash of inspiration, an epiphany.

'Grandmummy, why not let the wine room out to lodgers? Nobody uses it. Aunty Primrose and Aunty Celeste say it's haunted, and your wine pots are all gone. You're sure going to get a lot of lodger rent for it.'

'But what I am going to do next year, *boy*? I must have some place to store them wine pots if I start again, God willing,' protested Grandmummy, making a quick sign of the cross for good measure. (It was her wont to make the sign of the cross whenever she mentioned God.)

'Ha! Next year! Next year! Why, by next year, you will be making so much money on lodger rent you might as well go on to stop the wine business altogether – or if you start again, maybe you can store them pots in the garden shed,' said Rohan, thinking roguishly at the same time how much easier it would be for him and Mahan to steal the fermenting wine from this secluded spot, so conveniently detached away from the main house.

Nobody used the garden shed for anything. The boys occasionally read comic books inside it, preferring to read them in peace there instead of reading them inside the house. Grandmummy, who considered comic books the work of the Devil, always objected to the boys' reading that sort of literature, often making an almighty song and dance about it all. The little girls, Maria and Sussie, also used the shed regularly to play house with an obliging Poppsy, who was persuaded to stay on with bribes of small pieces of rock candy. The girls would dress him up in one of their old knickers, making a hole at the back to accommodate his tail.

Rohan and Mahan bought the comic books from Shorthand, a

pavement bookshop proprietor who ran a lucrative business at Galahad Street, a stone's throw away from the famous school the boys attended. Shorthand was aptly named – his left arm severed at the elbow. He was in no way restricted by his handicap, using the remaining stump with dexterity as though it had fingers. Shorthand had a murky past and was reputed to have been a notorious criminal before a home-made bomb accidentally went off, nearly taking away his sight and blasting half his arm off. Since then, in genuine gratitude to the powers above for sparing his sight and life, he had gone on the straight and narrow, abandoning his previous evil ways. The semi-crippled bookseller stocked his stall with popular American comic books, second-hand mystery novels, and innocuous fashion magazines showing scantily covered women in swimming suits or daunting lingerie. His chief income-bringer, however, were highly erotic American magazines showing full naked women in all sorts of poses, including centrefolds where the models posed with wide-open vulvas or clearly visible anal buttons. He had no qualms, or saw no moral impediments to selling the promiscuous magazines to anyone, but stopped short of selling them to the young and impressionable schoolboys, much to the latter's absolute dismay.

Shorthand had many adult customers, including most of the hard-core gang at the Nameless – Catnips especially standing out as a regular customer and expert connoisseur, to boot. The impoverished Nameless gang (Catnips apart) couldn't afford to buy the magazines since Shorthand put a rather high price on this particular type of merchandise, causing the always enterprising Catnips to initiate a new routine. Whilst pretending to pore over Shorthand's comic books, he would edge up to the famous shelf nearest the one-armed bookseller and rife through the sex magazines, sneak-previewing the centrefolds, which often pictured the 'juiciest' photo shoots. It didn't take long before he had the rest of the Nameless regulars copying his tactics, although for the most they just stood behind the mercurial Catnips. Catnips didn't stop at the sneak previews. He was aware that Shorthand frowned on customers' taking longer previews of his erotic literature, so he wisely bought a brand-new magazine now and then.

This he would take to the Nameless and rent it out to one person at a time for an hour or two, charging them a small sum of money for the privilege. Catnips, of course, didn't need the money. He did what he did out of pure altruism, knowing very well the emptiness of his colleagues' pockets.

Nearly all of Grandmummy's somewhat prosaic neighbours had a lodger or two, the extra money earned infusing their meagre incomes with well-needed boosts. Insufficient earnings were more often than not a nagging cause for worry, and letting out rooms seemed a simple yet effective way to make ends meet and to tidy over financial difficulties. Very often, lodgers were youngish men hailing from villages around Portopo who had succeeded in finding employment in the city and were in desperate need for a place to live. Short of sleeping out in the open, they rented any sort of abode with a roof over their heads. No official contracts or papers of any sort were signed. The normal procedure for landlords was just to ask for a month's rent in advance, whereupon the new lodger would be asked to move in. Everything, however, wasn't always above board between tenants and landlords. Often, there was trouble in collecting monthly rents, animosity frequently breaking out between the concerned parties, although very seldom resulting in tenant's actually being kicked out. It was not unusual for a lodger to be behind payments by a month or two, but arrears were eventually always paid back in full amidst feisty bickering between the warring parties.

Grandmummy contemplated Rohan's suggestion about taking in lodgers in thoughtful silence, her grandson looking on patiently, waiting for some sort of reaction. After a few minutes passed, she wagged a plump finger at Rohan, beckoning him to come closer. Rohan obliged rather gingerly, not quite understanding the gesture and what to expect from the Dragon.

Grandmummy looked around herself cautiously in a conspiratorial manner. Satisfied that nobody was close enough to eavesdrop, she opened quietly in an ingratiating low tone, anxious to win Rohan's trust, but also to be doubly sure the nosy Celeste or anyone else couldn't hear her from another room.

'Rohan, *child* (she conveniently dropped the '*boy*' this time). Can you ask around and see how much these fellows are paying for a room? Don't ask at once straight to their faces. We don't want that useless pack of neighbours of ours to think *we* want to take in lodgers, what? After all, we're not wretchedly poor like them, and we *are* English, aren't we? Just ask careless-like and try and get a rough figure. Now with the wine gone, maybe God wants me to take in these damn-blasted lodger chaps. Who knows God's ways, eh, *child*?'

The Dragon had a parting warning which she wasn't slow to impart. 'You keep quiet about this now, you hear me, Rohan! I don't want you going about babbling about this to anyone. Not a word, mind you! Just come straight back to me and let me know what you have learnt after you have finished.'

She concluded their discussion by clutching Rohan's shoulder lightly in a very conspiratorial fashion, sending out vibes to the effect that they were two closely intertwined plotters planning a great coup d'état in some distant troubled country.

Rohan was thrilled no end by the unprecedented honour of being taken into the Dragon's confidence and being given such a highly important task. He certainly wasn't used to being treated in this very amiable fashion by his unfathomable, crotchety old grandmother and decided on the spot – since such an enormous responsibility was thrust on his shoulders – that he would set out on the allotted task without wasting more time. Bridling with pride over the singular honour bestowed upon him, Rohan propelled himself into prompt action.

Unlike Mahan and the rest of the household, Rohan was on quite friendly terms with nearly all of Grandmummy's rather mundane neighbours, often having short chats with them on the most trivial of matters. Being a likeable child, he had no difficulty in getting people to talk. He genuinely liked most of the closest neighbours, except for a certain Mrs Fazal who lived next door, and his feelings were reciprocated. Almost everyone liked Rohan's friendly demeanour and easy-going ways, additionally quite flattered that a person from the grand 'English' lady's ménage would stoop to mingle so freely with the likes of *them*.

Rohan passed the 'hopper' house first and observed Baking Jane hanging out her washing. She was draped in a long bath towel, a garment she always wore when doing her washing, showing off her almost perfectly rounded figure. How convenient meeting up with Jane, he mused, recollecting instantly that she had a lodger to whom she was renting out her small front room. Rohan stopped abruptly in his tracks and hailed her. 'Good morning, Aunty Jane. What a lot of clothes you are washing today!'

Baking Jane looked up from behind a large bed sheet she was doggedly trying to get over the clothes line. Seeing Rohan, a firm favourite, she broke out into a welcoming grin, red betel stain showing prominently on her otherwise well-formed teeth – signs she had just chewed a plop of betel. She spoke to him in a pretended coquettish manner. 'Ah, Rohan, young sir! What are you doing here at this time of the day, eh? Come to court the old lady, have you?' she joked amiably, amused by her own sense of humour.

Baking Jane had been a great beauty in her youth and had a good many men all tied up in knots vying for her charms in those bygone days of thunder. Rohan, who was totally smitten by Baking Jane, pretended to be bashful upon hearing the intended joke, just to show its appreciation. Secretly, he would have loved to court Baking Jane, even marry her, but he knew he was far too young for that kind of thing as yet! He obligingly helped Baking Jane to put the difficult sheet over the clothes line and stood by afterwards watching her hang the rest of the washed clothes.

Baking Jane chatted on with Rohan, who listened politely, interjecting now and then with a few short monosyllables to show his interest. He was rather lost, far away in a state of wonder, gazing at the large stack of clothes his friend had just washed by hand. 'How on earth could one person wash so many clothes?' he pondered to himself. He had problems washing his own few shirts and trousers he was forced to do every single week and couldn't for the life of him fathom how one could get through such a large mountain of clothes. Baking Jane looked at him keenly as though reading his thoughts.

'Yes, yes, thems a lot of clothes, aren't they? I have to wash for *all* in this family, you know! Lazy bloody wretches, my daughters and son-in-law. One would expect them to wash their own damn clothes! Always burdening old Jane with their chores, the rascals,' she complained in a weary and abject manner, accepting her lot with resigned good grace.

'Who's washing your lodger fellow's clothes, Aunty Jane?' asked Rohan in an admirable attempt to steer the conversation to suit his present mission.

Baking Jane's brow darkened considerably at the mention of her lodger. There was considerable tension between her and the lodger over the latter's irregular payments of the lodging rent. 'Don't talk about that bloody stingy bugger, child! He wears just two shirts and one trouser a week, and when he travels home for the weekend, he gets his womenfolk to wash and iron them to be ready for the next week when he comes back here. God only knows what the bugger wears in the weekends in his damn village. Probably goes around naked, showing off his damn dangling dingle and dirty backside like most of them blasted villagers do. *Savages*, the lot of them! The only blooming clothes he washes here is his damn underwear, which he does at nights. The bugger doesn't do anything in the bathroom during daytime these days. Gets up earlier than me and shaves and washes! He's trying his best to avoid me, the rascal! Owes me rent money, you see – the damn village brute.'

Baking Jane's body shook with rage as she spoke, treating Rohan to a wonderful erotic treat. Her recent outburst had caused her bath towel to loosen. She immediately opened out the towel and rewound it around her body, but not before giving Rohan a full view of her naked breasts and familiar bald vulva. Rohan, who had only seen Baking Jane partially nude a couple of times before when the latter had forgotten to cover up her naked breasts at the breakfast buying expeditions, was bowled over by the highly erotic sight, especially enthralled by the bald vulva on view. How he longed to take matters in hand and cuddle Baking Jane's breasts and press himself against her 'thingie'! He was fast determined now, more than ever, to marry Baking Jane when he grew up.

Forcing his thoughts to matters on hand, Rohan digested Baking Jane's information for a few moments before proceeding to take the bull by the horns in a more direct sort of approach. He asked in a most casual manner, as if though just making idle chit-chat to pass away the time, 'How much do I need to pay you, Aunty Jane, if I become a lodger in your house? Is it a lot of money?'

Baking Jane laughed loud at the question and expertly squirted a sliver of red betel saliva from her mouth onto an unappreciative nearby bush.

'What a question you ask, child! Whatever are you asking that for, eh? Why do you want to go and be a lodger in my house? You don't need *that*! Aren't you living nice and grandly in the big house with Dona?

(Grandmummy's crooked house, although modestly large, was always referred to by the neighbours as the 'big house' and Grandmummy as 'Dona', a sort of superior title given to local women originating from the Portuguese period of usurpation.) Baking Jane continued. 'Anyway, if you really want to live with me, you can live for free, child. You're such a nice boy – not like that good-for-nothing bugger of a lodger fellow I have.' She paused here momentarily to ruminate upon her lodger's shortcomings, her normally amiable face darkening into a seldom-seen frown of annoyance whilst a harsh tone crept into her voice. She blurted out additionally, now with considerable venom, 'Why! Do you know, child? He's not even paid last month's rent and it's nearly the end of *this* month! As if *twenty* rupees is such a big sum for his pocket? The rascal has a gormant [government] job and can't even pay the rent in a regular way. I warned him good and proper, young Rohan, sir! I warned the dratted bugger last week. Told the fellow if he doesn't pay the money he owes me, I am going to kick him out by his backside at the end of the month!'

Twenty rupees! Rohan had made a good start. At least now he had some sort of inkling what a lodger paid in rent! He lingered a bit to chat more with Baking Jane, said goodbye after a while, and then continued on his very important fact-finding mission. He had made a satisfactory start and was fast determined to put together an accurate final report to present to the old Dragon.

Working shrewdly in this brilliant fashion with other families in the neighbourhood, Rohan soon obtained enough collective information to arrive at an accurate sum of rent a lodger was expected to pay. The results were very uplifting. His seemingly innocuous questions, craftily put to the closet neighbours, made them talk just as glibly as Baking Jane had. Nobody suspected his ostensible intentions and purpose ...

After just two evenings' work, he proudly reported back to Grandmummy. Choosing a quiet moment when no one else was around, he approached the Dragon who was sitting in her favourite chair in the front veranda. Grandmummy's general demeanour had become slightly better the past few days. She no longer went around the house muttering and cursing, although the disaster of the spilt wine was far from forgotten. It constantly preyed on her mind and tormented her endlessly. The partial recovery of her old zest made her even go back to her favourite pastime – solving the Sunday newspaper's crossword puzzle – although she did it now in a listless sort of way, more in automation than anything else. Rohan addressed her at once without further ado, saying with great pomp, pride, and alacrity, 'I made them inquiries, Grandmummy.' He then added for good measure, in case his old grandmother had forgotten the whole thing, 'About the lodger fellows' rents you asked me to find out, you know!'

Grandmummy craned her neck to come within closer earshot. She had far from forgotten the whole thing, as Rohan mistakenly supposed. On the contrary, she had become more and more enamoured with the idea of taking in lodgers ever since her young grandson had brought up the subject a few days ago. She said in eager anticipation, her flabby jowls quivering with excitement, her gaze transfixed on young Rohan, 'Yes, *my dear.*' (Her form of addressing Rohan had taken a remarkable form of ascent the past few times they had spoken, going from '*boy*' to '*child*' and now to this very respectable '*my dear*'.) 'What have you gone and heard? What have you found out for me, eh? How much are them damn chaps paying for a room? Our useless damn neighbours tell you anything worthwhile? Eh? Eh?'

Rohan answered eagerly, his findings gushing out in an eager torrent of words.

'Them lodger chaps are paying between twenty to sixty rupees for a room, Grandmummy. Baking Jane and all them others I asked say you must make them pay one month's rent advance in case the fellows do a bolt.' Rohan paused to gather his breath and continued. 'It also depends on what size the room is. If it's very big, you can rent it to two or three people to share and get more money. Both Mrs Plim and Mrs Roberts are renting out their big room to three boarders, and they get sixty rupees a month! Mrs Appu, who lives in the first house at Montague Street, rents out her small front room to two fellows for forty rupees.'

Grandmummy gasped in wonder at Rohan's detailed information. Her mouth opened and closed repeatedly like a goldfish in a bowl. She was more than pleasantly surprised – almost dumbfounded. 'What! What! *What!* So much! Who would have thought that! Why, *boy* (she was back to calling Rohan '*boy*' again), this means we can rent the wine room to two or even three lodgers and get about sixty rupees a month! Our wine room is so big! It's bigger than Mrs Plim's and Mrs Roberts's. Only hope the damn fellows will not drink alcohol or smoke inside the house or mess up the toilet and the bathroom. These fellows have never seen the insides of a decent toilet or bathroom in their entire lives. Everyone knows what village fellows are like! Country bumpkins and louts, the lot of them!'

How Grandmummy knew Mrs Plim's and Mrs Roberts's rooms were smaller than hers and how she could possibly know that 'village fellows' had never seen a decent toilet in their lives was a mystery to young Rohan. He had never socialised with a 'village fellow', nor, for the life of him, did he know what 'they were like', as Grandmummy so contemptuously put it. On and off, whilst buying hoppers at Baking Jane's, he had seen the latter's lodger and, on reflection, didn't think he differed too much from anyone else. He seemed a decent sort of man and looked quite capable of using a toilet.

Grandmummy pondered over her last statement in silence for a while, weighing the pros and cons of having a 'village man' living in her house. Besides the unsavoury possibility of the mess one could make in her toilet and bathroom, or indulging in alcohol and smoking, the rather more dangerous prospect of a prospective lodger getting attracted to or, worse still, getting romantically involved with her two younger daughters loomed ominously in the background. The whole matter was a bit risky as she saw it, but the constant image of the spilt wine flowing from her broken pots swirled continuously around in her head. With no extra cash forthcoming for the year from anything else, she quickly made a decision.

The matter was decided right then and there and settled. The empty wine room *was* to be let out to a lodger or maybe two – possibly even three. Grandmummy was determined to give the young aunts a stern warning to keep out of the way of the expected tenant or tenants. Swearing on the Bible would be needed, she reflected. Yes, yes, she would get Primrose and Celeste to swear they wouldn't unnecessarily flaunt their charms in front of the new lodger or lodgers, intentionally or even accidentally. Grandmummy's brow wrinkled in concentration as she pondered over this move. In hindsight, perhaps Primrose could be excluded from the Bible-swearing, she reasoned. The girl was punctilious – putty in her hands – and could easily be manipulated, but controlling the outspoken and bold Celeste was another matter altogether, a different kettle of fish! These days, she scarcely knew where she stood with Celeste. Only the other day she had a blazing-hot row with her divorced daughter – a noted young heretic – over the latter's absolute refusal to attend the previous Sunday's High Mass in memory of a great saint whom the church absolutely adored and revered.

Grandmummy wasn't slow in putting her plans into action. The rest of the household were brusquely informed that evening after dinner of her decision to rent out the wine room to lodgers. The information came as a complete surprise – a total bolt from the blue. As Rohan heard the Dragon's announcement to the rest, he bridled with pride, knowing it all was his doing. *He* was the master instigator!

Everything went according to plan, except that Grandmummy failed miserably in her efforts to get Celeste to swear on the Bible, the latter vehemently refusing to be curtailed in such a drastic and degrading way. Celeste burst out in indignation when Grandmummy brought the subject up.

'Why the devil do you want only *me* to swear on the Bible? You think I'm some kind of loose woman who wants to fool around with men all the time? I'm the bad one in the family, eh? What about Daisy, Primrose, and Rebecca? Are they bloody saints, or what? Your damn precious Primrose parades her arse at those netball matches of hers, while goody-goody Daisy just loves to show her knickers and whatever is inside them to just about anyone! It's just me who's the damn sinner, is it? Is that what you are saying here, eh, *eh*? Answer me, Mother! Go on, give me a damn answer!'

Grandmummy had no answer to Celeste's outburst. It was getting increasingly difficult to control her headstrong daughter, who seemed capable of doing just anything she wanted these days. She reluctantly let the matter go, making a mental note to keep a hawk's eye on Celeste after the new lodger, whoever he may be, arrived.

After a few days, Grandmummy put an advertisement in the *Jellico Journal,* a local English daily. The advertisement drafted by Grandmummy and carefully edited by the 'ladyships', who were rather proud of their written English, read as follows:

LODGINGS AVAILABLE

Highly respectable English family willing to rent large room for single or two lodgers. Bath and toilet facilities available. Limited cooking allowed. Alcohol drinks and cigarette smoking strictly prohibited. Reply giving personal details and background. Applications to: No. 9824, c/o Box 3254, *Jellicoe Journal*, Jellicoe Junction, Portopo.

Celeste protested loudly about the 'English family' bit, but she was shouted down into submission by the Dragon, who submitted the advertisement as it was. The newspaper's modus operandi was to provide the box number, collect all the replies over a week, and then post the lot to the hopeful advertisers.

Grandmummy received at least twenty replies the following week in a large brown envelope courtesy of the *Jellicoe Journal*. The entire household, fired on by the exciting prospect of having lodgers in the house, had entered into the spirit of things and were in a fever of excitement. The young aunts, Rohan's mother, and the children pored over the replies, reading them carefully and exuberantly over and over and over again. Finally, after an assiduous elimination of replies from those whom Grandmummy considered unsuitable for some reason or other, the Dragon wrote back to the rest, asking them to come over for an interview. There were differences of opinion regarding her final choices, Primrose, Celeste, and even Rebecca not really approving. To her credit, Grandmummy refrained from abruptly dismissing the dissidents as one would have expected, given her authoritarian nature and dictator-like tenureship of the clan. She listened patiently to what her daughters had to say, but at the end she stood firm on her original choice of candidates, dismissing her young acolytes' opinions and counter choices. Celeste continued to protest, being the firebrand she was, but her protests fell on deaf ears. Grandmummy completely ignored her.

The big day of interviewing the prospective candidates arrived. The entire household were in a state of excited anticipation, wondering what the applicants would look like and who would be finally selected.

Daisy, who had casually dropped in to return a Pyrex dish she had recently borrowed from Grandmummy, was thrilled to stay on, at least for the first interview. Oswald would be back in fifteen minutes to pick her up, so she would have a short while to preside over events.

Grandmummy, befitting her rank, had the pivotal role as undisputed chairperson of the interview board – Rebecca, Celeste, and Primrose serving as board members. Even the two little girls, Sussie and Maria, who were informed that some new 'uncles' were coming to stay, were allowed to be present in the living room, where Grandmummy intended to hold the interviews. The tots were always quite interested in the grown-ups' activities. More often than not, they promised good entertainment, if nothing else.

The first candidate arrived for his appointment sharp on time. He was a rather dark-skinned middle-aged man dressed in white cotton trousers, white cotton shirt, and black shoes. Rohan noticed he did not wear socks, which immediately put him on *his* disapproval list. Besides, there was a distinctive smell of mothballs on his person – a smell akin the urinal cakes at the pissoirs in the school toilets. The applicant had a great comb of greyish black hair parted in the middle, well smoothened with cheap pomade, giving it a greasy look. After the initial introductions were done and completed, Grandmummy took the applicant on a brief tour of the house, showing him the vacant wine room, the bathroom area, and the kitchen, where she told him he could boil water for tea or coffee or do simple culinary chores of a lesser time-consuming nature.

Arriving back in the living room, Grandmummy got down to the serious business of controlling the man's credentials, setting about the task on hand without further ado. She had decided before the interviews to put off the usual bludgeoning tactics she practised on all and sundry, so as not to half scare away her interview objects.

Grandmummy forced herself into a 'joie de vivre' frame of mind. When the occasion demanded, she could, and did, metamorphose into her own little benevolent avatar. She had five candidates to choose from and was supremely confident to have a lodger safely contracted and bagged by the end of the day. She put on her most benevolent face, not unlike the popular image of the grinning Cheshire cat of *Alice in Wonderland* fame, amidst the surprised looks of the others, who had never seen this grinning look of hers before. It seemed kind of macabre – even surreal – to see the old Dragon grinning away the way she did. The two little girls, Sussie and Maria, were quite frightened by the spectacle.

'Where you employed, Mr Bagshaw?' asked the Cheshire cat abruptly. (The applicant had introduced himself as A.S.S. Bagshaw.)

Mr Bagshaw coughed a few times, seemingly to clear his throat before answering. 'I'm doing part-time work at Murgortroyd and Sons in the mornings, madam, and in the afternoons I go freelance. Lots of big business people run after me to do insurance and import and export documentation work, you know. They know I'm the best man in the city to do this kind of work!'

Mr Bagshaw grinned in contentment after his declaration of employment, showing several missing teeth at the sides of his mouth, but then stopped abruptly as his gaze shifted to Daisy, who was sitting on Grandmummy's high chair in front of him.

Throwing caution to the winds, Daisy had taken this heaven-sent opportunity to show a complete stranger her knickers. Spreading her legs wide apart, she allowed Mr Bagshaw a more than generous look at her flimsy knickers, her partially visible vulva peeping out from one side.

'My God, is the woman doing what she is doing for just me? Or is it just carelessness? Why, I can see almost everything! I hope the old lady gives me the room. All these beautiful women and not a grown-up man in sight!' Mr Bagshaw thought to himself.

Daisy's knicker treat was visible only to Mr Bagshaw – the others sitting in a row beside Daisy and facing the applicant directly. Rohan and Mahan stood behind the grown-ups whilst the little girls sat on the floor beside their mothers.

Grandmummy frowned, not exactly pleased with what she had just heard. The man's commercial credentials seemed a bit dodgy, especially the part about working only in the mornings. It all sounded rather suspicious. Was he going to loiter around the house in the afternoons? The bit about Murgortroyd and Sons, however, seemed above board. Murgortroyds' was a fairly well-known commercial establishment at Jellicoe Junction, but then again, a man who worked only in the mornings surely couldn't be that well paid? Would he delay in paying the rent like the boy had warned?

The missing teeth also went badly with Rohan and the rest, especially the young aunts, who were watching and witnessing the cross-examination in fervent earnest.

Grandmummy put aside her negative ruminations and decided to give the interview and her doubts about Mr Bagshaw's viability a new chance. She went on to question him casually in a pretended uninterested manner about his immediate family and private interests, hoping something positive would emerge to cancel the seeds of doubt in her mind. Her questioning revealed Mr Bagshaw to be a practitioner of the art of yoga, was divorced, and that his former wife was living in Singapore. The penultimate bit of news was most discerning. Divorce was a taboo subject as far as Grandmummy was concerned. She had suffered agonies on end when Celeste got a divorce from her absconding husband. It brought back bad memories – very, very bad memories. The moment divorce was mentioned, Mr Bagshaw's goose was cooked. The poor man didn't know he was committing a colossal gaffe when he divulged the fact that he was divorced.

After a few more exchanges, Mr A.S.S. Bagshaw left suddenly, highly disappointed. Disappointed because he was never going to see Daisy's intentional flashing again, and suddenly because Grandmummy asked him for the princely sum of one hundred rupees for the room, knowing very well he could never afford it. Nobody in their right mind would ever pay such a huge rent. He didn't go quietly, though, hurling a phalanx of juicy invectives at the Dragon as he left, invectives that left Grandmummy totally unperturbed. Her many skirmishes with all sorts of door-to-door tradesmen and the like had hardened her almost to the point of impregnability against any type of verbal abuse.

Everyone was quite relieved at the first applicant's abrupt dismissal, chanting silent hosannas of thanks – immensely grateful. Mr A.S.S. Bagshaw was roundly disliked by all. In the distance, the sound of Oswald's Morris and car horn was heard. Daisy bade everyone goodbye and left, pleased as Punch at having exposed herself so wantonly to Mr Bagshaw.

Rohan, who related all that took place at the interviews to Salgado at school the following day, was in for a minor surprise. Salgado, mischievous and inventive as ever, immediately spotted the hidden gaffe in Mr Bagshaw's initials and wasn't slow to point it out.

'Ha! Why did he call himself Mr A.S.S? Didn't he have a proper first name? And you know what?'

'What?' asked Rohan.

'Can't you see, Rohan? Them initials are the same as *ass*. Why, the fellow must be one great big blooming jackass or something!'

Rohan, who hadn't really seen it *that* way, laughed out loud together with Salgado at the absent Mr Bagshaw's expense.

The second applicant was a salesman at Barnabas Wine and Spirits shop, a popular establishment amongst the European diaspora, who patronised it mainly for its impressive stock of imported wines, whiskies, cognacs, and the like. He had long greyish nostril hairs protruding in gay abundance from within a somewhat large nose – a sight highly offensive to Rebecca and the young aunts. 'Why the devil couldn't he trim those awful nose hairs?' they thought in unison. To make matters worse, he spoke so ebulliently on the products he sold that Grandmummy mistook him for a tippler. Needless to say, he was unceremoniously dismissed after just a very short interview. Grandmummy tolerated people's drinking alcohol but was wary of, and detested, overindulgence. She would often watch in horror and disgust at the frequent stream of vociferous guzzlers passing the house in the evenings when returning from serious drinking sessions at Ali Baba's – the infamous tavern situated just a few blocks away.

As the hour approached for the third applicant's interview, Grandmummy found herself visibly agitated. Never a patient sort of woman, she had now, even at this early stage, lost much of her put-on benevolent manner. The Cheshire cat smile and poise was fast disappearing, and in its place the old Grandmummy scowl and demeanour was metamorphosing back in place. Her increasingly deepening stare, darkening countenance, and impatient manner made the unfortunate third candidate quite nervous and fidgety. He was a rather timid young man who kept blowing his nose into a much soiled handkerchief – an act that worried the head of the interview board considerably. Grandmummy, who had seen a lot of tropical illnesses in her time and was terrified of ill health, suspected the young man of having some serious lung disease. (He was just experiencing a very bad cold.) Grandmummy's fast-deteriorating humour, which by now had started its dangerous descent to the rude, did no favours for the young man's cause. In addition to the nose blowing, he started to sweat from his temples and to stutter whenever he replied to any of Grandmummy's now standard questions on employment and background. The constant nose blowing, small rivulets of sweat, and incoherent answers did not please Grandmummy and the interviewing committee, hastening the third candidate's summary dismissal. Unlike the first candidate, the sock-less, yoga-practising divorcee Mr A.S.S. Bagshaw, the somewhat gormless young man was not at all displeased by his abrupt dismissal; on the contrary, he was almightily relieved just to get away from the Dragon's presence.

Grandmummy was clearly disappointed by the three candidates she had interviewed so far. She had entertained high hopes that all her interview objects would be above board, that it would have boiled down at the end to her having to choose from a fairly decent lot. After all, their written replies to her advertisement seemed so proper and correct! That the three she hitherto interviewed hadn't passed her criteria was a critical blow. The risk of nobody being selected, unthinkable at the onset, was a distinct possibility now – looming dangerously ahead.

The Dragon fixed a malevolent stare on young Rohan. If all went badly, she would give the boy a jolly good ticking off, she mused vindictively, mildly comforted that there would at least be someone to blame for the fracas – if fracas indeed it turned out to be. The cheeky brat was the chief instigator of the whole damn lodger business with his sneaky damn investigating and spying, she ruminated, conveniently forgetting that Rohan had investigated and spied at her explicit command.

A fourth candidate was interviewed. He was an elderly man, well past middle age, soberly dressed in a white cotton suit and well-polished brown shoes. He wore a tie of a dull maroon colour and, together with the rest of his attire, reminded Rohan and Mahan of their schoolmasters who dressed similarly – stubbornly clinging to the dress code of their last colonial usurper, the British. The young aunts instantly disapproved. They absolutely and positively hated the prospect of having an elderly lodger, which was in sharp contrast to Grandmummy, who had no such qualms – *her* primary interest being only a man of sound financial means and good morals. The old gentleman did indeed appear to meet the chairperson's criteria, answering the Dragon's questions to satisfaction. His physical appearance, though, made the aunts, Rohan, Mahan, and even Rebecca frown. There were tufts of salt-and-pepper hair sprouting out from his ears, whilst his bushy black eyebrows met together in the centre of his forehead, giving the impression of one curving great mass of hair. The heavy black eyebrows were in sharp contrast to his snow-white hair and greying ear foliage. They looked suspiciously pencilled over. What did it for him at the end were his false teeth which one could not but help noticing. In between answering Grandmummy's now standard questions, he would roll in and roll out his frontal false teeth with a flip of his tongue, a gesture sending shivers of revulsion and disgust through all on the interviewing board. Even Poppsy, who was watching the man keenly, barked in surprise and fear at the spectacle when it first came. Grandmummy, who had seriously considered letting out the room to the candidate, quickly changed her mind, completely put off by the flipping teeth. The old gentleman was soon sent on his way, Grandmummy subtly proclaiming she had a long list of candidates to interview and would contact him if necessary after all the interviews were over and done with.

Grandmummy's earlier concern of not being able to contract a lodger had spiralled into a definite worrying one now – a worry she shared with the entire interviewing board. All of them were very much subdued by the time the fifth and final applicant presented himself. Their initial enthusiasm when setting upon the task of interviewing the candidates had waned considerably, almost grounding to a standstill. Even the children seemed to have lost interest. As fate would have it, matters changed in a sensational fashion with the arrival of the fifth and final candidate. A postern of dazzling hope opened up...

He was a good-looking young man, carelessly dressed in quality clothes and genuine leather shoes. Rohan noted with satisfaction that he wore light-grey nylon socks of an expensive quality, the kind his father, Rainier, used to wear in the good old days. He had a rather handsome countenance and fine well-groomed hair smoothened back with a light application of a gentle-smelling hair cream. There was an aura of quiet confidence about him that augured well for his prospects.

The young aunts leapt out of the lackadaisical mood they had descended into the very moment he entered and presented himself. They were instantly thrilled, and so was Rebecca, who was rarely impressed by men these days. Grandmummy too, seemed taken in, as were Laura and the boys. The two little girls took an immediate shine to the candidate, whilst Poppsy, who had barked with zest at all the previous candidates the moment he saw them, refrained from barking at the newcomer. He nosed the young man in a fawning fashion, wagging his little tail all the while. Everyone was absolutely bowled over by the new arrival.

Grandmummy, although unwilling to rent out the room to a younger man for fear of Primrose or Celeste getting romantically involved, caved in almost instantly to the youthful applicant's infectious charm – a wonder in its own right. The young man's easy and relaxed manner even succeeded in bringing back her 'benevolent' Cheshire cat grin and poise. In any event, Cheshire cat or no Cheshire cat, Grandmummy was by now absolutely alarmed at the prospect of having no more candidates to choose from if this last one was sent packing too. The financial costs of placing another advertisement loomed ominously ahead, as was the prospect of going through the motions of conducting interviews all over again, which, in hindsight, she realised wasn't such an easy thing after all. There would be so much delay too. Placing another advertisement would require waiting another fortnight, even a month – a month without lodger rent! The Dragon was desperately anxious to wind up affairs. It wasn't just repeating the financial costs of a new advertisement and a subsequent delay in collecting rent that bothered her. Physically, she didn't feel too good either. Her constant efforts to smile and look benevolent had so far only succeeded in causing her jaws to ache, her neck to throb with pain, whilst a right royal headache was just inches away, waiting to break loose in full force. She had no desire to go through all that a second time around.

Grandmummy's subsequent probing of the final candidate's credentials proved to be pleasantly revealing – very much so. The young man was from the country and belonged to a landowning family of some means – at any rate, he purported as much, and was most probably true considering his manner and style of dress. He even spoke much better English than his unfortunate predecessors, whilst an aurora of contentment and class oozed from his person. Further probing from Grandmummy revealed that he had a better position in a governmental department – a position of some considerable importance – and would be travelling home for the weekends if he was allocated the room.

There was no further interrogation. There was no need, as the man met every criterion the Dragon had preset when embarking on the interviews. Besides, Grandmummy's jaws were aching terribly now after all the Cheshire cat grinning she had done. She was longing to retire to the kitchen, make herself a cup of steaming-hot tea, and relax on her favourite chair in the front veranda.

Grandmummy asked the young man to move in a week's time. Rohan's pioneering investigation revealing that it was the custom to ask for one month's rent in advance came well in hand. She even improvised, insisting, in a shrewd business move, for *two* months' rent in advance. A sum of forty rupees a month for the room was agreed upon, much more than normally required for a single lodger. Grandmummy told the young man that the room was large and could be rented to two persons for that sum or to three persons for sixty rupees to justify her somewhat high rental demand.

The young man readily agreed without so much as a whimper of protest, paying Grandmummy the requested advance on the spot in crisp new currency notes taken from an impressive-looking leather wallet he fished out from his rear pocket. Finally, a deal had been struck and a lodger contracted! As soon as the impending lodger said his goodbyes and left, a babble of comments broke loose amongst the interviewing board. Grandmummy hurriedly retired into the bowels of the kitchen, leaving the others to discuss the events of the interviews amongst themselves.

The whole ménage was thrilled in anticipation of the lodger's moving in. The divorced Celeste was confident she could induce or even seduce the rather good-looking young man into an intimate relationship. An extra effort would be needed, she mused, her thoughts drifting to a very special sleeveless low-cut blouse she had spent a lot of money on, one that showed her ripe, well-rounded bosom and descending cleavage to great advantage. She also decided not to wear a brassiere.

'Let the fellow get a good eyeful. Even my nipples show through in that blouse of mine! That ought to take his mind off blooming sugar-and-spice Primrose and her damn netball-playing fat arse.'

She ruminated further on the power of her sex appeal. 'Maybe I'll wear my semitransparent skirt too, the one through which my knickers can be seen! I'm sure he'll never look twice at Primrose or Rebecca after *that*.'

Primrose considered wearing her netball shorts on the day the lodger arrived. She had a host of admirers ogling at her whenever she played for the office netball team – drooling and lusting after her shapely legs and ample buttocks packed in tight shorts rather than appreciating any special playing skills, of which she hardly had any. She ran about the playing court nimbly enough and passed the ball reasonably well, but she had no real talent for the game.

In addition to their choice of clothes, both women took extra care of their hair and facial grooming in anticipation of the new arrival's moving in. Rebecca didn't do anything special to enhance her looks, nor did she ponder over her wardrobe, but she did have an extra spring in her step the entire week since the lodger was contracted. Rohan and Mahan too were quivering with anticipation, curious to see in what way the newcomer could benefit them. There was bound to be something, they deduced. There just *had* to be with a well-dressed, good-looking fellow like that, one who, besides, did seem to have a good deal of money to strew about! The crisp bundle of currency notes he fished from his wallet to pay Grandmummy was still fresh in their minds, the action and the money impressing them enormously.

On the practical side of things, Grandmummy got the room ready for the new arrival. She had the original lock on the door repaired, doing away with the padlock she used for locking the room when it was used for storing her wine. She also furnished the room with a simple bed and a dressing table which had an imposing round mirror mounted on top and several drawers for storing clothes underneath. Everything else, she left to her new lodger – that is, if he wanted to add anything else.

The big day arrived at last. As evening fell, a Morris Minor taxi drove up in front of the pavement curb directly opposite the house. The new lodger alighted from it and after settling the fare with the cabby, walked up to the house carrying a huge suitcase with some difficultly. Rohan and Mahan, who were watching through the front windows, rushed to open the door and allow the new lodger to struggle in with his heavy suitcase.

Grandmummy was first in line to greet him, rising from her favourite chair in the veranda as he came in. 'Ah! Good morning, Mr Sera. I hope you had a pleasant trip.'

'Yes, Mrs Trescoot, thank you! I travelled by train from home and took this taxi from the central station. Had to take a taxi, you know! My suitcase is too big and heavy to carry in buses, what with all them crowded passengers and all.'

The boys giggled loudly in amusement. People very seldom addressed Grandmummy by her real name, and 'Trescoot' did sound rather funny.

Grandmummy continued to address Mr Sera, but not before giving the boys a withering glare of rebuke for daring to giggle at her expense. Nothing escaped her eagle eye…

'Well, you better get settled then, Mr Sera. Take your suitcase into your room and then come back to the living room. The door is unlocked, but I have left a key on your dressing table if you want to lock the room behind you whenever you go out. My daughters and the children have been awaiting your arrival. Come and join us all for a while.'

Rohan and Mahan followed the lodger, both rushing eagerly to open the door and let him into the empty wine room – his new lodging. They were keen as mustard to make a good first impression, worm themselves into his good books.

The whole household gathered in the living room to greet their new lodger. Mr Sera mumbled a few words of greeting whilst shaking hands with Primrose, Celeste, and Rebecca. Celeste squeezed his offered hand extra-tight, but he didn't seem to notice, or pretended not to, although he was riveted by the sight of the latter's almost see-through blouse, which showed the contours of her alluring breasts and nipples.

'God! Just look at that! The woman might as well not wear a blouse at all! That flimsy garment of hers looks like it might collapse under her breasts at any minute!' Mr Sera thought.

With an effort, he averted his gaze, aware that all eyes were upon him. He was unusually tongue-tied – in all likelihood overawed at meeting three beautiful women at the same time, in addition to his formidable landlady and the children. Grandmummy broke the ice much to his great relief and began to explain a few house rules, Mr Sera nodding his head now and then whenever the dragon made a particular point. An awkward silence followed, the household still assessing their new lodger from head to foot, whilst the object of their scrutiny hemmed and hawed a bit before mumbling an excuse and retiring into his room. He didn't really *want* to leave the present company, but, betrayed by his frozen tongue, which didn't permit any casual conversation, he decided withdrawal was the best alternative for the moment. He would work on his social skills and find something interesting to say the next time around, he vowed silently; it just wouldn't do to remain tongue-tied in the presence of such beautiful women! Its being Sunday evening and with work starting only the following day, there was ample enough time to make a comeback of sorts later on that evening.

Well inside the solitude of his room, Mr Sera decided to take a shower before taking on the household again. Perhaps a cold-water shower might help loosen his tongue's temporary rigour mortis and temporary brain freeze, he mused. It *had* been such a long and tiresome trip from his village.

After his shower, the lodger, whose full name was Don Simon Sera, dressed and groomed carefully before emerging into the living room once again. Celeste ogled at him shamelessly, whilst Primrose put on her most dainty and delicate air, walking about like an opera ballerina. Rebecca smiled at him politely, as did the children. Mr Sera did not miss Celeste's bold invites but kept a low profile, watchful and wary of Grandmummy's intense gaze, which seemed to follow his every move – especially when in close proximity to Celeste. Finally, finding a topic to talk about, he inquired politely of the assembly if there were any recommendable restaurants in the neighbourhood where he could get a decent meal for the evening.

Celeste started to speak, but she was abruptly cut short by the Dragon, who spoke for them all, waving away the lodger's eating concerns airily. She replied with a condescending smirk, as if to give an impression that she knew everything about the entire neighbourhood.

'No problem at all with your meals, Mr Sera. We have a good many eating houses in the neighbourhood to choose from. Rohan and Mahan here can show you the very best ones.'

'Oh! Thank you very much, Mrs Trescoot,' said the young man gratefully. 'I'll just pop into my room and and get my wallet. The boys can show me around. I'm quite hungry. Haven't eaten anything since breakfast, you know!'

As soon as he went into his room, Grandmummy turned her attentions to her grandsons. Putting on her most stern face, she instructed them in no uncertain terms. 'Mahan! Rohan!' she barked out. 'You take Mr Sera and show him the good eating houses where he can eat some decent food. Don't diddle-dawdle like blooming gadabouts all over the countryside, but just show him the good places and come home immediately afterwards, you hear me!'

The boys nodded meekly in ready compliance, the 'diddle-dawdle' bit falling on deaf ears. They had no intention of 'coming home immediately afterwards' either, as they were secretly hoping Mr Sera would treat them to mouth-watering cake and frothy milkshakes for their trouble whilst *he* ate his dinner.

They took him to the New Modern Café, the only eating house at Jellicoe Junction serving archetypical European food like rolls, pastries, cakes, and varieties of meat pies and sandwiches – even sirloin steaks with French fries. Besides the Western food it made available, the New Modern Café boasted an excellent Victorian rice and curry dish – a spiced concoction of rice, vegetables, and meat.

Mr Sera ordered rice and curry and, as the boys hopefully

anticipated, asked them to keep him company whilst he ate. He offered the boys the same he had ordered, but Rohan and Mahan bashfully refused, requesting creamy cakes coated with mouth-watering sugary icing instead – the kind they were anticipating and always had room for in their young stomachs. At the end of his meal, Mr Sera ordered milkshakes all around, boosting his standing amongst the boys to an absolute zenith. They thought him a jolly fine fellow indeed and would have done anything for him right now in the present ebullient mood they found themselves in.

In between mouthfuls of dinner, Mr Sera skilfully questioned his dining companions on most matters concerning Grandmummy's household – Celeste's bold looks and semi-visible breasts still fresh and constantly preying on his mind. With cunning yet discreet coaxing, he eased out information from the boys as to the martial status of the aunts and Rohan's mother. For good measure, he even probed further, asking subtle questions about the rest of the household's affairs. The boys enlightened him with uninhibited, cub-like enthusiasm, having already taken a great shine to their new lodger, even trying to outdo each other in the information stakes to keep their new patron interested and happy. They considered it a small price to pay for the excellent creamy cake they had greedily finished off and the wonderful milkshakes they were now sipping through a straw. The brothers' information was more than eagerly snapped up by a delighted Mr Sera, who barely needed to coax anything out of them any longer.

The result of the dining excursion was that, upon arriving back at Grandmummy's, Mr Don Simon Sera knew that both aunts were 'available' – that the older Celeste had been married before and had child, and that Primrose had never had a steady boyfriend in her young life. He also knew of Rohan's mother's position, Grandmummy's ruined wine business, and many other things as well. He considered himself wonderfully well armed for his up-and-coming tenancy.

That Sunday evening passed like no other in the Dragon's den. Mr Sera sat with the family in the living room, chatting away politely on all manner of things. He had grown in confidence after his little chat with the boys and had recovered a great deal from his initial bout of tongue-tied awkwardness. After some time, Celeste boldly invited the new lodger to join them in a card game of slapjack, which the aunts sometimes indulged in during the evenings together with the children and sometimes with Rebecca, if she was in the mood.

Grandmummy never joined in the card games, preferring to pore over the local newspaper's weekly crossword puzzle instead. On instances when the crossword puzzle was complete and there wasn't much else to do, she would listen to BBC plays aired over the radio – even the others abandoned their card games to join her whenever a popular radio play was broadcasted. Currently, a very popular BBC detective series was broadcasted on Sunday evenings, narrating the exploits of a certain detective dubbed the 'Dark Detective'. The popular radio sleuth had a particularly mysterious signature whistle heralding the start of the program, fascinating radio audiences no end. Everyone listened with bated breath the full forty minutes the program ran, rooted to the spot in tense excitement. The mesmerising whistle was even played at crucial dramatic moments in the episodes, increasing the hair-raising tension no end. The amazing doings of the Dark Detective had not bypassed Grandmummy's household. Sharp on time on Sunday evenings at eight, everyone gathered around the radio to follow the daredevil detective's exploits.

The hour was now approaching for the radio program to begin prompting Celeste to boldly invite Mr Sera to listen too. Primrose, not to be outdone, timidly seconded her sister's motion...

The radio was placed on a wooden bracket mounted on the wall in the dining room, and as they usually did, the whole party pulled the dining table chairs closer to the radio to hear better and not miss out on anything. Primrose, attired in her netball shorts, demonstratively turned her back on Mr Sera, ostensibly to screw up the volume, but intentionally to allow the lodger to have a superb view of her much-admired rear end. The chairs were not enough to go around, necessitating an additional one to be brought in from the front veranda for Mr Sera, Celeste cunningly overseeing it was strategically placed in a position sandwiched between her and Primrose.

Grandmummy was not too happy about Mr Sera's joining the radio party. She wasn't happy at all, but she said nothing, not wanting to spoil anything on this, the very first day of her lodger's tenancy. She didn't like the little charade played out right under her nose, orchestrated to a very large extent by Celeste, deeply resentful of the growing intimacy obviously taking root between her daughters and the new tenant. She was itching to give Celeste a piece of her mind for her boldness, looking on disapprovingly at her headstrong daughter, admonishing her silently in her mind.

'Always that dratted damn Celeste making trouble. Why the devil did she go and invite the fellow to sit with us and listen to the radio play? And bending all over like that to settle the chairs, practically showing her blooming breasts jutting out from that dang-blasted blouse of hers for the wretched fellow to see! Blasted villager! What the devil does his kind know about them BBC plays, anyway? Probably doesn't even read a newspaper or a damn book, the damned ignoramus!'

There wasn't much Grandmummy could do about the events unfolding before her very eyes. She was forced to watch on as her younger daughters shamelessly flirted with the new lodger, feeling utterly helpless, but comforted herself somewhat knowing that evening would soon pass. Tomorrow, come tomorrow, she would put a stop to all this tomfoolery. She was determined to get Celeste and Primrose to swear on the Bible the very next morning that they would leave the lodger alone! She would not brook a second refusal from Celeste, she mused – not this time around, not even if her headstrong daughter brought the whole damn roof down with her violent protests. It wasn't only her daughters' behaviour she intended to curtail, but she was also hell-bent on giving a severe warning to Mr Sera to the effect that he conduct himself as a lodger, explicitly a lodger, and nothing more. He would be told in no uncertain terms to refrain from over-fraternising with the family and that he was at all times to stay inside the confines of his room when not using the toilet or the kitchen. Her plans laid out, Grandmummy steeled herself to the task ahead the next day, all the while scowling in distaste at her two younger daughters and Mr Sera, especially at Celeste, itching to knock her difficult daughter's block off, if only she could.

As the evening drew to an end, a growing feeling of closeness and intimacy prevailed between the new lodger and the others, except, of course, for Grandmummy, who longed for nothing better than retiring for the night. Both Celeste and Primrose were clearly enamoured by young Sera and it was left to see who would win his ultimate affection. Grandmummy's worst nightmares were being realised – unravelling before her very eyes – although she didn't quite know the half of it as yet. One thing seemed inevitable. There *was* going to be a romance between the lodger and one of the young aunts – but which one?

Meanwhile, life teemed on as usual at the Nameless. The weekend after the lodger's arrival, Rohan trudged along on Saturday morning to bathe Strangefellow, according to his 'contract' with Sonny, Poppsy following at his heels. Local gossip flew around swiftly at Jellicoe Junction, and it was inevitable that Grandmummy's new lodger came up in the initial conversation between Sonny and Rohan prior to the dogs' bath.

'Heard the old bird's gone and got herself a lodger chap from one of them faraway villages,' opened Sonny curiously, fishing shamelessly for details.

'Yes, yes, Uncle Sonny. That's true. He's a very nice fellow and is the manager at the government waterworks department at Coronation Park. He paid Grandmummy two months' rent in advance and has lots of money, too. He told Grandmummy his father owns a cinnamon plantation in his village and has acres and acres of tea bushes. They must be very rich people!'

'Bah!' ejaculated Catnips, who was listening to the conversation keenly. 'Them village buggers are all a bunch of no-good liars and thieves. Who is to know what sort of family the fellow has in his blooming village? Cinnamon plantation, indeed. Ha! Your stinky old grandmother's going to travel there to check all that humbug, eh? Answer me that? And who's to know for sure if the fellow has a government job or not? Maybe he's some sort of criminal chap who's up to no good! That old she-devil of a grandmother of yours is just stupid and foolish to take some unknown bugger into her house, a complete stranger she knows nothing about! Why, the fellow might rob you all and take off while you sleep! Might even slit your damn throats!'

Catnips's negative tirade stemmed primarily from the fact that the new lodger would be in close physical proximity to Primrose and Celeste. He was jealous – very, very jealous. Some time ago, besotted by Primrose's and Celeste's great beauty, he had become infatuated, completely bowled over by the two sisters. He tried several times to get a foothold into their lives and affections, but had failed miserably on each attempt, largely due to Grandmummy's watchful vigilance, but also because neither Primrose nor Celeste wanted to take him on, the sisters dismissing him in no uncertain terms. Catnips was a good-looking man and they were drawn to him initially, but when the truth of his idle life, suspected criminal connections, and purported cannabis addiction became known, they shied away, uncomfortable that a man of such shifty background and assuetude should even dare to vie for their affections.

Rohan didn't quite like Catnips's vindication of the new lodger. He defended Mr Sera stoutly. 'You're wrong about the lodger fellow, Uncle Catnips. He *really* has a government job. He took Mahan and me to his office one day and gave us a jolly good ice-cream treat at their department canteen. Everyone in that office place knows him well. And he sure is rich, all right. He's got a car in his village too. He said he won't bring it into the city because he's not used to the traffic here and doesn't want to meet with an accident!'

'Pish-posh!' said Catnips portentously, unimpressed by Rohan's confirmation of the lodger's credentials. 'So what if the bugger's got a government job? Any damn goat can get a dang-blasted government job these days. Why, I myself turned down several offers because them government chaps offered me such a ridiculously low salary for a man of my calibre! And why can't he get his car down to the city, eh? I've driven plenty of times in our heavy traffic! Once you learn to drive a car, you can drive it anywhere. That fellow sounds like a no-good liar to me! He's sure going to rob that foul-mouthed grandmother of yours and rape that high and mighty Celeste, and Primrose too. Serve them good and proper, the snooty damn bitches! They think they are royalty, the way they go about with their damn noses in the air and their fat arses wriggling behind!'

'Where ever did you learn to drive a car? We've never seen you drive no damn car. And who offered you a government job, eh? If anyone's a liar, it's you and not the old bird's lodger! Why the devil do you want to go and tell us all such damned fibs, God only knows. Driven plenty of cars, indeed! The only cars you've been in are those damn taxis you take from Ali Baba's taven when you are too damn drunk to walk home,' commented Uncle Pongo from his special corner at the breakfast table, while the rest of the breakfast-eaters nodded in assent, giggling in mirth.

Catnips wasn't pleased by Uncle Pongo's words, nor was he amused by the giggling, which he took as an affirmative acknowledgement of Uncle Pongo's comments on his driving prowess and alleged untruthfulness.

'Why do I need to show a damn useless nincompoop like you I can drive a car, Pongo? And what the devil do *you*, of all people, know about cars anyway? I may take a taxi now and then from Ali Baba's, yes, but when was the last time *you* drove or even *travelled* in a car, eh? You wouldn't even know a brake pedal from a clutch! And why do you want to know which government department offered me a job and all that? Do I come and ask you things about *your* private life, Pongo? All *you* do all day is sit on your damn arse on that stool of yours at your workplace, pretending to be a security guard, while you secretly study the blooming horse-racing sheet. When you're not doing that, you keep loafing all over the bloody countryside with old

Bellakay, or you hang about here in this damn place! And as for you, young Rohan, my boy! I'm telling you once again, that lodger fellow of yours is going to seduce both those aunts of yours. You better tell your mother, Rebecca, to watch out, too! Those village buggers have no respect for married women, either. Sex maniacs, thieves, and liars, that's what they are, the lot of them!'

Here, Sonny interfered and put an abrupt end to Catnips's ill-tempered tirade. The insinuations about seduction and sexual offence especially, irritated Sonny. It was not a subject to use in a conversation with a young child like Rohan, he decided.

'Now look here, Catnips! Look here now before I take my foot to your backside! You shut your blooming mouth at once, you hear me! Why do you want to go and talk to the boy about seducing women in that vulgar fashion, and drag his good mother's name into it too? You want to corrupt the fellow, or what? Can't you see he's just a young fellow and doesn't understand any of those dang-blasted things? He can't even know the meaning of the word *seduce,* you damn useless fool!'

Here, Rohan made an instant mental note to look up the word *seduce* in Grandmummy's dictionary, the very same she used to solve her crossword puzzles. Perhaps it was another important matter related to the mysteries of women he ought to know about before he grew up and married Baking Jane.

'Bah!' muttered Catnips in vexation, rising from his chair and storming out in the direction of the open grass patch under the banyan tree to calm down. He had a venomous parting shot, though. Directed at no one in particular, it was audible to all.

'No bloody good will come from that bloody village bugger moving in with that family, I'm telling you. He's sure like hell going to seduce those women and cause one big damn scandal. Mark my words and see. Serve the horrible old woman right for all the damn foul words and unpleasantness she showed me. The mad old cow!'

That night, Rohan did look up the word *seduce* in Grandmummy's dictionary. It was a bit difficult at first, as he started off at the letter *C,* thinking the word was spelt *ceduce.* Gradually, realising his mistake, he looked under *S* instead. He found the meaning of the word quite puzzling. The dictionary said, 'To lead astray, or corrupt'. *Astray* was a word he knew well enough, but he pondered long and hard how Catnips could have come to the conclusion that Mr Sera could lead Primrose and Celeste astray. Why! His young aunts knew their way about the city better than anyone else he knew. Besides, Mr Sera was new to the city and certainly didn't know *his* way about to lead *anyone* else astray! He started to look up *corrupt* too, but the effort of it all had made him rather drowsy. Putting the dictionary aside, he did a quick wash, cleaned his teeth, and got ready for bed.

One hot Friday afternoon, Rohan returned home after having done the hated marketing chores, entering the house stealthily with a sigh of relief. He was pleased by his successful market trip, having negotiated it without being detected by any of his school chums or teachers, nor had anybody seen him dart into the Dragons house both he and Mahan were so ashamed of. Passing the new lodger's room on his way to the kitchen, he heard voices from within. The door was latched from inside, but he clearly heard Celeste and Mr Sera in intimate conversation of sorts. Rohan approached closer and put his ear to the door. He didn't mean to eavesdrop, but his curiosity got the better of him. Celeste's voice could be heard clearly from within, an unusual sweet clang to it, quite unlike the usual fighting, spitting, and snarling Celeste he knew.

'Darling, darling, *darling!* Must you go to the laundry now? And why do you send your good shirts to the laundry for washing? Isn't it expensive? I can wash them together with my blouses when I do my own washing.'

Mr Sera's quixotic riposte was also heard clearly, even more clearly than Rohan's aunt's. The sweetness of his tone was equally unmistakable, just as Celeste's was. 'It's not so expensive, dear. I can easily afford it, but if you really want to, you can do that for me. How nice you are to me, my dearest girl. You know, you truly are a princess!'

A puzzled and staggered Rohan pondered over this brief exchange of words. True, he had not yet reached actual puberty and was still very innocent and inexperienced, but something kept hammering in his head, telling him that a new development – something serious – had happened between his aunt and the lodger. Why did Celeste call Mr Sera 'Darling'? At the pictures which he and the school gang regularly cut school to attend, only lovers called each other 'Darling'! And why did Mr Sera call his aunt 'Dearest' and a 'Princess'? Surely mean old Celeste couldn't be a princess? What on earth could be the meaning of all this? Could it be that his aunt and the lodger had fallen in love, like in the pictures? A fine kettle of fish that would be, he thought in abject discern. Why, if old Grandmummy ever found out, she would bring down the whole house! His young mind swirled around and around in a gushing turmoil of thoughts, confusion reigning supreme the more he thought about it all.

Entering the kitchen in a trance-like state, he deposited the purchased groceries onto the rough kitchen table and turned his attention to his hard-working mother, who was busy cooking the evening meal. He inquired innocently, in a far-off sort of manner, his mind still trying to solve the intricate meaning of the alarming conversation he had just overheard. 'Mummy! Is Aunty Celeste going to marry Uncle Don?' he blurted out in his usual forthright and bold manner.

Rebecca took her eyes off a steaming pot of rice she was cooking and looked up sharply. The question jarred her considerably. 'What do you mean, Son? What on earth do you mean?' she asked in surprise and a trifle shortly.

Rohan replied dutifully, further enlightening his aroused mother. 'Aunty Celeste called Uncle Don "Darling", and he called her "Princess" and "Dearest" – and she's inside his room right now, Mummy,' he blurted out in quick succession, the words gushing out in a torrent.

'What! Whaaat?! Are you sure, Rohan?! Or is this one of your, or your brother's, stupid tales again?'

'No! Mummy, it's the truth! I know this for sure! I heard them talking when I passed Uncle Don's room just now. I heard her calling him "Darling", and he called her a "Princess". Mummy, if you hurry now, you can hear them from outside the door. And if you peep through the keyhole, maybe you can see what the two of them are doing inside the room all alone.'

Rebecca had no desire to eavesdrop or 'peep through the keyhole', as Rohan boldly suggested, but she pondered long and hard over the shocking information she had just been the beneficiary of. Since her forcible move into Grandmummy's, her two younger sisters had treated her with mounting indifference, but she meant them well and did not want either to be taken advantage of or to suffer in any way. Rohan's surprising and alarming bit of information could only mean one thing. There was some funny business going on between Celeste and the lodger – this was for sure. In retrospect, she had half expected something like this would happen ever since the young man had moved in, but she thought Primrose the more likely candidate for the lodger's attention. After all, Celeste, although pretty enough, was divorced with a child in her baggage, an automatic deterrent for any young man looking for new love and romance.

Rebecca was in a dilemma, wondering what course of action to take. Though her boys often had a vivid imagination and could fabricate many half-truths, she totally believed all that Rohan had told her. Finally, after pondering a long time over the situation and at the risk of being considered a sneak, she decided to inform the Dragon. She had no scruples over her decision, just considering it her duty to inform her old mother. Let Celeste stew it out with Grandmummy, she reasoned. The days of sibling intervention, counselling, and talking over matters with her younger sisters had long since passed and would in all likelihood never return, not after all she had to put up with recently. She recalled bitterly how Celeste and Primrose would often visit her in the good old days – how she would ask them to stay for lunch or dinner or even over weekends, and how they would more than readily accept, fawning all over her. They would even unscrupulously borrow her best clothes and shoes, feigning they had an occasion of some sort to attend, but they wore them to work instead to impress their office colleagues. Sometimes, they, especially Celeste, even borrowed large sums of money that were rarely or never repaid.

Having tended the pot of rice, Rebecca cleaned up the fireplace, threw the hot ashes into the back garden, swept the kitchen floor clean, and went off in search of the Dragon.

Grandmummy worked herself into an elephantine fit of rage when she heard about the alleged affair from Rebecca's well-meaning lips. She had only recently come to terms with Celeste's scandalous divorce – learnt to accept it and move on. Now, on top of *that*, this new shame reared its ugly head. It was all a bit too much to bear. Her troublesome daughter, always a colossally headstrong person, was a constant thorn in her side – regularly causing untold worry and concern. The very fact that she was divorced – her fault or not – was proof enough of the trouble she had caused and was capable of causing. Celeste's lifestyle and actions always remained a bitter blow to the Dragon. Very few people in Victoria divorced, and divorce amongst the Christian community was even rarer, practically unheard of, and almost taboo. Now, after hearing the news of this most recent trespass, it seemed to Grandmummy that Celeste had flung herself from the proverbial frying pan and into the fire by getting herself into a romantic liaison with a 'village fellow', one who, besides, wasn't even of the family's ethnic heritage or practised Grandmummy's beloved Christian faith.

That same evening, when Celeste had finished eating her dinner and was making her way into the living room to listen to the radio, Grandmummy lashed out, firing on all cylinders. 'Celeste,' she yelled out from within the living room, 'come here at once. I want to speak to you.'

'Why are you shouting like a madwoman, Mother?' answered Celeste with some spirit. 'I'm not deaf, you know! What do you want?'

The very sight of Celeste and the tone of her spirited answer made the Dragon even more incensed. She thundered forth without further ado, her face apoplectic with rage. This was the original Dragon in action, unfettered by norms or boundaries.

'Madwoman, eh? Deaf, eh? Shouting? What I want? You troublemaking bloody wretch! Why the devil have you been in Mr Sera's room alone with him, and why did you call that damn village bugger 'Darling'? And why did he call you 'Dearest'? Have you lost your bloody mind? What the devil is going on? Is there no damn decency left in you at all?'

Celeste knew right then and there that the cat was out of the bag. Someone had been spying – eavesdropping on her conversation with young Sera and had ratted. With no options at all, denial being useless and stalling meaningless, she decided to come clean. Putting on a defiant front, she answered boldly, her young daughter, Maria, clutching onto her skirt in sheer fright.

'Lost my mind? And what bloody decency, eh? I'll show you decency! Plenty of it! A *decent* man wants me. Yes, me! Me! Me! Me! A bloody divorced woman with a child around my aprons! Am I to be alone for the rest of my life? Is my little girl never going to have a proper father again?'

Celeste's riposte didn't please Grandmummy at all. It confirmed now for certain that there *was* indeed something going on between Mr Sera and her troublesome daughter. There was no doubt about that – not anymore. 'Eyoooooo' Grandmummy wailed. 'What shame you bring upon our family, you bloody ingrate! Isn't it enough you have already divorced one man and disgraced us all? Are you now going to marry a man who is not even one of our own kind? The man's a heathen! Will you live with a man who is not a Christian? Who will see to the little one's upbringing? Will she grow up godless? What will people say? What will Father Clement say? What will *all* the family say? What will our bloody neighbours say, eh? You're only going to bring more disgrace to this family! Wasn't your sinful bloody divorce enough?'

The divorced Celeste wasn't noted for her religious beliefs – far from it. She wasn't over-concerned about her immediate family members' feelings either, often mocking Daisy (and Oswald) behind their backs, besides being cold, distant, and lacking in respect with her other siblings and relatives. As for the neighbours, she considered them plebeians – a laughing stock hardly worth a second glance. She replied boldly, her eyes flashing dangerously, hands on her well-shaped hips as though good and ready for a jolly good fight – even a physical one, if it came to that. She looked like a Spanish bullfighter standing erect on his toes with cape flowing and estoque in hand.

'What will people say, eh? What's our dang-blasted family going to say, eh? What's namby-pamby old Father Clements going to say, eh! What the devil do I care for that old goat of a priest and my useless damn family? What do I care for religion and all those stupid neighbours of ours? What decent man wants a divorced woman with a child, eh? Stupid old Father Clement's going to find a nice Christian man for me, is he? Is he? Do you want me to wait till I'm fifty or sixty to get married again, Mother? Don wants to look after me and little Maria. He's a good man and has a bloody good job, so what the deuce do I care for religion and him not being one of our own kind and all that other poppycock you always keep bringing up?'

Grandmummy, highly incensed by this most disrespectful reply, took a step forward in sheer frustration, brandishing her arms as if to strike her rebellious daughter. Celeste didn't skip out of reach this time. She stood her ground and didn't veer an inch, deciding on the spot that if her mother struck her, she would take young Maria and walk out immediately. Don was sure to follow – she knew that instinctively.

Grandmummy wavered between giving Celeste a resounding slap and holding back her hand. She wisely decided on the latter course of action, reverting to her verbal admonishing. Bitter words were said on both sides. No holds were barred in this mother of all arguments. The gloves were completely off as insults and invectives from the warring parties filled the air, shattering the otherwise peaceful evening.

The argument proceeded back and forth for a good hour or so, both combatants refusing to give in so much as an inch. Finally, exhausted by their efforts and having nothing further to say, the two antagonists quietened down and went sullenly about their respective ways. The rest of the worried and tense household who had witnessed the whole spectacle did likewise before retiring for the night. Nobody spoke.

Grandmummy made a fresh assault the next day after Celeste returned from work, continuing from where she left off the previous day. Weary and exhausted after a hard day at the office, Celeste felt something finally snap inside. She had reached the end of her tether. 'One more word about this, Mother, and I'm taking Maria and walking out this instant. I'll send for our things later on. I just can't take anymore. Don will come with us. I discussed this with him last night. You can find yourself a new damn lodger and a new damn daughter!'

The bold ultimatum astounded the Dragon, stunning her into silence. She had had her share of arguments with her children before, but nobody – nobody – had ever dared threaten to leave the flock. How she regretted her decision to take in a lodger! If only she had stayed her hand and sorted out the lost wine business in some other way instead of listening to her grandson. Her thoughts shifted to young Rohan, blaming him for all that had transpired. 'Dratted boy and his dang-blasted suggestion about lodgers. Always was a cheeky damn fellow! Just like that useless father of his! Never did like the brat. See what his bloody suggestion has gone and done! I have lost a daughter and a granddaughter because of that filthy damn scallywag and his bloody suggestions.'

Grandmummy reluctantly called a truce. She knew well enough the kind of mettle her headstrong daughter was made of. If Celeste said she would leave the fold, then she was sure to carry out her threat. The Dragon decided to ignore the liaison between her daughter and Mr Sera, putting on a distressed face whenever her errant daughter was in her presence, even shedding a few manufactured tears to show her disapproval and grave disappointment.

A few more days passed in the troubled household. Grandmummy, now partially reconciled with Celeste, still fumed and fretted over her ignominious defeat at the hands of the two lovers. She yearned to take out her ire on Mr Sera, but nothing came out of her desires, failing constantly in her efforts. The Dragon was totally foiled in her endeavours to pick up a jolly good fight with her lodger by the combined actions of the enterprising young man and the boys. Mr Sera paid Rohan and Mahan twenty cents each morning to spy and inform him when Grandmummy was not at her usual position on her favourite chair in the front veranda near the entrance door – absences that always coincided with Grandmummy's visits to the toilet after morning coffee had set her bowels in motion. During these strategic moments, Mr Sera would cautiously slip out of the house to work. It wasn't that he was gormless, afraid to square up, but he was determined not to pick up a quarrel with his intended mother-in-law. In the evenings, he would arrive together with Celeste. After a shower, the couple would go out and spend a few hours at the nearby seaside esplanade – a popular trysting place for lovers – or go to the cinema, where they fondled and cuddled, scarcely watching the movie. Returning home, they would boldly spend a lot of time together in Mr Sera's room, caring tuppence for the Dragon or anybody else. Anyone peeping through the keyhole of the door could witness Mr Sera grappling playfully with Celeste, on occasions putting his hands under her flimsy skirts or plunging them deep into revealing blouses. Sometimes Celeste's skirts rode up her knickerless bottom, enhancing an imaginary voyeur's viewing pleasure. As the days went by, the couple, unable to control their carnal desires, performed full-blooded coitus, a mind-boggling deed at the Dragon's lair. Don and Celeste never got completely naked, savouring that pleasure for the privacy of their many trysts at local motels in the weekends. They disappeared on Friday evenings only to come back home very late on Sunday night, looking flushed, sheepish, and dishevelled.

The Dragon gradually gave up all opposition to the affair and, in time, grudgingly caved in, accepting Mr Sera as her impending new son-in-law. Although her antithesis never wavered an iota, she resigned herself lackadaisically to the situation. In hindsight, and all things considered, she reasoned that young Sera wasn't such a bad catch after all! True, the man wasn't a Christian and belonged to another ethnic community, but he *did* come from a wealthy family and he *did* so much seem to have honourable intentions. Besides, as Celeste pointed out, who on earth wanted to sully their family name and reputation by marrying a divorced woman with a child?

In time, the rest of the family adjusted too. Primrose pouted for a while, resenting the fact that Mr Sera had overlooked her charms for her sister's, but she gradually accepted her defeat and, in time, became fairly good friends with the man, as did the rest of the family. In a way, Primrose felt kind of relieved that she was now the sole contender for a husband. There would be no more sibling rivalry from Celeste or any of her sisters – at least not where men were concerned. Rebecca and Daisy were already married, and now Celeste was 'taken' yet again.

Back at the Nameless, recent events at Grandmummy's somehow came to light through Sonny's inquisitive probing whenever Rohan came along to bathe the dogs. Catnips descended into a bittersweet mood upon hearing the news. On the one hand, he was jubilant because his prediction about the lodger's seducing the womenfolk at Grandmummy's was spot on – or at least partially spot on – for it turned out that it was *only* Celeste who was 'seduced'. But on the other hand, it hurt him considerably to learn that yet another woman whom he had fancied was now 'taken'.

'Huh! Told you damned lot, didn't I? Did I, or did I not, tell you, Sonny, and you other useless lot, that the lodger chap was going to seduce them womenfolk at the old bird's place? You asked me to shut up and threatened to kick my backside, didn't you, Sonny? And you others all sided with him, didn't you? Well, now, who was right, eh?

Well, speak up now! Speak up! Don't feel shy! Cat got your tongues? Go on, then, tell me if I was right or wrong?'

Neither Sonny nor anyone else spoke up. The way Catnips put things, especially his using the word *seduce,* sounded as though a very bad thing had happened at the Dragon's den. But after hearing what Rohan had to say about the whole incident, Sonny and the others came to the obvious conclusion that the 'old bird's' daughter had gone and gotten herself a mighty fine deal – a mighty fine deal indeed.

Still, good deal or not, and all things considered, Catnips did sort of predict a correct outcome, and the breakfast-eaters weren't slow to acknowledge it. They were, to a man, a rough and coarse lot, but they were also good sports at heart. Their silence at Catnips's questioning was meant to acknowledge the latter's partially correct prediction.

The mercurial mischief-maker looked around himself fiercely to see if anyone would contradict him, but seeing that nobody did, he put on a very pleased look, savouring his 'success'. He talked incessantly about it the whole morning until the regulars went on their separate ways and only Sonny was present. He continued to jabber about it to an irritated Sonny, who finally lost his patience and asked him brusquely to shut up. Catnips didn't – a fatal mistake. Shortly afterwards, a fully aroused Sonny, a favourite club in his hand, was seen chasing a fleeing Catnips out of the Nameless, shouting out expletives in his most explosive Captain Haddock-like manner.

Strangefellow, who disliked Catnips immensely, happily joined his master in the chase, barking his head off.

CHAPTER 4
Young Love and a Tyrant

The rose is red, the violet's blue,
The honey's sweet, and so are you.
Thou are my love, and I am thine;
I drew thee to my Valentine.

ONE HOT SATURDAY AFTERNOON, GRANDMUMMY'S eldest daughter, Daisy – Rohan's dark-skinned married aunt – came visiting along with her husband, Oswald. The duo's proud possession, a second-hand Morris Minor of a dull mauve colour driven exclusively by Oswald, was duly parked with unnecessary and exaggerated care beside the curb in front of Grandmummy's house. Morris Minors, or 'Moggies', as the British diaspora loved to call them, were very popular cars in Victoria. They had a top speed of just under sixty miles per hour and were economical on petrol, boasting a good forty miles on the gallon, give or take. Although Alex Issigonis, the car's British designer, had in all likelihood intended the car to be a sort of 'workers' car' in Britain, it wasn't so in Victoria, where ownership of *any* car was a privilege enjoyed by, and confined only to, the affluent classes.

Oswald, a tall, very dark-skinned, weak-jawed man in his late twenties, had only just recently received his driver's licence. Faithful to the code of newly examined drivers, he drove at a slow speed and with exaggerated caution. He was especially well noted by those who had witnessed his driving prowess, or rather his lack of any, for his terribly bad skills in the art of curb parking – or any sort of parking, for that matter. He was insusceptible to improvement and, for the life of him, could never quite manage to park a car properly in a pocket between two parked cars – or any other space. When parking in the first-named fashion, he always managed to park his car with the rear end sticking well into the parking slot and the motor end jutting a fair bit into the roadway, or the other way around. Oswald's bad parking skills were just the tip of an iceberg of monumental motoring discrepancies. He was a naturally poor motorist who possessed a peculiar driving style, squinting intensely in front of himself with his shoulders all hunched and body well forward, almost to the point where his chest would rest on the steering wheel.

The sound of screeching car tyres scorching the rough pavement curb did not escape the hearing of his wife, Daisy, causing her to snort in irritable annoyance. Daisy had this uncontrollable habit of snorting whenever she was annoyed. Her snorts sounded exactly like the grunting of a young pig and whenever they came, her whole face went through a sudden metamorphic change, her usual horse-like facial features turning into a distinct piggy-looking one.

'I always keep telling you, Oswald – I keep telling you a million, billion, trillion times – not to drive too close to the bloody pavement when parking! Why you never listen to me, God in heaven knows! We'll soon be needing new tyres again, the way you go about parking like a damn fool.'

Her husband deigned to answer, preferring instead to mutter inaudibly under his breath, terribly annoyed over his wife's comments. In addition to the criticism over his parking prowess, his being called a 'damn fool' didn't appeal to him either, especially since he considered himself to be a man of great intelligence, one possessing immense nous. He was very much aware of his wife's razor-sharp observations, living in a constant state of silent resentment at her many acid-like criticisms, which were not only confined to his motoring skills. He had over the years *learnt* to be silent through trial and error, discovering it was futile talking back to her. Daisy's dominance over him was unequivocal from the very first day they married. Friends, relations, and especially all at Grandmummy's were well aware that he lived under the dominating whim and command of his demanding wife.

'Petticoat government,' sniggered the firebrand Celeste behind Oswald's back. The rest of the family heartily agreed, although they were always careful to do so out of Daisy's auditory range. They weren't over-concerned if Oswald heard the jibes or not. None of them really liked the man in the least bit – not for want of trying though, as they *did* make an effort in the early stages of their acquaintance to be warm and friendly, but they had come up against a brick wall. Oswald put on a cold and distant front, almost openly sneering at them as though they were inferior beings – children of a lesser God.

Oswald hailed from one of the more prosperous middle-class families in the island and had lived all his life in a sheltered world free from the squalor and difficulties that less-fortunate families experienced at Jellicoe Junction. He wasn't a popular man and didn't have any real friends at all. Even at his workplace, colleagues went out of their way to avoid him, abhorring his pontifical manner and ultraconservative views. His union with Daisy had jarred his utopian world somewhat. It brought him into contact with Grandmummy's dominion – her immediate neighbours' struggles – and the raw, pulsating, day-to-day world of the lesser privileged. It was an alien world to him, appalling and contemptuous.

Daisy was well aware that Oswald held her family in contempt and was always on the lookout to see if Oswald slighted her relatives in any way. She had insisted early on in their marriage that they visit Grandmummy every weekend, brooking no refusal, sticking firmly to her guns despite her supercilious husband's periodical whining and disapproval. Oswald would have gladly given his right arm to avoid visiting his mother-in-law, but there was no way out. The weekly visits were an anathema – something he had to grind up and bear for the rest of his married life.

Oswald's protesting chunter over his wife's comments did not escape Daisy's super-sharp hearing. It only served to aggravate her more. She spoke out shrilly in between her standard piggy snorts. 'What are you muttering for, eh? I said something wrong, did I? Why are you always so damn stubborn and foolish? If it wasn't for me, we wouldn't even be able to afford any damn motor car at all! It was only two months ago we bought them new tyres, didn't we? You think money is growing on trees? Who pays half the bills in this household, eh? Answer me that! I'd like to know! You think we can do all *this* on *your* bloody salary alone eh? *Eh?*'

Oswald did not care to answer that particular question. He didn't want to risk answering and getting Daisy into a more agitated state than what she already was. He knew from past experience that whatever he attempted to say in his defence only served to fan the flames of Daisy's verbal bombardments. Still, Daisy was quite right of course, he reluctantly conceded. She *did* indeed pay half and sometimes even more of the domestic bills in their liaison – what with her damned big fat salary and all that!

'Tchah! I'm not muttering anything bad about you, Daisy. I'm just annoyed by the state of the pavement. How can anybody park a vehicle beside that dratted pavement when it's all slanting and crooked like that?'

Daisy, never one to be outdone in an argument by anyone, especially her husband, snorted in contempt. 'Fiddlesticks! How can other people park then, eh? All them other drivers manage to park so well! The curb's slanted and crooked for them too, isn't it? It's only you who finds fault with the damned pavement. Why don't you just admit you're just one big useless blooming driver instead?'

Oswald had no answer as to how other people parked so well, resigning to keep his mouth shut instead. He usually lost all arguments with his spouse and was never given the satisfaction of having the last word in anything.

The couple, having parked the car to their mutual dissatisfaction, made their way into Grandmummy's house, momentarily setting their little tiff aside so as to put on a façade of matrimonial unity for the benefit of Grandmummy and the rest. Daisy put on her most elusive air as she entered her mother's house, knowing fully well how much everyone looked up to her. The whole family gathered around whenever Daisy visited. Despite Celeste's 'petticoat government' jibes, she was very much respected and knew it only too well.

Daisy was a senior secretary at the main Portopo bank. Earning a large salary, and as she had commented earlier, she did indeed pay half or possibly more of the bills in her union with Oswald. Together with Oswald's salary, they had a large combined income by any local standard, which also explained their ownership of the motor car.

Oswald's almost coal-black skin colour was unusual for the people of Victoria, who generally were of a golden or light brown pigment, except for the Eurasians and close descendants of the British, who were as fair-skinned as any Caucasian European. Oswald was heartily disliked by Grandmummy for several reasons, but chiefly for his lordly and overbearing ways. Of course, Grandmummy quite conveniently forgot her *own* lordly and overbearing ways, which were almost as atrocious as Oswald's, if not worse. Behind his back and whenever referring to him on occasions, she spitefully called him 'that black bugger' – a very unladylike comment with racial undertones – but then Grandmummy, although treated like a great lady by almost everyone, never really did behave like one...

Daisy's skin was a light chocolate brown, a far cry from her mother's and two younger sisters', which was almost creamy white just like the Caucasians or Eurasians. Rebecca possessed the same complexion as Daisy, but there any comparison stopped. Rebecca hadn't Daisy's horse-like facial features – far from it. She possessed a beautiful and finely chiselled face, something she had passed on to young Rohan. Some even considered Rebecca the best-looking woman in the family – a consideration that spoke volumes, as both Primrose and Celeste were absolute beauties in their own right. The contrasts in family skin pigmentation were largely due to the fact that Grandmummy's late husband *was* a dark-skinned gentleman of aristocratic ties who had come to Victoria as a young man from Singapore to seek employment and make his fortune. He was colossally successful in both, becoming a prominent figure in society before sweeping a very beautiful young Grandmummy off her feet and marrying her eventually.

The resulting union between the unusual couple accounted for a genetic hotchpotch, the family possessing both white- and chocolate-coloured offspring. Strangely enough, the alliance didn't produce a blending of the two skin pigments as one would normally have expected. Either one possessed the light chocolate colour or one was creamy white, nothing betwixt and between.

Grandmummy kept a very low profile on her late husband's family background, only conceding reluctantly that he was Singaporean. It was as far as she would go, although she would often chastise someone or other, saying, 'If only *big Daddy* were alive. If only big Daddy were alive, I wouldn't have to put up with all the bloody devilment you lot are dancing. Big Daddy would have thrashed you all black and blue. You can consider yourselves a lucky lot that big Daddy's not around anymore.'

Despite her horse-like face, Daisy had a filling figure, generously curved in the right places – almost a perfect eight. She was fashion-conscious to an extreme, always wearing the very latest-style dresses and skirts, invariably shortened above knee length, as was her wont. Additionally and amusingly, she was quite famous within the family for flashing her knickers when sitting to reveal parts of her vulva through the sides of the undergarment – a trait that annoyed the somewhat prim and proper Oswald a great deal. She would sit all prim and proper initially, but as a conversation developed and time flew by, she would fidget about in her chair and uncross her legs, showing more than generous glimpses of the cavity within. On one occasion when a small mouse was observed running across the living room floor, she had screeched out loud and lifted both her legs high up on her chair, showing almost her entire vulva, which somehow managed to creep out of a very loose knicker. On many occasions when the couple visited Grandmummy, Oswald would complain to Daisy in a shrill, bleating voice, insisting she keep her legs crossed tightly like a woman ought to.

'Can't you sit in a decent way, woman? The way you sit, everybody in the damn room can see those ridiculous knickers you are wearing! Why can't you sit like other women do? What the devil is the matter with you?'

'Bah! What other women? I know how to sit. It's them old chairs of Mother's that're to blame. The legs are so long that you can't sit properly on them!'

It was a standard riposte Daisy made whenever challenged by Oswald, and it was always made in good spirits. She played coy, strangely amused by Oswald's protests, even appearing to welcome them in a twisted sort of way. Primrose and Celeste suspected that their sibling deliberately showed off her knickers and that she rather enjoyed the sort of outraged reaction, indignation, and attention her husband showed. Grandmummy and Rebecca accepted Daisy's indiscretions, though, shrugging them off as faux pas and nothing more.

Oswald and Daisy made themselves comfortable in Grandmummy's living room after the usual greetings were finished and done with. Daisy had sensational news to impart. She positively glowed with pride as she began, her recent spat with Oswald about the parking incident seemingly long forgotten. 'Ma! Oswald and I have decided to move out from Nanna's home.' (Daisy called her mother-in-law 'Nanna'.) She continued amidst initial gasps of surprise from the assembled family members. 'We've been to see a house in Meadows a few times now – Oswald and I – and it seems just right for us. We have signed the contract and have paid the advance the landlord fellow asked. I wrote the chap a cheque for three months' rent only just yesterday.'

Her sensational news notwithstanding, Daisy just *had* to mention the cheque she wrote out, unable to contain herself. Possessing a chequebook required a substantial deposit at the banks, and Daisy was not slow to imprint and impart on all and sundry that she could afford such a luxury. She was immensely proud of her chequebook, often bringing it up in a conversation through casual quips like, 'Oh, I paid them with a cheque,' or 'I just cashed a cheque at the bank only yesterday,' or something relevantly similar.

The news Daisy so proudly blurted out was received with more than avid interest by all. Grandmummy especially beamed with pleasure and pride. Meadows was a solid community a fifteen-minute drive away from Portopo City, quite well known as a fashionable settlement for upper-middle-class bourgeois families. Although it was officially designated a village with an elected village council, most people deemed it more an extension of outer Portopo – a posh extension by any standard. It had developed an excellent reputation in recent times as a citadel for the emerging rich – housing prices having doubled and then trebled in the area in a short space of time.

Grandmummy was the first to make a longer comment on the matter as she looked benevolently upon her eldest daughter, her eyes all misty. 'Why, Daisy! My dear, dear girl! That is such good news! It's so good for you and Oswald to start a home together. At last, you can leave Vernon and Gladys's house and live on your own. It is high time, too! Can't live with your in-laws forever, you know! Maybe now you can plan for a child too, eh? It will be so nice for all of us with a new grandchild.'

Daisy was a trifle jarred by Grandmummy's talk of a child. She hadn't thought of *that* option in the first instance. A child or children were the furthest thing from her mind, prompting her desire to move out of her in-laws' house. The truth of the matter was that she was getting rather bogged down by Oswald's well-meaning parents' constant advice and interference in almost everything she did, longing for more privacy and space for herself and her husband. Additionally, and what she found most irritating in her present situation, was that Oswald's parents, Vernon and Gladys, were fanatically religious – super-fanatical at times. It drove her to distraction. The constant prayer sessions at their home, the mandatory churchgoing, the pungent smell of burned offertory incense every evening, and other related nomenclature connected with her in-laws' religion made her believe that she was living inside a cathedral rather than a normal home. To top it all, her husband's annoying slave-like adherence to every house rule his parents imposed was not in the least bit pleasing to Daisy. It was copacetic to Oswald, but an anathema for her, increasingly getting on her nerves. She felt shackled, trapped in a situation not to her liking, and yearned to cut loose and flee from it all. She wasn't a godless heretic like Celeste, but it was all a bit too much to bear. Daisy often imagined how wonderful it would be to have a prayer-free evening and get away from the smell of burning incense, far away from her pontifical in-laws to someplace where she could curl up on a chair in her short skirts, relax with a good book, and give a tinker's curse about exposing her knickers, accidentally or otherwise. Perhaps she wouldn't wear any knickers at all, she mused, chuckling amusedly and thinking of the surprised look on Oswald's face if he ever discovered her thus. Daisy doubted very much that Oswald would object to her showing off her knickers or being knickerless when no one else was around. Her Oswald could play erotic games as eagerly as anyone else, his prudish ways notwithstanding.

'Is it a big house, Daisy?' asked Celeste, all the while keeping an amused eye on Daisy's knees and skirt. Daisy was most prone to show off her knickers when she was agitated over something or other. The knicker-showing performances could commence any moment now ...

'Yes, yes,' chorused Rohan, carried away by the moment. 'Is it very big, Aunty Daisy?'

'Yes, child, it is big. It has three bedrooms, a big kitchen with an electric stove, a modern bathroom, a garage for the car, and quite a large garden with an iron gate in front. There's a barbed-wire fence from the gate going all around the garden too.'

Rohan was impressed, as were the rest of the ménage. Only the wealthy had garages and large gardens. *His* parents had a large house with a garage and a garden before their downfall, and if Daisy and Oswald's house was anything archetypical, then it just had to be grand indeed, he reasoned.

'When are you moving in, Daisy?' bleated Primrose timidly.

'Next week. The office and services are closing for bank holiday on Friday, so Oswald and I decided to move in then.' Daisy continued, giving more lavish details. 'We made a down payment on a set of hall chairs and a dining table. The furniture chaps promised to deliver the lot the same day we move in.'

Next came the icing on the cake, the pièce de résistance that Daisy was savouring for last. She said with overwhelming satisfaction, a superior smirk flashing across her horse-like face, 'We also put a down payment for a new refrigerator and a telephone. The former tenants had a phone, and the phone chaps said they only had to reconnect the line. The fridge is coming on Friday morning. Oswald and I will travel down early so we'll be there to take charge of it.'

There were further and louder gasps of admiration from the assembled family at this additional bit of news. It was stunning, to say the least. Except for Rebecca in her glory days and Robert, who actually had a telephone connection at the moment, nobody in the family had owned a telephone before. The refrigerator impressed them all likewise. The acquiring of these magnificent items coming on top of their recent purchase of the motor car made Daisy and Oswald's stock climb even higher in the eyes of the family. Both Rohan and Mahan were already yearning to visit.

Daisy's knickers were plainly on view by now. They appeared to be of some very transparent pink material that left nothing to the imagination, showing a suspicious darker patch in the centre that seemed to wriggle and jiggle as though alive. Daisy was facing just Grandmummy and Primrose directly, her indiscretions visible only to them. Oswald and Rebecca sat beside her, and the children sat close on the bare floor. Grandmummy, lost in admiration of Daisy's triumphs, just didn't care, hardly noticing the intentional or unintentional flashing, but Primrose gazed on in shocked horror. How could her sister not be aware of her constant exposures, she mused, not for the first time.

Daisy turned her attentions to Rohan's mother, addressing her directly. 'Rebecca, my dear, could you send Rohan to us for a few weeks? We need someone to do a few small jobs and errands for us at the start. He'll only be needed for a short time, maybe five weeks or possibly six. Could you, Rebecca?'

Daisy purposely asked for Rohan, knowing very well that Grandmummy and the younger aunts would object to sending their favourite, Mahan. She was well aware of the unfair ranking hierarchy existing in her mother's house, which had young Mahan well in front, in terms of affection and everything else. Rohan was a dogsbody as far as Grandmummy and the younger aunts were concerned.

Rebecca wasn't too keen to let anyone make use of her younger son or, for that matter, any of her children for the purpose of doing domestic chores, but her dependence on her mother for having a place to stay and her reduced social circumstances didn't give her the necessary leverage to refuse Daisy's high-handed request. If Daisy had made such a request when Rainier was around, she would have found herself frog-marched out of their house and additionally roundly admonished by a furious Rainier, but things had changed. Rainier was gone, their home was gone, and Rebecca and the children were one step away from a life on the streets. It was hard for Rebecca to refuse Daisy's request – high-handed as it sounded – for another reason too: Daisy was the only person who helped out regularly in *any* sort of way. True, she lived under the Dragon's roof for free and Robert had helped quite generously last Christmas, but Daisy did, in many instances, generously hand out a welcome cash donation. Once a month or so, she would casually slip two ten-rupee notes into Rebecca's hand and mumble, 'Keep this for your expenses,' or something similar. The money proved quite welcome for Rebecca, who was constantly strapped for cash these days.

Rebecca reluctantly acceded to Daisy's request to send Rohan over for the stipulated weeks. She didn't relish the idea but saw no way out – refusal not an option. A 'no' would most certainly jeopardise Daisy's regular cash donations.

Rebecca's reservations apart, Rohan really looked forward to staying at his aunt Daisy's new house for a while. He was eager for change, wanting to get away from his idiosyncratic grandmother, his horrid aunts Celeste and Primrose, and the doldrums of living under the Dragon's roof. True, he would miss Baking Jane, his mundane neighbours, and pivotally, his little sister Sussie whom he loved above anything else, but a change of air would do him a world of good, he reasoned. There remained, however, an unknown impediment to the impending adventure that lay open before him. His euphoria and elation over leaving the Dragon's lair notwithstanding, he wasn't quite sure in his mind just *where* he had his aunt Daisy. Upon introspecting, he realised that he didn't really know her *that* well. Turning the matter over more deeply, he came to the conclusion that he didn't know her at *all!* She seemed friendly enough on her visits with Oswald, but one never knew, he mused. She could turn out to be every bit as nasty as Grandmummy, Primrose, and Celeste! Oswald, on the other hand, was a proven tyrant. Both he and Mahan had marked Oswald down as an out-and-out rotter a long time ago. Both brothers had experienced countless brush-offs and ignominious insults at the hands of Oswald almost from the very first day they moved into Grandmummy's house. In the days prior to Rainier's downfall, the siblings hardly had any contact with their uncle, seeing him sporadically at Christmas or at other family gatherings. He seemed friendly enough on those occasions, often patting them on the head when Rainier was watching, giving off an impression of benevolence and love. All that had disappeared after Rainier's fall from grace and the family's banishment into Dragon country. Oswald hadn't patted them on the head ever since, and he wasn't even remotely civil anymore.

It was agreed that Rohan be picked up by Oswald on Friday

afternoon after school was over. A stay of six weeks was decided upon between Rebecca and Daisy, with Grandmummy's rather reluctant consent. It was also agreed that Rohan continue his schooling as usual. Oswald would drive Daisy and Rohan to Daisy's workplace in the city in the mornings. From there Rohan would take a bus to school and back again in the evenings to meet up with his aunt and uncle.

Grandmummy's demurring wasn't due to any excessive love for Rohan (she hadn't any) but stemmed solely from the selfish fact that her grandson actually did do a lot of chores for her, which she would otherwise sorely miss when he was gone. Faced with a dilemma of sorts, her thoughts drifted to old Sakkala the street cobbler, whose dogsbody-like services were solicited before the arrival of the brothers. Sakkala, a chronic alcoholic, used to do all of Grandmummy's marketing chores and other 'dirty' work for a small retainer before Rebecca and her young family moved in.

Faced now with the prospect of having the sole services of Mahan at her disposal, Grandmummy sent word for the old cobbler and reinstated him on a temporary basis. Sakkala was over the moon over his reinstatement, seeing how much he missed the money he once used to get. Although the emolument Grandmummy paid him was small, it was a wonderfully welcome contribution for the old tippler in his efforts to maintain a regular rendezvous with his drinking buddies at Ali Baba's toddy tavern. Getting back on track again delighted Sakkala no end. He was getting on in age, but he still managed to dance a little jig whilst walking the short distance from Grandmummy's house to his little shoemaking spot by the big drain near Sir Francis Drake Street after the news of his new 'contract'.

Rohan spent the rest of the week in the close company of his little sister, Sussie, as much as he could. Whilst at school, he airily told his classmates that he would be spending a few weeks with his rich aunty and uncle at their home in Meadows. He did not forget to bring up the large house, refrigerator, telephone, garage, motor car, and fenced garden, subtly mentioning everything in an off-the-cuff sort of manner, knowing deep within himself that his school chums – scions of rich families – wouldn't be too impressed by refrigerators, telephones, and the likes. He knew the boys had fathomed out some time ago that he was living in reduced circumstances after his father's disgrace and plunge from society and was shrewdly trying to balance the books in a small way by mentioning his new living circumstances. Besides, Meadows was bound to impress, scions of rich families or not. The settlement, or rather 'unofficial' suburb, of Portopo was fast earning a reputation as a solid retreat for the bourgeoisie, boasting many high-income earners and rising society lions.

Friday afternoon arrived to find Rohan standing behind the front door, his meagre belongings packed in a solid leather suitcase – one of the few items Rebecca had managed to salvage from their old home. Oswald arrived shortly and, without bothering to get out of his car, tooted his horn several times in an impatient tact to signal his arrival. He was hoping Rohan would hear his signals and come out, saving him the bother of going in to fetch him. The horn blasts went badly – very badly – with Grandmummy, who had been sitting peacefully in her favourite chair in the veranda, absorbed in the newspaper's weekly crossword puzzle. She opened the front door and yelled out at Oswald, her face livid with anger.

'Why the devil are you blowing that damn-blasted horn like a big lord, eh? Can't you move your bloody carcass and come inside the house instead? Who do you think you are? Just you wait till Daisy comes around next time! I'll tell her how you were tooting that blasted horn of yours for all the damn neighbours and everyone else to hear.'

Oswald, quite used to Grandmummy's insults, wasn't overly upset about her rude comments, but the threat of 'telling' Daisy, however, sent off alarm bells. He cared a fig for Grandmummy, her neighbours, and her insults (he had learnt to ignore the Dragon's jibes the four years he had been married), but squaring up to Daisy was another matter altogether! He hastily tried to pacify Grandmummy yet made the fatal mistake of not heeding her advice to come inside the house, stubbornly sitting behind the wheel of his old Morris.

'Why, my dear ma! I'm just tooting for the boy to hear! We agreed to pick the fellow up at this time, you know!'

'Poppycock!' thundered Grandmummy, who wasn't buying any of Oswald's excuses. 'Rohan's not deaf. Why can't you come inside and help him with his suitcase? He's been sitting here with me and waiting for you to show up a long time now. You think Rohan's a servant fellow for you to command with your mighty big horn blowing, eh?' The boy's my grandson and not your blasted slave! Move your bloody arse and come in at once if you want to take him. Otherwise, start up your bloody useless old car again and buzz off home!' (Grandmummy cared nought for Rohan's being her grandson, as she put it, conveniently using that fact just to put Oswald in place.)

Oswald made a split decision. A part of him yearned to tell Grandmummy where she could shove her advice, but the yellow stripe on his back, the one that cringed at Daisy's many scoldings and criticisms, urged him otherwise. Changing his imperious horn-blowing tactics, he reluctantly stepped out from the Morris and came in to fetch Rohan. Besides, threats to tell Daisy or not, prescience told him it was futile to expostulate with Grandmummy when she was in this sort of warring mood. Fuming with well-concealed rage at having to get out from the car, he marched briskly up to the front door and into the veranda. Picking up Rohan's suitcase, he took the boy by his hand, curtly motioning him to come along to the waiting car. Rohan, though, was not quite ready to leave as yet. He broke free from Oswald's grasp, ran back into the house, and fondly embraced his mother and Laura, kissing them goodbye. Mahan was present too, sullenly watching on, but the brothers didn't say anything to each other – each knowing exactly where his boundaries of affection lay.

Rohan didn't want to, but he dutifully kissed Grandmummy on the cheek, and then turned his attentions to his little sister, Sussie. He had saved up his breakfast money that morning and, with the proceedings, had bought a small bag of sweets for the little girl. Sussie did not understand much of what was going on, but she knew that her beloved brother was going somewhere and wasn't too happy about it. She brightened up a bit, however, when Rohan presented her with the sweets, hugging him fondly. Rohan shed a little tear. He hated to be parted from his little sister even for a short while, but he comforted himself with the thought of the impending adventure that beckoned and the fact that he would be back again after six weeks. Saying a final goodbye to Sussie, Rohan got into the back seat of the Morris, his suitcase beside him. Oswald, still fuming over his defeat, drove off, taking a good five minutes to look into his mirrors and over his shoulder with meticulous exaggerated care to watch out for the dangers of approaching traffic. The driving-school purists were most adamant in insisting that this very important precaution be followed, fiercely propagating that the beasts of the traffic jungle were most dangerous at this particular motoring moment and that caution was of the essence. Satisfied that no marauding tigers were lurking about in the guise of speeding cars and all was well, he started off, driving extremely slowly, as was his irritating wont. He drove a considerable distance on first gear before the whining sound of his protesting engine made him realise he hadn't changed gears. He quickly changed to second and then to third in a haphazard manner, the car's gearbox groaning in protest at his inability to press down properly on the clutch.

Oswald drove past the city limits and entered the South Central Road, an important highway also popularly known as the SC1, similarly marked on all Victorian road maps. The new house at Meadows was only accessible by driving along the busy highway a few miles and then by turning into a small branch road at an important trifurcate junction. Oswald had picked up a bit of speed by now but was still lagging behind other motorists, his hands rigidly fixed on the steering wheel in the 'ten and two' fashion highly recommended by the driving-school instructors.

Finally, after what seemed an eternity to Rohan, Oswald turned off at a point where the road divaricated. Following the much narrower new road, he drove on a short distance and then turned into a dusty gravel lane. Not very far down, he stopped in front of the new house.

It was exactly as Daisy had described. The house, the front gate, the fenced-off garden – all of it was there. An impressive iron gate sandwiched in between two concrete posts signalled the entrance.

The iron gate had to be opened for the car to be driven in and Oswald, after barking out a command at Rohan to get down and open the gate, drove down the gravel path and parked the car immediately in front of the house, a good bit into the small green lawn. He couldn't park the car in the awaiting empty garage; a big moving truck containing his and Daisy's personal possessions blocked the garage driveway.

Daisy emerged from within the house and hailed them. She looked bubbly and fetching, dressed in a very short tartan skirt and a deep V-cut T-shirt that showed more than a glimpse of her plunging cleavage. A colourful bandana adorned her head, projecting a gay and debonair effect. The short skirt showed off her shapely legs and sat loosely over her well-rounded buttocks to perfection, while her breasts and bottom jiggled appealingly as she walked about.

'Ah! Rohan, so you're come at last! That's good! That's good! Lots of work to be done, child. Go! Drink some water from the kitchen tap if you are thirsty, and then come back here. I'll show you where to start.'

Turning her attention to Oswald, she pouted, a sliver of annoyance passing her brow. 'As for you! Why did you get so late? It's only a fifteen-minute drive from the city. The furniture man was here a while back, and nobody was here to help lift the sofa and chairs into the house. I nearly broke my back helping that man. Hurry up now and at least help the moving-truck people to unload our other things. I have spoken to them, and they have agreed to lend us a helping hand. Hurry up! Hurry up! We're not having all damn day, you know!'

Oswald hurried to do as she bid. He was glad Daisy had scolded him out of earshot of the moving-truck men. To be chastised in public was the worst thing he could imagine or endure.

Oswald, Daisy, and Rohan worked hard. Aided by the moving-truck driver and his helper, they managed to get everything inside the house within two hours – most importantly, placing the items exactly where Daisy wanted. The driver and his helper were more than willing to bend company rules and offer a helping hand after seeing Daisy bend down a couple of times to pick up something or other – generous glimpses of her scanty knickers mesmerizing them to a point where they just couldn't refuse. Their contract did not include detailed unloading of cargo into specific rooms and corners of clients' homes, but, highly taken up by Daisy's exposures and hoping for even more, they acceded to her request to help without so much as a whimper of protest. It was as the younger of the duo enthusiastically confided to his fellow colleagues at the company's head office the next day. 'You know, the woman was wearing such a short skirt that we got to see her whole blooming knicker when she bent down to pick up them smaller packing boxes. Why, I'm telling you lot, half her blooming backside was jutting out from one side of her knicker, plainly on view! John [the senior man of the two] and I were treated to *that* the whole blooming morning!'

He continued to give his colleagues detailed information about the events of that day, but his audience had already stopped listening after the mention of Daisy's exposed knickers and the jutting half backside, lost in erotic fantasies of their own…

After the moving-van people were paid and sent off, Daisy, Oswald, and Rohan sat outside the house on a large wooden packing crate, enjoying chilled passion-fruit drinks taken from the brand-new refrigerator. Daisy was immensely content. At long last, she had a home of her own, and for once since embarking on her married life, she didn't have her religious and prim-and-proper in-laws hovering around to interfere in every single thing she did.

Oswald seemed content too. After finishing his drink, he walked over to his old Morris and started the engine. He managed to park the car carefully in the centre of the garage after a few wobbly attempts, Daisy watching on warily, disapproval written all over her face, her fingers fidgeting nervously around her empty drink glass. She knew her husband was a bad motorist, but she remained optimistic, hoping that someday, somehow, by some wonderful miracle, that he would improve his driving skills. She was fond of 'her' Oswald in spite of their mutual petty differences and was very much concerned for his safety, not to mention her own. Since the motor car arrived and the realisation slowly dawned upon her that her husband was a terrible driver, she considered their lives to actually be in some kind of jeopardy. Thank God, she would often muse, that she had the good sense to sign all those special insurance papers that would give her an elephantine sum of money if Oswald met with an accident and died, selfishly optimistic that it would be a single accident and that *she* wouldn't be in the car. A last will and testament had figured in her thoughts a couple of times too, but she had dismissed the idea as morbid. No, she pondered to herself, she was far too young to be thinking of death, Oswald's fathead driving notwithstanding. Additionally and selfishly, she hated the notion of leaving all her assets to anyone in the family. Those assets were hard-earned and were hers alone.

Evening fell. The sun slowly disappeared below the horizon, and as dusk broke out, the trio decided to call time for the day. Daisy's mother-in-law had, with loving foresight, prepared a food hamper expertly packed in a large wicker basket. It was a thoughtful gesture and a relief to Daisy, who was spared the additional task of seeing to everyone's dinner. Daisy unpacked the food from its sealed plastic containers and warmed it all up on the kitchen stove, using her brand-new cooking pans. It was a thrilling experience to use the stove and pans for the very first time, and even though she was just heating up food, it felt almost as though she had cooked it all herself – a culinary triumph!

They ate hungrily. After the meal was over, Oswald went out to the front porch to enjoy a smoke whilst Daisy went back to the kitchen to check out a few things, Rohan trouping faithfully behind her heels ready and willing to offer any assistance. They all had just one thought in their minds, and that was to retire for the night and rest their aching limbs. Oswald had already assembled the couple's double bed with Rohan's help, and as night fell, the two adults made their way to the beckoning bedroom, leaving Rohan to sleep on a mattress in the spare bedroom. They fell asleep almost instantly after their heads hit the welcoming pillows, utterly exhausted by the day's gruelling work they had jointly accomplished.

Oswald and Daisy's new residence was the first house situated a short distance into the gravel lane. Adjoining on the right-hand side was a detached twin house built in identical architectural style. Both houses belonged to the local squire, who had his own family mansion a hundred yards away from the twin houses.

The squire's house was verily a mansion in the true sense of the word. It was magnificent by any standards – a truly grandiose sight. The architect who built it had showed remarkable acumen in mixing together an architectural hotchpotch of Dutch, British, and local styles. The silhouette of the mansion could be seen in quite a large circle around the immediate area, dwarfing the smaller bungalows in the lane and even other modest buildings within the vicinity. The squire, an important local man well connected politically and socially, was in his early fifties and was married, with two teenaged sons and a daughter of twelve.

Back at Daisy's, Rohan caught a glimpse of the squire's great house and marvelled at its magnificence. 'What rich people must live there?' he mused, making a mental note to inform his fat friend Salgado and the others at school about the magnificent neighbour his 'posh' aunt and uncle had. He hadn't seen such a big house and garden, even during his father's heydays when the family had led a prosperous upper-class life and often visited important people in the city.

Moving away from the view of the great mansion, Rohan turned his attention to the twin house, which, in all probability, was occupied by tenants of his uncle and aunt's social calibre. A neat little garden with a close-clipped lawn and colourful flower plants in little plots surrounded by palisades of short wooden sticks, reflected the work of a keen gardener. Large French windows – exactly the same as those at Daisy's – boasted hanging green curtains of a silky material that rippled and flapped in rhythm to the gentle breezes blowing into the house. A well-polished red BSA motorcycle with an attached sidecar was carelessly parked on the cobbled footpath leading to the house.

Rohan awoke early the next morning. He located a pristine tin of coffee amongst the many unopened boxes in the kitchen and, using a brand-new kettle, boiled some water for coffee. He was quite adept at making coffee, having watched his sister Laura do it every single morning at Grandmummy's, and soon had a steaming pot of coffee ready. Leaving a very hot cup of coffee for himself behind on the kitchen table, he placed two cups on a tray and walked up to the main bedroom, fully intent on serving it to Daisy and Oswald. It ought to please them, he mused, perhaps even get them to like him and mellow down a bit – especially Oswald. Nearing the bedroom door, he heard his aunt calling out loudly in a strange voice he hadn't heard before.

'Yeow! Oh, Oswald, you mustn't! Oh, Oswald! It's soooo ... Oh, Oswald,' moaned Daisy over and over again in that mysterious voice.

Rohan was absolutely petrified. Was Oswald striking Daisy in a fit of rage? His nasty uncle was a head taller than Daisy and quite capable of physical assault, but turning the matter over in his head, Rohan dismissed that notion. Oswald wouldn't dare strike Daisy, he reflected. His nasty uncle may have been bigger and taller, but it ended there. Oswald was no match for Daisy, who probably could knock her pretentious husband out silly in a physical brawl. Although not very tall, Daisy *was* a very strong woman. Everyone in the family knew that.

Collecting himself, Rohan made a fresh attempt at serving coffee to his aunty and uncle. He was careful to knock on the door – several knocks just in case they were in the the middle of a brawl, and was rewarded when Daisy opened the door clad in a bathrobe. She looked all dishevelled and guilty, an odd smell of something eluding Rohan, emanating from her person. Daisy's initial dismay at seeing Rohan turned abruptly to pleasure as she saw the coffee. She beamed at him most pleasantly.

'Look, Oswald, the boy has made us coffee! Isn't that clever of him!' Daisy cooed, appreciating Rohan's efforts. Oswald for once forgot his trademark rude disposition and grunted in grudging appreciation.

Leaving his uncle and aunt sipping the hot coffee, Rohan went back to the kitchen, drank the cup he had left behind, and then went out into the garden. Peering over into the adjoining house, he noticed the two neighbouring girls in the garden along with their mother, who was bending down to inspect a flower bed with keen horticultural interest. Looking up and spotting Rohan, she waved at him, stood up, and then walked over to the barbed-wire fence separating the two houses. She hailed him loudly and clearly in a friendly voice. Rohan had rarely seen such an attractive woman. True, his mother, Rebecca, and his younger aunts Primrose and Celeste were definitely equally beautiful, but the familiarity of seeing them day in and day out had sort of diminished their attraction, making the woman in front of him seem perhaps more attractive than what she actually was.

'Hello, young man! We saw you arriving yesterday with your moving van and things. Your parents must be tired after all the moving and unpacking and all that. They're still asleep after all that hard work, I suppose!'

Rohan flushed a deep red. He was pleased and quite thrilled to be addressed as 'young man'.

'They're not my parents, Aunty. I'm just helping them to move. They are my aunt and uncle from the city.'

'Oh! Is that so! It does not matter, child. You are most welcome anyway. Here, meet my children. Girls, come along and say hello to the young man!'

The girls, thus encouraged, came forward shyly, gazing upon Rohan and assessing him carefully from head to toe.

The younger girl spoke first, saying boldly, 'Why haven't you combed your hair properly? It's hanging all over the place. And if you go barefoot in the garden without slippers, Mummy says you will only prick yourself or get bitten by ants!'

The elder girl demonstratively put her hand over her younger sister's mouth and said gently, 'Keep quiet, Shanna. His hair is all right. You shouldn't say such rude things to people.'

Their mother laughed. Her laugh had a slivery quality about it, which Rohan found rather magical. She was quite close to him and affectionately ran her fingers through his mop of naturally curly hair.

'What's your name, child?'

'Rohan, Aunty. My name is Rohan.'

'Hmm, what a lovely name! My daughters are Ida and Shanna. I'm Vanessa. You can come over and play with the girls whenever you like. I shall speak to your aunty and uncle later on, once they have settled down a bit.'

In the distance, her husband's voice could be heard calling out for her. Leaving the children to get acquainted as best as they could, she retired into the house to see what he wanted. Rohan looked closely and carefully at the older girl, Ida. He liked what he saw. The slightly rosy cheeks, aquiline nose, fair complexion, deep grey eyes, and the suggestion of a small bosom rising underneath her thin cotton top all bored a big hole in his head. He felt immediately drawn towards her. At last, he had met someone from the opposite sex who was around his own age. Ida was definitely going to grow up into a great beauty. The signs were already there – signs Rohan wasn't slow to notice. The younger girl skipped into the house, following her mother, but Ida stayed back.

'Here! You can creep through the fence at this spot. The barbed wire snapped away a few weeks ago. Come over to our garden. I'll show you our house!'

Ida showed Rohan the offending aperture in the fence where he could creep through, perfectly happy to do as bidden.

Ida was clad in her pyjamas. Rohan, who in recent times, ever since his family had taken a disastrous downward spiral from riches to poverty, did not possess any nightwear at all, was still clad in his short trousers and T-shirt from the previous day.

Ida was slightly taller of the two and gave an impression of being very mature for her eleven years. If Ida's appearance sent thrills down Rohan's young spine, his own natural charm and good looks electrified the girl like no other boy had done before.

A mutual liking was almost immediately established.

'What school do you go to?' Ida asked Rohan.

'Windsor Royale,' replied Rohan with some pride, knowing fully well that the much-celebrated place of learning would impress the moment he mentioned it.

'My! You're really going there? Why, that's the best boys' school in Victoria!'

Rohan, still glowing with pride, blushed and didn't say anything.

Ida waited politely for a similar question from Rohan regarding *her* schooling details, but there was none forthcoming from the latter, who appeared to be quite tongue-tied for the moment. Not one to diddle or dawdle, she volunteered, 'My school is Dawson's Girls' High. It's the most famous girls' school in the country, Mama says. I'm eleven years old and am in the sixth form. I'm captain of our junior netball team too. Daddy takes me and Shanna to school on the motorbike. Mummy is a housewife and stays at home.' Her information gushed out like a flowing stream.

Rohan was lost as if though in a trance. He noticed Ida's small, well-rounded lips opening and closing sweetly when she spoke. It was like watching a film in slow motion. Being so close to her, he noticed she smelt like local lavender soap freshly taken out of its wrappings. Infatuation hung in the air …

Ida's mother emerged from the house again, this time in the company of her husband, a slight, dapper man with an Errol Flynn moustache and a very cordial air about him. He nodded affably at Rohan and introduced himself. 'So you're the new people, eh? Hope you all settle down soon and enjoy your new house. Vanessa tells me it's your uncle and aunt who are renting next door. Well, tell them to come over whenever they feel up for a visit. Tell them Merv Pinto and my wife, Vanessa, would be most pleased to see them. And you too of course, my boy,' he added anxiously, not wanting to leave Rohan out of the equation. He spoke in a suave manner and looked directly into Rohan's eyes, a very friendly smile lighting up his countenance. Patting Rohan in an affectionate fashion on his back, he proceeded towards the cobbled pathway from whence the sound of kick-starting a motorbike was soon heard. Mr Pinto, his BSA in gear, proceeded to drive off to the local market to do some errands for his wife.

Vanessa bade Rohan a polite goodbye whilst Ida followed at his heels to the corner of the garden, intending to help her newfound friend back through the aperture. For a brief moment, their bodies touched whilst she helped him over. Rohan experienced a beautiful feeling of bliss, a new and strange feeling quite alien to him, one he had never experienced before. He almost stumbled in his efforts to squeeze between the aperture, causing Ida to hold tightly onto his arm to steady him. He looked her in the eye as a sort of thanks whilst the girl's penetrating grey eyes gazed steadfastly into his. A spark had ignited, a beautiful spark, innocent and wonderful for both children.

Well over on the other side, Rohan waved a final time to Ida and entered his aunt's house. Oswald, who was still clad in his pyjamas, gave him a fleeting glance of disapproval as he came in. There was no sign of his aunt Daisy, but she emerged soon enough from the direction of the bathroom, her hair wrapped up in a towel, suggesting she had just washed it.

'Where have you been, Rohan?' she asked inquiringly.

'I was speaking to the people next door, Aunty Daisy – the Pintos. Mr Pinto said for you and Uncle Oswald to come over any time for a visit.'

'What! What! Whaaat?! You gone and done what?' protested Oswald vehemently. 'Why the devil did *you* go and speak with the neighbours, you bloody busybody? Who the devil do you think you are? Who gave you permission to go and speak to them?'

'Oh, shut up, Oswald!' said Daisy. 'Let the boy speak. Maybe he learned something useful.'

Oswald obligingly shut up. He did not want to be in his wife's bad books, especially on this, their very first morning together in the new house. Daisy was clearly interested in what Rohan had to report.

ALAN JANSEN

She quickly took her nephew out of Oswald's reach and pumped him for details of his visit. Daisy was an avid reader of romantic novels and success stories in the *Reader's Digest* and other well-known periodicals, especially those featuring a superheroine. She often fantasised and put herself in the main character's shoes. She yearned to live out something similar so that people would admire her for her achievements and possibly write a glowing tribute to her in the *Reader's Digest* or, as she often superlatively went overboard, perhaps even mention her as a candidate for the Nobel Peace Prize!

After listening to what Rohan had to say, which really didn't amount to much (he could only repeat Merv's invitation and give the names of the young family), Daisy decided right then and there to visit the new neighbours already that very evening. She haughtily informed Oswald of her intentions, the latter having no objections at all, for once in complete unison with his demanding spouse. He was even keener than Daisy to impress his new neighbours or just *anybody* in their new surroundings, almost bursting with eagerness to start proceedings straightaway.

After a quick breakfast of last night's dinner leftovers lovingly preserved in the brand-new refrigerator by Daisy, the company spent the rest of the morning until lunch unpacking crates and smaller boxes. Daisy supervised the proceedings, knowing exactly where everything had to go, whilst Oswald and Rohan did most of the carrying, lifting, and placing. By lunchtime, almost everything was in place.

Oswald and Rohan, thoroughly exhausted by their efforts, sat outside in the veranda to take a well-deserved rest. Daisy excused herself and disappeared into her new kitchen to make the trio some lunch, excited about the prospect of making her very first meal in her brand-new home. Something in the shiny new kitchen, stainless steel pans, brand-new cutting knives, and other utensils infused her with a feeling of confidence, inducing her into thinking she could turn out a master culinary effort. She hadn't a cookery book handy and didn't know quite how to get about it, but was brimming with confidence that she could turn out something very tasty anyway. An ambitious career woman and not really interested in domestic chores like cooking, Daisy's culinary prowess wasn't much to hurrah for. She hadn't inherited any of Grandmummy's innate cooking acumen, nor had she hitherto been in a situation where she *had* to cook for herself and Oswald – or for anyone else, for that matter. In the early days of her marriage, she had cooked a few meals for Oswald at her in-laws' place, meticulously following instructions in a cookery book, but what she had conjured was slightly burnt, quite tasteless, and barely edible. Oswald, who had to eat the concoctions, was panic-stricken, finding himself in a sort of "catch-22". On the one hand, being newlywed and sickeningly in love with his new bride, he just couldn't bring himself to criticise her cooking, whilst the other option, going empty stomach to bed, didn't exactly appeal to him either. He had his postnuptial obligations to fulfil, and sustenance was imperative! Oswald did the best thing he could think of. He secretly approached his mother with his dilemma.

Oswald's mother, a very tactful lady, didn't condemn Daisy's efforts outright but, through a masterful diplomatic overture, effectively put a stop to Daisy's cooking adventures. She took Daisy aside and spoke out in a soothing yet affirmative manner, subtly using her cook, Alfonso, as a convenient scapegoat.

'Daisy, my dear. Alfonso has been much put off lately, you know. He thinks you started your cooking because you didn't like his own, the poor chap. The man's not at all well and has been brooding about it for a week now. I'm terribly afraid to lose the fellow, and I don't know how I will manage if he goes and does a bolt all of a sudden, leaving us all high and dry. I think it best, my dear, if you leave the cooking to him. After all, we're paying the fellow a big salary, you know! Besides, you must try and concentrate on your career at the bank, dear! I see you bringing a lot of them files and papers from the bank now and then. Attend to your work and let poor old Alfonso do the cooking. There's a good girl. He's sure to be a very happy man again if you stay away from the kitchen.'

Daisy reluctantly complied – reluctant not because she genuinely liked cooking (she deplored it), but because in those early days of her marriage she did ever so much want to impress her new husband. Overnight, all the cooking chores were reallocated to the faithful Alfonso, who had stood by stoically and watched Daisy's inept efforts with helpless dismay and abject disdain.

A modest lunch of cooked rice and curried tuna was prepared by Daisy, together with a cucumber and shallot salad. Daisy was happy in her new kitchen, thrilled to the core to actually cook a meal in it. Sadly for her, however, the tuna curry and cooked rice she conjured wasn't at all appreciated by her dismayed spouse. Oswald did not dare complain in Daisy's presence – he was too much of a coward for that – but well out of Daisy's earshot, when she had momentarily gone off in search of a box of paper napkins, he expostulated to Rohan.

'Bloody woman can't cook for two cents! We might all die of starvation soon. Look at this damn-blasted tuna curry, boy! I'm telling you, it really is uneatable. It has no taste, no salt, and it's all watery like damn soup! And the rice! Why, it looks more like damn porridge than decently cooked rice! Must ask Mother to hurry up and find us that cook she promised before the dratted woman starts cooking *all* our meals. Where the devil she learned to cook, God in heaven knows!'

Rohan listened patiently. He had had eaten worse and, being always glad for a meal, didn't venture an opinion, instead keeping mum. The tuna curry was indeed a far cry from the best he had eaten, but in fairness to Daisy, it wasn't uneatable. As for the rice, it was definitely a bit soggy, but then cooking rice could be a bit of a tricky business at times. Even his mother, Rebecca, botched it up sometimes.

Daisy remained absolutely resolute in carrying out her plan to visit the new neighbours that very same evening. Once dusk fell, she showered with a shower cap on, afterwards putting up her thick black hair in a fashionable style, and then carefully applying her best facial make-up. Wiping her hands clean, she removed a shimmering black dress from her wardrobe and put it on the bed before selecting the underwear she intended to wear. She deliberately chose her sexiest knickers, fully intending to show glimpses of it ('accidentally', of course) as and when a suitable moment came her way. Glancing at her voluptuous body in the wardrobe mirror, she hummed a little melody before putting on her dress cut very high above the knee and· then her favourite pair of patent-leather high-heeled shoes, smirking in satisfaction at the result. Daisy knew how to dress well and always carried herself resplendently – an achievement compensating for her somewhat horse-like facial contours. It was the provocative figure that first mesmerised Oswald, her knicker indiscretions coming in at a much later phase of their relationship. A prim and conservative man, Oswald was drawn to Daisy's well-busted, amply rounded figure like a moth to a flame. He was well and truly hooked the very first time he laid eyes upon her.

Oswald too spruced himself as best as he could. Not to be outdone by his wife, he put on his best flannel trousers, a favourite silk bush shirt, and a pair of sleek black Italian shoes he usually reserved for very special occasions.

Rohan's scanty wardrobe didn't leave him much room for navigation. He had three school trousers of a tough blue cotton material, two 'home' trousers of faded brown corduroy, and his 'Christmas' trousers and shirt of expensive, impressive weaves, strictly commanded by Rebecca to be worn only at Sunday Mass and special occasions. His possessions also included a pair of cheap leather shoes, another relic from last Christmas, when Rebecca – struggling enormously to make ends meet – had somehow managed to provide the children with new shoes in addition to Christmas clothes. His mind on Ida, Rohan decided on the Christmas raiments, trying his best to block out a mental image of a protesting Rebecca hovering inside his head. The clothes sat well on him, enhancing his natural good looks and charm. Dressed like he was, he once again looked the posh young boy from the good old days – the son of a wealthy and important man. His father, Rainier, had always kept a special eye trained upon his younger son, admiring the natural attractiveness and commanding air he seemed to generate. Rainier would often ruminate to himself that the boy would go far someday. Clad in their finery, the trio walked over to the Pintos'.

The visit went well. Mr Merv Pinto proved to be every bit the decent, polite, and well-meaning man he projected. The earlier impression he gave Rohan of being suave wasn't just an act. Most people felt immensely comfortable in Merv's presence, and it rubbed off on Oswald and Daisy too. Vanessa was her charming self, oozing glamour and talking all the while in the very same seductive, silvery voice Rohan had experienced the first time she addressed him in the garden. She made an instant and deep impact on Oswald. Throughout the entire evening, he had eyes only for her, ogling her shapely figure obliquely and shamelessly whenever he thought no one was looking.

Daisy found the visit an excellent opportunity to talk to people who cared to listen, rambling on and on about almost everything under the sun. She was in her very best *Reader's Digest* mode, talking and acting like she was one of the heroines in the famous magazine.

Mr Pinto soon discovered that Oswald was an accountant and, being of the same profession himself, he was more than pleased to find a brother-in-arms. Oswald, just for once, found himself very much in the thick of things, despite Daisy's attempts to dominate proceedings. Vanessa – an excellent host – seemed to sense Daisy's dominance over Oswald and, more out of sympathy than anything else, occasionally shot out a comment or two the latter's way to draw him into the general conversation.

It didn't take long for Oswald to become hopelessly besotted by Vanessa, thrilled that such a beautiful creature actually wanted to talk to him, even ask his opinion on matters. In his thick-headed, bigoted way of thinking, he had only one explanation for what he imagined was Vanessa's keen interest; the woman was definitely interested in him! He was convinced of it. All through the chatter and goings-on of the evening, he would, now and then, glance critically at Merv's somewhat slight frame and moustached countenance with distaste, concluding that Merv was a very poor-looking specimen of a man, unfit to be the husband of such a lovely creature like Vanessa. He wondered repeatedly how on earth his host had actually managed to marry the woman and live with her for as long as he had done. Of course, Oswald's ruminations were completely off the mark, as usual. Although Merv was wiry and rather slight in stature, many of his friends and associates considered him a charming, even an attractive, man. He had met Vanessa whilst at school and had remained in love with her ever since – a love totally reiterated by his attractive spouse.

Rohan had a splendid time too, compensating somewhat for his troubled life since his family's exile to the Dragon's den. Various quiz games, Meccano sets, magic lanterns, comic books, children's encyclopaedias, and a host of toys were displayed, demonstrated, played with, discussed, and discarded one by one.

The evening passed very pleasantly for all concerned. Cake, hors d'oeuvres, and fruit drinks were served and partaken of in between chatting. Afterwards, Merv offered Oswald some whisky, both men indulging in a few glasses. Surprisingly, and for all his nerdish ways, Oswald was a very good drinker and could keep his liquor down really well, the alcohol sustaining and even improving his present effervescent mood.

By eleven thirty, the guests said their goodbyes and went back home. As was the custom in Victoria whenever farewells were said, they embraced one another. Oswald was quite thrilled to clasp Vanessa in his arms, pressing more closely than the accepted norm – definitely much more than Vanessa expected. The tightness of the embrace startled Vanessa a bit, but she recovered quickly enough, putting down Oswald's excesses to the effects of the whisky, reading nothing into it. Oswald, on his part, made a grave misjudgement. For a fleeting moment when their bodies briefly interlocked, he wrongly imagined Vanessa's response to be akin something more than just a fond farewell.

'Why?' he thought to himself a short while later, conveniently forgetting that it was in fact *he* who had embraced Vanessa so tightly. 'Why did Vanessa press so hard? Could she have feelings for me? It just has to be! Must be all that clever talking I did. I always knew Daisy just wanted me to shut up and say nothing in front of strangers because she's secretly jealous of my social skills and all the international things I know about. Showed the damned all-knowing cow, all right!'

Oswald was primarily thinking of a number of matters he touched upon when the evening's conversation had veered to international affairs – facts he had learnt courtesy of the political articles he read in the latest issues of *Newsweek* and *Time* at the reception desk of his workplace. He was secretly vindictive, his lips forming into a contemptuous smirk after having called Daisy a cow in his private thoughts – the first time he had ever done so. Any woman seemed like a cow in comparison to Vanessa, he reflected, throwing an oblique glance at his unsuspecting spouse walking beside him. He muttered softly, his voice audible only to himself, 'If only Daisy wasn't in the way ...' He was already willing to discard the wife whom he lusted after and just made hot love to that very morning!

After breakfast the next day, Rohan set about weeding the garden at Daisy's behest. Now and then, he peered inquisitively into the Pintos' garden to see if Ida had come out, but as the lunch hour grew nearer and nearer, there was still no sign of the girl. Daisy had disappeared into the kitchen to see about lunch, whilst Oswald sat spreadeagle on a lounge chair in the veranda. Spying Rohan toiling away in the garden, he hailed him loudly to come over. Rohan hurried as quickly as he could, not wanting to upset the 'great man' and be in his bad books in any way. Oswald had just one known vice: he smoked cigarettes, almost finishing a packet of twenty each day. Putting his hand into his trouser pocket, he fished out a few currency notes and, counting them carefully, spoke out sternly to the approaching Rohan.

'Here, boy!' (Oswald never addressed Rohan by name.) 'Merv said there is a boutique selling groceries at the end of the lane. Go there and buy me a packet of cigarettes, a twenty-pack.'

'What brand do you want me to buy, Uncle Oswald?'

'Hmm! See if they have Golden Fleece, boy. If they don't, buy me a ten-pack of Three Stars. It will do for today until I buy some from the city tomorrow.'

Golden Fleece was the most expensive cigarette in Victoria, whilst Three Stars came in a jolly good second. Oswald was notoriously parsimonious, but he wasn't niggardly when it came to his own needs. He had decided ages ago at the very commencement of his smoking habit that only the most expensive brands of cigarettes would do – and nothing else. It wasn't that the expensive brands had any particular aroma or other property that especially favoured his nose or palette, but he had this intense and compelling desire to impress people that even spilled over to his choice of cigarettes.

A man who smoked Golden Fleece was one to look up to, one who could command respect, Oswald reasoned. He would quite often carry the recognisable packet in his hand or put it into his semitransparent white shirt pocket whilst at work so that its unmistakeable logo and contours were visible for all to see.

Oswald wasn't quite sure about what sort of cigarettes the lane boutique kept in stock. Merv had sounded enthusiastic enough about the quality of the boutique's tobacco assortment the previous evening when the matter of buying groceries at the village shops came up as a part of their evening's conversation, but Oswald wasn't inclined to put much trust in his neighbour's judgement.

'God knows what these blooming village chaps stock in their damn shops,' he mused. 'Maybe what they have is all well and fine for that damn fool Merv, but what the hell does he know! Fellow has no class at all, smoking that ridiculous blooming pipe of his! I really should have bought a few packets of Golden Fleece from the city before we moved over.'

His ruminations complete, Oswald handed over a crisp five-rupee currency note to Rohan, who promptly put it into his trouser pocket. Used to doing the marketing chores and running errands at Grandmummy's, he didn't think Oswald's request was unusual or unjust in any way. True, he didn't like running errands, a chore he never did in the good old days when his father was around, but just this once he was happy to acquiesce, seeing that it gave him an excellent opportunity to explore the lane and also have a first-hand look at the boutique to see what sort of things they sold. Excited about the prospect, he skipped eagerly on his way.

Arriving at the boutique, Rohan looked around curiously, taking in at a glance the well-stocked shelves of assorted groceries and a huge refrigerator near the cash counter. The proprietor, a pot-bellied, unshaven, middle-aged man dressed in not-too-clean white trousers and a faded black T-shirt, attended Rohan, appraising the newcomer from head to toe with shrewd and beady little eyes.

'Hey! Where'd you spring from, young sir? I've not see you around here before!' he said politely by way of conversation – always ecstatic to get a new customer and curious about the new boy. Rohan, although not very well dressed, and barefoot besides, projected a distinct aura. The proprietor immediately marked him down as belonging to the upper-middle class. He had a probing nature and a shrewd knack for fathoming these things. Years in the trade had given him a special sixth sense – an ability to 'smell' out the calibre of the customers who came and went, irrespective if they were well dressed or not. He sized up Rohan accordingly. Well used to scions of wealthy clients regularly popping in to buy candy and ice lollies, he knew instinctively that Rohan was 'elite' despite the latter's dishevelled appearance and lack of footwear.

Rohan replied respectfully in answer to the proprietor's question. 'My aunt and uncle moved into the house farther down the lane. We came only yesterday,' he said with some pride, knowing for sure this bit of information would surely impress.

The proprietor's rat-like face lit up immediately upon hearing what Rohan had to say. He put on his most benevolent look to instil a sense of security into the young client and put him at ease. Always on the lookout for an infusion of new and profitable customers, he rubbed his hands in glee at this stroke of good fortune. The house the boy had described was considered one with great potential. The former tenants bought so many groceries that he had granted them credit facilities and even consented to give them a small discount now and then. What luck for him that the boy had come here first, instead of going farther down the lane to that bloody communist lot at the cursed cooperative store! Bunch of filthy saboteurs! Ruining everyone's business with their damn-blasted low prices and all their treacherous socialist talk.

Putting his intense acrimony for the cooperative store aside, the proprietor rubbed his hands contentedly and spoke out in an even more polite fashion, almost fawning over young Rohan. 'Ah, so you're the new people what moved into our squire's vacant house, eh! Well! Well! Well! Ask your aunty and uncle to come here if they want anything, young sir! We have everything! All the finest groceries in the world, and our prices are very reasonable. No need for you people to buy anything from those terrible scoundrels at the cooperative store down the lane or from any of them fancy city stores!' He finished his little discourse by putting on an exaggerated all-knowing look, not forgetting to wag a finger in a cautionary manner as if to emphasise even further the dangers of indulging in any such foolhardy actions.

Rohan bought the cigarettes. The proprietor did indeed have stocks of Golden Fleece, promptly impressed that the new occupants of the house down the lane had such expensive smoking habits. Showing a shrewd eye for future business, he made it a point to carefully place the cigarettes in a crisp brown paper bag as a sign of goodwill. For good measure, and hoping to nurture Rohan's friendship, he took out a large caramel toffee from a huge bottle on his cash counter and gave it to Rohan free of charge, all the while putting on his manufactured benevolent look – the one he usually reserved for his very best customers.

Unfettered by any additional chores after handing over the cigarettes to Oswald, Rohan left the company of his aunt and uncle and walked over to the garden fence separating the twin houses. He spotted Ida outside on her front porch and hailed her enthusiastically.

'Hello, Ida,' he said, blushing a bit at hearing the sound of his voice calling out her name.

'Rohan!' exclaimed Ida, looking up in genuine pleasure and surprise. 'What are you doing now? Come over and play snakes and ladders with me!'

'Can't come now, Ida. Uncle and Aunty are going to have lunch soon, and they're only going to make one big blooming fuss if I am not at home.'

Ida pouted. 'Come after you have lunch, then. We already had lunch. Mummy and Daddy are taking their after-lunch nap, and Shanna is also asleep.'

'All right. I think Aunty Daisy and Uncle Oswald will sleep a bit after lunch too. I'll come over after I have washed the lunch dishes and plates.'

'You wash the dishes and plates?' asked Ida in surprise, a quizzical look of indignation creeping up her pretty face. 'What do you want to go and do that for? You're not a servant fellow!'

Rohan sighed. It would be difficult to explain to a family like the Pintos that he was a servant or a foundling in Oswald and Daisy's eyes and was treated as thus, rather than as a loved nephew. He tried to cover up a bit for the treatment he had to endure at the hands of his uncle and aunt.

'Aunty and Uncle will soon get a servant, Ida. Until then, everyone has to help out. I can wash up all them dishes quickly and come over. It's no trouble, really.'

'All right, I'll see you afterwards, then!' said Ida, still a bit nonplussed, not fully comprehending the dish-washing bit that Rohan had imparted to her. Why couldn't the grown-ups wash the dishes? Or why didn't Rohan just leave the dirty dishes as they were and come over to play instead? Surely they could be washed later?

Ida, her mind in turmoil over her young friend's strange situation, went back into the house while Rohan rejoined his aunt and uncle, who were just about to go over to the kitchen for Sunday lunch.

Oswald was a bit wary of the impending meal, but he put on a brave front. Surprisingly, Daisy's cooking was not at all bad this time around. She had put a little more effort into the Sunday lunch than the previous meal she had cooked, and even Oswald's demanding standards were met somewhat, at least halfway. She had even fried a few eggs, which, fortunately for her, didn't require any special culinary acumen and had also managed to boil the rice perfectly this time around. There was tuna again, but she had made it tastier, adding more spices and salt, adding cut tomatoes, and even squeezing a whole lime into the concoction.

After lunch, Daisy asked Rohan to do the dishes and scrub the pots and pans clean – a command which made the latter smile ironically to himself, thinking how easily he had portended it all to Ida only a little while ago.

Rohan and Ida sat on the gleaming waxed floor in Ida's bedroom, playing snakes and ladders. Rohan knew the game well, having played it a good many times with Laura and Mahan, sparing Ida the task of explaining the rules. Ida sat with her legs crossed in yoga fashion, her short skirt hovering well over her small, shapely knees – a pleasing sight that didn't escape Rohan's eager scrutiny. They played the game a few times and grew bored with it after a while. Ida suggested they go to the back garden and climb the cherry trees to see if any ripe or half-ripe cherries could be plucked. Rohan readily agreed. In his present exuberant state, he would have agreed to anything that his newfound friend suggested.

A gentle zephyr blew outdoors, cooling the effect of the hot afternoon sun, making the tree-climbing expedition quite pleasant. Ida, who knew the footholds of the trees very well, having climbed them many times before, started off first. There were five trees in all, and she started climbing the biggest one first. Rohan followed suit. Although a city boy born and bred, he had a good deal of tree-climbing experience under his belt, having, along with his best friend, Salgado, and the rest of the school gang, climbed nearly all the trees at the school gardens.

Ida was well above him when he started. Looking up, he saw her perched upon a trifurcate fork high above, eating a ripe cherry with one hand whilst gripping a solid branch above her for support with her free hand. Her short skirt had ridden up, and her legs were visible up to her waist. Ida's encouraging shouts jarred Rohan out of the shock of seeing what he saw, making him climb on higher until he almost reached her lofty perch.

The trees were loaded with ripened fruit, which hung conveniently on reachable branches for the children to pluck at leisure, eating as they pleased. A few green-and brown-headed parrots protested in alarm from the trees farthest away the one the children had climbed after first having had to abandon the tree now on siege by the bipeds.

'Mummy doesn't like me climbing trees,' Ida informed Rohan. 'She says it might give me bow legs.'

'What are bow legs?' inquired Rohan.

'Don't know,' replied Ida. 'I think it's legs that are very crooked from the waist down.'

'Your legs are not crooked from the waist!'

'Aha! How do you know that, eh? You've been looking up my skirt when I was climbing, haven't you?' Ida teased purposefully.

Rohan blushed, a bit perplexed and at a loss of words after Ida's true and telling dart. He didn't answer. They both remained silent for a while, momentarily lost in their own thoughts.

'Whom are you going to marry when you get big?' Ida inquired, breaking the silence, not caring for this trifling dip in the conversation.

'I don't know,' Rohan replied, shaking his head. 'Whom are *you* going to marry?'

'I'm going to marry a very rich man, richer than Papa! He can buy me anything I want then!' said Ida with perceivable vigour and an imperious toss of her curls.

'I'm going to be a very rich man someday soon, you know,' replied Rohan in great haste, alarmed at the prospect of being out of the running for this wonderful prize – and at such an early stage, too! He did not know how, but he was determined to become a millionaire and vie for her affections. There just had to be a way!

Ida, firmly reassured by her newfound friend that his financial prospects were promising and secure, said with feeling, 'That's all right, then. When you become very rich, we can get married and have babies just like Mummy and Papa.'

'But there are no babies in your house,' countered a puzzled Rohan.

'I was once a baby, Shanna was once a baby, and *you're* a great big baby for not knowing that!' said Ida, laughing – her laughter having the same silvery quality as her mother's.

Rohan winced as he instantly unravelled Ida's telling logic. He did not want her to think he was stupid. How could he have not reasoned *that* out?

Ida continued on the subject of babies. 'Mummy says it pains heaps to have babies. Babies have to come out from the woman's stomach, and it's something awfully painful.'

Rohan absorbed this information with keen interest. He had seen quite a few pregnant women before, but he had no idea as to how the babies inside them came out. However, Ida seemed to have it all worked out. 'From the stomach? Where from the stomach?' Rohan asked.

Ida looked in his direction obliquely in a shy manner, averting his direct gaze.

'Mummy said there's a special place in the stomach for babies to grow, and then they come out from that *other* special place girls have. Come closer. I'll show you.' Speaking thus, she adjusted herself, sat more comfortably on the fork, and pointed at the lower part of her dress to indicate the part of her anatomy from whence babies came forth.

Rohan couldn't help but be surprised. 'How can babies come out from *there*?' he wondered. Maybe Ida was just playing a prank on him. He looked up at the girl, expecting her to burst out laughing at any minute, but Ida maintained a straight face, dismissing the notion of an intended joke. Her information left him nonplussed. 'What a lot more there seems to be to learn about women,' he thought ruefully. 'Is there no end to it all?'

Rohan and Ida shared a definite closeness now after their chat about financial security, marriage, babies – where they came forth and all that. Although they didn't express it in any special way, they both knew they were friends of another sort now. They shared deep secrets – secrets that that linked them together somehow. The spark they had initially ignited had expanded beyond just a spark now. In its place, a growing sense of intimacy had taken root.

They climbed down from the tree. Rohan, standing at the bottom, helped Ida through the last branches with a new sense of care and manly protection.

'Let's go over to the squire's house. I can show you their huge garden,' Ida said after a while.

'All right,' replied Rohan, trooping obediently after her like a faithful husband.

They walked over to the squire's mansion, bodies touching quite often as they walked along. Ida boldly opened a massive front gate, signalling the entrance to the property, carefully closing it behind them. Rohan had seen a few gardens in his time – Vanessa's picturesque little garden recently, and Grandmummy's efforts in her back garden, not to mention Rebecca's very own large garden in the good old days – but what presented itself before him took his breath away. It was gargantuan, almost like an entire city park. An abundance of sequestered plots circled by small whitewashed limestone boulders and sprouting a panorama of exquisite tropical flowers dominated the huge garden. A wonderfully pleasant smell emanated from the plots, not too strong, yet fragrantly lingering like some mysterious perfume in an Eastern emperor's palace. Surrounding the circular plots in a large outer circle, a hybrid thorny rose creeper slithered its way all over the erected wooden crisscrossed arch-like structures. The creepers were inundated with red and yellow rose blooms, further enhancing the beauty of the garden and its lingering smell. Intersecting small pathways connected the sequestered plots, whilst a motorable road led right up to the mansion's front door. The squire's wife, a more than keen gardener, had designed the whole fantastic scenario with a passion and acumen second to none.

The young pair walked through the garden, waving at the squire and his wife, who were taking tea by the side of the house, outside on the front lawn.

'Who's your new friend, Ida?' boomed the squire.

'Ah! A boyfriend, is it?' joked his wife.

'This is Rohan, Uncle. He lives next door to us,' said Ida, blushing about the insinuation that Rohan was her boyfriend.

'Oh, so that's who you are, eh!' the squire said to Rohan. 'Your uncle and aunt said they would be bringing you along when we last met. You're most welcome, Rohan. Come over to the garden whenever you like.'

'Thank you,' said Rohan shyly, not knowing whether to address the great man as 'Sir' or 'Uncle'.

The children walked hand in hand, exploring the garden in detail until it was time to get back. Not wanting to leave through the main gate, which was a good distance away from where they were, they crept through the obtrusive barbed-wire fence on the side of the large mansion which bordered the lane and their respective houses. Rohan gallantly held up a rather loose-hanging upper wire in between two tightly strung ones, allowing Ida to creep through the aperture. He held her waist in a protecting gesture in case she would stumble, and was surprised by how small and soft it was. With his other hand, he held one of Ida's free hands to additionally support her, gripping her palm and fingers tightly, loving the sweetness of it all. Her hands were moist with sweat, and so were Rohan's, but neither seemed to mind – on the contrary, deliciously happy to enhance their intimacy through this modest exchange of bodily fluids. Once successfully over the fence, Ida did the same for Rohan. Walking closely, side by side, the short distance back to their homes, they were a trifle reluctant, knowing they had to soon part. Neither child wanted to be too far away from the other. They took secret pleasure as their bodies brushed close to one another, stopping briefly at Ida's front gate to say goodbye. As they walked away from each other, Ida suddenly sprang back and embraced young Rohan in a vice-like grip. They held each other for a brief moment and then as suddenly as Ida had embraced him, she quickly detached herself and ran along home, a bit red-faced, but immensely pleased at her bold imitative. Young love was blossoming, and Rohan's happiness knew no bounds.

The coming week went by swiftly and despite Oswald's petty tyranny, Rohan began to really like his new circumstances. He thought of Ida from the moment he awoke until he went to bed at night. She was his world, his love, his everything. They spent every evening together, playing various indoor games in Ida's bedroom, climbing the cherry trees in her back garden, or walking through the squire's immense garden. Once when climbing a cherry tree, Rohan helped Ida with her footing on a particularly difficult trifurcate branch, blurting out boldly, 'Let me help you, milady.' He didn't know quite where he had picked up the 'milady' bit, but he had a faint recollection of reading it in one of his sister Laura's pocket romances, which he sometimes read for want of anything better to do. Ida giggled shyly at the 'milady' quip. There was an embarrassed silence for a while after Rohan's display of verbal and physical chivalry; nevertheless, both were more than pleased about what had happened. They couldn't find anything else to say to each other, but they were deeply thrilled all the same. Rohan's romantic gesture and words had served as a declaration of love, and they both knew it.

Rohan's romance with young Ida bloomed and flourished with each passing day. The pair became nearly inseparable. Oswald and Daisy, eaten up in their own affairs, did not notice anything unusual, and the Pintos, being very broad-minded people, never gave such things a serious thought. On the contrary, it delighted them to know that their own little Ida had somebody around her own age to play with, consequently warming up to Rohan in an extra-special way. They were a clever couple, and it didn't take them long to observe and realise how Oswald, and to a lesser degree Daisy, choose to treat their nephew more like a servant than a close relative. As for young Rohan, he wasn't in any way unduly bothered by the Cinderella-like ill treatment he was on the receiving end of, having a lot of it in his baggage courtesy of the Dragon, Celeste, and Primrose. It was a grim *Oliver Twist* kind of scenario, with Oswald playing a more than convincing elderly Noah Claypole, and Daisy a somewhat milder Mrs Sowerberry.

As the days drifted by, Oswald found himself increasingly under Daisy's rule, a position he hadn't quite anticipated when he took the joint decision with his spouse to move out of his parents' house and start a home of their own. Compared to when the couple had stayed at his parents', where he was dominated only in fits and starts, he was now entirely in the hands of his sharp and bossy wife. Oswald took out all his pent-up disappointment over his situation on Rohan, tormenting the boy in every single way possible. There was an element of perverseness in his actions, asking his nephew to do all sorts of unnecessary household chores and marketing errands out of sheer devilry. One afternoon, after having driven home and parked the car in the driveway, he scolded Rohan thoroughly for the trivial reason that the boy was sweating a bit at the temples.

'Why are you all covered with sweat, boy? Decent people are going to think we are keeping a pig in our house. You are a passenger in *my* car! I don't like scallywags like you sweating in my car! It smells up the whole damn vehicle. Go and do a shower at once and clean yourself!'

Rohan, who had only a few small beads of sweat trickling down in a thin line from his temples, protested a bit. He was a clean boy and resented being called a pig. 'I'm only sweating a little, Uncle Oswald. It was very hot in the bus today from school, and the people were all packed in like sardines.'

Oswald did not veer an inch from his frontal attack. Rohan's answer only spurred him on, adding fresh fuel for further assault. 'So now it's all our fault, eh? It's our fault that you travel by bus, eh? Why are you so ungrateful, boy? Who took you into this house and gave you shelter and food, eh? Your no-good criminal father's helping you, maybe. Does he?'

Rohan, not one easily to cry, burst out in tears at the mention of his absconding father. He remembered his absent parent with love and affection. Normally, Rainier's recent mishaps and trials were a taboo subject in the family. It was an unspoken rule that nobody except Grandmummy should comment on or discuss Rainier's actions since his disgrace and disappearance, and nobody ever broke the matriarch's rule. It was infrangible. Oswald's frontal attack, especially the bit comparing Rainier to a common criminal, did *really* hurt. Rohan just couldn't stop the flood of tears. Sobbing, he rushed off into the kitchen and sat down by the small dining table, putting his head in between his elbows, cradling it back and forth like one demented. For a brief moment, he looked like an inmate in an asylum. He was truly miserable, hating Oswald so much that he wished the ground would open up and swallow his tormentor forever. His horrid uncle just *had* to be the worst of the lot in a long list of rotten family bullies, he thought bitterly, wiping the tears off his cheeks.

Oswald was gleeful. In recent weeks at Meadows, he had yearned to administer corporal punishment on Rohan but stayed his hand, fearing the wrath of Grandmummy and Rebecca if they ever found out he had laid hands on the boy. Instead, he reverted to using all sorts of scathing scoldings and cunning psychology to torment his young victim. Much to his chagrin and great disappointment, nothing he conjured up seemed to work. He just couldn't breach Rohan's defences. Here at last – at long last – he had found a postern of opportunity that really did the job! Oswald was delighted with his discovery. He would have liked to dance a jig, knowing he had discovered the last piece in the puzzle – the entire lay of the land!

Daisy, who was half-heartedly listening to what had just transpired, chipped in, more in automation than with any real feelings of sympathy for her beleaguered nephew. 'You leave the boy alone, Oswald. You're always nagging the fellow.'

'I'm not nagging. Isn't it the truth that the boy has a criminal father? Who embezzled his employer, eh? Who sat in the remand jail and shamed you all, eh? Who ran away and left his family to starve, eh?'

'Shut your mouth, Oswald. Insulting my family again, are you? What are you saying now? Our family are all criminals, are they? The boy's father was never found guilty in a court of law or sentenced to prison. How can he then be a criminal?'

'I'm not insulting your family, Daisy. It's just the boy's father who's no good. Why do you want to drag your family into it?'

'That boy's mother is my sister and a part of my closest family. My sister is married to a criminal? Is that what you are saying, you jackass?' replied Daisy, in real anger this time.

Oswald, realising that he had perhaps sailed too close to the wind, stopped his current persecution and went off to smoke a cigarette in the garden, muttering a host of invectives under his breath. He wasn't finished with Rohan, not by a long shot...

'Here, boy! Just look at the state of the garage! What are we feeding you for, eh? Go find a broom and sweep the damn place clean. It's such a damn mess!'

Rohan protested feebly. The garage wasn't at all a mess. It was clean except for the Morris's tyre imprints from the last time Oswald had parked the car inside.

'But Uncle Oswald, only yesterday you asked me to clean the garage. I cleaned it and swept the floor and put all those oil tins and things on the shelves like you asked me to.'

'The garage must be swept and cleaned *every* day! If the garage is not clean, the car smells too. You want to travel to the city in a smelly car, boy? Anyway, why are you arguing with me, eh? Didn't I ask you to do something? Why can't you bloody well respect your elders? Don't they teach you anything in that damn fancy Christian school you go to? Go! Clean the garage at once!'

Rohan looked around him ruefully. He could have easily disobeyed Oswald, but he knew that if he did, his tyrant uncle would somehow poison Daisy's mind and send him packing back to Grandmummy's. He would be glad to leave, even welcome going back, but the snag was Ida. By now, he was deeply in love with his newfound friend. It was a young boy's first love, the sweetest thing in the world. He never knew such feelings could ever exist. It was as if a whole new magical world had opened up before his very eyes, the enchantment of it all overruling all other options. For Ida's sake, he would have to somehow put up with Oswald's bullying and tyranny. His sweetheart's love came with a price – a price he *could* afford, but a hateful price nevertheless. His mother and Daisy had mentioned a six-week stay, and four weeks had almost passed. What would happen after the sixth, and how it would affect his relations with Ida, he didn't really know, but he was determined to at least see the stipulated six-week period out without incident.

Oswald wasn't exactly finished. He had additional chores in mind for Rohan. 'When you are through cleaning the garage, wash them car tyres too. They are all full of dirt and sand from the lane. And when you have finished, run along to the lane boutique and buy me some cigarettes,' he said roughly, malevolence written all over his Othello-like face.

Rohan sighed and said nothing. To do all this would mean at least an hour's delay in meeting up with Ida, but what could he do? He acquiesced in sullen silence.

After an hour, the last chore completed, Rohan handed over the cigarettes to Oswald and hurriedly made off to the bathroom, where he showered, dried off, and combed his hair carefully. He still had reduced, but ample, time left to spend in his sweetheart's company.

Left to himself, Oswald pondered over his present circumstances. The move from his doting parents' comfortable house hadn't the kind of effect he had expected. He had been keen to establish himself as a houseowner mostly because of the kudos he expected to earn from his colleagues at office. (He had no real friends.) His co-workers were well aware that he had been staying with his parents, a fact that didn't augur well whenever he entered into discussions in the canteen at lunch, during tea breaks by the water cooler, or whilst at other places during times when employees met and socialised for a short while. He was openly ridiculed for it, his colleagues often sniggering and saying, 'Mama's boy', behind his back with monotonous regularity, some even daring to say it to his face. Things had improved after he moved over to Meadows, the office bunch grudgingly conceding to show a little more respect. Still, Oswald's new circumstances, although a definite 'lift' in the eyes of many, didn't really give him the kind of satisfaction or leverage he had hoped for, despite the improved circumstances at work. As the days rolled on, he became increasingly disenchanted and uncomfortable being with Daisy all the time, not to mention missing Alfonso's cooking and his parents' succouring presence. His only solace was Vanessa. As with Rohan's love affair with Ida, this was an enormous comfort, one that automatically cancelled his homesickness each and every time it came to the fore.

Oswald's attraction for Vanessa had now become an obsession. He was besotted almost to the breaking point by Merv's free-speaking, vivacious wife, his infatuation deepening day by day. Not a moment passed without his feeling an uncontrollable urge to crush Vanessa in his arms and ravish her like some wild beast. The thought was both sweet and wicked at the same time, and it disturbed him no end, troubling him on account of the unpredictable consequences that such an action could bring. There were his parents – a staunch Christian duo – and then there was Daisy! Oh God, there was Daisy! He shuddered to think of an eventual showdown with his formidable spouse.

It never occurred to Oswald that Vanessa would decline his advances, that his feelings weren't in the least bit reciprocated. An easy-going sort of person, Vanessa was the life and soul of any gathering. Her bubbly enthusiasm and vivacity *was* her natural way of behaving, not just when Oswald and Daisy were around, but with anyone she socialised with. Her rippling, silvery laughter had a special ring to it that was very contagious and could put the most sullen person into a good mood. The unique laughter, easy smile, and bubbly ways was a tonic that Oswald wrongly imagined to be a show put on for his benefit, spurring him to come to the conclusion that she was attracted to, and possibly even in love with, him. The truth was far, very far, from what he imagined. Vanessa was blissfully and totally in love with her Merv and had always been, ever since they had first met.

For all her playful ways and vivacious manner, Vanessa was definitely no fool. A well-balanced woman possessing a sharp intellect, she had in early life given up a promising academic career to settle for the less glamorous role of being a full-time housewife and mother. Perceptive to an extreme, she didn't need too long to see through Oswald's shallow, petty, and often cruel ways. She observed the irritation and contempt Oswald showed Rohan at evanescent moments when the former least suspected that anybody was noticing or watching. She also knew quite early in their neighbourly acquaintance that Oswald, even Daisy, treated the boy more like a servant than a nephew. A good friend to her husband, she discussed the matter with him quite often. Merv always listened faithfully to her discursions. He was a kind of man, but he did not want any ill feeling to arise between them and his vexatious immediate neighbours.

'My dear Vanessa,' he would say with a sigh, 'we can do nothing about it. After all, what *can* we do? Just feed the boy plenty when he comes over and give him some pocket money now and then.'

Recollecting his own childhood, he would add after a few seconds' thought, 'A little money now and then is sure to cheer the poor chap up. Boys always want money, you know – for this and for that.'

Despite the placable front he showed his wife, Merv was fighting a dilemma of sorts in his private thoughts. For the past fortnight, he had been itching to expose Oswald as a mountebank, talk to the squire and other neighbours, or perhaps even lodge a complaint at the local police station alleging child cruelty, but he stayed his hand. He had no actual proof of any misgivings, and the consequences of his actions might only result in a disastrous outcome for Rohan.

After Rohan had left, Oswald showered, changed, and sat in the veranda to smoke a cigarette and await Daisy's summons for dinner. His thoughts drifted again to his ongoing crisis, which was deepening with every minute. Was Daisy really the right woman for him? Weren't carnal desires and carnal desires alone what had prompted his proposal of marriage? Had he made a colossal gaffe four years ago when he married her, not waiting for the 'right' woman to turn up – a woman like Vanessa? And then there was Daisy's family! God! What a bunch of illiterate degenerates! Why, that wretched mother of hers alone could make a saint turn in his grave!

As the week ran its course, Oswald continued to misread Vanessa's bubbling demeanour and natural friendliness in the build-up of their acquaintance. He had no doubt in his mind that she was secretly in love with him and would drop everything to elope if only he popped the question. He had recently in Daisy's company seen a romantic film featuring Cary Grant, a movie star he greatly admired, where at the end of the film, the actor had literally swept the heroine off her feet and carried her away into the sunset. He imagined himself carrying Vanessa off her feet and into a new life together. Oh! How wonderful it would be, he mused. He was so taken up with Cary Grant's film character that he even imitated some of the film star's mannerisms for several days, much to Daisy's chagrin.

Outwardly, and in spite of everything, Vanessa and Merv tried their very best to maintain a civil front with Daisy and Oswald. They were a peaceful sort of couple and were wary of bringing out matters into the open – a most unsavoury prospect. They reasoned they had to live with each other and that bad relations were not a very comforting platform on which to build neighbourly peace and tranquillity. Additionally, there were the children... It wouldn't seem right to expose them to any eventual neighbourly feud, especially now that Rohan and Ida seemed to get along so well with each other. Buckling down to the inevitability of it all, Vanessa and Merv continued to visit Daisy and Oswald for late tiffin soirées or for dinner on occasions, sometimes at Daisy and Oswald's and sometimes in the comfort of their own home.

One Sunday evening, Oswald's passion for Vanessa climaxed in a way that no one could ever have anticipated. The Pintos came on a visit. It was not a spur-of-the-moment visit, but a pre-planned evening dinner. Oswald and Daisy had made prior preparations. Some Chinese beef noodles and few meat dishes were bought from a reputed Chinese restaurant on their way back from work. Oswald also bought a new bottle of imported whisky – the one at home being half drunk – and a few packets of roasted cashew nuts. Well at home and just before the guests arrived, Oswald wheeled his drink trolley into the living room. He carefully extracted some ice cubes from the refrigerator's freezer compartment and placed them in an intricate little ice bucket he was immensely proud of. He placed both the half-drunk as well as his brand-new bottle of whisky together with the ice bucket and the cashew nuts on the trolley, took a long critical look at his handiwork, and grunted a deep sigh of satisfaction. The imported whisky was expensive, but Oswald bought only the best, in keeping with his uncontrollable desire to impress. It was like the cigarettes; only the best brands would do. Besides, he was pleased as Punch to flout the expensive whisky under Merv's nose, as the latter always offered Oswald the much cheaper local whisky whenever *he* visited. Oswald deliberately placed the bottles so that the impressive brand labels were visible, muttering softly to himself, 'That'll show that dratted little bugger what sort of whisky I drink. Hope the fellow gets shamed! A lout, that's what he is! Offering *me* that bloody no-good local stuff whenever I visit! Still, can't blame the fellow, I suppose. No breeding in the chap. And in any case, I don't think he can afford the expensive stuff. Why, the man can't even afford a decent vehicle, running around on that cheap, ridiculous motorcycle of his!'

Merv could certainly afford the imported whisky, but he was a pragmatic man, sincerely of the opinion that local whiskies more than held their own against the imported varieties. The motorbike and sidecar were logical choices too. Merv was a genuine biker, a keen enthusiast since his teens and a prominent figure at the Portopo Motorcycle Club. It would have also astonished Oswald to know that

Merv did indeed possess a motor car as well – a much better one than Oswald's modest Morris – keeping it safely in the garage of his parents' home the past four years. He really loved his bike, and after a discussion with Vanessa, had decided to use the less impressive vehicle until the children were a little older and outgrew the sidecar.

As the hour for the Pintos' visit approached, Oswald maintained a calm posture, but inwardly he was very much on edge and slightly hysterical. He had decided today *was* the day to cut the Gordian knot. He would take some opportunity later on in the evening to crush Vanessa in his arms and declare his love, an act he was sure would pave the way for a wonderful life in the company of this wonderful creature. His brain whirled in a spiral of thoughts as he lit up and chain-smoked cigarette after cigarette.

The evening started off well enough. The children went off to play in the garden, whilst the adults sat in the living room, sipping their drinks and making light banter. Vanessa looked stunning in a form-hugging dress of pale green that shimmered and glistened with every movement she made. Her creamy white skin, akin old alabaster, blended well with her flowing black hair. Oswald, who watched her every move with hungry eyes, was completely bowled over, his infatuation reaching an absolute zenith. He talked more than usual, flinging out opinions on almost every subject that came up. Normally, in the privacy of their own company and within her own family, Daisy didn't allow Oswald to air his opinions on anything – at least not for a longer while. She had seen through the shallowness of her husband a long time ago and, these days, usually cut him off in the bud whenever he started off on his grandiose ramblings. When in non-family company, however, a certain licence was allowed and a temporary truce was called in an effort to create an impression they were a modern, democratic couple, each allowing the other to expostulate and promote opinions independently. It was of paramount importance to Daisy that they project this fictitious front to the world, except of course when they visited Grandmummy, when the licence was temporarily revoked.

Oswald didn't mind in the least his 'free speaking' cancellation whilst visiting his mother-in-law, welcoming it instead. He had nothing to say to Grandmummy, Celeste, Primrose, or even Rebecca, considering them plebeians, a sort of subspecies. He showed some measure of respect for Robert, though, whenever they met, typically and only because the latter had a thriving business of his own.

In recent weeks, Daisy had been very much concerned about her increasing waistline. Most of her conversations these days veered on the trials of the extra weight she carried.

'You know, Vanessa, I just can't understand it. A small breakfast and two meals a day, that's all I eat, yet I'm always having weight problems. I don't even indulge in tiffin at office – just drink a cup of tea, that's all! Only last week, I checked my weight at the damn office canteen and saw that I weighed one hundred and sixty-two pounds. Yesterday, the same blooming scale weighed me in at one hundred and sixty-eight!

Vanessa comforted her distraught neighbour, offering some friendly advice. 'It's the sugar, Daisy. Maybe you're drinking too much tea a day. How many cups do you drink? Think! Besides milk, each cup has one or two teaspoons of sugar in it, right? Sugar's very fattening stuff, you know!'

Daisy pondered over this statement of fact, finding it highly enlightening. 'You know, Vanessa, I think you're right! It *does* make sense what you're saying. I drink about four cups of tea a day at the office and about three at home, and it's all with sugar and milk. But what's to be done, eh? The damn office work stresses me out so much, and my bloody manager's nagging makes it worse! The office tea really helps, you know, and when I come home, I like to relax with even more tea. Everything's so blooming stressful! Stress here and stress there – this to be done and that to be done. The tea calms my nerves. It really does!'

Oswald piped in. He felt that some sort of humorous intervention was needed, something to make Vanessa laugh. 'Maybe you should try smoking, Daisy! It calms the nerves and will keep you off the sweetened tea!'

Vanessa dutifully giggled at his comment whilst Daisy glared at Oswald sullenly. She hoped her husband wouldn't say anything more but was disappointed in her surmise.

Oswald continued, quite delighted by his silver-tongued suggestion. He remembered the Cary Grant film they had recently seen. 'If you put on more weight, I might not be able to carry you, you know!'

'Why the devil do you want carry me?' demanded Daisy in a sharp tone, momentarily discarding her standard truce with Oswald.

'Just fooling, Daisy, just fooling. It's just a joke, woman! No need to get all huffed up!' replied Oswald in a pacifying tone, glancing obliquely at Vanessa in a conspiring manner as if to say, 'Look, I can't even make a joke! The woman is completely impossible!'

Vanessa, a bit alarmed that a small domestic tiff was in the offing, tried a minor diversion of sorts. 'Merv carried me over the threshold of our first home when we were newly married, you know.'

Merv, sensing that his wife needed some support, dutifully picked up his cue. He joined cheerfully into the conversation. 'Why, Vanessa, I can still carry you quite easily, you know! You're still the same weight as when we were newly married.'

Oswald, thrilled with the very thought of carrying a woman like Vanessa and not wanting to opt out of the carrying stakes, blurted out boldly on the spur of the moment, quite without thinking. He wasn't going to be outdone by 'puny' old Merv. 'I can carry you too, Vanessa! I can carry you home if you like when it's time to leave.'

Vanessa flirted away these slightly alarming comments with ease. 'My, how gallant you are, Oswald. But I think I'll walk back home, anyway. No need for anyone to carry me.'

Daisy was itching to knock Oswald's block off or at the least give him yet another of her worst scoldings ever for his daring comments, but she kept her cool even though she was seething with well-concealed rage. She cunningly put an abrupt end to the subject.

'Talking about sugar, we're completely out of sugar for coffee later on. Here, Oswald, run along to the lane boutique and buy some,' she commandeered Oswald vindictively, pleased as Punch that she had found a way to manoeuvre him away from the conversation, even if it was temporary. (The couple never asked Rohan to do errands when Vanessa and Merv visited.)

There wasn't much Oswald could do but acquiesce. He doubted they were out of sugar, but he didn't have the courage to protest. Glaring bitterly at Daisy, he made his way to the front door, reluctant to leave the present company, especially Vanessa. He had never set foot in the lane boutique before and wasn't exactly looking forward to doing so now, but Daisy had to be obeyed. Just as he was about to depart, though, Vanessa surprisingly blurted out loudly, 'Wait, wait, Oswald. Wait a bit, will you! If you're going to the lane boutique, I'll join you. We are terribly in need of some butter for breakfast tomorrow. I used the last bit to make tiffin sandwiches, and we're completely out now.' She gestured to her husband and continued. 'Here, Merv! Give me some money, will you, dear?'

Merv obligingly pulled out his wallet from his hip pocket and handed over a currency note to Vanessa, a dismayed Daisy looking on haplessly. Instead of being exiled, her vexatious husband would now have Vanessa's company all the way to the boutique and back. As for Oswald, he could hardly contain himself, overwhelmed by this new development. He pinched himself to see if it all wasn't a dream, unable to believe his good luck – bracing himself thrillingly at the prospect of accompanying Vanessa on this sudden grocery-buying expedition. Here was the opportunity he was waiting for to get Vanessa alone and declare his feelings! Surely it was a sign from above? God must be with him, he thought excitedly. It just had to be so. There was no turning back now!

The couple walked along the footpath leading to the lane boutique. The pathway was narrow in certain places, and the surrounding foliage barely permitted two persons to walk side by side. At these intersections, Oswald did not give way and walk in single file like he ought to have, resulting in their bodies touching and bumping into each other on more than one instance. Vanessa thought little of it, but to Oswald this was crucially further confirmation that the woman was indeed in love with him. Besides, why did she want to come along to the lane boutique too? He did not for one instant believe it was the need for butter that had prompted her actions; it had to be because she *wanted* to be alone with him, just as he longed to be alone with her. There was no other explanation.

Oswald was really on fire now. Before he met and married Daisy, he had had no intimate contact with women whatsoever, although not for want of trying. No real romance had lightened up his early life – no puppy love, no teenage romance, nothing! His pre-marriage love life was a blank canvas. Daisy was his first and only venture into the field of romance and serious physical relations – until now. True, he had wanted, lusted, and yearned for Daisy ever since he first met her, and he probably still did, but right now, ever since he had met Vanessa, it all seemed more a mere physical need than anything else. This thing with Vanessa was something on a much higher plane, something he couldn't quite explain.

There was a full moon out that night, the whole area bathed in eerie yet magical moonlight – a setting made for lovers. Even the crickets and cicadas that usually made a regular din at dusk seemed unusually contained, allowing only a single nightingale to serenade in isolated splendour whilst the gentlest of zephyrs kissed the trees and foliage like a lover's caress. Oswald braced himself. Unable to bottle up his feelings any longer, he decided right then and there that it was crucial to act and get it all over and done with.

At a suitably broader spot on the narrow footpath, he cast a furtive oblique glance at Vanessa, whose perfect silhouette seemed even more enhanced by the magical moonlight. Putting his hand on her shoulder, he drew her roughly to himself – almost forcibly – in a tight, awkward embrace.

'Vanessa, Vanessa, darling,' he bleated passionately. 'I love you, darling. I know that you love me too. We were meant for each other! Tell Merv you want to leave him and let's go away together. We can stay somewhere in the city until things blow over. Find a new place afterwards, a new home for just you and me.'

Vanessa, normally the coolest of customers and never at a loss of for words, was thunderstruck – flabbergasted by what sounded to her to be one of the most incredible statements she had ever heard. For the first time ever in her life that she was struck dumb. In what seemed an age, but which in reality took just a second or two, Oswald's amazing words really sunk in. Her initial amazement turned to annoyance, then to resentment, and finally into real anger. The very impudence of the man! The *very* suggestion! Where on earth did *that* come from? Had he gone completely mad? Fully recovered now, she answered back with venom, her mouth puckering in distaste as though she had drunk a foul-tasting medicine. Gone was the charming, bubbly Vanessa of old. Her silvery voice had turned into a harsh rattle of discord.

'I love you?! Whatever made you think that, fool? Never in a hundred years can I ever love a blasted pig like you! And we are going to find a new home for just us, eh? What about my children? You ever thought of them? And how dare you suggest that I leave Merv? He's my husband, and we love each other. You say nice things to his face, whilst behind his back you are trying to seduce his wife? Nice state of affairs, this! I hope Daisy really fixes you good and proper when I tell her all about it!'

Oswald was devastated, total surprise written all over his face. He was never in doubt that Vanessa cared for him in the same way he cared for her. Was all the interest she had shown him in the recent past just an act? A charade acted out for nothing? And what about her fond and tight embraces whenever they parted company, her obvious enjoyment of his jokes, her infectious, bubbly manner in his presence, the enthusiastic urge to join him in his sugar-buying expedition, and all that rubbing and jostling against him on the footpath? Was everything a sham? Didn't any of those things mean anything? Anything at all? Vanessa's words and reaction came as an absolute surprise. It was agony, a death sentence! He did not know quite what to say or do. Like a snake's intended victim, unable to move or make a sound, he was paralyzed, unable to react at all.

Vanessa didn't proceed any further. Abandoning Oswald and giving a tinker's curse for the butter and the morning's breakfast, she rushed down the pathway back to Daisy's. Once there, she summoned her nonplussed family and stormed back to their own home. Merv, sensing the intensity of her actions and feeling that something drastic had upset her, followed without saying a word. He knew something serious had happened, but didn't probe, wisely waiting until they were back in the privacy of their own home for Vanessa to explain. Vanessa had given Daisy a sympathetic look on her way out, but she had said nothing. She wanted to discuss the matter with her husband first before deciding on a suitable course of action.

Daisy was flabbergasted – confused, to say the least, over her neighbour's strange behaviour. Whatever was the matter with Vanessa? What had happened? Had Vanessa got suddenly ill? Why had she run off like that? And where was that damn Oswald? She waited patiently for her husband's return to get more facts on the matter, brooding all the while over what could have caused Vanessa to leave the way she did. It all sounded so very odd and intriguing ...

It didn't take long before Oswald limped back into the house, ashen-faced and forlorn like a man in a trance, barely able to walk or pull himself together. He rued his actions bitterly, realising now what a colossal misjudgement he had made in thinking that Vanessa was as much in love with him as he with her. He had made a complete and utter ass of himself – this he knew for certain now. Looking around and noticing the guests had scooted off, he assumed the worst, that the late object of his affections had spilt the beans and left him high and dry to face the music. He decided right then and there to come clean with Daisy and confess the whole sordid story to her, his love for Vanessa, his proposal on the footpath, and Vanessa's violent reactions. It was the last thing he wanted to do, but there was no way out. He had finally manoeuvred himself into an emotional cul-de-sac of his own making. Shuddering in apprehension, he gathered the remnants of his wits to face the music.

Daisy felt that she was hit by a mega-thunderbolt upon hearing Oswald's complete confession. She knew her husband well, even educated him in the more intimate intricacies of sex, but never even in her wildest fantasies could she have envisioned such a scenario. Oswald had sobered up greatly by now. He was still shaken to the core, but his reason seemed to have returned. Normally a careful man, love, or rather infatuation, had given him wings. His uncharacteristic behaviour surprised even him. Realising the ghastliness of his situation, he decided to grovel effusively and unreservedly.

'Oh, Daisy, Daisy,' he bleated. 'I was bewitched by the woman. I don't know what really came over me. Forgive me, please. It was a moment of weakness. It will never happen again. Don't break up our marriage, and please, please, please, don't tell Ma and Pa.'

Daisy, fuming with rage, was like one beset. She had never been so angry in her whole life as what she was now. 'You spineless bloody jackass! Who do you think you are, eh? Look around carefully, fool! Nobody likes you! Nobody except your damn parents! You think you're one big Hollywood star, don't you? Like that Cary Grant chap, eh? You think you are better than everyone else in the world, repeating like a parrot all that blooming hogwash you get from those magazines you read at office. Why, if I didn't marry you, nobody would ever have had you at all! You blithering idiot, can't you see that?'

She continued, a nerve throbbing alarmingly in her right temple. 'How can you shame us all by making such a fool of yourself? Where are your brains, you donkey? Is it all gone down your bloody arse, or what? It's that easy to leave me and go off with Vanessa, eh? I mean nothing to you, do I? All that we built together is nothing, eh? You're ready to run away with Vanessa without so much as a thought for me, huh? And why *shouldn't* I tell your precious ma and pa? I am sure as hell going to tell them. They have the right to know what sort of jackass they spawned into this world.'

Her temper getting the better of her and completely out of control,

Daisy actually rained a few well-struck blows on her husband's cowering body with her bare fists. Oswald, his arms outstretched in protective sublimation, fled pell-mell into the bathroom, where he managed to latch the door behind himself to avoid further corporal punishment.

Daisy did not know really what course of action to take. She continued to rain insults and scoldings on Oswald in a prodigious fashion, whilst the latter, safely secure in the confinement of the locked bathroom, barely listened – sunk in his own misery and degradation. Finally, ceasing her scolding and insults more in exhaustion than anything else, Daisy went off in the direction of the bedroom, a myriad of thoughts swirling in her head at the sudden influx of events which had turned what seemed a promising social evening into a nightmare from hell. She closed the bedroom door behind her, sensing a need for solitude and to decide on what course of action to take. Feeling faintish, her feet wobbly and her whole body shaking, she flung herself face down on the large double bed, placing a pillow over her head to shut out all light and sound.

Rohan, a comatose witness to all that had transpired, was speechless. He was perceptive enough to gather that Oswald had wanted to run away with Vanessa and leave his aunt Daisy high and dry – a deed that shocked him enormously. He had always disliked his mean and cruel uncle, but this latest act of his made him detest him even more. How could Oswald sink so low as to want another man's wife? he mused. Wasn't it enough he had a whole cartload of other sins as well? And then there was his *own* situation. Whatever would happen to him now? It was beyond doubt that his uncle's actions would result in a total falling-out with the Pintos. Would this mean he would never see his beloved Ida again? He shuddered in apprehension at the thought, unable to imagine a life without his beloved sweetheart.

The evening dragged on slowly, very slowly. Oswald, after a while, cautiously emerged from his self-inflicted exile in the bathroom, keeping a wary eye for any sign of his enraged spouse. He made it to the front veranda, where he sat on an armchair, pulled out a fresh packet of twenties from his pocket, and started chain-smoking, ashes from his cigarettes piling up beside him on the floor. As for Rohan, he could only walk nervously around the house, too tense and worried to do anything – just watching and waiting for Daisy to emerge and for something conclusive to happen. He was trembling like a leaf, knowing instinctively that his love affair with Ida was in all likelihood doomed, that his wonderfully exquisite bubble of happiness could burst at any moment.

After what seemed an eternity, Daisy came out from the bedroom. Her eyes were all red and puffy from crying. She had a determined look on her tear-stained face that made Rohan fear the worst. He shivered uncontrollably with a premonition that his whole world was just about to crash all around him.

Daisy addressed Oswald in a chilling yet composed voice, a tone she had never used before. 'We're packing our clothes and things and clearing out now. Tomorrow morning, I will phone the squire and give him notice. I shall give no reason, but just say that we are leaving immediately. I'll ask your pa to hire a van, and you can stay away from work and help them pack our furniture. We'll put everything in your pa's extra garage and in his backyard until I decide what to do. I shall speak to your precious ma and pa, telling them how you shamed us all. They have a right to know why we had to leave and what sort of a son you are. We cannot stay here one single moment longer!'

Oswald shivered. He shuddered at the thought of his beloved parents getting to know what had happened, although deep within him, he knew that Daisy was right in her decision to move out straightaway. Their position was untenable. They would not be able to face Merv and Vanessa again ... ever! Besides, the story would probably reach the ears of their landlord, the squire, and even other immediate neighbours. He would be a laughing stock, a butt for neighbourly jokes, a cuckold of sorts. Daisy wouldn't fare much better, even though she was the innocent party in the whole sordid episode. Everyone would pity her for not being able to hold on to her man. There would be much whispering and sordid gossip behind her back.

Oswald had one last miserly concern however – archetypical of his parsimonious nature. Daisy's intention of immediately vacating the tenure-ship of the house meant an unnecessary forfeiture of some of the rental advance. He said softly, almost reverently, not wanting to aggravate Daisy any further, but concerned anyway about the loss of money they would incur, 'You know, we did pay the squire three months' rent in advance, Daisy. Such a loss of money it's going to be! Such a loss!'

It was a foolish and near-fatal thing to say, a sort of trademark complaint that a disappointed Fagin would make to the Artful Dodger for bringing in a poor haul of stolen handkerchiefs. It sounded even more foolish coming on top of the ruckus he had only just recently orchestrated.

Daisy leapt like a tiger. She bounded towards Oswald and gave him a resolute blow on his head that actually made him stagger back a few feet.

'You bloody, stingy, tight-fisted damn bugger,' she screamed, 'you're thinking of losing rent money at a moment like this when you've gone and disgraced us all? Is *that* your main concern? The humiliation doesn't bother you, does it? How can we live here even another single day? Can you face the Pintos? Answer me that, you jackass! Who threw us out, eh? Who's the criminal now, eh? You're always going on and on about Rohan's father's being a criminal. You're a thousand times worse than he is, you, you, you ...'

Daisy was getting alarmingly apoplectic, almost choking on her words, dangerously near to a seizure. Oswald, extremely frightened now, backed off hastily to the garage, where he opened the door of his car, got inside, and sat down in the back seat to escape yet again – and to think.

Rohan was shattered upon hearing Daisy's decision. If they were to leave now, he would never get a chance of seeing Ida again. He grew numb with shock, his eyes growing misty with tears.

Daisy, true to her word, hurriedly packed a suitcase with a few clothes and other necessities required for the next day or two, and asked Rohan do the same. Rohan did not have much to pack, but he reluctantly complied. He was heartbroken, the unjust and cruel vicissitude of his young, turbulent life filling him with utter helplessness and profound misery.

Oswald too packed some things and at Daisy's behest, started the car in the garage and drove up to the front porch, where they all dumped their things into the boot and partly in the back seat. Rohan looked in desperation in the direction of the Pintos' house, anxious to see if he could catch a glimpse of Ida, but she was nowhere to be seen. He panicked briefly, thinking to make a bolt for it and throw himself at Vanessa's mercy. It was now or never. If he ran quickly enough, it could be done, but at the last moment he just couldn't bring himself to do it. His legs froze, a sober inner voice dictating that he stay where he was.

In the house, Daisy switched off the lights, latched the windows, and locked all the doors, afterwards getting into the car without saying another word. Rohan got into the back seat as though in a trance as Oswald started the car and drove off towards the city.

Daisy was very bitter. What had intended to be a triumphant and permanent shift to living on their own had turned out to be a short and terribly truncated stay – no thanks to her tortuous, foolhardy husband. She made Oswald drive to Grandmummy's first, where Rohan was unceremoniously dumped off. She did not go in, being too upset for the moment to explain the situation to her mother and family. It could wait for tomorrow, she mused, but tonight – yes, tonight – she was going to tell her fine in-laws what a jackass of a son they had brought into the world. How they would cringe in shame to hear the whole sordid tale! That was the only thought that offered any sort of solace right now.

Everyone was just about to get ready for bed at Grandmummy's – the household extremely surprised to see Rohan arrive at this very late hour. Rohan offered no explanation. He just rolled his old mattress onto the floor and then sat upon it fully clothed, shoes and all. Everyone tried to get him to throw some light on his unexpected presence, but to no avail. He was too traumatised to say anything. His mother could not get a word out of him, and not even Grandmummy's threats of corporal punishment had any effect.

'You tell us what happened, boy, or I'll take the cane to you,' threatened the Dragon.

Something snapped inside Rohan as he looked upon Grandmummy's scowling, heavy-jowled face. For the first time in his young life, he felt really angry at the way he was constantly subjected to misery and ill treatment from nearly everyone who stood him nearest. The additional agony of being parted from his precious Ida filled him with hatred for and resentment against the whole world. He had just about had enough of his relatives and their incessant bullying. He cared an iota for Grandmummy's cane and her threats. Unlike the rest, he wasn't afraid of her – never actually was – and was definitely not going to be submissive now. He had reached the end of his tether. Turning around to face Grandmummy as though he were going to lash out at her, his fists tightly clenched like a boxer's, he said, 'You hit me one more time, Grandmummy, and I'll go to the police straightaway. I'll tell them you hit me *all* the time! Leave me alone, all of you ... you ... terrible, horrible devils, or I'll run off to the station right now and report you all.' He yelled in great passion and with trembling limbs, a thin film of froth drooling from one corner of his mouth. Small as he was, he looked alarmingly threatening. The assembled family felt frightened – very frightened. Never, ever had they seen him like this before. Even Grandmummy, sensing that something had really upset the boy, reluctantly decided to leave him alone. Everyone wisely decided to let matters lie. They retired for the night, now and then throwing looks of bewilderment at Rohan's quivering small person huddled in a foetus-like position and sobbing on his mattress.

Rohan couldn't sleep, his mind shattered by the terrible events of the day. Never in his young life had he been as disconsolate and miserable as what he was now. Lying on his old mattress, he sobbed incessantly, his thoughts constantly centring on his precious Ida. He knew it was not possible to meet her again. True, he knew what school she went to, but he couldn't just show up there and ask her to marry him, could he? And how on earth was he going to support Ida, even if they got married or ran off together? Still sobbing softly, his face suffused with tears, Rohan tossed and turned on his thin mattress until he finally fell asleep in the early hours of dawn.

CHAPTER 5

Primrose Catches a 'Sir-John', and Meena

Little Arabella Miller found a furry caterpillar...

MEENA, THE EIGHTEEN-YEAR-OLD DAUGHTER OF Mr and Mrs Fazal, Grandmummy's next-door neighbours, was sitting on the chair in the front veranda, to all purposes well and truly engrossed in a book she held in front of her. A solitary youth, his back to the Fazals' front gate, stood immobile, his gaze riveted on the young girl sitting demurely on her chair. Rohan, who was on his way to run an errand for Grandmummy, couldn't but help noticing the youth. The latter's gaze was intense – very much so – prompting the always bold and inquisitive Rohan to open a conversation.

'What are you looking at, eh? Has anything happened in Mrs Fazal's garden? A grass snake, is it? Or is it one of them huge bandicoots?'

'Mind your own business, boy! Just get going on your way!'

'Why should I mind my own business? Who are you to tell me to mind my blooming business! Shall I shout out for Mrs Fazal that you are planning to rob her?'

It was a shot in the dark, but it went home. The youth didn't retort or challenge Rohan's threat. He had good reason …

Young Meena, sitting very reticently in her chair, gave the impression of being immensely wrapped up in her book, but suddenly, as though trying to change her sitting position, she raised her two legs high in the air, her skirt climbing up well up to her waist and exposing her naked genitals. Absent undergarments revealed her most intimate assets, leaving nothing to the imagination. As quickly as her legs went up, they were put down again. It was a lightning-quick gesture, bold and alluring, elevated knees joined tightly, thighs apart. In between the erotic gestures, all that one could see was a demure young girl engrossed in reading a book.

The youth at the gate did not want Rohan or anybody else to know just why he was standing outside the Fazals' gate. Meena, meanwhile, who had espied Rohan in conversation with the youth, stopped her erotic antics at once, fast determined to reserve her indiscretions only to complete strangers. Besides, she mused, her brain whirling frantically, the boy was far too young and, more alarmingly, might rat on her to that strange old Englishwoman living next door.

Getting no answer from the lone vigilant at the gate, Rohan shrugged his shoulders and went on his way.

Back at Grandmummy's after his traumatic stay at Meadows, life went on as usual for young Rohan. He tried hard to put the painful episode of his lost love, Ida, behind him as best as he could, miserable for a long time afterwards, while lugubriously lamenting what might have been. Although in time he did get back to being his normal self, he could never quite forget his adored Ida, her charming ways and piercing grey eyes. She always remained the sweetest of his memories – an unforgettable part of his life as long as he lived. Often when alone, he would philosophise and come to the conclusion that if there was any divine justice, then surely he had to meet up with Ida again someday, somewhere, somehow. The thought comforted him enormously.

Ida was devastated too, crying almost every day for several weeks afterwards. Unlike Rohan, who had nobody to confide in and be comforted by, she was smothered with love and support from Vanessa and Merv, who understood the child's devastating sorrow. A few weeks after the squalid incident, Merv took the entire family on a holiday to the hills, where the novelty of the mountain air, the luscious green scenery, and everything else helped Ida tremendously. Ida learnt to ride a pony and laughed again, much to the relief of Merv and Vanessa. It took some time, but gradually Ida's young mind healed too, although, like Rohan, she never quite forgot the enchanted weeks they had spent together.

Daisy wasn't slow to tell Grandmummy and her sisters of the whole sordid incident that had prompted her hasty departure from her very first home. She left out nothing. As expected, Grandmummy was ferociously incensed upon hearing of Oswald's atrocious behaviour, even though she secretly triumphed at his folly. She had a permanent weapon to use against Oswald, and its emoluments would come in very handy, indeed. Afterwards, and whenever Daisy and Oswald came to visit, she always made it a point to subtly bring up the matter in some form or other just for the pleasure of seeing Oswald squirm.

'Daisy, my girl', she would often say, 'perhaps you should try again and find a new place to live.' Glancing obliquely at Oswald, she would continue slyly. 'Find a house a good bit away from *young* neighbours. Can't have Oswald running amok again, can we?'

Daisy, who by now was totally reconciled with Oswald and had forgiven him totally, would protest wearily. 'It was a moment of weakness, Mother! Just let it go, will you, for God's sake! Oswald's suffered enough as it is! It will never happen again.'

Oswald would remain silent during these discourses, trying his hardest to maintain a stoic countenance, although for the life of him he couldn't help wincing – a sheepish look of shame creeping up to cancel the stoic expression he so desperately tried to maintain. He suffered agonies at the ignominy of his situation, but there was nothing he could do. There was no way out of the emotional cul-de-sac he had so unwittingly got himself into. His arch-enemy, Grandmummy, held all the aces, and it was utterly futile for him to say anything in his defence. Maybe with time it would all blow over, he often reasoned to himself, a sliver of hope flashing through his mind. After all, the wretched old woman couldn't live forever …

For a while after his degradation, Oswald was akin a lost soul. He couldn't quite face up to Daisy, feeling immensely guilty in her presence – additionally resenting the condemning eyes of his parents, boring into him accusingly. Returning from work in the evenings, he would do a quick shower and then take long walks on the streets near his parents' home for hours on end, his hands in his pockets, his head bent low. For many weeks, he was subject to the most stringent cold-shoulder treatment from his parents, and *that* really did hurt; it was the deepest cut of all. He had always been the adored son, loved and pampered as long as he could remember and losing that status made him feel lost and alone. In hindsight, he came to the conclusion that Vanessa had bewitched him in some way, that he didn't really love her, and never actually had. How easy it was to be beguiled, and how easier still it was to see the light once everything was over, he reminisced bitterly. He hadn't felt a thing for Vanessa these past few weeks and often wondered what really possessed him to act in the way he had done. It all seemed a horrible dream, a nightmare from hell, where all his senses were screaming silently, urging him to wake up. Daisy's forgiveness in due course, as well as his parents, came as a relief, but the incident left a bad taste in the mouth for him and his nearest. It remained a stigma destined to be borne the rest of his life.

As for Rohan, he never spoke to his uncle again – ever. He deliberately ignored Oswald and treated Daisy with a dignified coldness as well as a twelve-year-old boy could possibly muster. His uncle and aunt felt his contempt, very much so. They felt guilty in his small presense whenever he was around, which was not very often, as Rohan always made it a point to 'disappear' whenever the horrid duo came on visits, but not without first demonstratively turning his back on them immediately after their arrival. Never a vindictive boy, he refrained from sneakily telling Grandmummy that Daisy had made him wash dishes and that Oswald had given him numerous horrid chores to do, but he never quite forgot a wrong done to him – a trait he maintained all through his later, adult life.

The house adjoining Grandmummy's belonged to a respected Moor gentleman who had a minor executive position in one of the many commercial companies operating at Coronation Park, the busy industrial and business citadel at Jellicoe Junction. The house was as large as Grandmummy's, but, in contrast had a little walled-up front garden and a gate. The garden, signalling the entrance to the house, was a major deviation from Grandmummy's own mouse-hole-like entrance constructed at the twisted behest of some mad architect with a lunatic's sense of humour. The vast difference between the entrances of the two houses notwithstanding, both structures were equally big and roomy.

Mr Fazal was around fifty or so and was married to a much younger wife. The couple's teenage daughter, Meena, around Laura's age, was the apple of Mrs Fazal's eye. The latter was a terrible snob and bigot, a trait she took great pains to hide, ostensibly putting on a show of being a great humanitarian. She was not unlike Grandmummy in her ways, although Grandmummy, to her eternal credit, never pretended to be anything other than what she actually was. Apart from this divergent fact, the two women were almost like two peas in a pod. If Grandmummy considered herself to the manor born, then Mrs Fazal acted in an even haughtier fashion, almost as though she were royalty...

Mrs Fazal, just like Grandmummy, considered herself and her family to be all too good for her simple neighbours. She had grand designs for Meena and went a step further, taking meticulous care in forbidding her daughter talking to, or keeping company with, any of the neighbours or their offspring, including Rohan's elder sister, Laura. Grandmummy was different that way, never objecting to Primrose, Celeste, Rebecca, or the rest greeting their somewhat mundane neighbours or having small chit-chats on occasions, although she did keep a wary eye on Primrose and Celeste in case there were any young men involved.

Incipiently, when Rebecca and her family first moved in with Grandmummy, Mrs Fazal had invited Laura, Mahan, and Rohan for a visit after having learnt through her network of contacts that Rebecca's family once enjoyed a very superior social status. She thought that her daughter could benefit from befriending such a refined family, even though they seemed to be in a temporary spot of trouble. Mrs Fazal changed her mind very quickly after that initial visit, deciding that the siblings were absolutely unfit to keep her daughter's company. When the children were being taken on a tour of the Fazals' house on that first, last, and only visit, Mrs Fazal, after careful and shrewd questioning, learnt that the young family were truly destitute – without any immediate hope of recovery. She also observed the faded, much-washed clothes the children wore, the boys' feet sans any 'home' footwear, whilst heartily disapproving of Poppsy, who somehow or other had managed to follow the visiting party into the house and was sniffing all over the place with great curiosity. All in all, Mrs Fazal decided that it was extremely injudicious on her part to have invited the children. There was far too much imparity between her daughter and Rebecca's children for any relationship to build and blossom, she wrongfully concluded. Like a decadent Roman emperor of old, she gave a definite thumbs down, effectively sealing off any further fraternising between the children. It didn't all quite fit into the grand designs she had planned for her beloved daughter.

The boycotting of the children, especially Laura, was seen as an unforgivable slight by Grandmummy and indeed by all the others in her household. When Grandmummy heard of it all, she launched into a fearful tirade. 'Where the devil does that bloody heathen woman get off? Laura is not good enough to keep that fat daughter of hers company? Is that what that wretched damn woman is saying?'

Rebecca joined in the abuse. 'Not good enough, eh? My Rainier was once a *prince* in this damn city! What the devil has that wretched woman got to boast about? Sitting on her fat arse all day and passing judgement over decent people, the illiterate bloody cow!'

The others in the ménage, Primrose, Celeste, and even Daisy when *she* got to know about the incident, were incensed too. The boys, in all honesty, one could understand, but Laura?

Grandmummy was livid with rage over the deliberate ostracising of her granddaughter. It wasn't just the actual slight on Laura that rankled her; she also couldn't quite get over Mrs Fazal's daring to sit in judgement over anyone in *her* august ménage. All her life, she had looked down haughtily on almost everyone who crossed her path, considering her imperious self and household sacrosanct, above reproach from anyone. But now the tables were turned. Someone actually had the gall to look down upon *her!* Although it was Laura and the boys who were ostracised, Grandmummy deemed Mrs Fazal's act a personal slight directed at her. She decided to fight back.

Grandmummy could quite frequently be heard to raise her voice and rain down choice insults upon Mrs Fazal. The two houses, Grandmummy's and the Fazals', although detached, were separated by a very narrow aperture, barely enough for a person to walk through. Often, the occupants of the respective houses could hear each other's voices and whenever one spoke in a higher octave, it was quite possible to hear an entire conversation – the walls separating the two houses rather thin. Grandmummy used this highly novel eavesdropping tool to her advantage, her high-pitched, telling jibes and insults well within the auditory range of the Fazal household.

Mrs Fazal chose to ignore Grandmummy's many unpleasant and hard-hitting comments, not caring to retort and considering it beneath her dignity to do so. She maintained a stony silence, although whenever she had visitors and they couldn't but avoid hearing the insults, she would wave aside their concerns aloofly.

'Don't take any notice of that old woman's vulgar talk. She's not right in the head, you know! Almost a lunatic! She talks ill of everyone in the neighbourhood. A mad old Englishwoman, you see! Everyone knows that! We would complain to the police, but we do feel so sorry for her – poor wretched old soul!'

As for Mr Fazal, all he wanted was to maintain a trouble-free, tranquil, and respectful household. He was a prodigious worker, leaving for work quite early in the mornings and coming home late in the evenings, much tired by his efforts of poring over company ledgers all day long. The only thing on his mind when he got back home was to take a shower and relax in his favourite lounge chair in the living room, armed with his beloved newspaper and awaiting his wife's summons for dinner. Mr Fazal supported his spouse's policy of maintaining a determined silence in their feud with Grandmummy, saying and doing nothing to aggravate the matter any further. On occasions when he met head-on with Rebecca, Primrose, Celeste, or any of the children on the streets, he would politely nod his head and mumble a quiet greeting – quite in contrast to Mrs Fazal, who would slyly pretend to be looking elsewhere or give the impression she was lost in thought, oblivious to the rest of the world.

Secretly and to himself, Mr Fazal thought that his wife's attitude towards Laura, the others in Grandmummy's household, and the rest of his immediate neighbours ludicrous to say the least, but inured as he was by his wife's snobbishness, he kept his thoughts to himself, concluding that it was wiser to remain impartial and keep his own counsel. It was not that he was afraid of his spouse (he wasn't), but he distinctly disliked domestic squabbles of any sort, judiciously deciding like the three famed monkeys of Toshogu, not to see, hear, or speak any evil!

Grandmummy was considered a colonial dowager duchess of sorts, even though the English usurpation had ended a decade ago and the majority of the former lords and masters of Victoria had departed back to the old country for good. Although her self-imposed seclusion meant she rarely left her house, she was yet quite well informed of the comings and goings of the neighbours living around her. Nobody quite knew where her sources of information originated.

One suspected she learnt a good deal from her monthly visits to her friend the parish priest and a great deal more by shrewdly cajoling all sorts of information from the stream of door-to-door tradesmen she encountered on a daily basis. The Dragon was quite clever at this sort of gentle persuasion, her victims feeling quite drained after a session with her, wondering just what had happened and why on earth they had talked so glibly.

As for the neighbours, they all knew who Grandmummy was. They respected her enormously but also took great care not to cross her path. On the rare occasions when Grandmummy did leave the house and would by chance meet a few neighbours head-on, they would lower their eyes and pretend, like Mrs Fazal, to be looking elsewhere. They didn't dislike Grandmummy – far from it – on the contrary immensely proud to have a person of her pedigree living amongst them, but they felt uncomfortable in her presence, not quite knowing whether to courtesy or bow, say hello and smile, or just nod a greeting. They felt small in her presence – a kind of class-adulation thing inbred through generations of living under the British yoke and where super-conservative Englishmen insisted that everyone should know their 'proper place'.

Mrs Fazal, on her part, had no claim to any significant ethnic descent. She possessed quite simple ancestry, hailing from a family of nondescript Moor settlers with origins in the Middle East. She spiced her ancestry considerably, though, sending out discreet signals purporting that her extended family were oligarchs connected to royalty.

Grandmummy staunchly believed Mrs Fazal portentous, a social misfit who hadn't a clue about etiquette and other trimmings qualifying one to the ranks of the upper classes. Nothing could dislodge her from this opinion. Greatly put off by and irritated about her rival's persistent insistence that her family was vastly superior to *her* own English lineage, she scoffed openly and often at the 'pretender'.

'Bah!' she would say in contempt whenever anyone spoke well of Mrs Fazal. 'What utter balderdash! That woman's an illiterate humbug with no class or breeding. Her people came from some outlandish country, and they practise some un-Christian heathen religion – yet she thinks she's good enough for decent company.' A few mutterings of an unpleasant nature would follow, her brow dark in anger and resentment.

Mrs Fazal, not to be outdone, was just as much in contempt of Grandmummy as the Dragon was of her. She never missed a clue to bad-mouth Grandmummy to anyone caring to listen. There was a feud going on between the two women – a sort of cold-war type of feud – but an intense feud nevertheless.

Needless to say, the whole family faithfully and staunchly rallied around Grandmummy in her battles with Mrs Fazal, especially Rebecca, who was every bit as cross as Grandmummy over the way Mrs Fazal had snubbed Laura. Rebecca had high hopes for Laura, especially in the academic field, and was immensely proud of her daughter's scholarly progress at school, where she outshone most of her classmates, often bringing home brilliant monthly report cards filled with glowing tributes from her teachers.

The Fazals, to Grandmummy's chagrin, were the only people in the immediate neighbourhood who possessed a telephone – a possession which gave them an enormous boost and considerable social kudos in the area. The family were rumoured to have influential connections in high places through wealthy merchant relatives who were credited with being in some great business venture or other. One suspected that it was these grand connections, and these alone, which made Mrs Fazal behave the way she did. Her husband's steady job apart, she did not have anything else to crow about.

Occasionally, a grand car of an expensive Mercedes model would pull up beside the curb by Mrs Fazal's house and a well-dressed, silver-haired old gentleman would step out to visit the Fazals, spend a good hour or two inside, and then drive off. The car was driven by a liveried chauffeur, giving the visitor and his visits additional pomp in the eyes of the awestruck neighbours.

The old gentleman was one of the grand relations, in all probability the kingpin of the clan. His visits – needless to say – figured regularly in the neighbour's day-to-day banter. They were often undecided which of the 'eminent' families were to be revered more – Mrs Fazal's or Grandmummy's. The Fazals' telephone and the grand relative in the Mercedes weighed heavily, but Grandmummy's British lineage, which everyone was aware of, probably gave her a thin edge.

Grandmummy openly sneered at the enemy's 'grand relative' whenever anyone brought up the subject.

'That withered old bugger is just the damn landlord who owns the Fazals' house. The blooming fellow comes to collect the rent. I suppose that damn humbug of a woman hasn't paid the damn rent for ages and ages and prostitutes herself to the old fellow to get out of the mess she is in. A humbug and a prostitute, that's what the wretched heathen is!'

Of course, nobody believed Grandmummy's version of things, not even her staunchest allies, the members of her own family. Everyone in the Dragon's ménage took her version of matters for rancorous rhetoric and nothing else. There were limits to what they were willing to support, and Grandmummy's landlord theory was wafer-thin. Together with the entire neighbourhood, they knew that the Fazals had *bought* their house outright ages ago.

The Mercedes was a hard pill to swallow for Grandmummy and couldn't easily be explained away – wealthy landlord or no wealthy landlord. The only motorist who visited Grandmummy these days was Oswald, in the company of Daisy. Grandmummy was quite disappointed over the fact that Oswald's old Morris couldn't match the grandeur of the old gentleman's Mercedes – really put off by it all. She was often heard to vent her disappointment over Oswald's poor choice of vehicles, a withering look of disdain crossing her countenance. 'Why on earth can't that womanising bugger [she had taken to calling Oswald a 'womaniser' after the affair at Meadows] buy a decent car instead of driving about in that damn old contraption of his, God in heaven knows! They have such a good income together, him and Daisy. Surely they can afford to buy a better car?'

Sometimes she would blame Oswald's parents. 'The fellow's family are so rich, yet they can't buy him a decent bloody vehicle. Shameful lot! Always throwing their blooming family wealth in our faces with their bloody boasting; talking big about their blasted cooks and servants and all that, yet they let their only son drive about in that disgraceful old crock of his! Why can't they buy the fellow a Mercedes? What are those wretched people hoarding all their damn money for?'

The household would listen discerningly to the Dragon's complaints about Oswald's choice of vehicle, except for Rohan and Mahan, who heartily agreed. The boys were crazy about motor cars and supported Grandmummy's views all the way, fervently hoping Oswald and Daisy would have a change of heart, take notice of their grandmother's constant complaints, and buy a new car. In actual fact Grandmummy's and her young minions' opinion on Oswald's car were somewhat unfair and not in keeping with the general consensus. Oswald's car was second-hand – true – but it was not an 'old crock'. The Morris Minor, although not a vehicle in any luxury class, was still a car a good many people in Victoria would have given their right arm to possess. Oswald just made it *look* ancient by driving it so slowly and so wretchedly. Besides, Rebecca, Celeste, and Primrose were quite proud that their sibling Daisy was part-owner of a car. Except for Rebecca and Rainier in their heydays, nobody had ever owned a motor car in the family. Grandmummy's father was reputed to have owned a one, but nobody ever knew if this was true or not – a horse and carriage a more likely prospect in those bygone colonial days.

The Fazals' telephone burnt a hole in Grandmummy's head – the ownership of such a device a luxury by any Victorian standard. Grandmummy constantly bombarded her son, Robert, with requests to get her a connection, but they fell on deaf ears, as there was a huge sum of money involved to cover the costs.

'I am an Englishwoman, Robert! Is it a luxury for an Englishwoman to have a telephone? If your father was alive, he would have installed a telephone ages ago! I can't get about and do things on my own, you know! Is it so damn hard for you to lift your damn backside and get me a phone connection, or are you too damn stingy to do it?'

'But, Mother! Whom are you going to call? You're not on speaking terms with any of Father's people or your own people, and you don't have any friends! Do you want a phone just so that it can gather dust in the house?'

'Huh! What the devil do you know about my affairs, Robert? I have plenty of friends! Only the other day, Father Clement was saying how nice it would be if I had a telephone! And what about Celeste and Primrose, eh? They need to call their workplaces when they get sick, don't they? And they have friends too, don't they?'

'Mother, please! A phone connection costs more than a refrigerator and as much as a quarter year's income. You have a nice arrangement with Father Clement already. Why do you want to phone him? And if Primrose and Celeste need a phone so badly, why the deuce don't they save up enough money to get a connection? Must I always be the one to spend money on you all?'

There were regular arguments about the telephone connection, but Robert stood his ground. He knew it was the Fazals' telephone connection that irked his old mother, inducing her demands to possess one.

The Fazals did not possess a motor car for some reason or other. Mr Fazal did possess a driving licence, a relic from his youth, but he no longer felt comfortable driving in the fast-moving city traffic. When he had successfully obtained his licence ages ago, there were just a scattering of motor vehicles making their way serenely along the streets of Portopo. He drove about like any other proud new-car owner then, but with time he found traffic to be so congested that he dreaded driving every day. Besides, travelling by public transport had become quicker and less costly. In due course, he sold off his motor car and never drove again – ever. Mrs Fazal protested for some time, but she was ignored by her spouse, who told her flatly that she could take a taxi for short-distance travel and use the public transport system whenever she wanted to travel longer distances. Meena, the Fazals' young daughter, was driven to and back from school in another relation's motor car – a much more modest affair than the famous Mercedes.

Meena was neither fair- nor dark-complexioned, neither pretty nor ugly, but something in between. She was rather plump, though, a condition brought on by staying at home most of the time without any form of physical exercise whatsoever, not even at school. Her doting mother wrote letters of excuse to the girl's headmistress, citing ailments her daughter was supposed to be suffering from which, she firmly declared, didn't warrant the girl's participation in sports or physical training sessions of any sort. Her actions were solely prompted by her terribly flawed opinion that strenuous workouts for a young girl weren't ladylike. Additionally, she insisted that the hot sun (school physical training exercises were always held in the open air) would affect the girl's complexion negatively. Another factor that influenced Meena's extra pounds was Mrs Fazal's feeding her all sorts of purported health-enriching foods. Whenever the daily newspapers printed, or the radio broadcasts trumpeted out glaring propaganda for new nutritional food, Mrs Fazal went for it in a big way. Fresh milk in the morning was delivered to the door by a well-known local grocer, whilst rich food was always on the daily menu. Thickly buttered bread, fried eggs, beef sausages, rich porridge, and candied fruit were always on the breakfast table, whilst choice steaks accompanied by rich sauces together with potatoes and roast chicken steadily made the rounds at dinner – all inevitably followed by sweet pastries or heavy puddings for dessert. For good measure, Mrs Fazal made her daughter swallow a host of vitamin pills of assorted colours, shapes, and sizes, which pharmacies and visiting medical reps firmly propagated were essential for growing children and adults. Nothing was spared in Mrs Fazal's efforts to raise what she considered was a 'healthy' child.

A consequence of Mrs Fazal's flawed parenting was that Meena, now sixteen years of age, led a very prosaic kind of life. She was a very, very lonely and isolated child. Her mother's contempt of her neighbours made it impossible to have any contact whatsoever with children around Meena's own age, and the ostracising of Laura made matters even worse. Meena would watch whimsically each morning as Laura made her way to school, chattering away with other neighbouring children in her company. Meena would often sigh to herself, regretting the fact that she wasn't even allowed to be friends with a girl of her own age, one who, besides, lived next door! Lonely and segregated, she had only her own company to keep, courtesy of the self-inflicted frayed relations her mother had kindled and maintained with all her neighbours, including Grandmummy and her household.

Mr Fazal, a prodigious worker and excellent provider, was also something of a loner, spending evenings and weekends at home. He had just a very small circle of friends, whom he met up with sporadically. A very habitual sort of man, he led a ritualised life, travelling to work by bus in the mornings and coming back home in the evenings in the same clockwork-like manner. If he had a flaw, it was a tendency to be fastidious. He was always splendidly attired in a colonial-style three-piece white suit and brown or black leather shoes – the kind the English diaspora wore and which were imported from England. On really hot days, he would wear a stiff colonial hat of khaki – another relic from the British colonial days – to protect his face and head from the glaring tropical sun. When the monsoons broke, he was conspicuous in a grey overcoat of genuine waterproof material. He kept a black umbrella tucked under one arm or folded out if it was raining. Armed with a well-polished brown leather briefcase, he gave the impression of being a successful career man, yet somehow always managed to maintain a vacuous, aloof air about himself, discouraging conversation of any sort from strangers and even people he knew.

Mrs Fazal tolerated Primrose and Celeste, as they were always fashionably dressed, but also because they represented a step up in the ladder, higher than most of her other worldly neighbours. She graciously allowed the sisters to use her famous phone now and then when absolutely necessary, carefully wiping it after they had finished speaking. Mrs Fazal's action in wiping the telephone wasn't just a fad. She had a mortal terror of illness and always suspected Rohan, Mahan, or other neighbourhood children of having some sickness or other. It petrified her no end that someone would pass on infectious germs to her daughter or herself, conveniently and callously forgetting her poor husband – an action that wasn't really surprising. Throughout her married life, she had taken Mr Fazal for granted, keeping him on a tight leash – a leash Mr Fazal wasn't even aware existed. She always got her spouse to do whatever she wanted in such a subtle way that Mr Fazal wasn't in the least bit aware he was being used. Mrs Fazal, like Grandmummy, ruled the roost, Grandmummy through sheer bulldozing, and Mrs Fazal through more Machiavellian sort of methods.

Meena had attained womanhood rather late, and although some time had passed since then, she was still struggling to come to terms with it all. The physical changes that went hand in hand with her metamorphosis from girl to woman, apart from manifesting itself in her young body, had also affected her mentally. Right now, she was finding it difficult to control all the urges and changes her newfound sexuality demanded. Having no friends to talk to or even joke about on such matters, she had to fathom for herself why her body was behaving like it did and why her mind had such erotic cravings. Speaking to her mother was completely out of the question. She did not have *that* kind of relationship with her strict and conservative mother. It never occurred to Mrs Fazal's self-centred ego that she ought to have a face-to-face talk with her young daughter to discuss the latter's ascent to womanhood or explain the facts of life in general. She would come to regret her actions gravely in the days to come …

Grandmummy's immediate neighbourhood at Jellicoe Junction was not a fashionable or prosperous one. It wasn't the worst place to live at Portopo, but it wasn't the best either, at the most probably between fair to middling. Although the great and famous school which Rohan and Mahan attended was located plumb in the middle of the area, nothing else stood out in terms of prominence or prosperity.

The vicinity surrounding Grandmummy's house especially, was a troublesome microcosm – a good number of families struggling to make ends meet and unemployment rising to dizzy heights. Loiterers and ne'er-do-wells sprouted in abundance, having little or nothing to do most of the day. Some of them were minor criminals engaging in pickpocketing and petty theft, whilst a few others – more daring than the rest – indulged in crimes bordering the nefarious, crimes that sometimes turned extremely ugly and violent. Youths, especially, took to just hanging around in small gangs in convenient nooks and corners, horsing around with each other or indulging in acts of petty rowdyism. A good many played football or cricket on the streets, often inconveniencing passers-by and traffic, sometimes even damaging windows and walls of buildings.

The youth holding sway at the Fazals' gate couldn't keep his mouth shut for long. Unlike most of his peers who were unemployed or didn't want to take on an ordinary job, he did a few odd jobs for the market's shop owners, which included delivering fresh milk to customers in the mornings. The Nameless was his last point of delivery. As fate would have it, the little eating house had just started serving breakfast for the day, when he showed up with Sonny's modest milk order. Everyone at the Nameless knew him, of course, but they found him uninteresting and unworthy of the effort of entering into any meaningful conversation, which irked the budding voyeur no end. He would often stop to listen to the breakfast-eaters' boisterous palavers, wishing he could come up with something sensational to impart and be a part of the jolly group. Today, at long last, he had a wonderful story to tell. 'Let's see if these fellows can top this,' he mused as he started off on his tirade.

The gate voyeur, known as 'Milkfellow' by the clientele at the Nameless, rattled off his tale of how he had seen Meena expose herself so shamelessly. His listening audience were shocked, enthralled by the events related – none of them doubting it was just reverie. There weren't many listening to Milkfellow's little discourse, just Sonny, Catnips,

Uncle Pongo, Pina a blind beggar, and Karolis the fish vendor. It was a very sunny morning, and the others were eating their breakfasts out in the open under the shade of the banyan tree. Milkfellow's narrative appealed strongly to Catnips – the others only interested in a platonic sort of way – except for Sonny, whose flamboyant sexual conquests and adventures were legendary. Karolis, a staunch family man, didn't care for these kinds of things, whilst Pina had abandoned any sort of sex life ages ago and, in any event, couldn't see. As for Uncle Pongo, he was a paragon of moral virtue and was far too embarrassed upon hearing of Meena's exploits.

Catnips, normally haughty and contemptuous of Milkfellow, was most humble and endearing as he spoke up after the latter had finished his erotic tale. 'I say, my dear Milkfellow. I say, look here now. What if I come over and join you at the gate, eh? Please, dear boy! How about it, eh? There's a good chap!'

'Oh! I suppose you can come, Catnips, but not any of you other chaps. Too many persons at the gate might scare the girl off and draw attention from passers-by, besides. Come today at around three in the afternoon. The girl usually sits in their veranda around that time.'

Uncle Pongo, Catnips's chief antagonist, butted in acidly. 'So! At last you are shown up for the dirty peeping Tom and predator you are, you scoundrel! Can't resist, eh? Crumbs from the table, eh? You come here day after day and talk big of your luxury living, how you buy luxury wines to drink, the cars you used to drive, even boasting of your female conquests, but here you are sucking up like a cur to Milkfellow just to see this poor girl's indiscretions! What a useless bloody wretch you are!'

'Oh, buzz off, Pongo! It's you who is the useless wretch, you old fool! What a dirty mind you have! Can't you see I am just going there to check out Milkfellow's story? If it's true, I'm going to contact the girl's parents and let them know what's going on. I'm just doing my civic duty, you ass!'

'Bah! Civic duty indeed! I'll bet a day's wages you are just going there to satisfy your lust and nothing else. We all know your ways!'

Here, Sonny interrupted, not wanting a minor ruckus so early in the morning. Promiscuous to an extreme, he was immensely stirred by Milkfellow's narrative, but he wasn't prone to acts of voyeurism, preferring actual sexual coitus instead. He had some sympathy for Catnips though, and played out a masterful diplomatic overture.

'Let Catnips be, Pongo. Maybe he is telling the truth and just wants what's best for the girl. Maybe he can check out Milkfellow's story and if it is true, inform the girl's parents about it all. Catnips will then only be doing his civic duty, as he says. We have to trust him on *this* one. You can't go on mistrusting old Catnips all the time, Pongo!'

Catnips clutched this straw like a drowning man. 'Yes, yes, Sonny. Old Pongo has a dirty mind. I'm just going to see that things are put right.' Turning directly and squaring up to Uncle Pongo, he demanded sternly, 'Anyway, why are you always butting in my affairs, Pongo? It's as Sonny says. I'm really trying to help the girl. If I see things are as Milkfellow says, I can always have a confidential talk with the girl's father. He is a respectable man and deserves to know what's going on. You have a dirty mind, that's what. Always suspecting me of this and that! And do I come and see what you are up to at that stupid workplace of yours, eh? I know you keep on ogling at those young women who work there, you blithering lecher!'

'Bah! Talk to the girl's father, indeed! Ha! I know why you want to join Milkfellow at that gate. You can fool Sonny, but you can't fool me! And *you*, Sonny, shame on you for encouraging the fellow. That's your trouble, Sonny. You make all sorts of excuses for lechers like him whenever women are involved. You have no respect for women, Sonny! Never have and never will!'

Uncle Pongo was truly upset. He led a blameless life and, although not a complete paragon of virtue, had been faithful to his wife for the past forty-odd years.

Sonny didn't counter Uncle Pongo or come up with a reply. Secretly, he was ashamed that he had sort of half-supported Catnips. He didn't know why, but he always saw women as sport – a kind of super-fault in an otherwise honest and empathy-inclined life. If Catnips wanted to watch an erotic cabaret, then let him! *He* wasn't going to stop it...

Catnips departed the Nameless shortly afterwards, one arm around Milkfellow, to all appearances in animated conversation with him, whilst Uncle Pongo looked on haplessly, his contempt for the Machiavellian mischief-maker increasing in leaps and bounds.

The sensual, erotic performances at the Fazals' veranda went on for more than a week, Meena performing like clockwork at a certain time in the evening after she returned from school. There were two in the audience now – Catnips having joined Milkfellow, who took to bringing his milk-delivery bicycle with him, leaving it by the Fazals' front gate to give an impression he was delivering extra milk in the afternoons. They were in cahoots witnessing the performances, careful to watch out for young Rohan or Mahan whenever the brothers left the Dragon's house to go on their marketing chores or other errands. The Englishwoman's boys would rat on them if they discovered the truth, and then *everything* would be spoilt – lost forever– they reasoned. The old lady was much respected in the neighbourhood. Besides, her stern hauteur and massive frame didn't augur too well. She looked perfectly capable of thrashing the living daylights out of the voyeurs if it came to that.

Both Catnips and Milkfellow would have dearly loved to climb over the gate and take matters further, even have coitus with Meena, but fear of the prominent Mr Fazal and the long arm of the constabulary, which was never quite far off, kept them at bay. Wisely, they decided the watching duo was adequate, as they didn't want any further interested passers-by to join in and spoil the fun. They acted out a charade of normalcy to cover their surreptitious actions, feigning intense conversation in between smoking cigarettes, whilest keeping an eagle eye trained on the erotic cabaret going on in the background.

Around this time, a new and singular situation had developed at Grandmummy's. Primrose had been complaining of a pain in her abdomen and sides for some time, prompting Grandmummy to take her to a nearby doctor for treatment. Doctors' visits – yet another rare occasion Grandmummy left the confines of her home – weren't often, but they did happen now and then. Of all her children, the Dragon loved young Primrose the best, doting on her and taking a close personal interest in every little thing she did. She was especially worried about and often brooded over what sort of a young man would ultimately win her daughter's heart – worried because she wanted only the best for her favourite offspring, fearing Primrose would end up with a bad choice. It was heartbreaking and shameful for Grandmummy that both Celeste and Rebecca had made such poor marriages despite all her nurturing and advice, although, in retrospect, neither Celeste's nor Rebecca's choice was actually bad. Celeste was reputed to have driven her husband away with her ill-tempered nature and Rebecca's husband, Rainier, was acquitted in a court of law of the embezzlement charge brought against him. He had only 'disappeared' to be left alone, to concentrate on salvaging his former career, get his life back on track, and reunite with his young family.

The physician of Grandmummy's choice, a certain Dr Nader, was a highly successful GP. He ran a medium-sized consulting chamber and dispensary on a busy street near the main general hospital and was Grandmummy's family doctor – originally introduced to her by Father Clement. Dr Nader didn't count as a close friend, as Father Clement and Mr Macmillan were, but the Dragon had consulted him professionally for many years when seeking medical assistance for herself, Primrose, or Celeste, whenever it was absolutely necessary. The doctor's patients, with a small exception, were all Jellicoe Junction people, born and bred. Nobody knew the standard ailments or collected idiosyncrasies of his patients better than he did.

Dr Nader's waiting room was always crowded. A decent and popular man, he enjoyed a good reputation, having cured many grateful patients – additionally earning kudos from the community in general for not charging fancy prices from his poor and middle-class clientele. He wasn't popular with his fellow medical practitioners, though. They frowned upon the low consultancy fees he charged in comparison to their own – which were almost treble and sometimes even four times as much. Behind his back, they viciously called him 'that damned Bolshevik', referring, of course, to Dr Nader's going against accepted medical norms, or rather the run-of-the-mill, by charging the modest consulting fee he did.

Of course, Dr Nader wasn't a communist. An ardent Christian and family man, Sunday Mass always found him in one of the front pews of the parish church alongside his wife and children.

Not all the good people of Jellicoe Junction could afford visits to a private doctor. Generally, whenever anyone fell ill and home remedies had no visible effect, the cost-free outpatient section at the government-run general hospital was the only available choice. The general hospital treated patients from the entire city and even those hailing from far-off villages, who, poor souls, travelled long distances to arrive on time. No fees were charged for either consultation or medicine, the incumbent government's policy being to provide free medical services to *any* patient, irrespective of the geographical area one hailed from. There were, of course, large government-run hospitals even in far-off villages, but village folk for some reason believed that the general hospital at Portopo was the ultimate citadel of medicine in the whole island – a glaring misconception. When the general hospital at Portopo first opened its doors many decades ago, it was the only hospital of its kind in Victoria – sick citizens rushing to be treated at this 'magical' place of healing. It was in those early days that the 'citadel' reputation arose. Almost everyone knew today that the hospital was no better or worse than any other. The doctors at the supposed citadel were as likely to make mistakes as their fellow colleagues in the countryside or anywhere else.

Doctors at the general hospital, young and old, ranged from the clever to the mediocre to the really incompetent. A few ageing dinosaurs fitting the incompetent label just went through the motions and were particularly dangerous. They had tried really hard to break into private practice ages ago but had never quite made it, subsequently resigning themselves to the permanent payroll of the government hospital until the day they retired. Often, they were too jaded and downright uninterested to make an extra effort to look deeply into a patient's condition, just ordering random tests in a Micawber-like fashion, hoping something would come of it. As for the patients, their fate was a lottery. They couldn't *choose* the doctor they wished to see, but were ruled by and subjected to a rigid ticketing system. Whilst in the waiting hall, an attendant would call out ticket numbers in an ascending order, resulting in a patient's being directed to a doctor who happened to be free just at that particular time. It all boiled down to one single fateful ticket number, or 'instant karma', as ancient Sadhu at the Nameless described it whenever the subject arose during the feisty breakfast palavers.

Grandmummy, and everybody else who could afford to, avoided the government hospital like the pest – hence her visit to the affable Dr Nader. The doctor's waiting room was always filled to capacity, primarily on account of his modest consulting fee, but also because he was extremely successful in his diagnosis and treatment. Additionally, and pivotally for the patients, he possessed an uncanny ability to judge just how much they could afford to pay. He would generously charge a lesser consulting fee whenever he concluded that a particular patient couldn't afford much – a Good Samaritan quality endearing him to many, one that had first drawn the attention of the benevolent Father Clement.

The waiting room at the doctor's clinic was filled to capacity when Grandmummy and Primrose arrived. There were about fifteen patients clutching ticket numbers, waiting patiently to be called up. Grandmummy wasn't over-perturbed by the long waiting line, which meant she would have to wait a good hour or so. Ignoring the suffering souls in the queue, she put on her most domineering demeanour, took a firm grasp on Primrose's hand, and proceeded to march her off directly into the doctor's consultation room under the verbal and physical protests of the irked attendant in charge.

'Madam,' bawled out the incensed attendant, attempting to stop her with his bare hands (a fatal mistake), 'You must take a number and wait in the queue like everyone else. You can't just walk into the doctor's consulting room like that! Please take a number and *sit* down!'

Grandmummy squared up to him and fired a quick verbal salvo of her own, brusquely brushing aside the attendant's grabbing hands for good measure.

'Don't you know who I am, *boy*? Get out of my way at once! I'm a personal friend of the doctor! We're not standing in no damn queue with all them other sick people. God in heaven knows what germs and things we can catch from that wretched lot!'

The angry attendant – an elderly silver-haired man – incensed at being called a *boy*, tried to hold back Grandmummy's large person by physical force, but he couldn't quite manage it. He was a puny specimen of a man and no match for the heavyset Dragon, who stormed into the doctor's waiting room together with a clutching Primrose, much to the chagrin of the waiting patients in the queue.

The doctor, who was in the middle of a consultancy with another patient, looked up in surprise as the trio burst into his room – Grandmummy grasping a tottering Primrose's hand, whilst the irritated attendant, both arms half wrapped around the matriarch's large torso, was trying his very best to pull her back.

Dr Nader sighed as he recognised the intruder. He knew Grandmummy from previous encounters, ever since Father Clement had first introduced them. He waved aside his angry employee with a few conciliatory words and motioned for Grandmummy and Primrose to step into a curtained section of the room, where a single bed was placed for examination purposes. He politely asked them to wait there until he finished his attentions and discussions with his current patient.

They did not have to wait too long – the doctor appearing after a while, white coat flapping gently in the breeze generated by the ceiling fan, his stethoscope around his neck in true doctor fashion. He decided not to admonish Grandmummy for her queue-busting terrorism. He had learnt from past incidents that it was futile – of no avail. He said graciously, but in a resigned and weary manner, 'My dear Mrs Trescoot. We were only talking about you the other day, Father Clement and I. What seems to be the trouble, eh?'

Grandmummy nodded her head and acknowledged the greeting. Pointing at the blushing Primrose, she said, 'Ah! Dr Nader, it not me who's sick. It's Primrose here, who has been having some pain in her stomach for some days now.'

'Pain in the stomach, eh?' said the doctor, putting on his best bedside manner. 'Well, let's see now. Come! Lie down on the bed here and let's examine you a bit then.'

The doctor proceeded to examine the young aunt after first asking her to strip down to her underwear under the watchful gaze of Grandmummy, who didn't budge from the room. The good doctor did not protest Grandmummy's presence. He was used to the prudishness of some of the local people, a quality he had learnt to tolerate. Quite often, he was forced to examine younger women in the company of their mothers or other womenfolk.

After asking a blushing Primrose some questions regarding her condition, he pushed and pressed her abdomen and sides a bit, hemming and hawing as though pleased with what he discovered. Completing his examination, he asked his patient to get dressed again and then requested that both mother and daughter take a seat beside his nearby consulting desk away from the curtained examination room. He washed his hands and reappeared shortly. Primrose, who had whimpered a bit under his gentle probing, was pale-faced and drawn, not looking well at all.

Grandmummy spoke first. 'Well,' she demanded, 'what's wrong with the child?'

'My dear Mrs Trescoot, nothing's seriously wrong with the young woman – nothing to worry about, that is – but she needs to have her appendix out.'

'What? This means an operation and all that, doesn't it?' quipped Grandmummy, consternation written all over her face.

'Yes, yes, but I have no facilities for operations of that sort here. I can give you an emergency referral to the government hospital. They will do the job in no time, and the young lady will not have much to bother about afterwards.'

Grandmummy and Primrose, momentarily struck down in silence, let this bit of information sink in. The mention of the government hospital didn't augur well.

'That damn government hospital is like a bloody cattle shed, always crowded with them sick villagers and everyone else. Is it safe to send the child there?' asked the Dragon anxiously, highly concerned for her favourite daughter's well-being.

Dr Nader replied with a look of sobriety on his face, his manner gently persuading. 'True, true! It's very crowded for outpatients, Mrs Trescoot, but once you get admitted, the wards are fairly all right. And they do have all the equipment needed for this kind of standard operation. Besides, I will dispatch a personal emergency referral to a doctor whom I know personally there – a first-class surgeon. My referral will also mean that you don't have to stand in any queue and won't need to wait. The young lady will be admitted at once.'

Grandmummy and Primrose were relieved by the doctor's comforting assurances. After the latter had written his professional referral, Grandmummy thanked him cordially and left the consultancy room, with Primrose trailing daintily behind her heels. She conveniently 'forgot' to pay Dr Nader's consultancy fee before leaving and had to be hauled back by the attendant just as she was leaving through the rear exit. Having come off a poor second in his earlier tussle with the Dragon and adamant not to brook any more nonsense this time around, the harried attendant had recruited the stronger and younger clinic clerk to assist him. Well and truly cornered by two persons, Grandmummy grudgingly paid up, the long-suffering attendant still smouldering over her arrogant behaviour earlier. He gave her a parting scowl that would have put a normal soul to shame – but not Grandmummy. She was far beyond threatening looks or anything else anybody threw at her, a condition brought upon ever since her husband had passed away so many years ago.

The operation was a grand success. Primrose was admitted the very same day to the government hospital and was re-examined by a doctor after he read the referral notes of Dr Nader. Primrose was operated on that evening and had to stay a few nights at the hospital to recuperate.

Celeste was ordered by Grandmummy to stay with her sister at nights, a privilege extended to close relatives of warded patients whenever circumstances permitted. After five days, well and truly recuperated, Primrose came home in a taxi along with Celeste, who had earlier on tended to her sister's discharge papers and helped pack her things. Primrose did not look too bad for her ordeal, on the contrary, radiating a mysterious kind of glow – a far cry from her usual prim and distant manner. For once in her young life, Primrose found herself the focus of everyone's attention. She revelled in her new role, exaggerating a great deal on her surgery, which she purported – quite untruthfully – to have been very painful and horrendous, conveniently leaving out the anaesthetic that had knocked her out for the duration of the operation. The special aureole-like radiance she emitted went quite undetected by everyone except Rohan, who sensed something alien in his young aunt's manner. It seemed to him that a 'new' Primrose had come back in place of the old one. She seemed to have gone through a giant metamorphosis of sorts, he thought, and was now looking much happier, talkative, and confident – traits she had never shown before. She appeared to have become extremely benevolent too, another leaning alien to her parsimonious nature. Just that afternoon, she sent Rohan on an errand to buy an egg-and-bacon roll from the New Modern Café and had tipped him ten cents, a deed that left Rohan flabbergasted. He had never got a tip from her before, not even any pocket money, so the ten cents really surprised him. Additionally, that evening after dinner, Primrose distributed chocolates to everyone, breaking her hitherto tendency to share such treats with only Grandmummy and occasionally with Celeste. It was as if though the hospital had kept the old Primrose and had sent out a clone – a modified and improved clone. Primrose's sudden burst of altruism made it apparent to Rohan that something more than the operation was responsible for his aunt's current state. In hindsight, he thought that she did appear to have the same moonish sort of look Celeste wore in the days immediately after she had entered into a liaison with Mr Sera a few months ago.

After another two days of convalescence, Primrose dropped a minor bombshell. She chose a quiet family evening to come clean and blurt the news she had been itching to impart to her mother. The boys were busy doing their homework. Rebecca was discussing the next day's cooking agenda with Laura, the little girls, Sussie and Maria, had fallen asleep on the couch.and Celeste was away at the seaside esplanade with her new paramour, Don.

Primrose approached the Dragon gingerly, opening warily. 'Ma, I met a man in the hospital, and he wants to come and meet you and start seeing me here at home.'

Grandmummy, who was reposing in her favourite chair in the veranda, jumped out of her temporary inertia with a dexterity alien to her bulk and age.

'Whaaat?!' she thundered. 'You did what? Who the devil told you to go and get involved with some blooming fellow at the hospital? Here you go to have a serious operation and things done, and you go and get yourself involved with some bloody man! How dare you, you wretch!'

'He's not just *any* man, Ma. He's a doctor,' replied Primrose, playing her trump card with supreme confidence, knowing fully well that her mother would definitely approve of such a wonderful liaison.

The Dragon swallowed this last bit of information with surprise. She had always entertained high ambitions for *all* her children and was very bitter and disappointed with the results so far. The family's matrimonial record was not a good one; only Robert's marriage was satisfactory in an actual sense of the word. True, Daisy had also made a good marriage with Oswald, but Grandmummy disliked the latter intensely and couldn't stand the sight of him, especially now after his sordid behaviour at Meadows. Celeste's divorce still rankled and caused her a great deal of pain, as did Rebecca's abandonment and Rainier's public trial at the local assizes. As if things couldn't get any worse, Celeste's most recent liaison with the lodger Mr Sera, a man not even of Grandmummy's beloved Christian faith, and a 'village fellow' to boot, seemed almost intolerable. It was all just too much to bear at times. Her last and only hope for salvaging some her lost family honour was for her youngest daughter to marry really well. Primrose's last statement sent a contented thrill down the matriarch's aged spine. Grandmummy was inundated with relief, overjoyed beyond words.

'A doctor? How did you get involved with a doctor, child?' she asked in a much more condescending tone and a definite gentler manner.

'He's the doctor fellow that operated on me, Ma. He came several times to see me in the ward afterwards and asked me all sorts of questions.'

'What sort of questions?' demanded the old bird.

'Just questions, Ma, like where I live, who my parents are, if I was working or not, and things like that. Then he said after a while that he likes me very much and that he wants to come and meet you and the family.'

'Why does he want to come and see us? Did he say he was interested in you, then?' asked Grandmummy, hoping to high heaven that such was the case.

'Oh, Ma! He must be interested in me! Why does he want to call otherwise?' bleated young Primrose, blushing several shades of crimson.

Grandmummy digested this information in silent contemplation.

If the man was a doctor and if he wanted to call publicly without any hanky-panky behind the family's back, then surely he must have honourable intentions? Perhaps this operation of her daughter's might just well turn out to be heaven-sent after all! She decided on the spot to give her consent.

'All right, Primrose. All right! You may ask the young fellow to come if he wants to, but you will sit and talk to him in the living room. No taking the man into any corners or to the back garden or anything like that, mind you, missy,' she said, wagging a fat, cautionary finger at Primrose for good measure.

Primrose was deliriously happy. She knew she was beautiful and couldn't for the life of her understand why so many men had dismissed her as they did. It remained an enigma. Only recently, Celeste's love affair with Don had succeeded in breaking down her self-confidence to an even lesser degree, plunging her into a tenebrous mood. She found it terribly hard to swallow that Don could have overlooked her in favour of Celeste.

Primrose *was* an enigma of sorts – not a hopeless enigma like Grandmummy, but an enigma nonetheless. More than often, she stubbornly waited for a lover to fall into her lap – a man who would make the first move. The doctor at the hospital had seen the beauty there was to be seen and was besotted, fast determining to put his bachelor days behind him. Having studied a good deal of psychiatry in his student days at Portopo's medical school, where he had qualified as a surgeon and spent an additional year in general psychiatry; Primrose's taciturn kind of nature didn't bypass him. Not one to let an opportunity slip by and a man who, besides, knew his own mind, he didn't dither. After a few initial prods and pleasantries, he openly declared his interest to a blushing Primrose, who was both thrilled and flattered at the same time. The doctor's bold approach was just the kind of opening gambit Primrose had always wanted and longed for. The fact that he was a professional medical man only served to enhance his appeal.

Primrose's conquest was hot news in the family. Word gradually got around amongst family, friends, and neighbours, courtesy of Grandmummy, who would have sung it out from the rooftops like a rampant 'fiddler on the roof', if only she could. The doctor was no longer Primrose's private prerogative. Everyone wanted to know details about him: what he looked like, how old he was, where he lived, and so on and so forth. The boys were especially interested to know if he had a motor car and, if he did, what sort of car it was.

The rest of the family continued to give Primrose the third degree whenever an opportunity arose. Questions poured in a never-ending stream, a harried Primrose answering them as best as she could. In truth, she herself had limited information to impart – practically nothing! She hadn't asked her intended fiancé detailed questions about *his* family, his age (he was thirty-five), or general background, being much too timid to do so. In any event, she was terribly cautious that intense questioning on her part might inadvertently put the great man off. She was in awe of her medical conquest, quite overawed that a person of such high station was enamoured by her charms. All she knew was the bare minimum the doctor had cared to reveal in the short time they had got acquainted – precious little, as she realised in hindsight. Thinking the matter over, she came to the conclusion that she ought to have asked the man at least *something* about his family and a few other personal details. She worried about it a while, a sliver of concern crossing her brow.

Grandmummy informed Primrose that the doctor could come to visit that very same week on Friday evening. Primrose hurried over to the Fazals' house, called the doctor at the hospital, and informed him of the news, which was exactly what her conquest had been hoping for.

Thursday evening found the house swept spotlessly clean, the furniture dusted, and the floor polished with a colourless wax Grandmummy carefully hoarded, using it otherwise only during the Christmas season to keep the living room floor spotlessly shiny. Everything else was tidied and made ready for the occasion. Primrose had bought some flowers from 'Flower Power', the neighbourhood florist down at Montague Street, and put them in a glass vase, placing it on the little coffee table in the hall. The little girls were dressed in their best finery, whilst Rohan and Mahan were told in no uncertain terms to wear their better clothes – the Christmas clothes bought last year. Laura needed no special instruction. Everyone knew she always dressed in a sober, yet stylish, fashion to suit any occasion.

Grandmummy, not to be outdone, put on her favourite dress, a black velvet one with a white lace collar she wore on her confessional trips to Father Clement and to Christmas midnight Mass. She looked stately in that old but dignified dress, the light around her highlighting the white lace collar to perfection amidst the sheen of the black velvet – quite reminiscent of a Rembrandt portrait. Primrose had informed the family that the doctor had a car and everyone was peering anxiously through the small windows in the veranda to see when his vehicle would pull up beside the curb. The boys especially were thrilled, wanting to see what sort of a car Primrose's young man possessed. They were also curious about the suitor's parking skills, having witnessed their uncle Oswald's miserable attempts to park his car in an acceptable fashion beside the uneven curb outside Grandmummy's crooked old house.

At last, after what seemed an eternity, a brand-new Austin Princess pulled up beside the curb. To Rohan and Mahan's critical satisfaction, the driver, who could be no other than Primrose's suitor, made a perfect parallel parking, expertly manoeuvring his car in between a parked lorry and a similarly parked van. The boys' assessment of his parking skills climbed to a very high level, and with it their opinion of his viability as a prospective partner for Primrose. A man who could park a car like that must surely be a grand chap, they thought in unison – one thoroughly fit to be a family member.

A youngish, somewhat portly man stepped out of the car, hesitancy written on his face as though uncertain of his whereabouts. An aura of well-being hung around him, auguring well for his prospects. A closer look revealed a not-too-handsome face slightly pockmarked on both cheeks, in all probability an heirloom of boyhood pimples. He had thick black hair parted in the middle with the aid of some glistening pomade applied quite liberally. Despite the pockmarks and overweight, he had a commanding air about him, a kind of granite quality generating respect. It was not surprising that the shy and taciturn Primrose had fallen so heavily for him.

Primrose stepped onto the doorstep and waved at her conquest. The young man waved back in acknowledgement, relieved to see the object of his affections. and that he had found the right house. He locked the car, walked up to the house, and stepped in.

The suitor was duly presented to Grandmummy by a nervous and stuttering Primrose. After the initial introductions were done with, Grandmummy waved the other family members away airily and sat in the veranda together with Primrose and her young man.

'Primrose has told that me you're a doctor,' she said, opening the conversation.

'Yes, yes, I'm a doctor,' the suitor replied in a gruff voice and lofty manner.

He appeared rather brazen, not in the least bit overawed by Grandmummy's large and looming presence, nor did he appear to approve of the old house and drab furniture, looking around himself with a faint air of distaste. Earlier on, when driving in search of the address, he had frowned at the surroundings he found himself in – not quite approving the fact his would-be fiancée lived in such a shady-looking neighbourhood. He wasn't – as it came to be known later on – a genuine snob like the wretched Oswald, but he was genuinely used to being in more grandiose places. He was a short-tempered young man too, used to having his own way and resentful of being cross-examined by anyone on any matter. Grandmummy and the rest of the family were quickly to discover this special trait of his in the days and months to come.

Grandmummy continued to speak. She didn't quite like her intended son-in-law's manner, itching to lay down the law and stamp her authority on him, as was her wont with everyone who crossed her path. This time around, however, she didn't quite get away with it. The doctor was made of sterner stuff.

'If you're seeing Primrose, then you must speak with her only in the living room. She's not allowed to go out with you anywhere until she's good and ready,' Grandmummy said to the doctor.

'Good and ready? Good and ready for what?'

Grandmummy pierced him with her famous gorgon's stare. Short of turning everyone into stone, the very same stare had achieved resounding success with neighbours and others, petrifying them into instant subjection to the Dragon's iron will. The suitor, however, remained unfazed. The famous stare that had made many a challenger bite the dust did not affect him at all. He remained unperturbed, displaying no fear. Looking away from Grandmummy as though having nothing more to say to her, he calmly turned his attentions to Primrose. He started to chat with his lady love as though Grandmummy wasn't even there.

Grandmummy, disappointed by the failure of her staring tactics and not used to be treated in this flippant fashion, made a fresh assault, attempting to regain the initiative. 'Young man! Didn't you hear what I said? No gallivanting around with Primrose until I say it's all right.'

The doctor, a man who knew his own mind, was not afraid to speak it. If he had seemed short and had bordered on the rude in his initial prod with Grandmummy, then there was no mistaking his abject rudeness now. 'Now, look here, Mrs Trescoot. Just look here now. I did the decent thing and called on Primrose in your own home, right? I had earlier on asked your permission to see the girl, didn't I? Haven't I done the right thing? I'll be damned if I have to sit and talk to her in your blasted presence all the while. I will take the girl out now and then if she agrees, but I'm not asking your permission for that. The girl's an adult and can make up her own damn mind. It's quite enough I've made my intentions known to you without you throwing some goddamned bloody rule book at me as well.'

'If you go and do those things, then I'll forbid Primrose to see you again,' said the Dragon threateningly. Doctor or no doctor, Primrose's prospects or no prospects, she disliked coming out second best in any situation and wanted to crush the young man. She wanted him to grovel before her like everyone else did.

'Fine! Then I'll go now. I won't trouble your daughter again. No use in me waiting here anymore,' said the doctor heatedly, retreating towards the front door.

Grandmummy was flabbergasted. Never in recent years had anyone treated her like this and gotten away with it. It seemed the young man cared tuppence for her terms. The lack of respect astounded the old Dragon – the suitor's quickness to abandon such a prize as Primrose, likewise. One side of her wanted to give this young daredevil the worst scolding of his life, consequences be damned. Another, the sensible side, the one hoping for a grand husband for her beloved youngest daughter, urged her in an inner voice, 'Do this and your daughter will lose this splendid opportunity to reel in such a fine catch.' Grandmummy made a split decision – not an easy one for her to make. She decided to grovel and, for once in her life, eat humble pie.

'Wait, wait, young man. Why are you getting all angry and huffed up like that for?' she countered with mounting panic. 'If Primrose is willing, then I suppose she can go out with you for a dinner or something. Wait and talk with the girl and see what she has to say. You can talk to her alone. We will not disturb you.'

'Harrumph,' said the suitor, peeved. He stood still by the open doorway for a moment in an undecided fashion, momentarily lost in space. Finally, after what seemed an eternity to the eavesdropping household, but which only took a few seconds, he retraced his steps and walked inside once again. Glaring testily at Grandmummy, he steered Primrose into the living room, where the rest of the family had been surreptitiously listening to the conversation in rapt attention. Grandmummy's easy defeat came as a shock to her minions. She was their queen and commander-in-chief, and her being treated as the doctor had treated her was unprecedented. None of them imagined – even in their wildest dreams – that the Dragon could fold up so easily and be beaten in her own steamrolling tactics. At the approach of the doctor and Primrose, the eavesdroppers fled discreetly back into the bowels of the house, leaving the living room entirely at the disposal of the young couple. The distance to the living room was too far away for any decent eavesdropping, so they reluctantly stayed put where they were, each one yearning to know what was transpiring between the pair they had so hurriedly left behind. Rohan and Mahan, commanded by Grandmummy, made regular sallies into the living room and back into the veranda, where the Dragon sat licking her wounds. All they could see was the doctor in intimate conversation with their aunt. The couple appeared to be quite absorbed in one another, in complete oblivion to their surroundings and everyone else. The boys reported back faithfully to Grandmummy all of what they saw, which amounted to hardly anything at all...

Rohan and Mahan soon tired of their spying manoeuvres. They were expecting to see daring kissing and fondling, the kind they had witnessed in the many adventure matinees they faithfully attended at the Elphinstone and Empire cinema halls, but in that surmise they were profoundly disappointed. All the doctor and Primrose seemed to do was to hold hands and talk softly to each other. Deciding that enough was enough, the boys went outside to have a closer look at the doctor's car instead, much to the chagrin of Grandmummy, their assignment-giver and 'chief of intelligence', who yelled at them to come back, but to no avail. They pretended not to hear.

'It looks like a new car. Much better than Oswald's shitty old car,' volunteered Mahan.

'Yes, yes, it's so much bigger, too. Sure to have one big powerful engine, not like stinky old Oswald's small Morris,' said Rohan, the 'Morris expert', in lieu of the fact that he had, during his sojourn at Meadows, spent a good deal of time inside his detested uncle's vehicle.

'Them Austin cars are blooming expensive, too,' countered Mahan, putting on a solemn and knowing air, although he hadn't the foggiest notion what an Austin could cost.

'Yes, that's true! Austin cars have leather upholstering and a six-cylinder motor.' Rohan had no clue as to what a six-cylinder motor was. He had picked up some motoring jargon from Oswald and Merv whilst at Meadows, and six cylinders sounded a grand thing worth repeating.

Mahan didn't know anything about cylinders, either, let alone six. He wisely kept his mouth shut and did not offer a comment, not wanting to betray his ignorance and give Rohan the upper hand – sibling rivalry always in the fore where the brothers were concerned. Instead, he instinctively put out a finger on the dust-covered surface of the car and drew a dust line. Rohan, not to be outdone, drew a funny face. Mahan copied him, and soon the duo were busy drawing all sorts of dust figures on the car, laughing, gesturing, and commenting on each other's artistic efforts. The boys' merriment was abruptly shattered by the sudden emergence of the suitor in the front doorway. He yelled out instantly at the unsuspecting boys, who were quite busy drawing even more dust figures, this time on the car's bonnet and rear.

'Hey, you bloody wretches! What the devil are you writing all over on my car, you good-for-nothing young scallywags! Get away from that vehicle at once, you hear me!' he bellowed, advancing threateningly.

Rohan and Mahan fled the scene of the crime, leaving the enraged doctor to wipe out the offending works of art with a clean cloth retrieved from the boot of his car. They were easily wiped off, but he was angry nevertheless, not fancying driving back home in congested traffic with all those funny faces and lettering all over his vehicle. The doctor looked on helplessly at the fleeing boys. He had better keep a close eye on those two in future, he thought – bloody young hooligans.

Well away from the house, Rohan and Mahan stopped to gather their breath and ascertain the situation. They felt slighted, angry about being called 'bloody wretches' and 'damn scallywags' by a man they had only just met. What a pompous fellow, they thought in unison. Why, he was no better than their stinky old uncle Oswald! After some moments of anxiety and indecision, the siblings retraced their steps and made their way cautiously back, avoiding the front door for the comparative safety of the kitchen entrance.

The doctor, whose original purpose was to go to his vehicle and fetch some vitamin tablets out of his medical bag for Primrose, re-emerged soon enough back into Grandmummy's living room. He was still visibly annoyed by the boys' pranks.

'Hey, Primrose! Those boys who are staying here, the ones you said were your sister's children, where is their father?' he inquired angrily of Primrose, adding for good measure, 'I would like to have a word with him. Doesn't seem to me he is disciplining those fellows like he should, the damn young rascals.'

Primrose wisely and conveniently ignored the query about Rainier's whereabouts. It was not appropriate to let her new fiancé know *that* part of the family history, especially now in this early stage of their relationship. Instead, she inquired in a subdued fashion about the nature of the boys' offences, assuming her young nephews had somehow or other annoyed her suitor through some prank or mischief. The doctor explained that they had been mucking about with his car, but conceded gruffly, to Primrose's relief, that there was no real damage done. The episode of the dust drawings had soured him somewhat, but he recovered quickly and turned his full attentions once again to his lady love.

So ended the first visit of the suitor. All in all, it went rather well, Primrose heaving a sigh of relief when it was all over. She visualised wedding bells ringing in the near future and, in her momentary state of bliss, generously didn't rat, or perhaps forgot to rat, on the boys' misdeeds to Grandmummy or the others. If she had, Grandmummy would have surely boxed their ears – even Mahan's. Primrose's success was pivotal and superseded everything. Nobody would be allowed to jeopardise that!

The boys aptly nicknamed Primrose's young man 'Dr Piles', courtesy of his angry behaviour over the dust figures. It seemed an ideal name and a jolly good joke to them, as his given name turned out to be the very English-sounding Giles. In time, and as they got to know the doctor better, they discovered that his verbal assault over the dust figures wasn't just a temporary thing. The young man *was* short-tempered, so the sobriquet stuck. Doctor Piles, or 'Giles-Piles', slowly became a nickname the whole family used whenever talking about the suitor, much to Primrose's annoyance. As time passed, the ménage gave the doctor a wide berth whenever he came courting, discovering quite early that he did not want anything to do with them. He was very good to Primrose, though, always bringing her a present whenever he came to visit, as well as behaving courteously and lovingly.

Dr Piles, as the boys sarcastically dubbed him, soon settled down into a routine where he would visit Primrose, take her out to see a film, and afterwards enjoy a cosy romantic dinner at one of the many exclusive restaurants in the city.

Grandmummy, who was treated in the same disdainful manner by Giles as he did for the rest of the family, did however, put her foot down on the film-and-dinner routine when it first came up, insisting that someone from the family always accompany the lovebirds. She brooked no refusal, knowing jolly well that it was rather late in the day for Giles to threaten walking out as he had done on the first occasion they clashed, where she had come off a poor second. That boat had sailed for Giles. He was far too much in love with Primrose now to do anything as drastic as that; he simply couldn't. Giles may have won the first round in his battle with Grandmummy, but the Dragon was slowly wresting back the initiative. As with the tortoise and the hare, the race didn't favour the swift. She was well on her way to the winning post, leaving a gasping Giles far, far behind. Giles grumpily agreed to the chaperoning business, seeing no way out. He longed to be rude and crush Grandmummy with some acidic comment or other, but restrained. Grandmummy was overjoyed. She knew she had got the rather testy young man exactly where she wanted him, where she had wanted him right from the start. She was firmly back in the saddle…

There was a small hitch in the chaperoning stakes. Both Rebecca and Celeste peremptorily refused to be an unwelcome third wheel in a date between the two lovers, whilst Laura – always shy of socialising – withdrew quite early on, saying she had far too much schoolwork as her senior exams were approaching. This left only the boys, and Grandmummy reluctantly had to settle for them, as did Primrose. There was a bit of a snag, though, as neither Rohan nor Mahan was trained to eat with a fork and knife; nor were they familiar with high-class dining etiquette – imperative if one was to dine at the better and more posh restaurants. In the glory days, when their father Rainier was around, there were many parties and functions at Rebecca's stately home, the elite of Victorian society always well represented. Rebecca always maintained correct table etiquette, including assorted knives and forks, soup spoons, dessert spoons, wine and brandy glasses, starched napkins, and all the trimmings of correct dining. On more grandiose occasions, she even engaged a professional butler and serving staff from a service company specialising in such matters. The children – Rohan, Mahan, and little Sussie, with the exception of Laura, whom Rebecca had already initiated into the intricacies of proper dining etiquette, were always made to eat separately, much earlier, and were not allowed to participate in the grand doings that followed. Rebecca hired a nanny to see to the children's needs whilst they were confined to another section of the house.

Apart from serving spoons and an occasional spoon and fork, neither Rohan nor Mahan had ever used cutlery of the type expected in posh dining etiquette. It was Rebecca's intention to start training the boys to eat correctly. 'All in good time,' she would often say calmly to her husband, but the latter's sudden financial collapse and its disastrous aftermath put all her well-thought plans into disarray. She had left it too late…

Grandmummy, never one to be stumped by a problem or to let the grass grow under her feet, decided to take matters into her own hands and train the boys without further ado. Although a recluse of sorts, the fine upbringing and circles she had moved in as a young woman in the distant past served her in good stead. What she didn't know about dining etiquette could be written on the back of a postage stamp. Still, however, the grandiose dining etiquette of earlier generations was a bit obsolete and considered extravagant in restaurant circles these days. Well aware of this, Grandmummy prudently decided to teach the boys just the *basics* expected in the trenching stakes, basics that had survived international etiquette's many chops and changes the past few decades.

It was agreed that the brothers take turns in chaperoning Primrose. Mahan would accompany the couple on the initial date, and Rohan would follow suit the next time around.

Grandmummy informed the boys that she was going to train them to use a fork and knife, to identify plates for the main course and starters, scoop up soup in an accepted fashion, place a cloth napkin on their laps or under their chins, and a few other elementary matters. She used a loaf of white bread bought from the 'New Hotel'. Cutting it into thin and thick slices, she took out her prized butter from her food cupboard and applied liberal coatings on the bread, serving the result to the two bemused boys. Rohan and Mahan were rather perplexed over the bread and butter. Was this all they served at fancy restaurants? Were they expected to eat just bread and butter when they went out with Giles and Primrose for dinner? Always the bold one and never shy to speak his mind, Rohan expostulated, addressing the Dragon in a stern voice. 'Are we only allowed bread and butter to eat at the dinner, Grandmummy? Everyone says they serve all sorts of foreign meats and Frenchy fries and things at the restaurants!'

'Don't be a silly jackass, boy! Of course you'll be allowed to eat proper food like European courses and things! Can't you see I am only trying to train you fellows to eat all that with a fork and knife? You think you'd be allowed to eat all those grand meat chops and things with just a blooming spoon like you do with your damn heathen local food? It would be disgraceful! Now be quiet and see how I'm using the fork and knife. Imagine the bread is a big piece of meat.'

Putting a slice of buttered bread on her plate, Grandmummy demonstrated how the cutlery was to be used. Rohan and Mahan, after some initial awkwardness, soon got the hang of it all, after some time becoming quite adept with their forks and knives, using them with the dexterity of one to the manor born. A rather watery soup was made and poured into deep soup plates, and again Grandmummy showed them how to properly scoop it into their mouths and then correctly tilt the plate at the accepted angle to finish it off. Further instructions and demonstrations followed.

Grandmummy conducted her crash-course sessions the entire week, repeating the process with the buttered bread and soup servings, even adding some cooked fish a couple of times for good measure. The boys had absolutely no objections. Although the bread was pretty much ordinary, it was not often in their present circumstances that they tasted butter, with the exception of Mahan, whom Grandmummy secretly allowed to share the culinary treasures within her food cupboard now and then. As for the soup, it did taste wonderful in spite of its watery consistency, as did the boiled fish, but then again Grandmummy was a master cook; anything she turned out did taste heavenly. The training sessions had a definite *Oliver Twist* aura about it all, the gaping ménage looking on in wonder. At the end of the week Grandmummy was fully satisfied that the boys would be able to hold their own and handle the coming restaurant visit with flying colours. She did not want her intended son-in-law to come to any hasty conclusion that he was marrying into a family without class or knowledge of rudimentary dining etiquette. She had enough of *those* kind of subtle insinuations from Oswald, who never missed a cue to bad-mouth Grandmummy and her household. Giles had to be shown what kind of mettle her family was made of, at least where dining etiquette was concerned. Mollified over the results of her crash-course sessions, Grandmummy informed Primrose that the boys were ready and that her suitor could choose a date for their first romantic outing.

The coming weekend was duly scheduled for the inaugural restaurant visit, and Mahan, as prearranged, was the first choice to accompany the lovers. Fate, however, decreed otherwise. On Thursday evening, Mahan came down with a heavy cold, which even brought upon a sore throat and a high fever the next day. Sick like a dog, he was in no condition to accompany Primrose and Giles. Rohan was ordered to step in as the first and only reserve.

'You get your clothes ready, boy!' commanded Grandmummy to a more than willing Rohan. 'And see that you are presentable, you damn scallywag! You always look like a street boy with those crumpled clothes of yours and that damn clotted head of hair your silly mother calls curls! Why can't you be a bit more like Mahan? See what a well-dressed, good-looking boy your brother is!'

Grandmummy, of course, was being spiteful – more than a tad dismayed that her favourite grandson, Mahan, couldn't accompany Primrose and Giles. In truth, Rohan was miles more attractive than Mahan, and his dark curls were much envied by almost everyone who noticed them.

Giles had picked Saturday for the restaurant visit, leaving ample time for Rohan to wash and iron his 'Christmas shirt' and 'Christmas trousers'. He even took full advantage of his brother's immobility to sneak away a pair of fancy nylon socks, a pair much prized by his fastidious elder sibling. He polished his only pair of leather shoes and satisfied that his raiments would more than do for the occasion, calmly awaited Saturday evening with eager anticipation.

Primrose dressed very carefully. She was rather tall and fair, with a head of pale light hair, some unknown Scandinavian gene in her lineage putting its hand up. Her natural good looks seldom needed any special make-up. For the occasion, she had a new dress sewn of a shimmering, dark-green material that showed off her excellent figure to perfection. On the advice of Daisy, the dress was shortened much more than Grandmummy usually allowed Primrose to shorten her dresses and skirts, the hemline eventually ending up well above the knees, much to Grandmummy's chagrin.

'You want everyone to see the girl's knickers, Daisy? Isn't it enough that *you* show off those ridiculous knickers of yours every time you sit on a blooming chair? Don't pass your damn bad habits on to your sister!'

Daisy and the Dragon protested back and forth about the bold alteration, but after glancing at the preliminary results, the latter shrewdly decided not to forbid it.

Rohan had dressed up too. He looked very smart and the onlooking family members approved heartily. Apart from the 'borrowed' socks, he had further rummaged into Mahan's things and sneaked some his brother's favourite hair pomade, which he had applied liberally to comb his hair in a backwards style. The resulting effect was a stylish, well-groomed head of thick, glossy hair – slightly curly still, as no hair pomade in the world could entirely smoothen out Rohan's wild curls. Normally, he wouldn't have dared to purloin any of his brother's things, but he knew Mahan would be bedridden for at least a week and would never know of the minor pilferage. The smell from the hair pomade would disappear after he had washed it out the next day, and the exquisite socks he would put back in their place that very night.

At five thirty on Friday evening, Giles's impressive new Austin Princess pulled up outside the house. Giles did not bother to get out, tooting his horn instead to signal his arrival. What was taboo for Oswald in Grandmummy's rule book was hypocritically deemed acceptable for Giles. She was desperate for Primrose to keep her catch, and a horn blast or two wasn't going to spoil any of it. Besides, as she saw it all, he was a doctor and not just a blooming accountant like Oswald and compared thus, Giles had a God-given right to blow his horn anytime he wanted.

Primrose and Rohan rushed to join Giles in the waiting car. They were going to an evening film at the Empire Talkies, which started at six o'clock. The plan was to see the film and then proceed to a restaurant for dinner, after which Giles would drop off Primrose and Rohan at home.

The film, a much hyped Hollywood thriller about a daring jewel thief, turned out to be quite entertaining – at least for Rohan. Giles had bought expensive box seats for the trio, each box having a seating capacity for four persons in rows of two.

'Sit in the front row, Rohan,' said Primrose. 'If you sit behind us, you might not see so well.'

It wasn't concern for her nephew's viewing possibilities that prompted her remark – wanting Giles all to herself in the back-row seats, safely behind Rohan.

Rohan found the luxury of the box seats awesome. It was such a come-up from the rough-and-tough gallery section where the school gang always sat. His position in front of Giles and Primrose gave him a commanding view of the cinemagoers below. He felt grand and superior, a sort of monarch of all he surveyed. As the film progressed, Rohan completely forgot the duo behind him, engrossed in the doings of the daring jewel thief. Giles and Primrose, less intent on the film, cuddled and petted as lovers usually did at the cinema.

After the film was over, Giles drove them to a highly reputed Chinese restaurant where he had, earlier on in the day, booked a table. Chinese food was the restaurant's speciality, but they also served excellent English cuisine. The staff seemed to know the doctor well, welcoming him like an old and favoured guest, ushering the trio politely to their waiting table.

It wasn't Rohan's first restaurant visit, and he wasn't overly overawed by his surroundings. He had been to quite a few restaurants when much younger, in the company of his parents and siblings in the good old days, where he was allowed to use a spoon or just a single fork to eat his food, Rebecca fussing over him, cutting his meat, and keeping a watchful eye on his progress. Older now, he found no getting away from the fork-and-knife ritual this time around and was quite nervous as to how it would all turn out despite Grandmummy's elaborate bread-and-butter crash course.

Primrose and Giles ordered mixed grills and Rohan, not to be outdone, did likewise. 'I'll have a mixed grill too, Aunty Primrose,' he said after hearing what his aunt and Giles had ordered. He didn't know what a mixed grill was, but it sounded a grand concoction, judging by his fellow diners' enthusiasm when ordering the dish.

Giles completely ignored Rohan, both during the cinema visit and now at the restaurant. It was as though the third wheel didn't exist. He did not exchange a single word with the 'bodyguard', leaving young Rohan completely to his own devices, not out of cruelty, but mostly because he considered Grandmummy's chaperone service a slight to his impeccable character, tolerating it only for Primrose's sake. Looking obliquely at Rohan, he murmured very softly, his voice audible only to himself, 'Bloody hell! Just look at the boy! What the Dickens is he doing here? What is he supposed to put a stop to? Damn that blasted grandmother of his and her bloody prudish British ways! Ignorant old clot!'

Giles did not actually dislike Rohan, or even Mahan, for that matter, but he wasn't over-fond of children, and in any case couldn't quite understand for the life of him what anyone else was doing in the middle of his romantic outing with Primrose.

Giles's ignoring tactics didn't really bother Rohan. He was inured against ill treatment, having experienced the worst sort at Grandmummy's, and had come to the conclusion it was no use dwelling on the rights and wrongs of the horrid treatment of which he was constantly at the receiving end. It was part and parcel of his new life.

'Let old Giles-Piles ignore me! Why should I care? I have seen a good film sitting in the best seats, and I'm now going to have a grand dinner! Let the poxy fellow do what he blooming well wants, the mean old jackass!'

Reasoning thus, he stole a quick oblique glance at Giles, wondering just what Primrose saw in him. His aunt was admittedly, by any standards, a real beauty, whilst Giles looked like an ogre under the dim restaurant lights, the pockmarks of his long-vanished pimples standing out distinctly. Was it just the fact that he was a doctor that had bowled over Primrose? Rohan broke into a mischievous grin, his mind drifting to the picture-book story of *Beauty and the Beast,* which he had only that very morning related to young Sussie and Maria.

The couple made small talk, after which Giles ordered a bottle of beer for himself and a glass of wine for Primrose. Despite his ignoring tactics, he graciously ordered a bottle of orange squash for the 'bodyguard'.

The restaurant was half full. There were about five tables at the section where the trio sat. All in all, there were about twenty tables placed in three sections in the medium-sized restaurant. Elegant Chinese lion statues, fearsome-looking carved wooden dragons, and gigantic colourfully illustrated vases were placed in strategic corners. Intricate paintings depicting Chinese landscape scenes hung on the walls, whilst in the centre of the dining area a medium-sized fountain gurgled in peaceful tact, water sprouting gently through the mouth of an exquisitely carved gilded dragon with its head tilted high. Soft Chinese music, the distinct clang of the ruan dominating, could be heard floating gently around the eating area. The melodies were soothing and caressing, enhancing feelings of goodwill and contentment.

There were a few couples sitting at the adjoining tables a small distance away. Rohan observed that they too, like his aunt and Giles, appeared to be courting couples. It seemed that the establishment had purposely cordoned off and reserved the section where they sat especially for lovers.

The waiter in attendance arrived shortly with soup and a light salad, which were served as a starter. Small bread rolls and butter accompanied. Rohan, who was quite famished, quickly finished his soup using a soup spoon he had successfully identified, managing to do so in a discreet sort of way so as not to attract Primrose's or Giles's displeasure. He was particularly careful not to splash soup about or slurp it crudely, delicately wiping his mouth with his napkin after finishing. He didn't want Primrose to rat on him to Grandmummy, saying he had made a hash of things. As ever – and unlike the rest of the family – he didn't fear Grandmummy, but family pride was at stake. The code of the sons of Rainier and Rebecca was about to be tested and had to be upheld at all costs.

Besides the soup spoon, there were two sets of forks and knives neatly placed beside the plate of each diner. The smaller salad fork and knife came as an irritable surprise to Rohan. Grandmummy hadn't mentioned this in her fork-and-knife crash course. It was a temporary conundrum, but as with the ordering of the main course, he wisely decided to follow the grown-ups' example, doing as they did. Imitating Giles and Primrose, he ate the salad with the smaller fork and knife, avoiding a minor faux pas.

Giles and primrose ate slowly – very slowly. Rohan waited patiently for them to finish and the waiter to re-emerge with the mixed grills. 'How could people eat so slowly?' he thought to himself. He looked at Giles's large lips moving up and down whilst chomping down on his salad in an irritable slow motion, noticing the strong yellowish white teeth as he opened his mouth wide for each mouthful.

"Why, the fellow could easily eat a horse. Maybe he *is* an ogre and will swallow up nasty old Primrose on his wedding night,' Rohan thought, chuckling to himself. His chuckles turned to irritation shortly afterwards as he watched the couple put down their knives and forks several times to make small talk, ogling each other like a pair of doves. He sighed in exasperation. Hadn't they come here to *eat*?

Tiring of waiting for Giles and Primrose to finish, Rohan shifted his attention to the couple sitting nearest them. The lady at the table was thirty-five or so, and her companion was a bit older. From where he was sitting, Rohan could see that she was a big-bosomed woman and the sight of her large breasts made his mind wander to Baking Jane. The woman was well dressed, her smartly cut gown showing the cleavage between her big breasts to perfection. Rohan wondered if the breasts possessed the same huge nipples Baking Jane's possessed, the ones that he had seen on a few occasions when Baking Jane was too slow to cover her bare bosom during Rohan's breakfast-buying expeditions.

After a short while but what seemed like an eternity to Rohan, their waiter came along and cleared up their soup plates, salad plates, and used cutlery after first inquiring in the time-honoured maxim if the starter was to the table's satisfaction. Receiving an affirmative answer from Giles, the waiter informed that the main course would arrive very shortly. Primrose was too timid to converse with the waiter and left all the talking to Giles, who seemed to be very experienced in that sort of thing.

True to his word, the waiter re-emerged some minutes later, wheeling in a serving trolley, the mixed grills placed on hotplates ready for serving. There were equal portions for all.

The mixed grill was a concoction of beef and pork chops, chicken breasts, special sausages, and plenty of colourful vegetables with both roasted potatoes and French fries, served in separate dishes. The chops were well done, not too soft or tender, requiring a good deal of pressing and cutting with a fork and knife.

Rohan, with Grandmummy's training sessions under his belt, brandished his fork and knife with the air of an aristocratic continental count. He was hoping the other guests, especially the big-boobed lady and her companion at the nearby table, were looking on and admiring his highly sophisticated eating preferences and the superb dexterity he displayed with his fork and knife.

Giles and Primrose, unlike during the salad period, didn't talk much, just saying an occasional word or two to each other as they helped themselves to the sumptuous food. Soon, the trio were wading into and enjoying their meal.

Rohan found it quite a different proposition to work his way through a pork chop, unlike cutting and eating a slice of Grandmummy's buttered bread and boiled fish, especially since the chop in question had a trifurcate bone intact in its centre. He had some difficulty in mastering the required technique and pressed harder and harder with his fork in order to get a good grip on his large chop. Unfortunately, at one (as he related later to his great friend Salgado at school) unguarded evil moment he lost control of his fork and his pork chop, succumbing to excessive pressing, went airborne. The fork made a loud screeching noise as it skidded off the porcelain plate, whilst the pork chop he was attempting to cut went sailing over his arm and shoulder, landing plumb in between the breasts of the big-bosomed lady at the adjoining table.

Rohan was petrified, the damage seemingly irreparable. Other guests, attracted by the sound of Rohan's screeching fork and the volatile and highly audible reaction of the big-breasted lady, looked on in amusement. They smiled broadly, too well mannered to laugh outright, pretending as far as possible they hadn't seen or heard anything out of the ordinary. The big-bosomed lady, after initially screeching through chock and indignation, was now uttering choice invectives. The servile waiter in charge who had witnessed everything hurried to settle the matter and hush up the incident. He offered the distressed woman a million pardons and supplied her with fresh paper tissues to clean her slightly soiled cleavage, looking discreetly away as she did. Not knowing quite where the meat chop came from, the enraged victim glared around at the other restaurant guests, hoping to detect the culprit and to seek some sort of retribution, even give the offender a very resounding, unladylike slap. Her fellow guests diplomatically averted their gazes, making it impossible for the victim to identify a culprit or even form a suspicion. The small boy in the next table was shooting glances at her, but he had done that before a couple of times, seemingly staring at her bosom in a very interested and un-small-boy-like manner. No, it couldn't be him, she reckoned. He seemed far too young to have been eating such a big piece of meat. As for his curious glances, she put it down to a child's natural curiosity. An unusual event had happened, and the child, behaving like a child, couldn't help but stare, she erroneously concluded.

Primrose sat frozen still throughout the sudden commotion caused by her nephew, fearful as to how Giles would react to the situation. She sincerely cared for Giles but was aware of his hot-tempered nature and his apparent open contempt for her family. However, and to her great surprise, her anxiety proved gravely misplaced. Giles did not seem in the least bit ashamed, nor did he appear vexed in the tiniest bit. He appeared totally unconcerned that a future member of his family had committed such an embarrassing faux pas, slipping up crudely in elementary dining etiquette. His reaction was a revelation. Unlike the other discreet and well-mannered guests, he simply roared out in laughter until the tears rolled downed his rather chubby pockmarked cheeks. Neither Primrose nor Rohan had ever seen Giles like this before, rendered speechless by the spectacle.

The doctor was a quick-tempered man, true enough, but he was in no way a snob – nor was he a bad human being. Under his gruff manner and openly rude demeanour was, indeed, a strong sense of humour, as the family were also to discover as the years rolled by and their acquaintance with him deepened...

'The meat was not meant for throwing, nor is it a flying saucer, boy,' he said, his laughter subsiding, but still grinning and chuckling as though he couldn't quite forget what had happened.

'That was an interesting target you were aiming for, boy. You're trying to get hitched up already?' he asked Rohan whilst winking broadly at Primrose, who was extremely mollified over the sporty way Giles seemed to be taking it all...

Rohan squirmed uncomfortably in his seat, staring with rigid eyes at the napkin on his knees. He was ashamed of himself and dared not look up directly at Giles. The aristocratic continental count had slipped up badly, and there was no place to hide.

The code of the sons of Rainier and Rebecca had been tainted. Raconteurs in the family would narrate again and again the tale of the flying chop well into posterity so that they could roar in laughter. Even so, and despite his growing discomfort, Rohan could not but help think at the same time that Giles was not such a bad chap after all. He shuddered to think what his cruel uncle Oswald would have made of such a situation.

Rohan was generously given a fresh chop and a new fork by the waiter in attendance. The furore done with, the trio went back to the business of serious trenching. They ate with cracking appetites, Rohan pausing now and then to steal a quick glance or two at his fellow diners at the tables around him. Apart from his victim, the lady with the big bosom, who was still darting occasional accusing looks of angry reproof at those around her, everyone seemed to have settled down. Dessert was subsequently called for and by the time coffee was served, Rohan found himself very sleepy indeed. It was long past his usual bedtime, and the combined effect of the rather long film, the rich food, and the trauma of his flying chop contributed greatly to his drowsiness.

Giles paid the bill, tipped the waiter generously, and, together with Primrose and Rohan, walked out to the parking lot where his car was. The three drove home in comparative silence. The last thing Rohan noticed was Giles's free hand sliding around Primrose's neck whilst the other expertly manoeuvred the car's steering wheel. He fell soundly asleep...

Rohan awoke conveniently when Giles pulled up in front of Grandmummy's house. He was still sleepy, but his hearing was sharp enough to overhear what was going on in the front seat.

'Here, Primrose, I have a gift for you,' Giles said, his rough and deep voice booming out as he produced a small package from his breast pocket.

'Oh, Giles, you shouldn't have,' bleated Primrose. Inwardly she was quivering with excitement, wondering what the present could be.

'Open and see what it is.'

A rustling of wrapping paper was heard before the opening snap of a clasp on a box. An exclamation of wonder was heard from Primrose. 'Oh, Giles, why, it's a ring! It must have cost a lot of money!' She repeated, 'You shouldn't have.'

'Shouldn't have? This is an engagement ring, Primrose. I want to get married to you this year. First, you must come and see my parents. That's fixed soon enough. Then, we must fix a wedding date. You *will* marry me, eh?'

'Oh, Giles!' Primrose bleated for the third time. 'Of course I will marry you. You're the only man for me.'

'That's settled it, then. You better tell that mother of yours as soon as possible. We can settle the other details later.'

The abrupt proposal and its prompt acceptance over, Giles got out of the car and opened the door on Primrose's side for her to get out. Rohan roused himself sufficiently to open his side of the car, got out, and sheepishly thanked Giles for the evening before going inside. Giles kissed Primrose goodbye and drove off.

The household were already sound asleep as Rohan and Primrose made preparations to retire for the night, each lost in their own thoughts. Primrose had hoped the others would be awake so that she could announce the wonderful news of her engagement, but resigned herself to wait till morning. She was quivering with excitement, tossing and turning on her bed a good while before finally falling asleep.

Rohan suffered no such qualms. He fell asleep instantly on his mattress, dreaming of pork chops and salad forks coming alive and chasing him around and around the Chinese restaurant, followed by the angry lady with the big boobs sprinting closely after. Giles was in the dream too, cheering on and roaring with laughter.

The next morning was a personal triumph for Primrose. She showed immense exultation announcing the engagement and Giles's plans for an early wedding. The engagement ring was displayed over and over again and was greatly admired by the entire household.

Grandmummy was tickled pink. At long last, one of her children had pulled off the big one – the major heist she had always dreamt of. She could now proudly boast a doctor in the family baggage. It was a grandiose feather in her cap. She beamed cordially at Primrose the whole day, purring like a contented cat. The whole family were in good spirits that day, even Rebecca, who momentarily forgot her troubles. Primrose did not mention the incident of the flying pork chop to anyone. She didn't want *that* particular incident or anything else to diminish or outshine the news of her engagement. Mentioning it would have taken considerable gloss off her own triumph and shift a good deal of focus onto young Rohan.

Rohan set off after breakfast in the direction of the Nameless to do his dog-bathing chores. He usually bathed Strangefellow on Saturdays, but preparing for his dinner chaperoning duties had come in between. His belated arrival did not bother Sonny too much, although he did wonder where the boy had got to the day before.

It was past ten in the morning when Rohan showed up. Most of the breakfast-eaters had already eaten and departed. Of the regulars, it was only Catnips, Uncle Pongo, and Benjy who were present. Sonny offered Rohan breakfast as he always did on the days the latter came over to bathe Strangefellow. Rohan accepted despite already haven eaten the paltry breakfast that his miserable ten cents could buy. He excused himself for not turning up on Saturday morning, explaining the reason for it, and then proceeded to describe the events of the previous day in detail to a very attentive proprietor of the Nameless.

A hopeless gossip and busybody, Sonny loved nothing better than listening to the goings-on of all those he knew and even those he didn't, seeing how much he was confined to the Nameless nearly all week round with precious little time left over for socialising. Whatever free time he had, he usually spent frolicking with some woman or other, courtesy of his promiscuous lifestyle. Catnips, Uncle Pongo, and Benjy, who weren't sitting too far away from Sonny, couldn't help overhearing all of what was being said. Rohan took great care in describing the visit to the posh Chinese restaurant, but he warily kept out the incident of his flying pork chop. He knew that Sonny was always interested in other eating houses and restaurants and would be absolutely thrilled to hear a first-hand account of the doings at the famous Chinese establishment. He was well armed...

'It's a big place, Uncle Sonny, with large ceiling fans over each table and big statues of them Chinese dragons and funny-faced lions all over the place, and they have a big fish pond on a side by the wall, with fat goldfish swimming in it. There was a fountain, too! Right in the middle of the dining area, with a dragon spitting out water from his mouth.'

Sonny listened in open-mouthed fascination sighing hopelessly after Rohan had narrated all. How he longed to have such a restaurant! Whatever would those Chinese fellows come up with next, he mused – ceiling fans, fish ponds, fountains, dragon statues, and the likes, all in the confines of a blooming restaurant?!

'What did you order to eat, Rohan? Those posh places have all fancy names for food and stuff.'

'I ordered a mixed grill from the menu, Uncle Sonny,' replied Rohan importantly, a pompous overtone creeping into his voice as though he had read the whole menu card and had chosen the mixed grill himself. 'It said on the menu card that the dish had pork chops, beef slices, chicken, sausages, vegetables, and roast potatoes – and oh! They start you off with soup and salad. It was written clearly on the menu. There were lots of different forks and knives on the table, and as *you* know' – here, he fired a conspiratorial look at Sonny as though they both shared some sort of superior acumen in dining etiquette – 'one has to decide which fork and what knife to use for them different food they keep bringing you all the time.'

The words gushed out in a torrent. Sonny didn't quite know about the 'different forks and knives' Rohan had referred to at the end of his narrative, but he was very much taken up by the boy's apparent knowledge of the types of cutlery to use – additionally deeply impressed by the young fellow's ability to read a whole menu card. He immediately formed a new respect for Rohan from that moment onwards – not that he did not respect him before, but he hadn't realised the depth of the boy's abilities. The lad would go far, he reflected, maybe become an even bigger success in society than what his disgraced father had once been – poor man!

'How much did it all cost the doctor?' asked Sonny, turning the conversation from aesthetic dining to high finance.

'Oh! I don't know exact-like, Uncle Sonny. I only saw him leaving behind a five-rupee tip for the waiter after he had pulled out a big bundle of currency notes from his wallet and paid up.'

Rohan had that 'continental count' air about him again as he spoke, the very same he had at the Chinese restaurant before his pork chop went airborne. He also deliberately exaggerated the bit about the 'big bundle of currency notes'. The five-rupee tip, however, was indeed true, as he did see Giles leave behind the money.

Benjy, the xenophobic one, chipped in sourly, 'Bah! Five whole rupees! I can eat for four days with that money! And tell me why do we need to eat them pork chops and blooming beef slices and things? There's nothing better than our old Victorian rice and curry with them tasty fried fish and preserved lime pickle. It's tastier, it's healthier, and it costs just sixty cents! In any case, you don't know what them damn Chinese fellows use for meat. Old Fernando at the municipal council's meat stall told me the other day that them Chinese chaps never come over to buy meat from him or from anyone else at the market stalls! Never, he said! Where the devil do they get their damn meat from, eh? Now *that's* what I'd like to know!'

Catnips, who had said nothing as yet, spoke up. No discussion was concluded without some bombastic comment or other from the mercurial mischief-maker, and he didn't disappoint this time around either. 'I hear them Chinese chaps are secretly killing crows and using the meat as chicken in them noodles and things, and the rascals also chop up and use snails and things! I'm sure it's all snail flesh in those blooming soups of theirs! You see any small pieces of snail floating around in that soup you drank, Rohan, small heads with them little pin-like horns they have?'

Uncle Pongo protested this scandalous reputation-buster, thinking it all a bit too far-fetched. 'Bah! You always take things too far, Catnips. There's no proof about those crows and things, and besides, Chinese chaps don't eat snails. Its them Frenchy fellows that's the snail-eaters. Old Petrus, the cook at the parish church, says that Father Clement imports dried snail flesh from France and that the old priest himself has to prepare it. Father Clement wanted to show Petrus how to prepare the snail flesh, but Petrus was having none of it. He flatly refused to handle or even come near the dang-blasted vile stuff.'

Catnips wasn't put out by Uncle Pongo's talk of proof and all that. It all sounded pure poppycock to a genuine anarchist like himself. 'Huh! It's all very well for you to talk, Pongo. And, yes, thank you very much, but I *do know* all about old Father Clement and his horrible damn snails. But you can't deny people talk about them Chinese fellows, you know! It's not only me who says the rascals are slaughtering crows. Ask anyone at Jellicoe Junction! They all know about it. And another thing – why aren't there any crows in pecking sight around them Chinese fellows' dustbins outside on the street? Why is that, may I ask? Crows are very clever birds, you know! Maybe they keep away for a reason. Maybe they know from experience that those grinning Chinese devils are waiting to pounce on and slaughter them all!'

Perhaps there was something of veracity in what Catnips said. There was a nasty yet persistent rumour purporting that the smaller Chinese restaurants (there were quite a few at Jellicoe Junction) did indeed surreptitiously kill and serve crow meat as a substitute for chicken. Nobody knew if the rumour had any substance or if the Chinese restaurants were stealthily traduced by vicious nationalists. Municipal health inspectors who made surprise checks at all restaurants never once found a shred of evidence to confirm the wild claims, yet, on the other hand, a few inspectors were notoriously surreptitious and prone to taking bribes. Surreptitious inspectors or not, people talked and, as Sonny hinted in his next comment, there perhaps was some truth in the matter after all.

'You know, chaps, I can say just one thing as a restaurant owner.' (Sonny smirked in self-importance as he titled himself a 'restaurant owner'.) 'I can say but one thing. I don't want to bring down a fellow businessman,' he said, smirking again, 'but just tell me how them smaller Chinese restaurants at the market square can sell chicken noodles with lumps of chicken flesh for such low prices? We all know the damn high price of chicken! I've eaten at Poo Ping's place once, and he charged just one rupee for my chicken noodles with plenty of chicken pieces in it! And Fat Phuc and Fook Sook charge ten cents more – or so they say – at their restaurants at the market square.'

The conversation, fanned by Sonny's rather vindictive input, went on, back and forth, with signs of it turning into a lengthy discussion. Rohan left the debaters and went over to the outhouse tap near the banyan tree to tend to Strangefellow's bath, the breakfast-eaters' discussions ringing in his ears. The talk about crows and crow meat being used in Chinese restaurants was food for thought. Rohan, who hadn't heard the nefarious rumour before, decided that he just had to have a long talk about it with Salgado at school the next day. Maybe his fat friend could clear up the mystery and shed some light, he mused. If ever there was anyone who knew things about food, restaurants, and eating houses, it was Salgado.

The matter of young Meena's flashing episodes came to an unexpected and abrupt end, to the everlasting disappointment of the two voyeurs, Catnips and Milkfellow.

One day, Mr Fazal, having forgotten some important office documents at home, hurried back unexpectedly in the afternoon to retrieve them and saw for himself what was going on. Both Catnips and Milkfellow were so engrossed in the live cabaret on display that they didn't see Mr Fazal's looming presence until it was too late.

A lot of people took Mr Fazal for granted, but he was no fool. The little scenario enacted before his very eyes flabbergasted him. He knew instinctively it must have been enacted many times before and that the louts at the gate had witnessed it multiple times. Although a respectable man of a mild disposition, he reacted with a fury completely alien to him. He took his folded umbrella in a firm grip and literally horsewhipped the sex-struck duo with it, chasing them a good many yards down the road – no mean feat for a middle-aged man who had scarcely had any decent exercise the past twenty years. Milkfellow, much more agile than Catnips, got away with a few body blows, but Catnips felt the full front of Mr Fazal's attack, even being struck on his right ear with the umbrella. Luckily for him, the folded umbrella served as a sort of cushion, reducing the force of the blow and possibly saving him from a burst eardrum and severe injury.

Nobody knew what transpired between Mr Fazal, his daughter, and his wife, but a few months later a wedding took place at his house. He had pulled his daughter out of school (she was a mediocre student anyway) and arranged a marriage between her and a young man from within their own ethnic community. The wedding was a grand affair, magnificent, picturesque, and full of pomp and extravagance – exactly in line in with what Mrs Fazal had always dreamed of. There were many wedding guests, and the cars parked outside on the pavement that day were unusually large in number. Rohan and Mahan had a field day observing and commenting on the parked cars. They were most impressed that there wasn't a single old car amongst the lot. Even Giles's new Austin paled in comparison to the stately hunks of metal that caught the eye. Grandmummy was not invited; neither were Rebecca and the children. Primrose and Celeste were favoured with an invitation, but Grandmummy firmly put her foot down and forbade them to attend, despite Celeste's fiery objections.

The newly wedded Fazal daughter eventually moved out of her parents' and into her new husband's home on the north side of Portopo, quite a distance away from her parents and Jellicoe Junction.

The two voyeurs, deprived of their wonderful source of free entertainment, soon forgot the whole affair, although Catnips had to seek medical aid for his ear injury, which he nursed for a full week. They talked about it for a while, though, and spent a good many hours discussing and dissecting the whole incident, each voyeur having something different to say. The general consensus, however, was that they both had a rollicking time enjoying the sight of Meena's exposed genitals.

Of course, Catnips and Milkfellow couldn't keep their mouths shut for long, and soon the story of Meena's misdemeanours spread amongst almost everyone in the immediate neighbourhood to Grandmummy's great delight and Mrs Fazal's horrified chagrin. Grandmummy wallowed about blissfully in the shaming of her rival's family, often raising her voice in the kitchen area, where the walls dividing the two houses were at their thinnest, pretending to be discussing the whole sordid affair with a make-believe guest. Meena's name would come up often. On occasion, Grandmummy would maliciously pretend to warn an absent Primrose and Celeste of the dangers of behaving like Meena, strewing more salt into Mrs Fazal's wounds. Grandmummy immensely enjoyed this glorious opportunity to vindicate and torment her 'enemy' with the colossal weapon fate had so kindly provided her. At long last, after years of feuding and constantly being on the losing side, she had scored magnificently. It was something to crow about for years to come in their never-ending feud, a wonderful weapon – an enchanted sword. Poor Mrs Fazal could do nothing but suffer in silence. She kept a low profile. Not even the happiness of her daughter's grand but hasty wedding could hide the fact that she had lost face – quite a lot of face.

Mr Fazal pretended not to know or hear anything, although he was shaken by the whole experience for a long, long time afterwards. It was only after the appearance of grandchildren that the stigma of what had happened slowly disappeared for the Fazals, Meena included. In retrospect, she was thoroughly ashamed of her adolescent behaviour and went red in the face whenever she was reminded of her misadventures. As luck had it, her new husband never got to know of her 'exposures'.

Grandmummy's unequivocal success did not stop with the shaming of the Fazals. She also made it a point to pass on information of Primrose's forthcoming nuptials to influential neighbourhood gossips and anyone with whom she was on the slightest nodding terms. As a result, and in a short time, the neighbours came to know of the coming liaison between the Englishwoman's daughter and the doctor. As expected, this boosted Grandmummy's status even further in the eyes of her neighbours, Mrs Fazal excluded. A doctor in the family was something quite unheard of, unparalleled in neighbourhood chronicles. Some of the closer neighbours, like Baking Jane, plied young Rohan and Mahan with questions about the young doctor, questions the boys answered as well as they could. Rohan, especially, gave out quite a lot of details (all exaggerated, of course) to Baking Jane, who absorbed it all with absolute delight. He loved talking to Baking Jane, his intended wife-to-be. The longer he talked, the longer he could stay.

It was like their conversation a short while after Primrose's engagement. 'Heard that Dona's [Grandmummy's] younger daughter has gone and got herself a doctor fellow,' opened Baking Jane.

'Yes, yes, Aunty Jane. Him and Aunty Primrose are going to be married soon.'

'Really! Getting married already? Goodness me! So we're going to have a doctor living with us in the neighbourhood, then!'

'Ahhhh! I don't think he will stay with old Grandmummy. He's got some fancy house somewhere else and will take Aunty Primrose to live there after they get married and all that.'

'Oh!' said Baking Jane, a tad disappointed there wouldn't be any free or convenient medical consultations going a-begging. She continued. 'What sort of doctor chap is he? Is he any good, or is he like those useless damn humbugs down at the gormant [government] hospital?'

'Tchah! They say he's very good,' said Rohan, lying through his teeth, not really knowing much about Giles's medical acumen. He brightened up a bit though, recollecting Primrose's appendix adventure. 'He cured Aunty Primrose of her appendix thingie and has a huge black bag with medicines in it and all that. He also has a brand-new car, so he must be a really good doctor fellow.'

'Ah! Appendix, eh! That means he must be an operating chap,' smirked Baking Jane knowingly, not slow to share *her* acumen on the subject. 'You know, the kind that opens up people's chests and stomachs and fixes the tubes and thingies inside. So that's his speciality, eh! Just imagine that! An operating fellow in our very own neighbourhood! Old Bellakay told me last week when we were discussing the horrible state of our wretched gormant hospital that them operating chaps are called *sir-Johns* [surgeons].'

Rohan was momentarily stumped by Baking Jane's seemingly vast medical knowledge. He didn't quite know what a *sir-john* was, but he had a faint recollection that the school nurse had mentioned something similar when the boys at school were given a lecture on health and hygiene. The school nurse had carefully described various medical professions, from a GP down to a *surgeon*. Rohan went along with what Baking Jane said. If Bellakay said an operating chap was a *sir-john*, then it just had to be true. The old gentleman never lied. Rohan answered, 'Yes, yes, he's a *sir-john* fellow, all right. That's what he is!'

Baking Jane, relieved by this confirmation, continued to chat. 'Ah! That's really good, young sir! If one of us gets any of that dangerous appendix thingie, then we can ask Dona or your aunty Primrose to get your doctor chap to do the cutting and things. It's better *he* does it than those blooming jackasses at the gormant hospital. You know those rascals nearly killed old Mrs Plim once? They went and cut her up for something and left behind a small scissor in her insides. Poor woman went to several private hospitals to find out why she was still in so much pain until they finally found the scissor after those *ax-rays* [X-rays] or something they'd went and done on her!'

Baking Jane, who had already made out Rohan's order, had quite forgotten to make a parcel of it, distracted with her ramblings about Giles's medical acumen and Mrs Plim's unfortunate innards. Remembering quickly, she pulled herself together, hastily wrapped up the order, and handed it over to Rohan, who paid up and left, a tad reluctant to do the latter. He threw a final glance at Baking Jane's voluptuous body, making a mental note to have a longer conversation with her the next time around so he could stay a little longer.

CHAPTER 6

Member of Parliament

Sing a song of sixpence. A pocket full of rye.
Four and twenty blackbirds baked in a pie.

INSIDE A LARGE ROOM AT the abandoned railway station where the 'twilights', or rather the prostitutes, at Jellicoe Junction conducted business, the tall, stately, Amazonian Rooney tried her best to freshen up after her client had paid and gone his way. She had charged three times the usual price for having coitus with him without a protective rubber, something she did once in a while, knowing fully well the risks involved. It was the standard price that the twilights charged for unprotected sex, although a growing number of Rooney's fellow professionals refused outright to perform coitus unless customers wore a condom – the steady rise of venereal disease in Portopo a troubling cause. Condoms, a new method of birth control, had become very popular amongst Victorians a few months back and were even distributed free, courtesy of international health organisations operating on the island.

Drying her genitals as best as she could and wiping her bulging, sweaty breasts, Rooney put her knickers into her handbag, dressed quickly, and hightailed it to the red zone near the Ritzo Cinema and the De Luxe Hotel. Here on a street corner in a depilated building, the twilights collectively paid rent for a small flat, which they used to shower and refresh themselves in between servicing customers. Rooney showered vigorously, glad to get rid of the smell of her last client, who in fact had a pungent body odour besides appearing quite slovenly. Inside the shower whilst scrubbing herself, she turned over in her mind a master plan she had hatched for abandoning her line of work for something quite revolutionary and entirely respectful. She had long since cast her eyes on the abandoned railway station at Jellicoe Junction, wanting to convert it into a housing condominium for the many homeless souls who lived there, and partition off a section for a private spa and health centre for herself and her sisters-in-trade to own and run. Nobody knew the denizens of the abandoned old station as well as Rooney did. There were ways to reintroduce them into society and respectability, but this would require a new and strong political ally – someone who could wrest the station away from the parties battling for its legal ownership and thereby pave the way to attaining her goals. She was waiting for a saviour, a new entrant into the political arena, one whom she could cooperate with to put her plans into action. Perhaps that new firebrand from the Nameless might be a good option, she reflected, her thoughts shifting to Bellakay, who, against all odds and amidst great surprise, had become a candidate for third MP at Jellicoe Junction in the country's forthcoming general election.

One clear, fine morning found Bellakay and Uncle Pongo ambling along as usual on their way to the Nameless, the humble little microcosm that was their regular breakfast destination for so many years. It was quite possible to take a bus the short distance to the shanty eating house, but neither of them did. It was healthy to ambulate, but it wasn't a primary factor influencing Bellakay's and Uncle Pongo's decision to walk. Going about on foot was born out of necessity rather than choice since they could rarely afford bus fares. Walking together leisurely and seemingly engaged in pleasant conversation, they appeared to be very much at ease in one another's company. Both friends enjoyed a bromance of sorts, despite their having distinct and completely different personalities. Uncle Pongo, though extremely poor and living on the bottom rung of the local social ladder, was gregarious, the essence of buoyancy itself, whereas Bellakay, as poverty-stricken as his friend, was definitely (except when lecturing his fellow breakfast-eaters at the Nameless) the most stoic person one could ever hope to find at Jellicoe Junction. Another glaring difference between the two men was that Bellakay, a social rebel, firmly believed in a laissez-faire sort of doctrine, something that Uncle Pongo didn't give a toss for.

Irrespective of their differences and lifestyles, Bellakay and Uncle Pongo did share at least one unshakeable trait: neither of them was avaricious in the least, although both certainly would have welcomed a pot of gold with open arms if they ever found one or rather more realistically, a few more coppers to boost their meagre incomes. Bellakay was unemployed not by choice, and was on the brink of being a true destitute, at times barely managing to feed and clothe himself – often mistaken for a common tramp. Uncle Pongo, in contrast, was a tad better off. He was employed as a security man, or, as the good people of Jellicoe Junction called the profession, a 'watcher', at a large mercantile establishment. It was a job on the lower rungs of professions at Jellicoe Junction, one which inevitably paid a pittance. There was nothing in Uncle Pongo's appearance that could even remotely suggest he was in the security profession. No one in their wildest dreams could ever associate him with guarding life and limb, let alone property! His dapper mannerisms together with his frayed but rather spruce-looking clothes cast him more in the mould of a Wodehouse character than anything else – a sort of older Ukridge!

Bellakay and Uncle Pongo's breakfast rendezvous at the Nameless was a daily occurrence. They were looking forward to it enthusiastically, longing for the eating house's simple yet cheap and tasty food, the rough day-to-day banter, and the pleasing aftermath of being able to lounge under the huge banyan tree a stone's throw away from the eating house. The tree's protective beard-like foliage offered a wonderfully cooling lee from the hot tropical sun. It was a miniature haven, a place ideally away from the madding crowd for those seeking its magnificent sanctuary. Sonny would have loved to put up a signboard for the eating house, but erecting one would only serve to invite immediate attention and trouble from the municipal council authorities, seeing that he possessed no licence to run his business. Nor did he own the land around it.

Now and then, a well-meaning municipal council sanitation inspector would raid the Nameless along with a crew of paid labourers who would methodically demolish the rough shanty structure, razing it to the ground. This did not bother Sonny too much or deter him from continuing his illegal business. Apart from the obstreperous barking protests of Strangefellow, neither Sonny nor any of his clientele interfered with the inspector's demolition job. Sonny usually stationed himself a few yards away from the wrecking crew, hands folded across his chest in pretended sublimation as he patiently waited for it all to be over. The inspector had a sort of understanding with Sonny and didn't do too much damage, not that there was anything much of value to damage. The rough boards, mud-plastered wooden walls, poles, and pieces of plywood that made up the fragile structure, together with the thin corrugated metal sheets that was the roof, easily fell apart with a minimum of effort. Through the passing years, by trial and error, Sonny had learned to rebuild his little structure in easily detachable sections which could be fitted back into place with a minimum of effort.

The inspector's demolishing crew had simple instructions to see that the structure was not standing upright any more – and nothing else. The wooden walls weren't crushed or broken up, just loosened in their detachable sections. Even the rickety old chairs, tables, and benches weren't pummelled or destroyed, but were unceremoniously dumped in a heap by the banyan tree, alongside everything else. It took Sonny just a few hours to rig the demolished construction together again after the inspector and his wrecking crew had left. He was quite used to it, expertly putting the pieces together again like a gigantic jigsaw puzzle, knowing exactly where each detachable section and other diverse building materials should be placed. If the material, in spite of the wrecking crew's caution, was too badly damaged, he would improvise and use other building paraphernalia he kept hoarded in a heap by the outhouse. Sonny was often helped by Uncle Pongo or Bellakay in his rebuilding endeavours. Small cracks in the wooden wall sections would be refilled with mud and straw and then plastered over smoothly with an additional coating of mud. When it had all dried off after a few days, the walls would be whitewashed, making the surface glisteningly white and clean.

The only article of any proper value at the Nameless was the three-gallon boiler that was used to have constant boiling water ready for making tea. The inspector's demolition crew, following his punctilious orders, purposely kept the boiler intact whenever they raided the Nameless. Sonny always heaved a sigh of relief once the wrecking crew gently lifted the boiler to a safe area in the clearing beside the banyan tree before moving on to the actual demolition job on hand. There was an unmistakeable air of déjà vu over the regular demolishing and rebuilding; the process repeated several times over the past few years. As for the sparing of the boiler, it was not a deed even remotely connected to feelings of empathy. The inspector was rumoured to accept bribes from his 'victims' for not causing too much damage on his demolition excursions, and Sonny did pay him a small retainer for sparing the boiler. Government officials in Victoria were a poorly paid lot and were not averse to making a little money on the side. The inspector was no different from others.

Bellakay and Uncle Pongo had to walk by the municipal council's power station en route to their rendezvous at the Nameless. The power station was a bit obsolete – one of the first of a batch that were built in the city after the introduction of electricity to the island. Apart from the building itself, there were a good many cables, giant transformers, and other electrical paraphernalia inside the station, all much antiquated in comparison to the modern power stations that had mushroomed all over the country in later years.

Approaching the power station, the two friends pinched their noses and partially covered their mouths with their handkerchiefs to lessen the terrible stench hovering over the station and its immediate vicinity. An awful, revolting smell of putrefying flesh made everyone passing by quicken their pace considerably to get away from it as fast as they could. The more sensitive retched, unable to bear the awful smell.

Portopo had an abundance of crows, and for some strange reason a huge number of them had decided to make the power station their home. It was a sort of colony, a short flying distance from the city, where they would maraud for food. Many liked to roost on the exposed electrified metal cables stretching back and forth between the station's ancient, enormous transformers. Others built nests in convenient nooks around the transformers and other electrical equipment within the vicinity, serenely unaware they were inches away from a swift death. The rest paired off in nests in the huge tamarind trees that grew outside the fenced-off station. Inside the fenced area, a good many unfortunate birds were quite frequently mortally electrocuted and fell to the ground to rot as they lay. As and when a bird fell, the rest of the flock would start to caw and clatter in ceaseless unison, mourning their fallen comrade's demise. The terrible, obstreperous racket would go on for a good fifteen minutes or so, after which the infernal funeral rites would abruptly cease, the birds calmly reverting back to their daily lives, to all appearances and purposes no longer perturbed by their dead companion lying on the ground below. The crows never seemed to learn that roosting on, or nesting in, particular nooks near the electrical wires and cables was a dance with death.

There was another strange phenomenon concerning the crow population. It appeared that the area outside the fence enclosing the transformer equipment and buildings, apart from being a home and breeding ground, was also a sort of final resting place for the birds. They flew over from all over the city when sensing their mortal lives were about to come to an end through old age, but also when very ill from terminal disease. They came to die – a wheel-of-life thing – the young crows building nests inside the station and in the surrounding trees outside to ensure posterity, whilst the old and sick flew over to end their mortal days.

Once a month or so, a municipal council maintenance crew cleaned up the area within and outside the station and buried the corvine corpses in shallow graves a short distance away from the surrounding mesh-wire fence. The stench around the power station was a permanently vile one all the year round.

Elections for a member of Parliament at Jellicoe Junction (and other constituencies in the country) were fast approaching, and the community's political parties and independent candidates were in full swing in preparation for the event. The air bustled and crackled as never before with high-pitched febrile activity.

Jellicoe Junction was a fairly large electorate and had three seats in the offing. Normally, it was just the two mainstream political parties that stood a chance of winning the first two seats – the third usually an intense battle amongst the top-rung independent candidates. Apart from the two main political parties and independent candidates, another group consisting of local crackpots and fanatical amateurs threw in their lot, joining the fray. They formed their own political parties, often registering them with colourful and bizarre names. This year's crop was no exception, the names ranging from downright silly to utterly incomprehensible. The list was long, and some names were more absurd than the others. Glaring examples were the Wise Solomon Party, Freedom from Starvation Party, Red Blood Party, Abolish Slavery Party, Lime Pickle Party, No Knickers Party, and the Anti-Colonial Vegetarian Party. There was even a party in honour of the much loved Victorian national sport (cricket) – the Abolish Leg before Wicket Party! Even amongst the independent candidates, a few names raised an eyebrow – Doctor Crippen standing out prominently.

The names made no sense. The Freedom from Starvation Party, for instance, seemed quite a ridiculous name, as nobody really starved at Jellicoe Junction or, for that matter, anywhere else in the whole country! Then there was the Abolish Slavery Party, whose founder was known to be a keen student of early American history – immensely fascinated by the slavery issues of the American South. Slavery was alien to the people of Victoria, since its practice was never known to have taken place in the history of the country, not even during the Dutch, Portuguese, and British usurpations. The Red Blood Party was another connondrum. Many scratched their heads in wonder over the name. Bellakay, the acknowledged sage of the Nameless, was an irritated critic whenever the subject came up in the many debates and arguments during the morning breakfast sessions. He would contemptuously dismiss the party in a testy manner. 'Bah! Blooming nitwits! We all have red blood, don't we? What are these nincompoops hoping to achieve, eh? Who on earth has anything but red blood? If we're white, brown, or black – or even yellow like them grinning Chinese chaps that sell them damn-blasted cheap false teeth at Sir Francis Drake Street – we still all have blooming red blood! You chaps ever heard of people with green or black blood?'

The breakfast-eaters at the Nameless nodded wisely at Bellakay's aggravated lamentations, although Catnips couldn't resist a pun. 'Maybe them Red Blood Party chaps are all secret vampire fellows, you know, drinking blood and all that, like in that new *Dracula* matinee we saw at the Empire Talkies last week. You know, the one with that Christopher Lee chap.'

The assembly all guffawed loudly at Catnips's frivolous comment.

The breakfast-eaters, keen movie enthusiasts and regular patrons of the nearby Empire Talkies cinema hall, made it a point never to miss a horror film – vampire films especially – which they both loved and dreaded at the same time. They were ardent fans of Christopher Lee, the British actor who usually played the part of the demonic, bloodsucking Count, often debating amongst themselves if the actor was a real-life vampire or not. The *Dracula* films scared the living daylights of them, but they boldly put their fears aside and rushed to see the bloodthirsty vampire's gruesome adventures whenever a new film or even a rerun was screened. They were thrilled by the films, yet were terribly apprehensive afterwards for long, long periods. Right now, despite their mirth in the aftermath of Catnips's quip, they struggled inwardly to shut out the terror and mental image of the gruesome bloodsucking Count from their minds.

The breakfast-eaters were not unlike their fellow Victorians in their fear of all things connected, even remotely, to the dark powers. They were superstitious to the core, almightily afraid of ghosts, goblins, spirits, devils, vampires, and the like. Mercurial Catnips, especially, although never a man to back off from a jolly good scrape and who was often involved in drunken brawls at Ali Baba's toddy tavern, was the worst of the lot. For several weeks after seeing the very first *Dracula* movie screened at Jellicoe Junction, he had gone around with a sizeable crucifix around his neck, which he had somehow or another obtained from somewhere – no mean feat for him, especially since he was not known to practise the Christian faith. Additionally, and to be doubly sure the bloodsucking Count wouldn't enter his house, he had strewn a bunch of garlic pods together and hung them outside his front door. He hung a few more above his window in his kitchen – just in case – and as an additional precaution, took to sleeping with a lighted oil lamp beside his bed and a hefty double-bladed axe beneath it. There were times that entire month after seeing the film when he positively reeked of garlic upon entering the Nameless, causing Sonny and the others to shrink away in revulsion.

Election fever had hit Sonny and the rest at the Nameless, hit them really hard. The breakfast-eater's palavers – always hot and steamy – increased in sheer boisterousness as Election Day slowly inched closer, week by week, day by day.

Bellakay would come out of his shell during election time like a colourful butterfly emerging from its drab cocoon. He transformed into something of a grown-up enfant terrible, taking a break from his usual antigregarious ways to eagerly join in the conversation whenever the election was discussed. At the close of the breakfast session, Bellakay would proceed to make gurgling sounds from his throat as though clearing it. It was the much-dreaded start signal that he was about to give a speech, serving admirably well as an early warning system. The wary assembly, filled with apprehension about what was to come, hurriedly left the confines of the Nameless and hightailed it into the open clearing outside or underneath the banyan tree to be left in peace. Undeterred by these traitorous tactics, Bellakay would proceed with a fiery analysis of the current political doings at Jellicoe Junction, completely uninvited and completely uncalled for. Although a thin and wiry sort of man, Bellakay had a cavernous voice, and whenever he fired off one of his political speeches, it magnified several degrees above audible – even heard by the harried breakfast-eaters outside.

Normally and for the major part of the year, the breakfast-eaters respectfully accepted Bellakay as a very clever man, one having a scripted panacea for any problem or question. They would often turn to him to settle disputes or to seek his advice on a myriad of matters, but during the run-up to the local elections they remained most circumspect, endeavouring as far as possible to keep out of his way. Whilst light banter was much loved, always accepted, and was the regular order of the day, heavy political speeches at the drop of a hat were not always welcome or uplifting to the rough-and-tough breakfast-eaters, especially so early in the morning. Unfortunately, they had very little choice in the matter for like it or not, Bellakay would deliver his morning speeches. Nothing anyone said or did would deter him from spouting his mind-blowing rhetoric. A few bolder ones asked him quite curtly to shut up, whilst the odd violent one or two would even threaten him with bodily harm, but to no avail. The old warrior, streetwise and used to living on his wits, had, over the years, developed into a man of unbending steel. He was totally unafraid of physical combat, never willingly backing off from a fight. The violent ones, faced with the possibility of being counter-attacked, sulkily withdrew after a few moments of nervous staring. Physical combat, so early in the day and just after a hearty breakfast, wasn't to their liking. They usually muttered multiple obscenities and backed off. The lesser aggressive ones – the ones who asked Bellakay to shut up – also eventually put up with the nuisance, grudgingly paying him some attention in between smoking a cigarette or drinking an extra cup of tea.

On one occasion when nothing failed to stop Bellakay's post-breakfast speech, which on that particular morning had an even more annoying clang to it than usual, Uncle Pongo tried a more diplomatic overture. He had indulged heavily at Ali Baba's toddy tavern the evening before and was suffering a throbbing headache and a right royal hangover.

'Bellakay, old man,' he opened sheepishly, interrupting Bellakay's speech. 'We all know you're one hell of a clever fellow! Why, you know so many things you're maybe the most learned man in the whole of Jellicoe Junction! We *know* you can make one hell of a politician – what with all your talk of that Marx chap and all that – but we've still not started the day, you know! We just got up from our beds, dear fellow – just finished our breakfasts! All of us just want to relax, think over things, enjoy a smoke, or have a cup of tea, you know! Maybe you can continue this speech of yours later on in the afternoon, eh! Most of us come in for tea, you know! We're wide awake then, old chap!'

The long-suffering breakfast-eaters muttered in assent after Uncle Pongo's long statement, looking on hopefully at Bellakay with puppy-like pleading eyes.

Bellakay cocked one ear and listened carefully to what his good friend had to say, but he didn't find any of it reasonable or acceptable.

'Bloody lazy devils,' he thought to himself. 'Just got up from their beds, indeed! Why, I myself have been up since four in the morning! How these fellows could sleep away most of their time, God in heaven knows! Small wonder that most of the damn lazy lubbers can't find any decent work!' (He conveniently forgot that he couldn't find any 'decent work', either.)

Uncle Pongo's long appeal did not have the desired effect. Bellakay gave his close friend and the assembly a crushing look and went on stubbornly with his irritating ramblings. A defeated Uncle Pongo put his hands up in despair and walked out of the Nameless to repose in solitude under a special spot beside the banyan tree, where Bellakay's ranting was still audible but slightly diminished. Many of the others who had also been at the drinking session at Ali Baba's the previous evening followed suit.

It wasn't everyone, though, who was vexed by Bellakay's pre-election rhetoric. True, the morning's protesters at the Nameless were large in number, but there was a growing bunch of local dissidents at the little microcosm and elsewhere who had taken Bellakay to heart and really did understand the gist of his utterances. Thoroughly displeased by what they considered to be a government that did nothing to improve their lot, they secretly gloated whenever Bellakay mentioned phrases like 'the dirty rich', 'the capitalist merchant class', 'the filthy aristocracy', 'the downtrodden masses', the 'rotten banking system', and other inflammatory denouncements. They didn't quite understand much of Bellakay's excerpts from Marx's famous dogmas or the classical Greek philosophers' citations he regularly quoted, but they did understand, and did identify themselves with, many of the harsh situations of day-to-day life that Bellakay so effectively painted on his volatile verbal canvas. Bellakay spoke for *them*. He was 'their' man and was much admired, although they dearly wished he would abandon his Charlie Chaplin-like clothes in favour of dressing like a normal person.

Bellakay had another secret admirer. This was none other than Rooney, leader of the twilight brigade at Jellicoe Junction. The Amazon had listened to Bellakay in full flow on numerous occasions down at the market square (Bellakay's favourite oratory spot) and other prominent places, and had become a staunch fan. Like most of the downtrodden, Rooney was hoping for a shift in the political arena, but she had a secret agenda of her own, one she was ready to unfurl if things went her way.

Even Sonny was a secret admirer, thoroughly dejected like the others over the many atrocities the incumbent government was either directly responsible for or had cunningly orchestrated through various unscrupulous means. He had a very special bone to pick with the banks, especially. Over the years, Sonny had tried to borrow money from several prominent banks in order to open a genuine restaurant, without success. He was steadfastly refused and in no uncertain terms often even thoroughly bawled at by irritated bank officials for even daring to ask for a loan. Sonny's present establishment, the Nameless – an illegal structure in addition to being an unlicenced business venture – didn't do him any favours with the bank officials, who knew all about his 'business'. Permanently bereft of a bank loan, Sonny hated the banking system, his hatred spilling over even to successive governments that controlled the banks.

Around this time, a rather peculiar American was seen hanging about the neighbourhood, frequently engaged in earnest conversation with several locals. He was a gangling, grey-haired, middle-aged man who, it seemed, was making an intensive tour of the city, visiting and checking out government institutions, housing conditions, banks, and other important places and matters. An aura of benevolence radiated from the stranger, who seemed well disposed to all alike. He appeared to be a philanthropist of sorts too, prioritising visits to the poorer areas in the city, where he would stop and chat with people for hours on end, even giving generous cash handouts to a lucky few. Nobody knew why the American did what he did or whom he represented. Some thought he was just a kind-hearted foreigner who liked to help the needy with his little cash donations, whilst others reckoned he was an agent for an international social institution that provided him with carte-blanche funds to further their causes.

By chance and in an extraordinary twist of fate (as later events would reveal), the American visitor stumbled upon Bellakay in full swing, giving a fiery speech at the bustling market square near Galahad Street. When the mood took him, Bellakay could and did speak perfect English, this in strong contrast to his fellow Victorians, who were disposed to a rather sing-song-like approach to the Queen's tongue. The particular speech at the street corner was duly heckled by the impish youth who hung around the market square – always on the lookout for mischief, especially whenever Bellakay was involved. Bellakay, as was his wont, remained unperturbed by the heckling except when it got far too personal and vociferous for his liking, at which point he paused to hurl a series of quick ripostes at his juvenile detractors. Despite the intervening altercations between the warring parties, the American was greatly impressed by Bellakay's delivery. Standing under the convenient shade of a nearby shop's veranda, he seemed almost rooted to the spot, fascinated by the depth, content, and delivery of the scarecrow-like orator's speech. It had a profound and monumental effect on the visitor. A great admirer of Cicero, he appeared stunned, spending a good five minutes after the speech was over in complete immobility, turning over and over in his mind the remarkable address he had just heard. By the time the American recovered, Bellakay had already vanished into the shadows.

At the area around the Ritzo Cinema, Rooney was in close conversation with a fellow twilight who had just come out of the general hospital after being successfully treated for severe internal injuries caused by a horrific gang rape she had been on the receiving end of recently.

'Glad to see you well again, my dear! Don't worry about a thing! We shall all give you something to send home this month so you don't have to rush back to work. You must give time for your injuries to heal properly. Never fear, I have a plan for those bastards who savaged you. They will regret it till the day they die, and so will their blooming boss – especially him! I have plans for that fine-feathered fellow too!'

'Be careful, Rooney. Please be careful. That boss chap is a big-shot politician, you know, and has a whole heap of dirty thugs working for him! They're a dangerous lot.'

'Bah! Politician or no politician, I'll fix the bugger good and proper. Don't worry your pretty little head about that! Just take it easy now and lie low.'

The 'boss' the women referred to, a certain Mr Hazimudoo, was a powerful politician belonging to the incumbent government's party. Hazimudoo, a noted lecher, had contracted the injured woman for his pleasure, but after he had finished and done with her, had cruelly left the young twilight to the mercy of his thugs for their carnal pleasure as well. They had repeatedly raped the poor woman in an orgy of coarse, violent, and painful sex.

Rooney was not one to let harm done to her or any of her sisters go unpunished, always seeking revenge in some form or other. Sometime later, all the culprits who had taken part in the gang rape fell mysteriously ill and were admitted to the toxic-poisoning ward at the general hospital. All of them appeared to be suffering from severe groin problems, the doctors nonplussed by it all. It was rumoured that Rooney had visited the stricken men in hospital whilst they were in the nadir of their affliction, smiling sweetly and doing an excellent Florence Nightingale act. The suffering patients had no idea why she visited them but were very uneasy and wary of her presence. When news of their affliction and Rooney's angelic hospital visit got around, heads wagged knowingly. They all knew what the Amazon was capable of. Stopping short of actual murder, she was capable of just about anything. Her father, a reputed warlock back in her native village, had initiated his young daughter into the mysteries of the dark side, even making regular forages with her into the thick forest around the village to gather strange and little-known roots and herbs. A month later, all the gang-rapists were discharged from hospital, outwardly and to all appearances cured, but remaining impotent the rest of their lives.

A week later after Bellakay's speech at the marketplace, a fat, rather well-set police constable made a brief appearance at the Nameless astride an official black police bicycle. With an expert sway of his large torso, he swung one foot over the bicycle's front frame and dismounted. The breakfast-eaters, jolted by the sudden appearance of the long arm of the law, looked suspiciously at him. Strangefellow gave off a round of shrill warning barks directed at the stranger from his high perch on the banyan tree, putting Sonny, who was momentarily distracted with something else, on guard. Strangefellow didn't like the police who weren't always nice to him or his canine brethren down at the marketplace and elsewhere. Besides, he knew for sure that Sonny and the breakfast-eaters disliked them too, loyally trusting his human companions likes and dislikes implicitly. He skimmed down expertly from the banyan tree and 'greeted' the constable with an additional round of fierce barking, prancing around madly – snarling and snapping dangerously close to the lawman's fat legs and ankles – no danger to the intended victim, since they were firmly encased in standard-issue heavy police boots and knee-length woollen stockings. Keeping a wary eye on the dog, the constable looked around himself in a disdainful, aloof sort of manner. He didn't like what he saw... The sullen and hostile eyes of the breakfast-eaters, who without exception had all experienced a few brushes with the local constabulary, pierced him, causing his earlier aloof manner to disintegrate into one of profound wariness. He didn't like the looks of the present company, and the feeling was mutual. Putting on a stern face, he drew up his large torso into a forbidding posture and addressed the breakfast-eaters. 'Which one of you fellows is Don Peter Pintoo?' asked the lawman in a deep, booming voice.

The breakfast-eaters looked around nonplussed. They knew each other fairly well, but the name Don Peter Pintoo didn't ring any bells. From his corner at the bench, farthest away from the entrance, Bellakay stirred uneasily in his seat. He gave a surprised muffled verbal acknowledgement.

'Tchah! That's me! That's my name. What the devil do you want with me, eh? Can't we free citizens even eat in peace without your lot harassing us?'

'Who the devil's harassing you?' the constable responded heatedly. 'I was only asking if a certain Don Peter Pintoo is here or not. That sound like harassment to you, eh? Can't a fellow ask a simple damn question?'

Bellakay snorted gruffly at this logical reply but said nothing.

The lawman took a closer look at Bellakay and decided on the spot that this very oddly dressed fellow looked even more suspicious than the rest. 'What an unkempt-looking scoundrel!' he mused. 'A first-class criminal, no doubt, that's for sure. Better keep a careful eye on this one in the future!'

'Anyway,' continued the lawman, still gazing unpleasantly at Bellakay, 'there's this American gentleman – the chap who is wandering all over the place here at Jellicoe Junction – who wants to meet with you at the police station tomorrow at eleven o'clock. He will be coming with some forms and papers that he wants you to sign. It is some sort of offer he wants to make you. God only knows why!' He paused to look even more distastefully at Bellakay. 'What the damn offer is, I don't know. Our inspector made some inquiries and said I could find you here. The inspector ordered me to contact you and inform you to be present tomorrow. The American chap said it will greatly benefit you, so you better make sure you are there!'

After delivering this thunderbolt, the constable hurriedly took off on his bicycle, having other errands to run. In any event, he did not want to linger longer than necessary amongst what he considered to be an out-and-out suspicious and dangerous-looking lot, especially that odd criminal chap to whom he had just delivered his message and that damn-blasted dog with his incessant barking and snapping at his legs.

Strangefellow, who had many scores to settle with the local constabulary, gave the departing lawman a few ferocious parting barks before retiring to the safety of his high perch, still giving off small half barks of displeasure at the enemy's departing back. He had earlier on lifted a furry hind leg and urinated on the constable's bicycle whilst the latter was busy delivering his message – an act that pleased the tree-climbing canine no end.

An eerie calm descended upon the breakfast-eaters. Nobody stirred or spoke as Bellakay and the entire company slowly digested the lawman's surprising news in stunned silence for a minute or two. Once the reality of the information had sunk in, a babble of frenzied discussion exploded.

Although there were ambiguous theories about the American's reason for his strange summons, a popular school of thought amongst the breakfast-eaters was that Bellakay, by some strange twist of fate, was a legatee of sorts and that a small fortune had been bequeathed him courtesy of the philanthropic American.

Bellakay himself, although outwardly straining to be calm and collected, was for once in his life truly rattled and taken completely by surprise. Who on earth would offer *him* anything beneficial? he reflected. All his adult life, people had been taking one stab at him or another, and being treated like a pariah, especially in recent years, seemed almost a lifetime sentence. Besides, how on earth had this American fellow heard of him? Surely it had to be a mix-up of sorts? A case of mistaken identity? Or was it? His mind twirled around and around like a tornado to find a possible source for his sudden summons, without much success.

Sonny took the lead for the assembly and proceeded to speak with great authority on the subject of inheritances and fortunes, the breakfast-eaters listening in rapture, savouring every word he said. They had good reason. Many years ago, when an orphaned Sonny was just a small child of eight, an American tourist had wanted to adopt the little boy. Alas! Things went wrong. Responsible officials bungled, wrong forms were filled, and a whole crop of other irregularities emerged, resulting in the intended adoption plan's falling apart and disintegrating. The American tourist, terribly disappointed, went back home, but not before leaving behind a modest trust fund for the boy, bequeathed to the care of an uncle the child lived with. The uncle, a well-known philanderer and drunkard, duly embezzled the trust fund through unscrupulous means, the money vanishing within a few months' time. The story was told and retold amongst the locals.

Over the years, the trust fund had been elevated to a considerable fortune, and the American tourist, a woman of modest means, had been promoted to the status of a multimillionaire – an heiress with unlimited funds at her disposal. Right now, spurred by his own experience in matters of inheritances and the like, Sonny spoke up. He was in his element.

'I'm telling you, Bellakay,' he said, addressing the still-dazed and dumbfounded sage. 'I'm telling you, my good man, this just has to mean something big for you. If it is that same American chap who's been wandering all over the bloody countryside that's gone and done this thing, then he must have left you a huge damn fortune! These Americans are like that, you know! They fancy some fellow or another and then go and leave the lucky bugger a whole pile of money. I'm telling you as a friend – a good friend – you better be at that police station tomorrow and cash in the chips, old boy, or you're sure like hell going to miss out on a damn fine thing.'

The breakfast-eaters, to a man, murmured in assent, nodding their heads affirmatively at what Sonny had just said. In light of the latter's appropriate past, they considered him an expert on the subject of fortunes and inheritances. The acknowledged expert's words of advice sounded fitting and solid, very, very fitting and very, very solid.

Bellakay, however, wasn't convinced. Despite Sonny's confident prediction, he couldn't help feeling uneasy, a sliver of malaise creeping up his spine. For years, he had lived in a state of total nihilism – a condition thrust upon him – and his many moneymaking ploys had not gone down too well with the constabulary. He positively detested the idea of presenting himself to any authority at the police station, nor did he relish bandying words with one as high up as a police inspector – fortune or no fortune. Fortunately for the homespun sage, fate intervened in the guise of Uncle Pongo. His dapper friend, sensing Bellakay's fear of the long arm of the law, offered his protective services. At crucial times, Uncle Pongo had an uncanny knack of being able to read what went inside his best friend's mind. They had been together through thick and thin, and nobody knew Bellakay in and out as Uncle Pongo did.

'I think I'll join you tomorrow, Bellakay. It will be good if you have someone with you in case that police inspector or the American chap wants a witness or something,' said Uncle Pongo diplomatically, putting it as best as he could.

'Yes, yes, let Pongo go with you. Old Pongo's not easy to fool, and you sure will need a good man at your side,' added Sonny knowingly. 'I would come too, but who will run the old café when I'm away, eh!' he added, a proud smirk lighting up his bearded face when dubbing his rough eating house a 'café'.

Bellakay gratefully accepted Uncle Pongo's offer, much relieved by the prospect of his good friend joining him, although he remained apprehensive about the whole business. The impending visit to the police station continued to worry him – a bit less than before – but it was a nagging worry nevertheless, one he couldn't quite put out of his head.

Sadhu, the incumbent holy man who secretly believed in pantheism but outwardly appeared to embrace and practise all faiths, was amongst the gathering when the portly police constable had made his dramatic appearance and exit. He was dressed as usual in a saffron-coloured robe, a good deal faded from constant washing and exposure to the gruelling tropical sun. Around his scrawny neck hung a necklace of dried rudraksha seeds, harvested from *Elaeocarpus ganitrus* evergreens, pierced and strung together expertly with strong yellow thread. A true ascetic, he lived in great austerity, his only meal for the day being breakfast at Sonny's.

Sadhu had remarkable prescience, a gift he used carefully, never wanting to upset anyone or raise anyone's hopes with his abilities. He also had a genuine knack for reading people's thoughts, especially those of the rough-and-tough clientele at the Nameless, whom he consorted with every day at the breakfast sessions. Sensing Bellakay's reluctance to keep his appointment at the police station, Sadhu spoke out from his corner, everyone pausing to look up in deference as the holy man began. At this time in the morning, he was sans the little arrow he otherwise 'wore' pierced from cheek to cheek, enabling him to eat, drink, and talk in a normal fashion. Sitting at the long table and facing the open window, his face bathed in golden sunlight, he looked exactly like a silvery-haired saint in a biblical holy picture, the sunlight giving the impression of an aureole hovering over his slender person.

'It is karma, my dear Bellakay. It's karma. The great lords of the universe have spoken, and it is your destiny to see this American man. Do not go against the lords' wishes or it will go bad for you. The great ones have summoned, and you must obey,' he warned, wagging a bony finger at Bellakay.

Bellakay looked around himself wildly after Sadhu's little speech. He thought of making a bolt for it and hiding away somewhere the next few days where nobody could find him, but he decided against it. It would be quite impossible to face his fellow breakfast-eaters again and look them in the eye if he did. Besides, a strong inner voice kept hammering in his head, telling him in no uncertain terms not to rebuff the overture. 'Perhaps it really was a sort of summons from a higher power, or karma, as old Sadhu put it,' he mused, his agnostic leanings ruefully disliking the notion that such powers could, and did, exist.

The next day found a somewhat shell-shocked Bellakay and the dapper Uncle Pongo at the local police station a good forty minutes before the agreed appointment time. Uncle Pongo had decided to come a good hour early just in case, shouting down a protesting Bellakay, who didn't quite like Uncle Pongo's early bird tactics.

The police station functioned in a converted old British mansion by the seafront, one historically used as an official residence by a host of bygone British governors. It was an English manor-house-like structure, imposingly large and solidly built. Huge open arches, typical of most old buildings in Portopo, were a feature of the front veranda, which also happened to be the coolest room in the entire mansion caused by gentle zephyrs blowing in and out through the open arches.

Inside the mansion, the original hall and large rooms had been partitioned into smaller offices and interrogation rooms, and at the very back, where the former kitchen used to be, the walls had been reinforced with special concrete and sectioned off into a few detention cells, where the less fortunate were incarcerated a few days prior to coming up before a judge.

Bellakay, with beads of perspiration on his brow and trying very hard to master his natural fear, had come dressed as he usually was, although he had refreshed his bizarre wardrobe somewhat. He was attired in his standard frayed clothes, but wore a freshly washed white shirt, and had patiently cleaned the spots of dirt from his much-used tie. His perpetual Charlie Chaplin-like coat and thick woollen trousers had been carefully folded and pressed under his pillow before retiring the previous night. Despite his efforts, he still looked decidedly odd, and those present at the station gave him searching looks, arching their eyebrows somewhat upon beholding the spectacle.

Uncle Pongo, on the other hand, was as spruce and dapper as ever. He was dressed in a well-ironed corduroy trouser and a neat white shirt. Just for the occasion, he had put on an ancient bow tie that had been in his possession for many years, an heirloom from his younger days. He too wore a coat, but unlike Bellakay's thick woollen affair, it was a fashionable one of light flannel – a favourite he reserved for important functions like weddings, Christmas Mass, and sometimes the odd funeral.

The duo presented themselves at the reception desk to a burly-looking sergeant in charge and after their names were duly checked and confirmed in a large appointment ledger, they were given curt instructions to take a seat in the veranda and wait their turn until they were called up.

The veranda seats were already occupied by all sorts of people who had different matters to settle at the station. Some were clutching forms for registration of vehicles, forms for obtaining driving licences, notices of eviction, and whatnot, whilst others were present to make official complaints of a criminal nature. More often than not, the opposing party featured in the complaint would also be present, starting the disputes all over again. The desk sergeant and another constable kept a careful watch over the proceedings, not hesitating to use their heavy batons on the obstreperous if things got overheated, as they more often than not did.

The veranda was certainly not a peaceful waiting room to be in, and Bellakay was more than relieved when Uncle Pongo suggested they move over to the surrounding garden, where they could still be within earshot and hear their names being called up.

'Better we wait outside, Bellakay. Them chaps in the waiting hall are getting on my nerves with all their dang-blasted chatter and arguments.'

Bellakay nodded in agreement, although it worried him they would be to be too far away from the bawling desk sergeant to hear his name when summoned. 'I hope we can hear that damn sergeant fellow when he calls out my name; otherwise, we may miss the appointment, you know.'

Uncle Pongo snorted with feeling. He didn't share Bellakay's anxiousness in the least. 'Tchah! Man! Can't hear, you say? Why, the way that blooming sergeant keeps trumpeting like a damn elephant, you could easily hear his voice at the next bloody junction! We'll hear him, all right. Anyway, I don't see any sign of the American chap, so he hasn't arrived as yet. Them police fellows can't call us in until he comes. He's the big shot figuring in all this, isn't he?'

'Yes, I suppose you are right, Pongo. Let's wait and see when he comes. A millionaire fellow like that is sure to come here in some big fancy car, and the only place to park it is behind that police car at the front portico. We'll know when he arrives.'

A good five minutes later, a large limousine pulled into the driveway and parked, as anticipated, behind the police vehicle. A liveried chauffeur opened the door on his side of the car and then stepped out smartly to open the passenger door. Bellakay and Uncle Pongo looked on with interest as a tall, elderly man disembarked. The new arrival looked around him with an air of inquiry before stepping into the bowels of the building. Neither Bellakay nor Pongo had ever actually seen the American on his tours around Jellicoe Junction, but they concluded that it must be the man himself and no other. A few minutes later, the sergeant in charge at the reception desk bellowed out sternly. 'Number twenty-three, Don Peter Pintoo. Number twenty-three, Don Peter Pintoo.'

Uncle Pongo, unfamiliar with Bellakay's real name, did not respond at first to the sergeant's loud summons, having quite forgotten the name that the fat constable had used when visiting the Nameless to summon Bellakay. He quickly remembered, though. Bellakay's agitated facial expression upon hearing his name called out was more than enough to jar Pongo out of his temporary memory lapse. The two men presented themselves promptly at the front desk, and, on the instructions of the burly sergeant, a somewhat beleaguered-looking Bellakay and a jaunty Uncle Pongo were instructed to go to a particular section of the building, where they were received by a bailiff and quickly ushered into one of the better interrogation rooms.

Inside, the chief inspector was already seated in the company of the American, to all appearances, engaged in very amiable conversation. The chief inspector was smiling, seemingly in a relaxed sort of mood, whilst the American, completely at ease, was leaning back on his chair with an air of complete satisfaction, a look of benevolence written all over his wrinkled, suntanned face. They looked up keenly as Bellakay and Uncle Pongo entered the room.

'Ah,' said the American, his face lighting up at the sight of Bellakay. 'Glad you could make it, sir. I had the privilege of hearing you speak at the street corner near Galahad Street the other day, and I must declare that was one heck of a speech, mister!'

His greeting over, he shook Bellakay's hand, gesturing him politely to sit. The inspector nodded briefly at Bellakay, looked once Uncle Pongo's way, and then settled down, allowing the American to do the talking. Uncle Pongo's presence didn't cause a stir, the American nor the inspector reacting to his presence. It was not unusual for persons summoned to come along with a family member or a friend. There was no chair for Uncle Pongo though, but he didn't mind in the least bit – the watchful bailiff thoughtfully bringing in an extra chair a minute later.

'I will come directly to the point, Mr Pintoo. Dexter is my name. I am a professor of political science at the University of … (here, he mentioned the name of a prominent university in the States), and I am also a trustee of the J. J. Brooker-Straton Fund, which I am sure you must have heard of.'

Bellakay recognised the name of the university but hadn't the foggiest notion who J. J. Brooker-Straton or his fund were. Normally cautious, he had shut his vocal powers to a standstill, deciding to speak only if necessary. He was still filled with the same malaise he had at the onslaught of the whole business, more than a tad in awe of the events taking place around him. The sight of the chief inspector in his intimidating khaki uniform and shiny black pistol partially jutting out from a well-polished leather holster attached to his belt didn't help much to ease his natural distrust and fear.

'Yes, yes,' continued the American, beaming amiably. 'The J. J. Brooker-Straton Fund seeks out laudable politically engaged socialists around the world who want to improve the lot of the common man. We endeavour to advance their political careers by financing election and other campaigns whenever possible and if necessary. I heard your excellent speech the other day, sir, and I was deeply impressed by the clarity of your convictions, the theoretical pureness of your quotes, and your conscientious feelings for the lesser fortunate. It was masterful! I have also made some discreet inquiries about you – pardon me for that – after which I telegraphed the society in New York. On my recommendation, they have decided to pay your deposit and cover the costs of a forthcoming election campaign, that is to say if you decide to run for member of Parliament for the Jellicoe Junction constituency. If you win, we will then offer further financial help to promote your socialist cause. If you lose, we will stand the costs of your lost deposit and reimburse all your election expenses, so you won't be left short either way.'

The last part of his statement was said in a most anxious tone – genuine and not superficial, yet silkily projecting a clear message: 'Do not rebuff my overtures. Take my offer, for it is one you will never get again in your life.'

Bellakay, dumbfounded, digested Mr Dexter's news. He was flabbergasted, stupefied, yet wonderfully exhilarated – all at the same time. For years he had yearned to contest the local elections, but the large sum of three thousand rupees the deposit required was always far beyond his meagre means. He couldn't even raise *two* rupees on any given day! As matters stood, his was indeed a lost cause, but here suddenly, like a bolt from the blue, was a chance in a million! A complete stranger was offering to pay for an election campaign and was even ready and willing to forgo the deposit money if it should come to that! Not only did the American make such a stupendous offer, but he even seemed most solicitous that it be accepted! It all sounded too good to be true. After what seemed an eternity to a nervous Uncle Pongo, but in reality took only a few seconds, Bellakay condescended to reply. He spoke out in flawless English.

'Sir, on behalf of the suffering masses, I accept your generous proposal and place myself at your service to contest the seat. If I win, I will be at Your Worship's and the esteemed society's service at all times. You can rely on me, sir.'

The American smiled. 'No need for thanks, and no need to call me "Your Worship" or anything like that, my good man. We international socialists must stick together, you know! I will make the necessary arrangements through the banks to pay your deposit. The good inspector here will act as my witness and also help you in contacting a suitable lawyer, if you need such a service at any time during your campaign. You must, however, immediately and in our presence sign these papers that I have brought with me, which the society needs to set the wheels in motion.'

He turned and looked keenly in Uncle Pongo's direction before continuing. 'I see that you have brought an associate with you, Mr

Pintoo. That is good because we will need the signature of an extra witness.'

Uncle Pongo bridled with pride at having being referred to as an 'associate'. He hadn't the foggiest idea what an associate was supposed to do but deduced that it had to be something jolly important.

The American continued. 'You will also need the services of a good campaign manager – someone whom you can trust implicitly. Er, perhaps this associate of yours, eh?'

Bellakay didn't need the American's hint. He had no doubt in his mind who should be his campaign manager! Intervening promptly, he promoted Uncle Pongo to high office on the spot. It was not a precipitous act. Uncle Pongo was, alongside Sonny, the only person whom Bellakay really trusted. He couldn't think of anyone more suitable to run his campaign than his best friend. He formally introduced Uncle Pongo to the American for the first time.

'My associate here is Mr Adrian Pongo. He's a man of sound character and intelligence, and the most trustworthy man I know. His knowledge of local politics is immense. He will be my official campaign manager. I know he will do a perfect job, sir.'

The small matter of a pre-discussion with the proposed campaign manager and obtaining his consent did not occur to Bellakay.

Uncle Pongo, thrilled by his sudden appointment to high office, found it hard to retain his composure, but managed somehow to keep a straight face. He was much taken up by Bellakay's complimentary introduction – especially the 'sound character and intelligence part' – immediately squaring his bony shoulders and assuming an expression of superhuman intelligence.

'Ah, yes, yes, I see that you have things well under control. I am sure Mr Pongo will make an excellent campaign manager. Good, good, good,' said the American, nodding favourably Uncle Pongo's way.

The papers the American had brought were duly signed by both parties, the inspector and Uncle Pongo signing immediately afterwards as witnesses. The American instructed Bellakay to present himself at the Peoples Trust Bank, at Master Merrill Peavey Street near Coronation Park, the next day, whereupon, after presenting his identity papers, the deposit for the local election would be paid in the presence of the American and the bank officials. The American hadn't quite finished, though. He had some parting information that jolted Bellakay and Uncle Pongo quite a bit.

'I am staying at the Grande Hotel by the seafront, gentlemen. I would like to see you both there this evening around sevenish for cocktails and dinner. I shall be most pleased to be your host. You will come, I trust?'

The very mention of the Grande Hotel caused Bellakay's and Uncle Pongo's knees to wobble. The picturesque hotel was one of the most famous in Victoria and renowned around the world. Only elite foreigners and the highest in the land walked its proud corridors and dined inside its majestic halls and afternoon-tea rooms.

Uncle Pongo answered shakily for the duo. Demurring didn't seem an option, not now, not after all the American's generosity. 'What! Er, Grande Hotel, you say, eh? Er ... yes, yes, yes, of course we will be there, for sure, Mr Dexter. We *will* be there, sir.'

'Good, good, good,' said the American again. 'I'll expect you around seven, then. Ask for me – Conrad Dexter – at the reception.'

All matters at hand amiably settled to the mutual satisfaction of Bellakay and his benefactor, they shook hands again before going their separate ways. The American said he would be in the country a few more weeks and would be greatly interested to hear Bellakay speak again before he left for America.

A slightly shell-shocked Bellakay and Uncle Pongo made their way to the Nameless for a spot of tea and to digest the happenings at the police station in an ebullient state of mind.

The breakfast assembly, in the meantime, were anxiously waiting after the morning meal for news of what had transpired at the police station, glancing hopefully now and then at the top of the pathway leading to the eating house for a glimpse of Bellakay and Uncle Pongo. At long last, close on midday, the duo made their entry and were immediately greeted with gargantuan enthusiasm. Even Strangefellow, who normally didn't bark when regulars arrived, woofed a good many welcomes, as though sensing a special occasion. Salutations were exchanged as everyone waited with bated breath to hear what the old warriors had to report. Bellakay didn't say a word. He appeared bemused – in a nebulous state of mind – hardly noticing the quizzical, almost appealing, looks of his buoyant companions. It was left to debonair Uncle Pongo to relate the events of the morning, and this he did with a great sense of pomp and drama. A natural showman, he couldn't resist spicing up the morning's events a great deal as he rambled on.

'Ahhhh! Chaps, we did meet the American fellow! Rich like hell, the bugger is! Had a whole heap of them dollar notes bulging out from his pockets. And that inspector! My God! What a terrible man, boys! He had a whip in his hand, and his eyes were bloodshot like that terrible Dracula fellow! Had a nasty temper, too! Not a man to be trifled with, lads! Lucky for old Bellakay that I was around to control the beast.'

The clientele at the Nameless listened in open-mouthed incredulity as Uncle Pongo told his story. Nobody dared interrupt until he finished his much exaggerated account of events. Afterwards, an awed silence reigned for a full minute or two as the group allowed the bulk of the information to sink in. After what seemed an eternity, the eerie lapse in conversation – unnatural by Nameless standards – was broken by a triumphant Sonny.

'Ha! What did I tell you chaps, eh? Did I, or did I not, say the American fellow would leave old Bellakay here a fortune? Didn't I? Didn't I?'

He looked around fiercely, daring anyone to contradict him. The news of Bellakay's benefactor and his elevation to election candidate had them all tongue-tied. It was unprecedented, an undreamed-of occurrence. In retrospect, they *did* recollect Sonny's having predicted that Bellakay would be in for an inheritance of sorts.

Sonny continued, emboldened by the present company's silent

acknowledgement of his prediction. He was at his impetuous best, an inspired Cicero addressing the senate!

'It's all up to us now, fellows! It's all up to us now,' he thundered. 'We must put our thinking caps on and help old Bellakay here win this election. Bellakay has got the American fellow's backing and, most importantly, the money! No need for *us* to worry about expenses and the like. Once he gets elected and becomes a big-shot politician, all the wrongs we suffer under this dang-blasted government of ours can be put right at last.'

He spoke as though it was a foregone conclusion that Bellakay would win, Euphoria running away with him – galloping wildly. The rest of the clientele nodded vigorously at Sonny's comments, approval written all over their faces. To a man, nursing grievances and petty grudges against the incumbent government, they saw Bellakay as a genuine saviour who could usher in a new era of justice – a man who spoke for *them*.

Bellakay saw himself a saviour too, recollecting all the injustices he had borne just to eke out a living. His inability to secure employment despite his obvious intellectual qualities; the abuse, humiliations, and insults he had to bear to make a little money; his constant brushes with the police – all burned a hole in his head. His recent visit to the police station gave him fresh food for thought, a sense of *priority* for reforms in a *descending* order. If elected, he would start his term in office by reforming the police department. Yes! That's what he would do first. After that, he would introduce legislation to curb all the damn religious mania that consumed and held the whole country in a grip of iron. Secularism would suit the country well, he mused gleefully; time to get rid of religious mumbo jumbo for good, especially those pesky damn monks and priests preaching hellfire and damnation. A good dash of Spinoza's rationalism had to be infused into the masses' way of thinking and make them a more balanced lot, but he would start off with the police – get rid of the most vicious and infamous amongst them! He paused here, scratching his head to think of a new reform, but stopped after a few minutes, deciding a list would do better in case he forgot a reform or two. Yes, he would prepare a long, long list. Like Emperor Tiberius of old, he would make a list of his intended victims – write it all down first thing the next morning on foolscap paper and, after that, draft out a political manifesto. His eyes lit up like a true Machiavellian plotter, his little reverie complete...

A burning concern amongst the breakfast-eaters was the first political meeting Bellakay would have to hold after announcing his candidature.

'We must have a stage and them huge powerful loudspeakers those other candidate fellows rent from Swami Electricals down at the marketplace. Old Swami makes them speakers himself, you know, and doesn't need to buy any of that fiddly-diddly imported rubbish them big-shot foreign companies sell,' said Benjy in his most imitable xenophobic manner.

'Yes, yes. We will need loudspeakers. Bellakay shouts well and all that, but his voice will not carry far enough for the thousands that come to hear him speak,' piped in Trevor, Uncle Pongo's son, who happened to drop by for a cup of tea and listen to the latest gossip. Trevor had just completed his morning shift in the design department at the big shoe factory at Portopo where he was employed as an office boy. His work – running errands, bringing in the mail, and doing other menial tasks for the artistic staff – hadn't anything remotely to do with actual designing, but he slyly induced people into believing he was some kind of master footwear designer. To hear him talk, one would think he was a footwear-designing Michelangelo in the making.

Bellakay, who had kept quite all along, spoke at last. 'Thousands? What bloody thousands, Trevor? You fellows never talk any proper sense – never! How the devil are we going to get thousands to come and listen? Why, only the other day I gave a first-class speech on the need for a socialist revolution at the corner of Galahad Street, and just five or six persons stopped by to listen! How on earth are we going to get thousands?'

'Five or six? My dear Bellakay! Don't forget the stray dogs that hang around that place or that crippled beggar man who always sits at that very corner every single day,' said Catnips sarcastically, trying to bring Bellakay down a notch, jealous of the attention the latter was getting.

The gathering all guffawed loudly at this statement, except Bellakay, who glared in displeasure at the interfering spreader of mirth.

Even old Sadhu, the local holy man, did not quite appreciate Catnips's joke, blurting out in all seriousness, 'Ah, brother Catnips, it's not good that you go and joke about the stray dogs and the poor crippled beggar. It's all karma, you know! Them stray dogs were once human beings in another life, and as for that pitiful beggarman, why, he must have been a rich and evil king in another birth, one who practised great debauchery and cruelty and is thus grimly rewarded in this life. Who knows, eh?'

Bellakay butted in for the second time, peeved by Sadhu's comments about previous lives and karma. He didn't give a tinker's curse for the afterlife, which, he staunchly persisted – quite regularly – didn't exist. 'Bah! What blooming other life! Tell me, good Sadhu, has anyone you know returned from the dead to discuss the afterlife you are always going on and on about? Why the devil you persist in talking about afterlives, I really don't understand!'

The audience turned to Sadhu, hoping for an erudite comeback of sorts. They weren't disappointed.

'My dear friend Bellakay! My dear learned friend, perhaps soon to be MP! Hasten not to judge and proclaim, wise one! You ask me for proof, yet I have none to give. I can ask you one thing, though, if I may. I ask you most humbly, do *you* remember the nine months you spent inside your mother's womb, eh? Day for day? Minute for minute, second for second? You lived even then, didn't you? The world around you lived on too, didn't it? Do you know anything of that time in your life, or even before that when you were a seed in your father's loins? No? I thought not... There are some things, dear Bellakay, that are unfathomable. There are oceans and dimensions one can't cross even with the best ships and the cleverest navigators. There are places and lives we cannot reach or contact from this troubled little globe we live on, yet they exist! Live and learn, my friend. Don't hasten to judge or dismiss. We are all babes in the woods in this mighty cosmos we live in.'

The breakfast-eaters gazed in awe at Sadhu. The latter's reverie impressed them colossally, especially the bit about remembering the occupancy of their mothers' wombs and being seeds in their fathers' lions. It touched them deeply. As for Bellakay, he was totally and utterly stumped – thunderstruck. The all-knowing sage didn't have a riposte worth coming up with. In fact, he didn't have a riposte at all! The aesthetic beauty of Sadhu's words and their endearing philosophical depth touched him deeply. Henceforth, he vowed silently, he would have a revised and more respectful opinion of the holy man.

Karolis broke Sadhu's erudite philosophic spell in an attempt to steer the conversation back to matters on hand. 'Ah! Fellows! Afterlife or not, we must forge ahead with plans for old Bellakay's election. The American is a good start and will do us a whole heap of good. Once them newspaper chaps get wind of his involvement, they'll sure like hell rush off and write about the whole bally thing. That sort of publicity *has* to bring us *some* extra crowd. We must make sure the American is seen with Bellakay as often as possible, and we must inform them reporter fellows, who are sure to take photos and write about it in the newspapers. We've got to use the American well, boys! That fellow is pure gold, and that means publicity. The more publicity we get, the more crowd that's going to come! What do you say, eh, chaps? Surely we can do it, eh?'

The assembly started to see the situation in a new light, everyone beginning to see nebulous possibilities that weren't there before. There could, after all, be a goose for the plucking – a really fat goose.

Uncle Pongo, who was feeling a bit lost, felt he ought to say something to assert his authority. After all, *he* had been elevated to the important office of campaign manager, hadn't he? He couldn't just sit there and say nothing! Itching to speak, he finally hit upon a matter that would save him some face. It wasn't much, but it would do for the moment. He cleared his throat and said in a pretended stentorian voice quite unlike his normally gregarious tone, 'You know, chaps, them other big-shot candidate fellows always have their meetings on Saturdays. We've got to have *our* meeting on a Saturday too. That's the only day our lazy buggers at Jellicoe Junction will lift their blooming arses to go anywhere! We must start our campaign by fixing a date for the first meeting, and it *must* be a Saturday. That's important.'

Uncle Pongo paused dramatically for a moment to look around him. He had intended to stop there, but a sudden epiphany flashed through his mind, spurring him on. By accident, he hit upon a key tactic – one that could change the entire course of action. 'We've also got to find some way to get at least some of them crowds that go to those other chaps' meetings to change their minds and come to ours. We must *lure* them away somehow and make them come and listen to old Bellakay.' (Pongo emphasised the word 'lure' very strongly.) 'A plan – that's what we need, boys! We have to come up with a cunning plan! So put on the old thinking cap and figure out how we are we going to do it, eh!'

The hard-core gang at the Nameless reflected upon Uncle Pongo's telling words on crowd manipulation, wishing they could come up with something and be the hero of the hour. Karolis, the fish vendor, suggested enlisting the services of Fotheringill, a well-known warlock and spirit-exorcist, to cast a rain spell. Fotheringill's rain spells were legendary, especially in sporting circles. Whenever a team was in a losing position in long cricket matches, diehard fans would consult him to perform a rain spell and effectively end the match. The expected rain didn't always come, but Fotheringill did have some modest success.

'I say, fellows! I say, chaps!' Karolis shouted out enthusiastically. 'What if we get old Fotheringill to put one of his rain spells on them other fellows' meetings, eh? Exactly like the one he did for Uncle Pongo at that big school match that stopped the game. If it rains, those other buggers' meetings will all get washed out, won't they?'

The eyes of the faithful plotters lit up joyously at this suggestion, only to be instantly doused after young Trevor's immediate astute observation. 'Tchah! It's no good, Karolis! It's no good at all. We need to hold Bellakay's meeting the same day, the same time. If old Fotheringill puts his blooming rain spell into action, it would rain on Bellakay's meeting too, wouldn't it? You thought of that, Karolis?'

Karolis blushed, crestfallen. He thought he had come up with a brilliant suggestion – distraught to see his hopes dashed to smithereens.

Mercurial Catnips, a silent participant so far, stirred uncomfortably in his place on the long bench by the dining table as though making preparations to speak. He wasn't known only for mischief, outright lies, and distortions of the truth, but also for surreptitious deeds spurred by a keen dose of chutzpah. Often, when not peddling his strange merchandise at the school gate, he spent almost the whole morning and afternoon at the Nameless doing exactly what he wanted: showing off many skills that impressed his fellows no end. He could easily read a newspaper faster than most others, almost always won a game of checkers (except against the incumbent champion, Sonny), and could talk expertly on any subject, although he told a good many outright lies and stretched the truth a great deal. Sometimes he wouldn't turn up at the Nameless or at his spot near the school gate for several days on end, wicked tongues claiming rightly or wrongly that he was otherwise occupied in ganga (cannabis) smoking sprees lasting several days in a row.

Catnips spoke out boldly. 'You know, chaps, there's a heap of stinky old dead and rotting crows lying all over the place around the old transformer power station.'

Catnips's unexpected and sudden talk of rotting crow carcasses surprised them all. It seemed surreal and irrelevant, far detached from matters on hand.

'What about them damn rotting crows? What's it got to do with Bellakay's election campaign? Why the devil are you bringing that up for, fool? You've been smoking them ganga joints again?' asked Sonny testily, irritated by this seemingly useless line of talk.

'Hold on, my dear Sonny, hold on! Don't get excited over nothing, man! I'm just asking you to consider them dead crows for a minute,' said Catnips solemnly, sounding a bit like Jesus on the mount. 'Them dead crows are left to rot near the station, and people can hardly pass that place because the smell's so vile, right?'

'Yes, yes, but what's that got to do with Bellakay's dang-blasted election meeting?' thundered the nonplussed Sonny once again – even more testily this time – a twisted vein throbbing dangerously on his right temple.

'You know,' said Catnips imperially, ignoring the much-aroused Sonny. 'You know, chaps, them dead crows do really give off one hell of a bally stink, don't they? Imagine if those other chaps' meeting places could stink like that, eh! Why, nobody in his right mind would hang around for even five minutes! No damn crowd's going to stay around with a foul smell like that! Who can stand such a horrible stench? Why, it's even worse than old Karolis's stinking oysters that we have to put up with every now and then.'

Karolis, who occasionally sold rotting oysters, looked up sharply in displeasure at Catnips, incensed by this sudden attack on his precious merchandise. He was anosmic and couldn't even imagine how much his oysters stank. 'Bah! Why the devil do you want to drag my bloody oysters into this? My oysters smell, yes, or so they tell me. No good my denying that! You lot know I don't sell them to eat, but you people rush off to buy them, don't you? Didn't you yourself buy ten pounds from me last season to scoop out the rotting flesh and look for them pearls inside, eh? Didn't you? Didn't mind the damn stink *then*, did you? You bloody useless rascal!'

Catnips ignored Karolis. He hadn't meant to start a discussion about the oysters; comparing smells was just a convenient argument that came into his head and nothing else. The breakfast-eaters, though, pricked up their ears at the talk of bad smells. Something in Catnips's manner and his subtle inclusion of the rotting crows in the conversation told them he was on to something – something obviously quite significant. They all knew his mercurial ways only too well...

'How are we going to get them other chaps' meetings to stink?' asked Uncle Pongo, throwing out his hands in exasperation.

'Think, my dear Pongo, think. Use the old noggin, eh! If we can shift them rotting crows to another candidate's meeting, they will stink up the place something terrible, would they not?'

'You mean if we place them rotting crows at them other fellows' meetings?' asked Uncle Pongo, aghast at the thought, but with a thrill of hopeful excitement creeping up his aged spine.

Catnips said, 'Yes, yes, of course! Can't you chaps see? We *can* place them stinky crows in good hiding places. The best meeting to sabotage would be that big-shot independent fellow's meeting. That damn sly fellow and womaniser Hazimudoo, you know! The very same devil who did a jump from the prime minister's party only last month and whose henchmen did that awful thing to that poor twilight – almost killing the woman, I heard! There's sure to be a large crowd for that scoundrel's meeting. If we hold Bellakay's meeting some distance away from his, then anyone leaving blooming Hazimudoo's meeting in a hurry will have to bypass Bellakay's meeting. Isn't that so?'

The candidate Catnips spoke of – Hazimudoo – hailed from a family of Japanese settlers, Victoria boasting a few citizens of Japanese and Chinese ethnicity who had made the island their permanent home many generations ago. Usually in the restaurant business and sometimes even practising dentistry (false teeth, for the most), Hazimudoo had broken fresh ground by becoming a highly successful politician, the first of his ethnic race to do so in Victoria. He was also none other than the person responsible for Rooney's fellow twilight's gang rape, although he had subsequently denied any involvement and covered his tracks well.

'Aha! I see what you've been fishing at now! So *that's* why you brought up them cursed crows! But even if one stinks up Hazimudoo's meeting, his crowd aren't surely going to just stop over and listen to what old Bellakay has to say, are they?' said Sonny, a tad better disposed towards Catnips at this stage than what he was a few moments before.

Catnips was in his element – unstoppable. He seemed to have a scripted panacea for everything this day. 'Won't stop, you say, eh, Sonny! Won't stop? My dear fellow, there's always ways and means to *make* them stop! We just *have* to see that they *do* stop! Once Hazimudoo's crowd starts passing through, we can have free fruit drinks and snacks on hand ready to offer them. That ought to hold them awhile. You know how our fellows are always ready and willing to gobble a free meal! And after that ... well, after that, it all hangs on old Bellakay here. If he gives one of them "first-class speeches" he's always boasting about, then maybe they might listen whilst eating and drinking and even stay on for the whole meeting. It's not impossible, you know! The sight of the American fellow on the podium might also hold them. They might like to hear him talk too. Anyway, that's my suggestion. Why else do you think I brought up the matter of them rotting crow carcasses?' Here, Catnips stopped awhile to get his breath back. His explanations were long-winded, but he hadn't finished yet, not by a long shot...

'Hazimudoo's crowd are sure like hell not going to waste a good Saturday afternoon and go home if his meeting venue smells like excrement. After all, they had come for a meeting, hadn't they? Besides, old Bellakay here is a new candidate. They might be curious to know what he stands for – what his political message is.'

The breakfast-eaters listened right through Catnips's long-winded epistle without interruption. To a man, they were all dumbfounded in the face of this incredulously bold and devilishly cunning corvine plan. It was a far-fetched plan as plans went, but then *all* of Catnips's schemes and projects were far-fetched, often backfiring, but occasionally enjoying superb success. They all knew what an innovative fellow he was, but this scheme of his exceeded anything he had previously come up with. There was, however, the 'small' matter of collecting the rotting crows and doing the actual ghoulish deed – concealing them in undetectable places at Hazimudoo's meeting venue.

Sonny spoke for them all. For all his rough ways and Captain Haddock-like manner, he was the most squeamish person one could find in the whole of Victoria. 'Who's going to transport them stinky old crow corpses and hide them at Hazimudoo's meeting place? I'm sure like hell not going anywhere near that damn power station for any love of gold – so you can count *me* out,' he said, looking around at the other breakfast-eaters for support and instantly getting it.

The rest nodded their heads, turning their gazes away from Catnips sheepishly, avoiding looking at the corvine plan's creator in the eye. They weren't super-squeamish as Sonny, yet none of them fancied the idea of collecting putrefying crow carcasses, either. The smell would be too miasmatic to endure for *any* length of time.

Catnips remained tranquil. He seemed to have everything all worked out. 'Huh! Don't you fellows worry about *that*. I know them homeless boys down at the marketplace very well. Yes, yes, the very same young devils who work there all day! Those boys have done plenty of work for me before, and I can easily get them to do what needs to be done, but it will cost us. Old Bellakay here must set aside a sum of money for their services from that election fund money the American chap has promised.'

The breakfast-eaters, highly mollified *they* wouldn't have to do the dirty work required, gave Catnips their full attention again. They knew all there was to know about the Market Youth Gang. Stopping short of actual murder, the rapscallions didn't have any known boundaries. To a man, the breakfast-eaters heaped rapturous praise on Catnips, a few even thumping him approvingly on his back for good measure.

'What a plan you came up with, Catnips, old man. A cunning fox, that's what you are!' said one.

Another chorused in. 'Where the devil you come up with them

bloody ideas of yours, God in heaven knows! Rotting crows, eh? Whoever would have thought of that?'

And a third, 'Old Bellakay's lucky like hell to have you on his side! He should make you campaign strategist – put you in charge of it all!'

Several others joined in the flow of praise. Sonny even lit a cigarette of a brand he knew was Catnips's favourite, offering it to the Machiavellian plotter free of charge.

Uncle Pongo, the campaign manager, also approved of the rotten-crow plan, but he was seething with bottled-up envy. 'Why the devil couldn't I have thought of it all?' he mused. 'Didn't I pass by that blooming transformer station a million, zillion times in the company of Bellakay on our way to the Nameless each day?'

After further intense palaver, Sonny, Uncle Pongo, Catnips, Karolis, Trevor, Benjy, and the rest of the hard-core gang at the Nameless, including the candidate himself, were 'elected' as the top men to steer the fortunes of the election campaign.

Sadhu gave a spiritual blessing to the election campaign, making a great show of sprinkling water from a brass bowl over the assembly whilst muttering his trademark mantras and chants. For good measure, he rubbed holy ash taken from his little pot onto the foreheads of the assembled, concluding his ministrations. The unholy fact that the recipients of his blessing had connived and approved the sinful sabotage of a rival's election meeting for their own devilish ends did not deter the incumbent saint in the least bit.

Bellakay's election campaign was now, thanks to Sadhu's holy efforts, officially protected by the deities. Nothing could go wrong now, at least in the eyes of the breakfast-eaters. In due course, the core gang at the Nameless became the inner circle of the new political party. Bellakay, whenever surrounded by his loyal party henchmen, would look around him proudly, secretly likening himself to his hero Lenin in the run-up to the October Revolution.

Uncle Pongo retained the title given him by Bellakay and proudly presented himself with unwavering aplomb to all and sundry who crossed his path as Bellakay's campaign manager. He rummaged through his things at home and managed to fish out a worn-out leather briefcase from within a dusty metal trunk, polishing it to perfection with boot polish. The briefcase lacked a proper handle, inducing him to ingeniously construct a rope sling, which he attached to the original metal hoops still dangling on each side of the case. In the coming days and weeks, he would sling the case over his shoulder whenever he went on official business for the new party. The rather crude rope sling notwithstanding, the briefcase did make him look like a manager of sorts, albeit one who seemed to have fallen upon hard times.

Bellakay's party was duly registered and the deposit paid through the good offices of the American. The party was registered as the Anti-Capitalist People's Socialist Red Party. The lengthy name was a result of a compromise after long, drawn-out, ferocious disputes over a suitable name for the infant party. Every single person came up with a favourite name, confident it was the right one to use. Sonny favoured the 'Anti-Banking Workers Party' courtesy of the bone he had to pick with bankers and the banking system. Bellakay opted for a plain-sounding 'Lenin's People's Party' but was shouted down into submission, everyone agreeing the name would only serve to frighten voters – Lenin considered by many an out-and-out scoundrel. Uncle Pongo wanted the word *cricket* thrown in somewhere, which sounded immensely ridiculous to the others, who hadn't the same enthusiasm for the sport as did the flamboyant campaign manager. Xenophobic Benjy, the scourge of all things foreign, advocated an alarming 'Anti-Foreigners Party'. Even others who didn't belong to the hard-core Nameless gang – stragglers who now and then popped in for breakfast or just a cup of tea – put in their two cents' worth. The banter went on back and forth, continuing for at least a few days before they settled on the final name. On one matter, however, the breakfast-eaters were in unison. To a man, they all wanted the word *Red* included – *Red* considered by everyone as a political word and color for the downtrodden and the poor.

They shortened the name down to the acronym – ACPSRP – for practical reasons, mainly because the long name wouldn't fit into the space on the posters they intended to print. Bellakay agreed to be photographed at Olga Studios down at Parliament Street, after which the developed photograph was rushed to Jellicoe Printing & Publishing at Galahad Street, where a thousand election posters were printed. Trevor, who was considered something of an artist courtesy of his surreptitious claim to be a part of the designing team at the local shoe factory, had designed the poster, aided and abetted by the election committee.

The initials of the new party were spelt out in bold black letters on the poster, which was followed by a smaller font elucidating the acronym. Bellakay's grizzly face was centred in the space immediately below the bold initials. The candidate and party leader had a certain compelling hauteur about him, looking formidable and determined in the black-and-white contours of the photograph. His beard stubble together with his Gandhi-style spectacles held together with metal wire on one side added a slightly sinister touch.

Catnips became the undisputed leader of the corvine collaborators. He wasn't overly fond of Bellakay but had a good nose for anything that could promote his own stock. 'After all,' he mused, 'bloody know-all Bellakay might just go on to win the blooming election! Who could tell? He might even go on to be the blasted prime minister one day! You never know with that damn-blasted oddball – the chap is capable of walking on the moon if he puts his mind to it.'

As with everything else, the party's inner circle opted to give Catnips and his fellow collaborators – the Market Youth Gang – a name and after another lengthy discussion in their best boisterous tradition, settled for the 'Rotting Crow Syndicate'. The word *syndicate* had become quite popular with the breakfast-eaters ever since the Elphinstone cinema down at Master Merril Peavey Street screened an Al Capone reel. Most of the hard-core gang at the Nameless had seen the film featuring murderous Chicago gangs often referred to as 'syndicates'. The easily impressionable Sonny, Catnips, and Trevor went around for some time attired in fedora hats – the kind the shady characters in the film wore. The hats were easily obtainable down at the Salvation Army depot, where used Western attire of all sorts was sold at ridiculously low prices and sometimes even given away free by the silver-haired female commanders who were deemed a tad potty by many. Nobody had wanted the hats. The good ladies were only too happy to give them away, free of charge.

The not so small matter of the evening's cocktails and dinner with Mr Dexter loomed larger and larger as the afternoon dragged on and dusk slowly descended. Bellakay was uneasy – more than a bit worried about the impending visit to the famous Grande Hotel. The magnificent hotel didn't worry or overawe him, but his clothes did. He wasn't superficial, but was hopelessly aware that his hand-me-downs from the Salvation Army were a kind of embarrassment. The clothes he wore to the meeting at the police station would have to suffice, he reasoned, although he wasn't really comfortable meeting his American benefactor whilst wearing them. His shoes worried him much more. The offending footwear's heels were wasted almost to the upper sole on the sides of both shoes and were quite noticeable. It was no use seeking the services of Sakkala, the street cobbler, at this late hour, as he would have already packed up for the day and vanished into the comforting bowels of Ali Baba's toddy tavern. A quick talk with Uncle Pongo, however, resolved the problem. A master of improvisation – the kind born from living a hand-to-mouth sort of life – Uncle Pongo settled the dilemma with finesse and flair. He brought along a few strips of hard cardboard, a bottle of glue, a few tin tacks, and a brand-new razor blade, intending to repair the wobbly shoes himself. He proceeded to expertly paste layers of cardboard to the offending sides of the shoes and, after they had dried off a bit, firmly nailed them down, cutting his effort into shape with the razor blade. As a final touch, he applied black boot polish on the finished area. The resulting repair work looked all right, the cardboard adjudged to hold a few hours at the very least. In the dim lights of the hotel's foyer and dining room, the makeshift repair work would hardly be noticed. Uncle Pongo and

Bellakay crossed their fingers in fervent hope it wouldn't rain that evening. If it did, the cardboard repair work would definitely become soggy and disintegrate. They both decided conclusively that Bellakay had to buy a new pair of shoes once Mr Dexter released the money he promised – perhaps even buy a brand-new wardrobe.

The evening with Mr Dexter passed without tribulation. After inquiring at the imposing front desk at the hotel for their host and being asked to await his arrival, the somewhat odd-looking duo were very much relieved to see the American walking swiftly into the foyer after just a few minutes. Ushering them into the dining room bar, Mr Dexter politely gestured his guests to have a seat, seating himself after they were settled. He made polite conversation and did most of the talking, but after Bellakay had drunk a gimlet at the suggestion of his host, the budding politician's discomfort about his attire all but disappeared. His tongue loosened and out poured the old trademark socialist jargon permanently bottled within him. Uncle Pongo was relieved that Bellakay babbled on as he did and that he himself didn't have to say anything. Mr Dexter sat enthralled, listening to everything Bellakay had to say in rapt attention, now and then taking down notes in a small pocket notebook he carried on his person. After the gimlets were drunk, Mr Dexter ordered whisky – the waiter bringing in a brand-new bottle of American bourbon together with a siphon of soda. Uncle Pongo watched nervously as Mr Dexter poured a drink for himself, squirting soda from the siphon. Pongo had drunk whisky before, but the siphon, a contraption he hadn't seen until now, troubled him. Bellakay, though, was unperturbed by the apparatus, handling it like one to the manor born – a further confirmation that somewhere down the line he *had* enjoyed a somewhat epicurean lifestyle or, at the least, an upper-middle-class one. Sensing Uncle Pongo's discomfort, Bellakay poured a drink for his campaign manager as well, flushing the two glasses with the siphon, much to Uncle Pongo's great relief.

Luckily, the dinner was a buffet where excessive dining etiquette wasn't really needed. Still, dining etiquette or not, it all was outlandish for Uncle Pongo, who, for the life of him, didn't know exactly what he was supposed to do at a buffet. Not so Bellakay. The future candidate for member of Parliament walked up elegantly to the buffet table, trooping behind Mr Dexter and handling the food, the plates, and the rest of it as though he had done it hundreds of times before. In the end, Uncle Pongo did rather well, wisely copying Bellakay's and Mr Dexter's seemingly experienced buffet manoeuvres.

The dinner went amazingly well. Coffee was drunk after the meal, prompting Mr Dexter to conjure a small box of imported cigars from his coat pocket, handing the black projectles around generously. The company were in a mellow mood, the excellent dinner, drinks, and the satisfying smokes successfully infusing a strong spirit of camaraderie. No longer did the magnificent dining hall and its surroundings intimidate Uncle Pongo, nor did Bellakay's shabby wardrobe trouble him the slightest. The two chatted with Mr Dexter with ease as though they were the best of friends – the kind on an equal footing. Sometime later when most of the diners in the hall had all but disappeared and the buffet table was being cleared up by weary staff, Bellakay and Uncle Pongo bade a fond farewell to Mr Dexter and went on their separate ways.

A few days later, Catnips, seeking to satisfy his sexual needs, was at the abandoned railway station for a roundabout with Rooney the Amazon. Catnips didn't have regular romps with prostitutes, but he had developed a carnal obsession for Rooney, whom he saw quite regularly. Lying beside her on the mattress in the special room the twilights maintained for sexual encounters, he felt truly satiated after mind-boggling coitus. Fondling the naked Amazon's huge breasts whilst she stroked his still-hard member, he was totally relaxed and in excellent spirits. He told her all that had transpired with Bellakay, the latter's sudden elevation to candidate for member of Parliament, and how they were plotting to sabotage Hazimudoo's meeting. Catnips knew he could count on Rooney's discretion. She shared many secrets with him, as he did with her. Besides, it was common knowledge that Rooney hated Hazimudoo over the incident where her fellow twilight had her vaginal innards almost crushed in a gang rape by Hazimudoo's henchmen – a deed she blamed the surreptitious politician for. Rooney cocked up her ears as she listened. Bellakay's good fortune and his coming candidature thrilled her no end... Here was the new man and new political force she had been waiting for! She saw her plans for taking over the abandoned old station flying off the drawing board. Pulling the scrawny Catnips over to herself in a tight embrace, she whispered in his ear...

'The crow plan is good, but not enough... You may destroy his meeting, but you've got to destroy the man himself, you know! He has to be discredited, and his followers must be persuaded to abandon him and maybe go over to Bellakay – to join forces with your man. And you know what? I know just how to do it.'

'Whaaat! You! How? I mean, how are *you* going to do it? Every single one of us at the Nameless has racked our brains, but we haven't come up with anything other than the crow plan.'

Rooney bent over and whispered something into Catnips's ear, the latter vigorously nodding his head in assent, delighted at what his giant paramour was proposing. So excited were the two over their plans that Catnips found himself aroused again, inducing another bout of copulating – the Amazon shouting out her pleasure in the final throes. They departed shortly afterwards, Rooney refusing to take Catnips's money. Catnips didn't press her. It wasn't the first time Rooney had given him a freebie...

In addition to paying the deposit, the infant party's great benefactor, the American, also opened a current account at the People's Trust Bank in the name of the new party, designating Bellakay as sole archon. The money came in handy for printing posters, hiring sound systems (including the cone-shaped speakers they hampered over), and paying diverse expenses. Bellakay immediately paid over a generous sum of money to Catnips for securing the services of the Market Youth Gang. The total amount granted by Mr Dexter was not gargantuan, but it satisfied Bellakay's needs more than enough. Uncle Pongo too was allowed to draw a fortnightly salary of three hundred rupees from the same account throughout the entire pre-election period. He bought a stylish pair of trousers and a streamlined, well-cut coat from Mowlana, the most famous haberdasher shop at Galahad Street, and firmly dragged along a howling Bellakay to get him fitted for a full suit and a few other items of clothing, as well. Bellakay was quite hopeless in matters of fashion and although he knew he cut a comical sight in his funny baggy clothes – handouts for the most part from the Salvation Army Charity Depot – he disliked buying new clothes even though he could afford it now. He was, however, firmly cornered and shouted into submission by a determined Uncle Pongo to be measured for a new suit and four new trousers. Uncle Pongo was painfully aware of his friend's touchiness where his wardrobe was concerned, but decided to take the bull by the horns – and damn the consequences. Throwing caution to the winds, he told a bullheaded Bellakay quite sternly that it just wouldn't do to go about canvassing for votes 'looking like a damn beggar', as he uncharitably yet truthfully put it.

'Nobody's going to vote for a man who looks like a bloody scallywag! You are trying to be an MP, for God's sake! If you're going to wear them horrid old clothes of yours, nobody's going to vote for you. It's bad enough that so many people already call you a beggar, a madman, a tramp, and all those other wretched names. You better start dressing well if you want to get decent people to vote for you, or you can forget this damn election – and I'm certainly not going to be your bloody manager! In any case, you owe it to Mr Dexter, who has given you this chance!'

Bellakay hated to comply, but he knew Uncle Pongo was right. In addition to consenting to the suit and trousers ordered by a strict Uncle Pongo, Bellakay reluctantly acceded to buying a pair of imitation patent-leather shoes from one of the pavement hawkers operating outside the Smart Lord tailoring shop. Four new shirts, a few pairs of socks, and a dozen handkerchiefs followed in quick succession, completing the shopping expedition. For the first time in many decades, Bellakay found himself the possessor of a brand-new wardrobe...

The next Saturday was scheduled for four political meetings. The two mainstream parties were scheduled to gather at the town hall grounds, an area as large as two football fields and quite sufficient to accommodate two or even three meetings. The prominent independent candidate Hazimudoo, who was expected to get a large turnout, had decided to hold his meeting at a lesser-known venue – a cavernous grassy clearing not far from the marketplace sprouting a few trees here and there. Catnips and the Rotting Crow Syndicate opted to hold Bellakay's meeting in a sizeable clearing which one had to pass before arriving at Hazimudoo's venue. A gravel road led to both venues, culminating at the entrance to Hazimudoo's cavernous clearing – a cul-de-sac of sorts – beyond which lay inaccessible woodlands. Catnips insisted on the exact position of Bellakay's venue after a thorough reconnoitring of Hazimudoo's own choice, obtaining the relevant information through a spy ring he had organised in the best Machiavellian tradition. It was a strategy that would prove vital for the Anti-Capitalist Socialist People's Red Party as events unfurled.

Hazimudoo, together with his friends and supporters, erected his speaker platform, connected the sound system, and decorated the area around the podium with colourful blue paper streamers and flags – blue being Hazimudoo's official representative colour. The effect was pretty and professional. Completing their work, Hazimudoo and his henchmen set off home for a well-deserved rest and lunch, pleased as Punch with their results. They would only return again later on in the evening in time for the commencement of their meeting. The departure of Hazimudoo's men was the start signal Catnips (who had been watching, hiding in some nearby bushes) had been patiently waiting for. He hurriedly made his way to the market square and was soon seen in earnest discussion with the leader of the Market Youth Gang, to whom he had laid out his plans in minute detail much earlier on that week. It was only a final go-ahead that was needed, and this he now imparted to the youth gang's protagonist – information the latter eagerly lapped up.

Catnips's dastardly plan – collecting putrefying crow corpses from the vicinity of the power station and hiding them in cleverly concealed nooks and corners inside Hazimudoo's meeting area – was met with complete aloofness by the Market Youth Gang. Catnips kept out of the action as far as he could. He was a past master at keeping his hands clean, firmly believing in a strict policy of delegating. Besides, as with Sonny, he was revolted by the thought of handling the decomposing birds with his own hands. The Market Youth Gang, however, had no such qualms. Homeless orphans or runaways from remote villages, they lived on their small earnings at the marketplace, but also from any dubious work that came their way – work that often bordered on the wrong side of the law. The next generation of budding adult criminals, they patiently awaited their turn to join the senior fraternity. They worked and bonded well, having their own ranking hierarchy, the toughest of the bunch sitting right on top, bossing the boys beneath his command. At night, they slept in open verandas of street shops on rough reed mats or straw taken from packing crates and boxes. During the day, they sauntered off to the market square to help unload the many trucks and bullock carts that streamed in carrying fresh vegetables, huge joints of meat, fish, and other merchandise. They were paid a decent retainer for the work they did, which was a great help for their daily sustenance. The rough-and-tough street work kept the boys slim, sleek, and fit. They were a salubrious lot, rarely getting sick except if injured by a falling crate or in some other mishap. As for the job at hand, the small matter of tolerating the miasmatic stench emanating from the dead crows did not repel them. They were used to bad smells, not as bad as the crows, but they put up with the awful stench anyway, quite cheerfully as it turned out, seeing that Catnips had promised them such a handsome sum of cash for their trouble. The boys were sworn to secrecy and could be trusted implicitly, never, ever betraying an employer's confidence. Loyalty was a maxim they invariably exercised, upholding it as a very special code of honour. It was imperative for their existence. They had a reputation to maintain and could never be trusted to do any additional work if it became known they had ratted on any of their 'special' benefactors, who more often than not hired them to do some shady job or another. There were ten boys in the youth gang, between thirteen and sixteen years of age, and each had collected a large haul of their repulsive cargo from the area around the power station in roughly woven jute bags.

A few birds were dumped unceremoniously under Hazimudoo's wooden podium – strenuous work, as it took the boys' joint efforts to tilt the heavy platform. The rest were placed and cleverly concealed in nearby bushes, in patches of tall inaccessible grass, and inside thick and thorny shrubs, all within the area where Hazimudoo's supporters would gather. There were a quite a few trees inside the venue, which the nimble boys skilfully climbed to place their rotting 'cargo' in trifurcate branches high above prying eyes, increasing the stench considerably. By the time the gang had finished their gruesome work, the platform dais and its vicinity was already giving off more than a suspicion of a jolly good stink. The hot sun, humidity, and gentle breezes would gradually magnify the stench as the hours rolled on.

In the meantime, Bellakay and his helpers were busy mounting a podium of their own, hanging colourful paper streamers, flags, and small banners around it. Bellakay, Uncle Pongo, and the rest from the Nameless worked tirelessly under the noonday sun. The sound system and loudspeakers, hired from Swami's Electricals at Palang Street, were duly installed by old Swami himself, ably assisted by his nephew Baby Swami – his right-hand man and heir apparent. On the platform, a centre table (borrowed from one of Uncle Pongo's more affluent neighbours) took pride of place. This was neatly covered over with a red plastic tablecloth. On the table, a row of aerated water bottles were placed, all of the variety 'blood orange' to further distinguish and drive home the official party colour of the Anti-Capitalist People's Socialist Red Party.

Catnips paid the Market Youth Gang the sum of money agreed upon, after which they exited the scene of the crime, the perfidious deed done to perfection. Catnips had paid the equivalent of four weeks' wages to each boy, and they were in a God-almighty hurry to rush back and spend it all at the various attractions in and around 'their' beloved marketplace.

The egregious deed over, Catnips looked around himself with an air of contentment. Throwing a final and satisfying look around the area, he hurriedly made his way towards the Nameless, Bellakay's designated and official party headquarters. Oozing exhilaration, he excitedly informed the eagerly awaiting gathering that the surreptitious deed had gone according to plan – the ghoulish work done and completed. Bellakay and his inner circle heaved an almighty sigh of relief over the news. They congratulated their mercurial colleague heartily, keeping their fingers crossed in fervent hope that the rest of the proceedings would also go along as planned and expected.

Bellakay, although pleased as everyone else about Catnips's success, was still uneasy over it all. He was filled with malaise over the kind of foul tactics his henchmen had just deployed. It was even harder to swallow since *he*, the party leader, had approved and agreed to it all. Turning the matter over in his mind, he resigned himself to its inevitability, reasoning that it was for a good cause. Utopia and Shangri-La couldn't be accomplished through meek and laid-back methods. Wasn't there plenty of back-stabbing and violence in the aftermath of the October Revolution?

The hour, and then the minutes, approached for the meetings to commence, both Bellakay's and Hazimudoo's. The somewhat close proximity of the two venues to each other meant that crowds arriving to and returning from Hazimudoo's meeting would have to bypass Bellakay's and be forced to have at least a brief view of Bellakay's proceedings, whether they liked it or not.

Throngs of visitors started drifting into Hazimudoo's meeting.

The candidate, followed by his inner circle and a very large entourage of supporters, marched in procession up to the speaker podium. There was a whiff of a bad smell even as they entered the clearing, but nobody thought too much of it – bad smells in the city not an uncommon feature. Blocked drains, bad garbage disposal, the corpse of a rotting cat or dog succumbed to a road accident, all contributed to nasty smells. The smell of putrefying flesh from and around Hazimudoo's podium did not at first attract any undue attention from anyone. Gradually, however, as proceedings started and the first speaker got into stride, those sitting closest the podium were seen backing away a considerable bit, moving their chairs with them. Even Hazimudoo and his henchmen seated by the table on the dais found the miasmatic stench increasingly bothersome. On several occasions, some of them got down from the podium to probe for its likely source.

'What the bloody hell! Where did that smell come from? What's going on here, eh?' said one.

'There was no bloody smell a few hours ago when we were here and fixed up everything,' said another, scratching his head wonderingly.

'It's too far away to come from the purifying works. And in any case, the winds have been quite gentle today,' said a third, referring to the sewage-purifying plant on the outskirts of the city which blew a disgusting stench over Portopo whenever the winds blew directly over the metropolis. Mumblings of a protesting nature started trickling in from Hazimudoo's supporters. They were soon to explode and gallop into an avalanche of unmentionable expletives.

The Market Youth Gang had done their ghoulish work well. The cleverly concealed crow corpses placed under the podium and painstakingly hidden in well-concealed nooks and corners in surrounding green foliage, drains, ditches, high branches of nearby trees, and other undetectable places gave off their desired effect.

The crowd was now positively agitated and restless, backing farther and farther away from the speaker podium. (Some had already left.) Hazimudoo tried desperately to stop the rot. The smell – overpowering even to him – had now reached the cusp of intolerable. Several appeals to stay went unheeded by the disgusted crowd.

'Stay! Please, stay, good people! We will soon find the source of the trouble,' cried Hazimudoo desperately over and over again, but it was obvious even to him that nothing could stop the rot. Search as they did, nobody could find the epicentre of the stench, so well hidden were the rotting corvine carcasses. Besides, well concealed or not, the search party didn't really put much heart and soul into their efforts. The smell was as unbearable to them as it was to everyone else. Anxious to get away from the awfulness of it all, they just poked about listlessly in nearby bushes with sticks and without much enthusiasm – none of them really caring to put their backs into doing a meticulous search – never thinking of tipping the podium and looking underneath it. Such a thought never crossed *anybody's* mind – sabotage an unimaginable prospect.

Still, sabotage or not, the eventuality of Hazimudoo's men's tipping over the stage was a possibility that had not bypassed Catnips's astute thinking. Guarding against such a highly improbable possibility, he had shrewdly ordered two huge boulders to be placed leaning on the left and right of the podium, making the wooden construction nearly impossible to budge – not the slightest bit. The presence of the boulders raised no eyebrows – each of Hazimudoo's workers who had helped in erecting the podium concluding that others in the group had placed the stones as extra structural support – podiums well documented to have collapsed in the past due to poor carpentry efforts.

Everything went according to plan. Hazimudoo's followers made their way out of his meeting seething with anger and disappointment. Supporting their candidate was well and good, but enduring a most horrible stench was not a sacrifice they were prepared to make. There were limits to their enthusiasm. The most diplomatic ones mumbled some excuse or other and slowly vanished, whilst the bolder and more vociferous made loud and ugly statements of disapproval before leaving.

'What sort of a buggering damn place you jackasses chose for your meeting, eh?' said one.

Another chirped in, 'Bloody nincompoops.'

And a third, 'Why the Devil did you bring us to this miserable f****** stink hole, eh? You think we are f****** pigs?'

A tirade of ill-tempered insults streamed in from several others. 'Damn scumbags', 'f****** idiots', 'incompetent rascals', and even graver invectives of an unmentionable sort poured from Hazimudoo's irritated supporters as they angrily made their exits.

Hazimudoo and his henchmen were shattered. They hadn't the faintest clue where the horrible odour that unceremoniously disrupted their meeting came from or how it got there. Unable to bear the stench, which was strongest near the podium area, they followed suit, prudently deciding to return the next morning better equipped with home-made masks and protective clothing to make a more detailed search for the source of the miasmatic stench. Hazimudoo's tumultuous meeting had ended before it had started.

As Catnips had cleverly anticipated, Hazimudoo's fleeing supporters did indeed bypass Bellakay's meeting venue on their way back. Curiosity made them stop to have a quick look at Bellakay's proceedings, and this was exactly what Catnips wanted. The additional lure of mouth-watering fruit drinks swimming in crushed ice and of tuna and cucumber sandwiches didn't need a second invitation.

Bellakay stood, ready to speak. He looked an extremely viable candidate as he strutted about the podium surrounded by his henchmen from the Nameless. The presence of the American was a novelty – foreigners, without exception, keeping away from local politics unreservedly. Most of Hazimudoo's supporters decided to stay on impressed by what they saw, especially the American sitting on the podium beside Bellakay. After all, they reflected, what did they have to lose and what harm would it do? They had come for a political meeting and were damned if they were going home without getting one, even if it wasn't the meeting and candidate they rooted for.

The ACPSRP had, through the combined efforts of the organisers, managed to round up nearly two hundred persons to attend the inaugural meeting, including the regulars from the Nameless. Strangefellow was present too. He never left Sonny's side, following the latter everywhere he went. Strangefellow's presence attracted the attention of a host of Jellicoe Junction strays, the whole lot occupying a section of the meeting grounds, sitting quietly in a rough circle, nudging and licking each other whilst looking on inquiringly at the proceedings. The faint smell of tuna floating around and the presence of Strangefellow, a fellow mutt they greatly admired, kept them rooted to the spot. They knew there were tidbits to come from the 'two-legs'.

Bellakay had worn his new suit – a glistening seersucker affair, the very same purchased at Mowlana's tailoring shop – and had completed it with an equally glistening red silk shirt tightly buttoned at the collar. A conspicuous red tie, tied in the conservative Windsor knot he had a penchant for, sat slightly loose beneath the collar. The combined effect was a tad gaudy, but it certainly transformed his customary dour and indecisive appearance. He looked like a modern-day agitator who meant business – one with a specific axe to grind.

Uncle Pongo, the campaign manager, walked up importantly to the microphone provided by Swami Electricals and did as he had seen numerous others do at many election meetings. 'Testing, testing,' he boomed before recoiling violently, very much shocked at hearing his own reverberating, magnified voice echoing back at him. A master of resilience, he recovered quickly to repeat the process, taking good care this time around to ignore his magnified voice. He repeated his 'testing, testing' routine and, satisfied that the sound was all right, announced rather importantly to the watching Bellakay, with one eye trained obliquely on the American, that the speaker system was in order.

The candidate rose to speak. A round of polite clapping rippled through the gathering, followed by a hushed silence. All eyes were trained on the rookie contestant for member of Parliament. Normally,

Bellakay didn't care a damn for audiences or venues whenever he unleashed his standard tirade of political balderdash on unsuspecting bystanders. This time around, however, the gravity of the situation caught up with him as he experienced his life's first ever fit of jitters. There were butterflies in his stomach as the seriousness of his situation suddenly dawned upon him. Shakespeare's quip about 'greatness being thrust upon' never hit a truer target. Here he was – a near destitute and the butt of many jokes just a few weeks ago – speaking as a legitimate candidate vying for the important position of member of Parliament.

He began uncomfortably, stammering a few opening lines as the crowd looked upon him expectantly. The unfamiliar sound of his magnified voice was as much a surprise to him as it was to Uncle Pongo. It seemed surreal, like he was in a bad dream – clawing and yearning to wake up.

Rohan and the school gang were present too. Rohan, who, through his dog-bathing duties at the Nameless, knew all about Bellakay's sudden change of fortunes, had persuaded Salgado to come along – and where Salgado went, the school gang followed. The gang weren't abreast of Bellakay's newfound respectability – Rohan having carelessly neglected to impart *that* bit of news. The boys, well used to heckling Bellakay whenever the latter delivered his crackpot cricket match speeches, and not fully understanding why Bellakay was on a public platform giving what *they* thought was yet another crackpot speech, began heckling him from their corner of the field. The boys' comments, catcalls, and rowdy whistling – highly audible – had a completely unexpected and galvanising effect. As raconteurs would relate in later years, the heckling turned things around. It sparked off the street fighter in Bellakay, successfully breaking off the shackles of uncertainty and uneasiness he had suddenly and unprecedentedly found himself in. He stopped stammering, threw his chest forwards, and took a firm grip on himself. Growing in confidence, he was soon mastering the microphone like one to the manor born. His earlier doubts about his viability were a thing of the past as his speech became more and more explicit and polished. Soon, he was off and running, rattling off a resounding political tirade that only he knew how to deliver. This was the old warrior at his scintillating best, a passionate apostle of the proletariat who had suffered grave injustices at the hands of various bullying authorities.

At the onset of his delivery, Bellakay's hair was immaculately combed back in sleek, oily strands, but as his ebullient state got the better of him, he began to run his fingers through his scalp, causing the oily locks to fall in a wild shemozzle all over his forehead and ears. The collar of his red silk shirt burst open in glee from its restraining button. His red tie began a sagging descent, long below its original point of knot, whilst his shirt, struggling to remain inside his trousers, was now partially hanging outside. His arms gestured like a symphony orchestra leader's whilst his footwork was a confident Fred Astaire. The sight was impressive. He soon had the proletarian audience cheering, although his close followers from the Nameless hadn't the foggiest notion what he was ranting about. Quips like 'the suffering masses', 'the downtrodden poor', 'the 'rich getting richer', 'dirty rotten politicians', and 'banks only for the rich' they caught clearly, but the hard-boiled quips and quotes from Marx and other famous intellectual socialists eluded them – not a catastrophe, as they cared nought anyway. They all loved Bellakay's impetuous style when he was in this mood (except, of course, at their early morning breakfast sessions), and sensed and knew instinctually within themselves that whatever he was saying was all in their best interests. They trusted their man implicitly, cheering him on vigorously at suitable intervals.

Mr Dexter followed Bellakay's speech carefully, understanding perfectly well everything Bellakay was endeavouring to communicate – the very same that eluded the gang from the Nameless and some others. He listened like one mesmerised as Bellakay ranted and rattled off socialist principles from the International Movement, and sighed in appreciation whenever the candidate quoted philosophers like Socrates and put forward the rationalist views of Spinoza. The lithe orator's style of delivery could have come from Cicero. Perhaps

Bellakay *was* Cicero, mused the American – reborn by some strange twist of fate on this little tropical island.

Hazimudoo's truant crowd were equally impressed. Fascinated by the sight of the ranting Bellakay with his wild, unkempt hair, loose collar, and red tie flying in all directions, together with the unusual sight of an American on the podium, they decided to remain firmly where they were. They stayed on right to the very end of Bellakay's speech, the crowd swelling to as large as seven hundred or more.

The press, who usually covered the more important candidates' meetings, were also present, albeit by accident, being originally in the entourage that had fled Hazimudoo's miasmatic venue. It was Hazimudoo's meeting that their well-meaning editors had ordered them to cover, but fate had decreed otherwise. Following closely on the heels of Hazimudoo's fleeing supporters, they found themselves in the thick of it all and decided to make the most of their unique situation. They found the new meeting and its colourful speaker decisively intriguing. The sight of the American – just as old Benjy had predicted – proved an additional novelty. *Everything* seemed groundbreaking, a change from the humdrum, predictable meetings they usually covered. Staying on wasn't a difficult decision. After all, as they reasoned astutely, they were assigned by their editors to cover a meeting, and they were doing just that, even if it wasn't the intended meeting. Photographs were taken and extracts from Bellakay's speech were jotted down in small black notebooks – whilst interviews were desperately sought with this very novel candidate and the American.

Rohan and the school gang had long since stopped heckling Bellakay. Realising the crowd were actually lionising him, they changed tactics and cheered on instead. Of course, they understood very little of the party leader's speech, but they cheered anyway in puerile abandonment, just for the devilment of it all. They loved nothing better than creating an almighty ruckus, and no opportunity could have been better than this...

More refreshments were passed around amongst the gratified crowd, prompting Strangefellow and the other dogs to leave their chosen spot and mingle, begging for a tidbit or two. The venue was a riot of people: Bellakay's original supporters, 'stolen' Hazimudoo supporters, newspaper reporters, Rohan's volatile school gang, the marketplace youths, and Strangefellow's four-footed friends – all contributing in their own way to the sparkling success the event had now become. The crowd, well fortified with food and drink, were supremely content, cheering on Bellakay in no uncertain terms, whilst the candidate, sensing their supportive mood, fished out a few standard digs from his repertoire of tricks whenever he had an audience eating from the palm of his hand.

'All you fellows want a good meal each day and a decent roof over your heads to protect you from the elements, don't you? Let me ask you, then … Let me ask you good people. How many of you fellows and your families are eating huge steaks or other fancy meats and things at each meal, eh? When are *we* ever going to eat those dang-blasted imported roasts and other fancy food them rich people eat? You fellows eat bacon and eggs and imported sausages for breakfast every day? Anyone here can afford to buy any damn imported whisky and wine? Your government provide any of this for you? Answer me! Do they? And what about your filthy-rich landlords who only suck you dry for rent and don't fix any damn thing in your houses, eh? Your children all get sick because your blooming roofs leak like a damn fountain while our government big shots and their fat families live in mansions, eating fancy food and drinking dang-blasted foreign whisky and wine. Why, we can't even find a decent job to pay for *our* poor children's fish and rice or plain bloody boiled potatoes and salt!'

The crowd, highly incensed by these horrible gastronomical atrocities and the talk of bad housing, were enraged. Vociferous shouts of support burst forth from the lips of the agitated supporters. Sonny, who was sitting on the speaker platform together with the organising committee and Mr Dexter, couldn't control his feelings any longer. He jumped up from his seat and interjected, shouting for all his worth into the microphone alongside Bellakay.

'Down with them all! Dirty rotten scoundrels, that's what they are! Bloody good-for-nothing rascals. Devils, the lot of them! And don't forget the accursed bank thieves! Garbage-eating pigs, the lot of them! Hang them all by the neck, the bloody scumbags!'

Strangefellow, who had joined his master on the podium, heartily agreed. 'Oewwwww!' he drawled, howling like a wolf. 'Oeowwwww!'

Bellakay was on cloud nine. Supremely pleased with the almighty ruckus he had conjured, he continued in the same vein, jubilant and unstoppable. 'I'm telling you, good people, I'm telling you sincerely, if you vote for me, I'll see to it that all of you chaps and your families eat all that fine food that only them capitalist pigs eat! I'll see that you have decent housing so that the rain doesn't beat down on your heads during each monsoon shower. I'll reform our bullying police force and bring about social reforms everywhere and to everyone. I'll usher in a new era!'

'Carpe diem,' muttered Mr Dexter from his seat at the podium, sensing Bellakay had effectively seized the day – made the best of his opportunity. 'Carpe diem, carpe diem ...'

The crowd, now well and truly goaded, cheered in wild enthusiasm for the galloping candidate. Bellakay cunningly turned the talk from social injustice to bad smells, intending to propitiate the section of his audience who had fled their fallen hero's malodorous meeting.

'You see them bad drains that smell like hell at Jellicoe Junction? Why are they in such a state only here, eh? Why does the government only have good drainage in the rich people's areas or that big-shot Coronation Park complex, eh? Why? Can you tell me why? Can't? Cat got your tongues, eh? Well, let *me* tell you why. Our blasted government pigs only clean up them streets and areas where all the rich people live and work. The dirty rotters neglect the streets where we poor chaps live! Why must we always be the ones to always suffer, eh?'

A wild furore broke out in a large section of the crowd after Bellakay's last statement. Having just returned from a failed meeting due to an unbearable stench, the candidate's talk of bad drainage really touched a nerve.

'Hurrah for Bellakay! Hurrah for Bellakay! Bellakay for prime minister!' they shouted at their newfound hero, over and over and over again.

A belligerent Bellakay spoke on for two hours non-stop on the same themes, his audience completely under his spell, his meeting an unqualified success.

After the crowds had departed, the candidate and the faithful gang from the Nameless stayed back together with the American to savour all that had transpired. They eagerly discussed what had taken place, looking forward with glee to what the press would report in the following morning's newspapers. Mr Dexter was kept in the dark about the Rotting Crow Syndicate, the conspirators suspecting he wouldn't be all too pleased by such a dastardly election tactic. After a good half hour passed, Mr Dexter shook hands with Bellakay, bade goodbye to the rest, and went on his way.

A prearranged limousine arrived to pick him up, the chauffer having parked the huge car by the main road leading to the marketplace. He had walked the short distance to the meeting venue to escort the American back to the waiting car.

The initial meeting of Bellakay and his Anti-Capitalist People's Socialist Red Party was an august success. A series of meetings would be held later on at different venues, gradually contributing to Bellakay's rising status and growing popularity. The success of the first meeting and the exalting press coverage it received, together with several meetings that followed in its wake, made Bellakay's campaign, against all odds, a serious affair, one not to be taken lightly. Hazimudoo, whenever in the public eye, dismissed Bellakay contemptuously as an eccentric twit, although he couldn't help being jittery about the newcomer's growing popularity. The 'twit' label didn't augur well for several voters at Jellicoe Junction who gradually came to see Bellakay as a front-line contender. Sections of the press found an unlikely new hero, one whom they lionised as far as they could. Bellakay was given frequent publicity in the local newspapers, not on the same scale as the main parties' candidates or Hazimudoo, but decent and much welcome publicity nonetheless.

Soon after Bellakay's memorable meeting, Hazimudoo experienced the second happening that would ruin his chances of being elected and effectively end his career as a politician. A regular client of the twilights, he was, as was the case with many others, very much enamoured of the Amazon Rooney. One day whilst soliciting Rooney's services, he was offered a stupendous deal of group coitus with the Amazon and three other prostitutes whom Rooney declared were new to the trade, and had only just arrived from some remote village. Hazimudoo needed no persuasion. He admired Rooney's superb body, having had several romps with her before, and the prospect of a serial romp spiced with 'fresh' women from the backwoods aroused him as nothing else could. Rooney quoted a stiff price for it all, but he went along without a murmur of protest. Money was no object when it came to satisfying his carnal desires.

That very same afternoon, Hazimudoo agreed to come over to the twilights' room at the abandoned railway station – a rendezvous he had kept many times before. There was strong daylight streaming well through a large window in the twilights' room that day, ideal for filming even without a camera flash.

Hazimudoo stripped naked as he got ready for steamy sex with Rooney. The Amazon was as alluring as ever, her golden, bulging breasts and frontal vulva enticing as at no other time. Hazimudoo, filled with lust, grasped her tightly and then almost immediately entered her. The act was over as quickly as it began, Hazimudoo unable to control any decent tact, whilst Rooney made the usual obligatory noises expected of her. Inwardly, she detested the close proximity of this most vile man who had callously almost caused the death of her colleague, but comforted herself with the though that what she was doing now was for a good cause. Secretly, and as pre-planned, Catnips was filming everything with his Kodak Brownie from a sizeable hole in the wall. As if from nowhere, three other twilights appeared, all stark naked from head to toe, ready for sex. Hazimudoo was in seventh heaven, bowled over by the erotic sight. Although his ageing member had gone limp after he had entered Rooney and climaxed, he almost immediately managed an erection again. He asked no questions, assuming that what was taking place was all part of the act. Catnips continued to film it all. Finally, satisfied that he had got all the necessary dirt, Catnips put his camera into its case, slung the case over his shoulder, and walked out in the direction of the twilights' annex near the Ritzo.

Rooney visited the *Jellicoe Journal* headquarters that very evening. She told her story to an amazed chief editor and produced Catnips's film documenting her story. The editor just couldn't refuse to print – Rooney knew this instinctively. This was hot stuff, the kind that could destroy reputations. Hazimudoo would be finished forever. Rooney was thrilled beyond words. She had killed two birds with one stone – avenging her physically harmed colleague, whilest additionally well on her way to starting a housing centre and spa at the abandoned railway station. All that was left was for Bellakay to be successfully elected as third MP for Jellicoe Junction.

The following Monday, the *Jellicoe Journal* ran a breathtaking story featuring the prominent independent candidate Hazimudoo's serial romp with four prostitutes. A series of embarrassing pictures showing a fully naked Hazimudoo in all manner of lewd situations was splashed on the front page. After the story broke and was even taken up by other newspapers, Hazimudoo was effectively lampooned – a broken man forever stigmatised in political circles. As Catnips, Rooney, and the other conspirators expected, a third of Hazimudoo's supporters did start to support Bellakay, disgusted over their former idol's wanton philandering.

An Anti-Capitalist People's Socialist Red Party election headquarters was established. Although their American benefactor had provided adequate money for renting a suitable premises, the committee opted to erect a temporary marquee close to the Nameless, assembled by a group of professional craftsmen often involved in putting up similar structures at national festivals and grandiose weddings. It was a solid, sturdy tent that stood out majestically, dwarfing the dilapidated construction that was the Nameless, which stood beside it. Enthusiastic election warriors covered the marquee with banners and small placards citing examples of Bellakay's most common one-liners used in his fiery speeches. In front of the tent at the highest point above the entrance, a large cardboard cut-out of Bellakay took pride of place. It was an enlargement of the photo taken at Olga Studios, the one that made him look formidable and rather sinister. Red plastic flags were stringed together across the sides and roof of the semi-oval tent. Inside, tables and chairs on loan from Bertram's furniture-for-hire shop at the marketplace and a large battery-powered radio set – yet another acquisition from Swami Electricals – were suitably placed. The radio was intended for listening to the latest news on the election and for following election results on polling day. The radio's volume, powered by a car battery, was exceptionally high and its tone exquisite, courtesy of Swami, an electrical genius who had tinkered with it a few days. Permission to erect the tent was obtained from the municipal council, who issued a permit without reserve. The council committee dared not refuse the new candidate who was constantly featured in the newspapers. Besides, they were well aware of the influential American's involvement and were most solicitous – wary of crossing swords with Mr Dexter, who appeared to have powerful connections with the police and other prominent people.

Bellakay, now an important man in many people's eyes, had all but abandoned his 'residence' at the abandoned old railway station for the comfort of the tent, finding it easier to control matters on the spot. Besides, as Sonny and Uncle Pongo pointed out, it wouldn't augur well for Bellakay to continue living in that notorious haven for squatters now that he had found true legitimacy as a candidate for member of Parliament.

In the days immediately preceding Election Day, Bellakay and a few volunteers from the party's inner circle were seen driving along the area in a semi-open-roofed Morris station wagon they were able to rent for a modest sum of money from one of the fish barons at the fish market. The vehicle, quite an old model, had a lingering smell of fish, but it didn't deter the enthusiastic warriors in the least. A large twin-cone loudspeaker was attached to the roofed front of the van and was connected to a small but powerful amplifier in the open rear. A hand microphone completed the simple sound system. The sound equipment – also provided by Swami – cost a tidy bit to hire, but it was well within range of the available funds.

Catnips, now unofficially elevated to chief campaign schemer, was amongst the van's occupants along with Uncle Pongo, Sonny, Benjy, Trevor, Karolis, Strangefellow, and the candidate himself. Strangefellow was quite vociferous, barking constantly at almost everyone and anything the van passed. He seemed to be having a good time and appeared to have quite forgotten his tree-climbing passion momentarily, content to be the only official four-footed member of the ACPSRP. Sonny had fastened a red plastic rose to his collar, which the canine was immensely proud of, licking it gently now and then. He appreciated being included in the mobile touring party and would now and then flash a loving look at Sonny, whom he adored above everything. Bellakay, the proud candidate, was always dressed in a silk bush shirt of the brightest red – another purchase he had made at one of the pavement hawker's lots. Since Uncle Pongo had induced him into buying that new suit and trousers at Mowlana, he had broken years of restraint and gone on a completely unprecedented shopping spree, buying several new items of clothing and surprising the old campaign manager half out of his wits.

The van stopped wherever people were gathered in small groups at the market square and at other prominent places, including the central bus and railway stations. At each instance, Bellakay would stand on a wooden box in the open rear section of the van and lash forth a stinging verbal tirade – the kind of political 'mantra' he had now become unreservedly notorious for. His voice, which normally carried well, was even more enhanced by the powerful hand microphone, endearing him favourably to many onlookers.

The opposition indulged in mobile canvassing too, although on a much larger scale than the ACPSRP. Their mobile strategy was almost the same as Bellakay's, with one glaring exception. The leaders of the top parties never travelled in person in the vans, preferring to stay on terra firma rather than being jostled and roughened up in a moving vehicle – an inconvenience Bellakay had no qualms about. The spontaneous automobile excursions did actually have an effect, often helping a fairly large group of uncertain voters to decide whom they should vote for in the final days.

Bellakay's campaign, his many mass meetings, and the van excursions did appeal strongly, despite the opposition's more grandiose efforts. His volatile speeches at meetings, the very simplicity of the solitary old Morris station wagon, and even the physical sight of the hardened and streetwise candidate created a powerful election magnet. Bellakay made a telling impression. Those on the very lowest rung of society, especially, positively adored him.

At last, Election Day arrived. Most of the candidates, including Bellakay, made several last-minute appearances at the market square and other important places in a frenzied tempo of hope. As evening approached, the weary candidates and their nearest supporters finally blew the whistle on their activities and retired to their respective party headquarters to follow the election results on the radio. The hustle and bustle of serious campaigning was over.

An unusual calm descended upon Jellicoe Junction. There were very few people about on the streets. Many had followed the example of the candidates and their supporters and had gone home or to their respective party headquarters to listen to the election results, which were expected to be aired later on that night over the radio.

Bellakay, Sonny, Karolis, Uncle Pongo, Trevor, Catnips, Benjy, and other hard-core party supporters kept vigil at their election headquarters, the huge marquee beside the Nameless. They were joined by most of the eating house's regular clientele and other enthusiastic supporters who had grown considerably in number in the preceding weeks. Uncle Pongo's wife, Bella, his daughter, Toni, his close neighbours, and even voluptuous Rooney and her colleagues were present.

The budget allowed for refreshments. Piping-hot tea was served together with cucumber and corned-beef sandwiches and a huge cauldron of Chinese fried rice, enough to feed a battalion. Sonny had even prepared and laid out his famous fried fish, generously financed with party funds. Sweetmeats were also provided, an enormous plum cake standing out prominently. Although frowning upon excessive guzzling, Bellakay had even provided a few cases of the much loved Victorian beer, whilst a good many of the more vociferous types had brought along a bottle or two of the fiery Victorian whisky and arrack. Obstreperous discussions broke out as spirits soared in a crescendo of hope for their candidate.

By and by, the first election results started to trickle in – rural village results the first to be announced – followed by small towns and lastly the city of Portopo. The results were expected – almost déjà vu – repeating the results of preceding years. The ruling party, hegemonic in Victorian politics, was always in the forefront, closely followed by the main opposition party. The foreseeable results didn't affect or dampen the mood of Bellakay's followers inside the tent. They did not like either party – just interested in a haphazard sort of way – not really caring which of the big parties won. Both parties were considered equally evil, although they secretly rooted for the opposition, the incumbent party in power considered the more villainous of the two. Bellakay and his new party was their final hope of a genuine renaissance – an ushering in of a new era, or Shangri-La, as Bellakay so often put it.

As each electorate's result was announced over the radio, there was wild mock cheering and shouting that spilled over into derisive hooting, more in a spirit of sheer devilry than anything else.

Strangefellow, greatly excited by all the shouting and jeering, alternated between reposing on his high perch on the banyan tree and sitting inside the marquee. He couldn't quite make up his mind what to do. One moment, he was slithering down the tree to challenge some particular loud shout or another from the crowd, and the next found him climbing back again. Gradually, though, growing tired of this see-saw-like antic, he decided to stay put in the tent. His decision was enhanced – very much so – by the regular tidbits of fried fish, corned beef, and other tasty edibles generously tossed his way by supporters inside the tent.

Bellakay, not a particularly strong-drinking man, avoided the beer, whisky, and fiery arrack, confining himself to many cups of tea instead. Uncle Pongo, the campaign manager, had no such qualms, gleefully indulging in several drams of the free-flowing whisky, talking nineteen to the dozen with almost everyone present. Sonny, Catnips, and the rest of the election committee followed suit, throwing caution to the winds. They felt thoroughly justified in downing several glasses after all the hard work they had put in for their candidate and the new cause.

Bellakay looked upon the proceedings with a contented smile upon his lips. It was a genuine smile, unlike the manufactured one he wore during his intense campaigning. Uncle Pongo had insisted well in the early stages of the campaign that Bellakay learn to smile as often as possible so as to enhance his appeal to voters – Bellakay reluctantly complying. Smiling, as with laughter, was an effort for him – a long-forgotten physical function. He had smiled so much throughout the entire campaign that his lips and gums ached every single day from the effort. Even his back ached like the devil. Uncle Pongo had also driven home the importance to Bellakay of walking with his spine held erect – to eliminate his usual slouching gait. Win or lose, Bellakay mused, he would be glad for tomorrow. He wouldn't have to put on that dratted smile any longer or sashay around like a goddamned blooming peacock anymore...

Finally, the results of the Jellicoe Junction constituency were announced. The crowd hushed and went silent, grouping closer together near the large radio. They listened with bated breath, everybody's heart pounding louder and faster as the radio blared out the result.

'Results for Jellicoe Junction electorate district 527, as follows. Most number of votes in descending order.'

M.A.D. Cuckoo, United Popular Party, 12,000 votes
Ichalot Oliphant, Democratic Socialist Party, 11,000 votes
Don Peter Pintoo [Bellakay], independent, 7,020 votes
Vernon Von Vandura, independent, 350 votes
Miss Olive Oyl's Women's Party, 300 votes
New Jellicoe Party, 289 votes
Abolish LBW Rule Party, 51 votes
Doctor Crippen, independent, 25 votes
Red Blood Party, 24 votes
Freedom from Hunger Party, 20 votes
Bagshaw Baladona, independent, 7 votes
Wise Solomon Party, 6 votes
Freedom from Slavery Party, 5 votes
Lime Pickle Party, 5 votes
No Knickers Party, 3 votes.'

The assembly let the results slowly sink in. In their deepest, deepest hearts, they had hoped that Bellakay, or rather Don Peter Pintoo, would pull it off and be elected third MP – and how he had! They lifted Bellakay off his feet and carried him around and around the tent in triumph.

'Hurray for Bellakay, Hurray for Bellakay. Bellakay for prime minister,' they chanted on and on again in a mad crescendo of celebration.

Uncle Pongo and the hard-core gang from the Nameless were beside themselves with glee. Euphoria never ran so high amongst the breakfast-eaters as what it was that night. Dancing, singing, and celebrations continued throughout the night and into the early hours of morning, the nearly five hundred supporters inside the marquee refusing to go home.

The American, Bellakay's great benefactor, extended his stay in Victoria and was often seen in close conversation with his protégé. Further funds were pumped into party coffers, and a special team of advisors – all top professionals recruited by Mr Dexter – were busy drafting a strategy for the new party's political advancement. It was wildly whispered that Bellakay was a 'coming' man, a would-be national leader, a dark horse for the highest office of prime minister.

Uncle Pongo, who had lived well for several weeks on the income he disposed as Bellakay's campaign manager, also received a small boost upwards. He was made Bellakay's private secretary, a position mandatory for an MP.

Sonny didn't get the much desired bank loans he had hoped for, but he did hit a jackpot of sorts. A cunning petition sent to the Land Ministry composed by none other than Bellakay resulted in his being granted a life lease of the small plot of land housing the Nameless, including the clearing where the majestic banyan tree stood. The terms of the lease didn't allow him to sublease, but he couldn't be evicted as long as he lived. After years of flaunting his illicit restaurant in an egregious manner under the very noses of the municipal council officials, Sonny had at long last become a respectable, law-abiding citizen, practically owning a fully legitimate eating house. Bellakay had even hinted it would be possible to change the life lease into a deed of absolute ownership.

Rooney eventually got Bellakay, through his new political influence, to put an end to the dispute between the warring parties at the old abandoned railway station. She petitioned for and obtained a long-term lease for the property, renovated the entire building, and started a housing collective made up of formerly illegal squatters. The spa she hankered after was financed, built, and opened, too. Rooney's colleagues – all former members of the twilight brigade – became employees in respectful positions, although it was rumoured that sexual services were also available on a very hush-hush, luxurious sort of scale if one so desired them. Catnips was a frequent visitor to the spa, where he was always welcomed with open arms by Rooney.

The hard-core patrons at the Nameless continued to patronise Sonny's eating house. Bellakay and Uncle Pongo still ate their breakfasts there, Sonny always perking up extra-specially as soon as they arrived.

Sonny never did put up a signboard at the eating house, despite his newfound legitimacy, but he did replace the mud and wood walls with solid brick, bought new stylish tables and chairs, and had a modern tiled roof installed. An extra section was constructed beside the main structure to be used as a kitchen, an electric stove complete with a new ventilation system taking pride of place. Later on, the pièce de résistance – a solid refrigerator and freezer – was also bought and installed.

Strangefellow had made many new amorous conquests whilst on the election tours he had made in the company of the election committee in the old Morris station wagon. Never one to let the grass grow under his feet, and in the true tradition of a travelling (canine) rock star, he had regularly copulated with a few receptive four-footed 'groupies'. His canine debauchery resulted in one of his many paramours' permanently moving in with him, providing Strangefellow and the Nameless with a litter of puppies shortly thereafter. The pups were adorable. They gambolled about in prancing steps, falling now and then into small pools of muddy water brought on by the inevitable monsoon rains, inducing the bitch to lick off the dirt and mud from their little bodies in ceaseless fits of maternal grooming.

Sonny couldn't keep all the puppies. He had neither the space nor the time to keep an eye on all of them. He gave away all but one to his clientele, who, knowing the unique prowess of the father – Strangefellow – expressed a great desire to possess them. The puppy

Sonny kept bore a close physical resemblance to Strangefellow. As the young chap grew up, he showed the same tendency as his dad to climb trees. In time, both father and son could be seen high above the branches of the benevolent banyan tree, reposing on trifurcate forks. Perchance they were the only tree-climbing dogs at Jellicoe Junction. The bitch stayed wisely on terra firma, keeping a wary eye on her mate and son from the safety of the green, green grass in the clearing below.

CHAPTER 7

Beauty and the Beast

Give me to drink mandragora ...
That I might sleep out this great gap of time.
My Antony is away...

THE SHOE FACTORY WHISTLE BLEW for the end of the morning shift as Trevor and Adonis punched their cards and headed for the Nameless for a snack and a cup of tea. Adonis, the handsomest man in the whole of Jellicoe Junction and one of the poorest, lived a hand-to-mouth existence with no money saved whatsoever. Adonis wasn't his real name, but the breakfast-eaters at the Nameless had given him the sobriquet after Bellakay had one day told them the Greek mythological record of Adonis, of his great beauty and what came out of it. Walking beside his friend, plain-faced Trevor glanced obliquely now and then at the handsome youth beside him, wishing he could have even half his good looks. If only there were some magic potion to drink and become handsome, he thought wistfully, sighing softly to himself. Little did he know that his wishes were soon to be put to a severe test in the form of an exhilarating prophecy that would sweep the island.

Serendib, a local name for a specific variety of the plant species

359

Mandragora officinarum, or mandrake, as commonly called, could be found growing abundantly in the thick forests of Victoria – easily identifiable to those specifically seeking it. Rich in mandragorine, a powerful narcotic and hallucinative agent, it could be fateful if its root was crushed and consumed as a tea or if partaken in any other form. Two tablespoons of dried root powder or a small portion of the crushed fresh root would be quite enough to cause death from asphyxiation preceded by nausea, vomiting, and respiratory paralysis. Not many people in Victoria were aware of all these precise medical facts, although they were more than a tad wary of the root. Everyone knew it was a famous and commonly used poison used by nefarious villains in bygone days of the country's history, when poison was a preferred method of assassination to do away with enemies one preferred dead rather than merely maimed. Nobody spoke of it as a poison these days, however – not much, anyway – as it was more widely known and accepted in modern times as a herbal ingredient Ayurveda physicians used in microscopic quantities to treat an array of illnesses. The practice of Ayurveda healing – a medicine of Vedic tradition native to the Indian subcontinent – was a widely practised form of alternative medicine that was very popular in Victoria. Ancient as the hills, it had become, in modern times, world famous, even rivalling traditional Western medicine practised in the main hospitals in Victoria.

It was proving to be an excellent summer at Jellicoe Junction, but it wasn't the weather, or rather the pellucid blue skies that was a particularly spoken-of topic. Something extraordinary – completely out of the blue – had gripped the people's imagination, causing unprecedented feverish excitement. Almost everyone was in a state of turmoil – a condition brought about by the volatile and inflammable news that had only recently taken an iron grip on the citizens of Victoria.

A highly reputed sage and famed astrologer who boasted a

fanatical, adoring following had made a mind-boggling prophecy in conjunction with the forthcoming total eclipse of the sun.

The sage had no fixed religion. His teachings leant towards pantheism, making him all the more acceptable to peoples of *all* faiths. Even diehard agnostics were often swayed by his teachings, secretly admiring the man despite their godless beliefs.

The great sage's prognostication caught on like wildfire and spread to all corners of the island. It went something like this: 'All ugly persons and even those with average looks would become beautiful in physical appearance if they, upon the auspicious moment the eclipse begins, take a small portion of the serendib plant's root, preferably strained and drunk as a tea. Those already possessing beauty would become even more beautiful!'

The root's toxic properties were waved aside with bold disdain. The eminent sage declared with supreme and sublime confidence that if the portion was taken without expressing fear of any sort once the sun disappeared from view, the root's poison would be nullified, rendered innocuous, and have no adverse effect at all.

The great sage's reputation was countrywide, untarnished, and well established. Not a single soul doubted the veracity of his proclamations, although the British diaspora proclaimed it a pernicious prophecy, one that could have dire consequences...

It was not only the residents of Jellicoe Junction who were affected by the sage's bold proclamation. The whole of Portopo and, for that matter, the entire country was in a state of hitherto unparalleled excitement. Newspapers were full of the proclamation, whilst radio programs had panels discussing it on prime-time listening hours. Even foreign news agencies operating in the island pricked their ears, sending off gleeful faxes to their head offices. There wasn't a single soul in Victoria who didn't know about the sage's prophecy. The 'small' matter of the serendib root's being extremely poisonous was shrugged away in callous contempt, everyone blindly believing the old sage's prophetic words. Nobody had any fear or scruples about drinking the deadly tea.

At the British embassy, the ambassador Mr Godfrey Ramsay was in an absolute state. His good friend, the eminent and well-known international scientist Mr James Caruthers, who had made Victoria his home for many years, had told him over tiffin that afternoon that almost the entire adult population in the island were determined to drink a decoction of serendib tea according to the sage's recommendations. Ramsay was worried not only because he was a genuine humanist and dreaded a large death toll, but also because he feared for the many tea estates which his countrymen owned and ran. Loss of tea exports due to a dip in production would lead to severe commercial hitches in the business world and damage British interests internationally.

'I say, Jamie! What the dickens shall I do? How the devil can we stop this blasted madness? You know how much we depend on the estate workers and the factory chaps for our tea industry here on the island. If those superstitious fools were to die or get sick, all of us would be in for it, I'm afraid! The trade's going to get a terrific whacking! Might take us months to survive such a dip,' Ramsay expostulated, addressing his friend.

Caruthers replied, 'Can't be stopped, my dear Godfrey. Can't be stopped. Nothing can sway these damn chaps once their minds are made up. It's all that blasted mumbo jumbo that sage fellow stirred up – the rascal! Nothing short of a retraction of the proclamation from the man himself can pull this around as things stand. I'm afraid it's gone too far.'

'Surely something can be done, man? We can't just lie down and do nothing!'

'Harrumph!' said Caruthers, knocking the ash and blackened tobacco from his pipe into an ashtray. 'I don't know. We could take some sort of evasive action, I suppose.'

'What sort of evasive action, Jamie? Got a sort of plan?' Ramsay perked up, a gleam of hope in his eye.

'We could alert old Humphrey [another Englishman] down at the Red Cross to be ready with a few mobile first-aid stations on the tea estates and a few down here in Portopo. It's still a few weeks to the eclipse, and it's not too late to send for emergency stomach-pumping equipment and drugs and stuff, perhaps even some medical personnel from Singapore, Burma, and India. It would at least save *some* of these poor chaps' lives.'

'Why, Jamie! That's a splendid idea. I'll get down to it at once.' Here, the ambassador cut short his tiffin and rushed over to his desk to make a few important phone calls.

The island inhabitants, to a man, were all firmly in the grasp of practitioners of the 'dark arts'. Superstitious beliefs of any sort were sponged up with unwavering and unsatiated consistency. Astrologers, casters of spells, palm readers, devil charmers, wizards, witches, warlocks, and the like were firmly believed to have the ability to make anybody's secret desires come true. An unattainable woman, employment sought, success at exams, curing of illnesses – almost anything desired – was considered attainable if one consulted the 'right' practitioner. Such was the belief and faith that people had in the ability of their heroes that they would to a man, swallow hook, line, and sinker anything the charlatans chose to proclaim. The people of Victoria had been promised youth and good looks on the day of the eclipse by the country's most famous sage, and that promise was good enough for them. The sage's prophecy was accepted and believed without reservation. It simply *was* going to happen! Doubters (a small minority) were treated with scathing contempt and subjected to immediate ostracism. It was as though the masses were in some kind of gigantic hypnotic trance. All of them firmly and fervently believed everything their wonderful sage had prophesied.

The famous sage was renowned for leading, and he did indeed lead, a life of great austerity, although on the flip side, his great fame created an empire of parasite spin-offs. Dubious acolytes made an excellent living capitalising on the reputation of the holy one, making handsome incomes by organising prayer meetings, selling mementos, creating membership clubs, and doing practically anything that brought in hard cash. The sage himself was above all such dastardly moneymaking methods, nor did he have the slightest desire to probe into alleged misdeeds indirectly connected to him, preferring instead to live out each day as it came whilst fully absorbed in prayer and meditation. Now and then, some well-meaning follower would try to point out to him that his good name was being sullied by nefarious followers so they could make money, but he would shrug away such accusations in a sublime way, saying, 'Karma will take care of them. Nobody escapes karma! They may dance awhile with their ill-gotten gains, but they'll suffer for it later when karma strikes.'

The clientele at the Nameless, as well as Sonny, the colourful proprietor, were as excited as everyone else about the approaching eclipse and the sage's prediction. To a man, all of them – except old Fotheringill the alleged rain-maker at Jellicoe Junction who doubted everything, and the diehard agnostic Bellakay – were convinced that taking the serendib root in a drinkable decoction would instantly transform them into handsome human beings.

Sonny was constantly seen in front of the large mirror hanging near his cash counter, twirling away at his slightly grey-streaked moustache and beard, thinking all the while how grand he would look after the eclipse, when he had successfully transformed his middle-aged body into that of a handsome young man. He had, of course, long since decided to take a serendib portion and had taken the precaution of stocking an adequate supply of the deadly root in the drawer of his cash register.

Uncle Pongo, the most regular of Sonny's customers, though a devout Christian, was a firm believer in sages, fortune tellers, charms, and other un-Christian-like practices and practitioners. The bishop of Portopo had long since denounced the sage and his organisation as followers of the Devil – a denunciation Uncle Pongo conveniently swept under the carpet. Like Sonny, he had decided to take the plunge. Nothing was going to stop *him* from transforming his leathery old face into a dashingly handsome one.

Father Clement, the parish priest at Jellicoe Junction, was the only religious authority apart from his boss, the bishop, to speak out openly against following the famed sage's advice, branding it all as pernicious. In his usual Sunday Mass sermons, he repeatedly highlighted the risk of offending the good Lord and the dangers of meeting up with Satan in hell if anyone followed the sage's prognostication. He condemned the latter's prophecy sternly, warning his flock in no uncertain terms that following the sage's advice would mean not only joining hands with the Devil, but would also result in one's winding up stone dead in the hospital mortuary! His normally attentive congregation squirmed uncomfortably in their seats at the good priest's tirade, especially the bit of 'winding up stone dead in the hospital mortuary.' They were very fond of their beloved parish priest, nearly always listening to and guided by his counsel, but in this matter they remained fixed as stone, totally unmoved. Deciding to ignore the Frenchman's advice, considering it to be his own private insinuations and thoughts, they put on a stoic front during his verbal assaults. Most of them had already bought the deadly root and were determined to drink a decoction made from it on eclipse day – Satan or no Satan, parish priest or no parish priest, mortuary or no mortuary...

Meanwhile at the Nameless, steamy discussions were taking place almost daily at the breakfast sessions. Sonny was in the forefront of the palavers one morning as he groomed himself in front of his mirror beside his cash counter. 'You fellows think that our whole body is going to change, or only the face? That sage fellow spoke only of taking a *tiny* portion of the root. He didn't say how much! Maybe a tiny portion will only change our faces. How do we know what sort of dosage to take to change the whole body, eh?'

Sonny glanced down from the reflection of his face in his mirror to his portly lower body – especially his protruding belly – after speaking. Hardly any proper exercise had left him with a paunch of some considerable size – a matter that bothered him no end. His promiscuous nature demanded that he look good in the eyes of his many female beholders, and a large belly certainly didn't augur well.

Already his army of lovers was tottering, causing him much concern. Many of his paramours seemed to prefer the charms of younger, slimmer, and better-looking men. Sonny found it hard going to accept the natural way of things and the fact that he was ageing like everyone else.

Catnips, fresh from the impressive impact he had made during Bellakay's recently concluded election campaign, spoke out first in answer to Sonny's query, seemingly well informed of exactly how much of the root one had to take. 'Ha! My dear Sonny, that all depends on how much of the serendib tea you're going to drink. You drink a teaspoon, maybe just your nose will change. You drink two tablespoons, your face will change. Two and a bit more will even give you a new head of hair. And if you drink three tablespoons or more, your whole body will change.'

'Huh! How do you know all that stuff?' asked Trevor suspiciously. 'How did *you* suddenly go and become such a big-shot serendib expert?'

'Yes, yes,' chorused the breakfast-eaters in concerned unison. 'Who told you about them teaspoons and tablespoon measures, Catnips? How did you get that information, eh?'

It wasn't just idle banter or baiting Catnips that the breakfast-eaters were bent on – not this time around. They were deadly serious, genuinely in doubt, desperately wanting to know just how much of the poison to consume. The great sage had carelessly (or so it seemed) neglected to say exactly how *much* to take. He had only mentioned a 'small portion' – a statement that had caused much confusion. A common consensus most people arrived at was that two tablespoons would suffice to change one's entire body, but Catnips's unexpected comments about dosages in relation to one's face and other body parts had them all confused.

Catnips glared at the present company uncomfortably. He thought he had made a simple and clever observation about dosage quotas and hadn't expected such a ruckus. He didn't want to willingly retreat from what he considered was a brilliant piece of logical deduction on his part, but a suitable reply was needed if he was to save face. Luckily for him, one flashed through his mind just at that moment – a most inspired flash. He replied boldly, gesturing with his wiry, spider-like hands in an airy manner, as though he had some superior acumen for the subject.

'Who told me? Who told me? Why the devil should anyone *tell* me? *Nobody* told me! Why do I need other people to tell me things? I'm clever enough to know things myself! Any fool can see the serendib stuff is like a medicine. When you fellows get a headache or fever, you take Vincent aspirins or Coleman aspirins, right? You take just one tablet, the blooming headache and fever hardly gets better. You take two or three tablets, the headache eases off and the fever goes down, right?' He looked around the company inquiringly, arching his eyebrows in a Mephistophelian manner for theatrical effect. Expecting a contradiction but getting none, he continued confidently. 'You take six or seven tablets, you'll get severe stomach cramps. You take the whole bottle, you'll sure like hell kick the bucket and die. It's all the same with serendib. You must give yourself the correct dosage, like I said. If you take an excessive dose, why then—' Here, he stopped his bold 'calculus' to enhance his last sentence by swishing his right hand dramatically across his throat, indicating that death would follow the excessive drinker.

The assembled company digested this information in thoughtful silence. They could not find any immediate flaw in Catnips's reasoning, although they could not, for the life of them, fathom how he had worked out the teaspoons and tablespoons measures. It was common knowledge that the root was sheer poison, but teaspoons and tablespoons? The group remained silent, though, refraining from contradicting Catnips. None of them wanted to interpose and risk appearing stupid by openly showing they were ignorant about Catnips's portion table, which he somehow seemed to have worked out through some complicated mathematics. One never could be certain of Catnips, whether he was lying, joking, or telling the truth. He was all sorts of things rolled into one and could well have a professor's degree in mathematics and measurements in his baggage, for all they knew. To a certain extent, though, they concurred he had to be right, at least on the matter of portions, which drew their attention to the dangers of taking too much of the deadly decoction. None were anxious to 'kick the bucket', as Catnips so callously and ruthlessly put it.

Bellakay, the third MP for Jellicoe Junction and now a very important person in the city, thought different. In the past, he was not inclined to speak often, except when trying to correct his fellow breakfast-eaters' factual mistakes or nullify the blatant lies Catnips would often come up with, but his recent success at the local elections had rejuvenated his confidence. He was definitely talkative these days, always ready and eager for a discussion. The great man spoke out from his corner, intermittently sipping from a cup of steaming-hot tea.

'You fellows are all foolish to listen to that humbug sage chap and those cunning rascals who follow him all over the countryside while making tons and tons of money. It's nothing but a big scam, I'm telling you,' he opened, the cynical tone of his voice unmistakable, his manner almost sneering. He looked around himself fiercely, as though daring anyone to contradict him.

'How can that vile serendib stuff make anybody beautiful? The blasted root is pure poison – we all know that. The only thing it's going to do to you is make you sick like dogs. And if you drink more than a tablespoon or two, you're all risking kicking the bucket, that's for sure. You fellows are only going to cause the government hospital to be overcrowded, or give more business to them damn-blasted funeral undertakers – dirty capitalist scoundrels, the lot of them. Always waiting like hawks for someone to die!'

Bellakay wiped his mouth with a serviette in a gesture of finality after delivering his chilling prognostication. He said no more, retiring into his corner, a bit surprised by the fierceness of his tirade.

The breakfast-eaters were not amused by Bellakay's opinions. In their present eager state to become handsome Adonises, the incumbent intellectual's talk of death and funeral undertakers sounded rather rebellious, even downright perfidious – not in keeping with the general consensus. Normally, they all looked up to Bellakay, listening very carefully to whatever he had to say, but in this instance they scorned the great man's words of caution. The whole serendib business and the root's promised effects had taken such a hold on them that anyone propagating against it was instantly regarded with deep suspicion – an enemy of humankind – an ungrateful cur. All they wanted to hear were words of support for consuming serendib, not anything to the contrary. To a man, they were determined the matter should run its rightful course. Their respect for Bellakay had doubled and trebled ever since he had become an MP, but in this matter they ignored their hero, giving him withering looks of disapproval and outright contempt.

Catnips, who suddenly found himself elevated to the position of expert on serendib, spoke up for his fellow cronies who lacked the courage to verbally disagree with Bellakay. He had become the darling of the assembly, seemingly unable to say or do any wrong. Bridling with pride over his new status, he responded to Bellakay's venomous tirade in a condescending, mollifying voice, addressing Bellakay as though the latter were a little child who needed correcting.

'Harrumph! Bellakay, my dear fellow! Dear man! We all know you now sit in Parliament with all those big-shot politicians and all that, but don't lecture us about serendib, dear friend! We do *know* that that the serendib stuff is poison. We're not fools!' Here he stopped to wink at the listening breakfast-eaters in a conspiratorial manner before continuing. 'You see, Bellakay. You see, my dear friend, the magical thing is that the root's poison will not take effect on eclipse day – *that's* the great secret the holy sage has revealed to us! Strange things happen at eclipses! Remember the two-headed little one born to old Joolius's goat at the last eclipse we had?' How did that happen, eh? Can you explain that, Bellakay?'

Bellakay felt pressed to give Catnips an answer. He reluctantly spoke again and tried to pooh-pooh the history of Joolius's two-headed goat by offering a sound scientific theory instead, but the breakfast-eaters were having none of it. They shouted him down in unison – the very first time they had actually done so. Gone was the esteem they held for their resident sage and member of Parliament. Bellakay, sensing he was getting nowhere with his heavily indoctrinated cronies, retired gracefully to his seat at the corner of the table, allowing Catnips to take centre stage. 'Damn-blasted nincompoops!' he mumbled under his breath. 'They'll all die, that's for sure.'

It was still quite early in the day, and Parliament wouldn't open till eleven. Not wanting to remain and be a part of the ongoing discussion, Bellakay murmured a few inaudible excuses, pushed back his plate, and trudged off. The assembly scarcely noticed he was gone. They weren't usually a fickle bunch – the breakfast-eaters – but they just couldn't be bothered with Bellakay right now. MP or not, there were much more important matters on hand.

Catnips's comments about the two-headed goat only served to make the assembly even more convinced of the dark nature of eclipses. Thoroughly buoyed, they were now more convinced than ever that it would be absolutely safe to indulge in a small portion of serendib tea on the auspicious day of the eclipse. As with Sonny, all of them had unobtrusively, and unbeknown to each other, bought small portions of the root and stashed it away in the privacy of their homes. They meant to grind it into a pulp, make a tea-like decoction, and drink it on the day of the eclipse – all in accordance with what the national sage and his followers had propagated. They were especially mindful of Catnips's measurement tables, fully determined to do as the 'expert' had recommended

'Make sure that you take the stuff exactly when the sun disappears and before the sun appears again, boys,' quipped Catnips before the assembly trudged off to their respective destinations after breakfast. Those who remained reposed sedately on the grassy clearing under the banyan tree, lost in their private thoughts. To a man, they all fantasised, imagining how wonderfully handsome they would be after the eclipse.

Catnips was in a state of ecstasy. For many years, he had tried to topple Bellakay from the latter's throne of official sage and guru at the Nameless, without the remotest success. To make matters worse, it had become even more difficult after Bellakay's election success. But now – at long last – he had made a major breakthrough. Bellakay was momentarily out of grace, and he, Catnips, had become unanimously accepted as the group's official 'senior advisor', or so it seemed. It thrilled the mercurial one no end, although he knew it was only baby steps yet. Right now, he was in favour through the dosage business, but perhaps he could totally wrest Bellakay's crown from the old goat? Who could tell? One thing was for sure: he *was* moving in the right direction. After the eclipse, he would proudly boast how right he was and end Bellakay's influence permanently.

'Serve the all-knowing old bugger right,' he mused vindictively, 'always trying to correct me with his damn fancy facts and theories. The fellow ought to be grateful to me for getting him elected instead of putting me down every time I say some damn thing!'

In truth, Bellakay *did* indeed express his heartfelt thanks to Catnips for the latter's unsavoury yet decisive role in the rotting-crow business and the frame-up of Hazimudoo directly after the deeds were done, but Catnips had a short memory. He expected people in his debt to fawn over him forever and look the other way whenever he stretched the truth – something Bellakay wasn't too keen on doing.

None of the excitement had bypassed Rohan, Salgado, and the rest of the school gang. As expected, Salgado was perceptibly in the thick of things.

'Are any of you chaps going to buy any of that serendib root stuff?' he inquired of his inner circle after the Latin class was over, in-between waiting for the next class taken by Mr Bull.

His friends, bored to death by dreary Latin verbs Mr Cedric had drilled into them (unsuccessfully) the past forty-five minutes, were only too happy to engage in any diverting conversation. They pricked up their ears at Salagado's inquiry, welcoming the interlude.

Obadiah, the gang's regular sceptic, was the first to comment. 'Bah! All them holy fellows' talk just doesn't seem right to me. How can ugly people become beautiful if they go and drink that stupid stuff? It's not possible! There have been eclipses before, you know! Why didn't anyone say anything then? That holy sage fellow and the rest are one big bunch of humbugs, I'm telling you.'

Obadiah looked around himself daringly. Even as he finished speaking, he knew instinctively that a contradiction would come in some cutting fashion or other in the time-honoured manner he was accustomed to. Everyone regularly shouted down young Obadiah's utterances and proclamations in sheer exasperation over his tendency to doubt anything anyone proclaimed. Nobody could fathom why Obadiah was so gloomy and negative. He had wealthy and doting parents, did fairly well at his studies, and was a persistent, albeit unwelcome, member of the school gang, yet he always managed to air an array of dismal opinions in an endless Aladdin's cove of gloom.

The expected riposte came cuttingly and swiftly.

'Huh! What do *you* know about them holy fellows' and wizard's powers! They can do horrible charms and stuff. Once, back home, a fellow hired a charmer to put a spell on the bank manager because he was refused a loan. The manager chap became quite mad within a month. The fellow came to work fully naked with only his blooming tie around his neck and his dingle sticking out. Pa said another charmer chap had to do a special ceremony for him to get well again. Them wizards and charmers and holy fellows can do anything. They can make even fatty fellows like Salgado thin like planks if they want to.'

The pearl came from Moon, thoroughly enjoying his dig at Salgado's obesity. Moon was a fairly new addition to the class, having transferred from a distant village school after his family had moved to take up a new life and residence at Jellicoe Junction. He had mounds of pimples on his forehead and cheeks, which marred and dotted an otherwise good-looking face.

Salgado stared dangerously at Moon. Usually, he remained completely indifferent to jibes made by anyone touching on his corpulence, but nevertheless made it a strict personal rule never to let any insult on his obesity or anything else go unchallenged. He knew he was obese, but he adopted a laid-back attitude, discarding all comments about his portliness with genuine unconcerned aloofness. Rather than losing his cool, he welcomed the jibes. It gave him the necessary leverage to have a legitimised go at his critics – often engaging in physical combat, a pastime he thoroughly relished. He never, ever lost a fight with anyone.

'Fatty fellow, eh? Become thin as a plank, eh? It's better to be a fatty fellow than a blasted pimple-faced baboon like you, Moon. Maybe *you* should take some of that serendib stuff so your poxy damn pimples disappear for good.'

Salgado's reply was meant to lure Moon into physical combat, rather than seek revenge for the latter's comments on his obesity. He was a past master at manoeuvring boys into a fight.

Moon flared up in anger at the reference to his pimples, which, in truth, caused him widening concern every passing day. Unlike Salgado, who cared nought for his corpulence, Moon was extremely sensitive of *his* special affliction. Like Salgado, he could dish out insults with lightning-quick speed, but there all comparisons ended... He did not suffer insults well, especially those veering on the subject of his pimples. Moon was not as big and powerful as Salgado, but he was short and stocky, and very strong. He also had a fiery temper and had taken instant offence at Salgado's telling barb directed at his marred facial looks.

'You want to take this outside, you fatty old piece of dung?'

'Okay,' said Salgado jubilantly, thrilled to the core he had successfully manoeuvred Moon into combat. The additional insult didn't bother him. He was not in the least bit concerned about being likened to a piece of dung.

'Maybe you don't need to drink that serendib stuff after all, Moon! I can knock out all them pimples on your face for free.'

Here a scuffle took place between the two. Salgado was definitely having the better of the exchanges, landing a few lusty blows, but he was caught unawares by the tenacious Moon, who went into a clinch and bit the fat one's upper arm expertly, almost drawing blood. Salgado yelped in pain just at the arrival of their strict and demanding history teacher, Mr Bull, who pulled the gusty combatants apart by their ears.

The two antagonists retired to their seats in momentary resignation. Moon was not entirely unhappy over the timely intervention of Mr Bull. One side of Moon's face was bright red from expert pimple bashing whilst Salgado checked his bitten arm to see if the skin was broken. Mr Bull did not punish the young gladiators. He was known to be strict and demanding but also for *not* punishing boys indulging in physical combat. He was considered a good sport by the students at the entire school, often ignoring scraps unless they went too far. Moon and Salgado didn't resume their fight after the history lesson was over and Mr Bull had left. Moon, having experienced Salgado's massive strength, was wary of a second round, and Salgado just couldn't be bothered.

Ruminating on his position during and after Mr Bull's excellent history discourse, Moon was quite desolate – almost at the end of his tether. He had suffered immeasurably at Salgado's insulting yet telling words. His pimples really did bother him no end, and the frustration of trying remedy after remedy without any visible success had taken its toll. Maybe that serendib stuff could help him, he mused. After all, nothing else did! So why not try? He decided to have a talk with Rohan, for whom he had acquired a good deal of respect in the short time since he had transferred over. Rohan had shown a very friendly front and had generously helped him initially to settle down in the new school.

'Hey, Rohan,' he said, addressing Rohan after school was over that day when the boys were departing to their respective homes. 'Rohan, what do you say about that serendib stuff, eh? You think it's really going to make people who take it look beautiful? That famous holy sage fellow and all them other wizards and charmer chaps can't be wrong like Obadiah says, surely?'

Rohan was flattered by Moon's obvious yearning to get *his*

valuable opinion on the matter, thinking his classmate must surely consider him a genius of sorts. He knew that the boys in his class thought him clever, but none of them had ever asked for his advice directly. Putting on a look of superhuman intelligence, he answered airily, befitting one whose opinion was so eagerly sought. 'Hmm! Maybe it will work, Moon. Maybe it will work. All them astrologer fellows and everyone else say it's going to work. Don't take any notice of silly old Obadiah. That fellow never agrees with anything! Why, at home, my aunt Primrose and my aunt Celeste and even Mother are secretly planning to take the stuff.'

Nothing going on under Grandmummy's roof escaped the inquisitive nose of Rohan or for that matter even his brother, Mahan. The fact that his mother and his aunts had already bought small portions of the root had not escaped their stern vigilance.

'Whaaat?! Your aunts and mother, you say? Why, then, that settles it! I mean, if *they* are going to take the stuff, then it just *has* to be all right! They're adults, aren't they? They should know.'

Rohan – slightly bemused by Moon's keen questioning – could not for the moment connect the dots but managed to do so after a short while. He said to Moon, 'Ha! You're thinking of taking the stuff, aren't you? You want to go and get all beautiful and everything like everyone else!'

'Noooooo!' drawled Moon untruthfully. 'Why do I need to do that? I look all right. Mother often says that I'm going to turn into a handsome young man soon! Them pimples I have will all go away once I get older, she says!'

'Hmm. I suppose that will happen, Moon,' said Rohan, scratching his young head, his thoughts drifting to Giles, whose pockmarked cheeks – a result of boyhood pimples – stood out prominently. 'Yes, I suppose it will happen as your mother says and those pimples of yours will go away someday. Mothers know an awful lot of things, you know!'

Here, the boys paused to contemplate the magical powers of

mothers for a moment or two before parting company amiably to go their separate ways.

Moon was impressed and relieved. Spurred on by the knowledge that Rohan's aunts and mother were going to take the plunge, he decided right then and there that he would somehow obtain a small portion of serendib root and take in on the day of the eclipse, as recommended by the sage and his followers. He wouldn't tell his mother but would do it secretly. 'No more pimples for me,' he thought with a great sigh of relief, grateful for Rohan's soothing counsel. Feeling much better, he walked on with a lighter step, his head held high, his mind drifting into a future scenario after the eclipse. After his pimples were gone and once he had transformed into a dazzling young prince, he would call Salgado a 'fatty piece of dung' again, and this time Salgado would not be able to insult him back by referring to his pimples – or any part of his anatomy, for that matter. He visualised a life without pimples – a life as a superbly handsome young boy – the world at his feet. What good times beckoned! 'Thank God for that wonderful sage, the eclipse, and all them astrologer fellows,' he mumbled under his breath, his joy knowing no bounds.

Another boy in Rohan's school gang who had decided to take the plunge was Lizard, whose ugly skin condition on his lower legs caused him endless agony. Like Moon, he was the constant butt of many a hurtful jibe from his callous schoolmates. Quite a common affliction in Victoria, the condition manifested itself in scale-like, dried-up dead skin, forming for the most below one's knees and down to the ankles. Lizard's scales, which his wicked school chums likened to the rough skin of Victoria's largest monitor lizard of the genus *Varanus*, gave rise to his moniker. Lizard was sick and tired of being called a reptile, especially one as ugly as the *Varanus*, and despaired of his blemished lower legs. He had tried wearing longer socks, but they wouldn't stay as high at the knee as he wanted, eventually sliding down to display the blemished skin. Besides, it was very uncomfortable wearing long socks in the withering tropical heat; only the school's Scout contingent managed to pull it off somehow.

'Huh,' said Lizard to himself, 'we shall see who's a lizard after the eclipse! I'll show them fellows a thing or two. They're going to have one jolly big surprise!' Like Moon, he visualised himself free from his affliction, his legs smooth as silk. Once his awful scales were gone, he could take part in the school's swimming activities, something he had decisively opted out of quite early in his school career because of his shameful condition.

Meanwhile, monks, priests, and other religious dignitaries at their respective places of worship did not officially volunteer to make any statement about the safety, morals, or religious implications of believing and following the great sage's proclamation. Their stony silence was interpreted by everyone in Victoria as an unofficial nod of approval. Citizens nodded their heads wisely, deducing that religious protocol must have made it impossible for the holy ones to trumpet their approval and that their silence was meant to convey nothing less than a very definite 'yes'. They weren't so far off from the truth. The otherwise passionate and outspoken clergy had their own reasons for keeping their mouths shut and maintaining a low profile. The great sage was not a favourite in their books. They frowned upon him disapprovingly, chiefly because he had rejected all *their* respective religions and had gone on to propagate pantheism, a philosophy they detested and considered highly dangerous – one that could end individual secular beliefs. The sage's prediction made them angry at first, but they soon changed their tune, seeing it all in a different light altogether. Giving the matter further thought, they reasoned that there was something really big to be gained from the whole situation – an opportune moment like no other. They had good cause to arrive at such a conclusion.

Victorians always suspected illness, misfortune, and accidents to be a direct result of the 'evil eye' – or rather that someone or other had put a jinx or curse on them, possibly through a hired professional warlock in exchange for a considerable monetary price. A spin-off effect of this superstitious hotchpotch was that, in a twisted sort of way, it helped to keep noses firmly grounded in religious matters. Adversities of most kinds were inevitably attributed to sinister forces of the occult. Alleged charms, spells, curses, and other such ungodly matters, proved to be a wonderful gold mine for clergymen whose religiously mundane congregations nearly always suspected an enemy was behind their misfortunes. Frightened by the belief that they were under the influence of dark forces, sufferers frequently turned to their respective clergy for solace and advice. Irrespective of whatever religion clergymen represented, they profited a great deal preying on the frightened minds of their prosaic flocks, often demanding hard cash for performing 'cleansing' ceremonies and the like. It was a seemingly ceaseless source of income, the well never running dry. As things stood, every single clergyman believed that something profitable would emerge from the whole serendib business, too. It was only the resilient French parish priest, an ardent Christian, who openly propagated against the holy – or rather, in *his* opinion, *unholy* – sage. He thundered out from his pulpit at Sunday Mass, denouncing and chastising in no uncertain terms the dangers of the sage's 'beauty' theory, which so callously required his congregation to willingly drink an outright poisonous brew. His rants proved a complete waste of time, the congregation just staring ahead into empty space, stoic and unfazed by his shouting. They ignored his denouncements patiently and just waited for him to get on with the actual service.

Joolius, the 'city' farmer whom Catnips had mentioned in the recently concluded conversation at the Nameless, was in turmoil, a myriad of thoughts running through his greying head. The whole affair of the sage's prophecy bothered him no end, gnawing deeper and deeper into his soul and causing him to soliloquy often and long. Like Hamlet – an aged Hamlet, but Hamlet-like nonetheless – he was steeped in uncertainty over whether 'to be' or 'not to be', or rather to take the plunge or not, the plunge being, of course, drinking a portion of serendib and even giving his precious livestock some.

Joolius had twelve goats, eight of which provided a steady income in fresh milk. He would rise early each morning, milk the goats, have his breakfast, and then push off on his pedal trishaw to distribute bottles of milk to his many customers. The four remaining goats, far too young to be producing milk, remained a solid investment for the future.

From time to time, Joolius took one or two nanny goats whilst they were in the midst of their reproduction cycles to his only friend, Vincentius, who lived in a small house with a neat garden at the other end of the city. Vincentius kept a fertile billy goat for the express purpose of siring. Many goat-owners came to him to have their nannies impregnated by his admirable animal, hoping for a new fold of kids and a subsequent guarantee of posterity. Joolius was no exception. He had managed to get his four present kids by having his goats impregnated through the famed billy's efforts. It felt comforting to know that his milk business was more or less guaranteed for a decade more to come – or thereabouts. Apart from the goats, Joolius also kept a large number of hens, whose eggs added to his excellent income from the milk. Now and then, he would slaughter a few old hens, selling the meat at the marketplace for a handsome profit.

Joolius was a greedy man, one extremely inclined towards avarice. As the years rolled on, he had managed to put aside a considerable sum of money which he had no earthly use for, hoarding it with Scrooge-like zeal. He had no family of his own nor any extended relatives, not even a distant cousin or two – or so he professed – although no one knew this for certain. Not averse to practising dubious business methods, he would regularly and carefully water the goat's milk in a careful way to prevent arousing his customers' suspicion. The eggs he regularly dyed in portions of dark brown tea on account of his customers' having a peculiar aversion to buying white eggs. Nutritional properties of white eggs were supposed to be lacking in comparison to those of brown eggs – considerably cheaper to buy at all retail shops.

Joolius's livestock provided a more than sufficient income for the old miser. Most of his hard cash he hoarded in a local bank, for which he received a solid rate of interest, but he was still not satisfied. His yearning to make more and more money was insatiable, dominating and surpassing every other thing in his life – even women. He decided at a very early stage of his adult life not to marry, horrified by the thought of sharing his wealth with a spouse and eventual children. Joolius wasn't a misogamist, but he callously ruled out a martial relationship, preferring instead to regularly solicit the services of prostitutes a couple of times a month. As time went by, even his promiscuous romps came to an end as advancing age took its natural toll – his potency flying through the window.

In addition to being avaricious, Joolius was one of the worst cowards at Jellicoe Junction – horrified of getting illnesses or exposing himself to danger of any sort. Although the ongoing serendib theory appealed strongly to both his vanity and conniving nature, he was at the same time terribly fearful of the root's poisonous effects. He would have loved to take some of the stuff and become young again, but fear stayed his hand and made him circumspect, unable to decide if the great sage was right or wrong. There would be nobody to take care of him if the serendib proved to have adverse effects, he reasoned. At such times, and when tropical fevers racked his body, he would often wonder if it hadn't been a mistake not to take a wife in his younger days.

Joolius's fear of the serendib root's poisonous properties and possible repercussions did not extend to his goats. Over the years, he had watched his goats eat everything from rusty and crumbling tin cans to any kind of litter they came across, without the animals' showing the slightest tendency to fall ill. He was seriously considering giving his livestock reasonable portions of serendib disguised in their fodder. After all, he reflected, hadn't his animals survived after eating all that blooming muck? What harm could serendib possibly do when the damn creatures stuffed themselves with the worst kind of refuse on an almost daily basis! He cunningly reasoned that if he gave his goats, who were getting on a bit in years, a dose of serendib, then they would become younger and extend their milk-producing years considerably.

Joolius was a bit jittery, afraid to actually go ahead with the deed – sorely in need of counselling from a third party. His mind drifted to Vincentius, the closest human he could call a friend. He needed to talk to somebody discreetly about it all, and Vincentius was the only person he knew who would keep mum or even condescend to talk to him, for that matter. Apart from not having a wife, Joolius dearly regretted that he never bothered to make more friends. Everyone he knew (apart from Vincentius and his customers) disliked him, shying away from any friendly advances he made.

One late afternoon after the strong tropical sun had waned and disappeared beneath the horizon, Joolius pedalled off on his milk-transport tricycle to visit Vincentius. Well at his destination, he parked his tricycle by the pathway leading to his friend's ramshackle old cottage, which stood in the middle of a small clearing, and knocked on the door.

Vincentius was a bit surprised to see his part-time friend, not expecting company – not Joolius's, anyway. The last time Joolius visited was when he had brought along his goats for a tête-à-tête with his randy billy. They had since met a few times at the marketplace, exchanged a few pleasantries, and departed on their separate ways – Joolius never showing an inclination to take things to a higher level. Nevertheless, he welcomed his visitor, wondering what on earth had brought him so suddenly. He didn't have to ponder long before Joolius came briskly to the point.

'I say, Vincentius, my dear fellow,' began Joolius in an obsequious manner, accepting an offer to sit on a comfortable rocking chair in the veranda of Vincentius's home. 'You heard about this serendib thing? What do you make of it all, eh?'

Vincentius looked up startled, a bemused expression on his face. 'Heard? What I've heard? Why, my dear Joolius, that's all these people are talking about these days. Serendib this and serendib that! That's all I hear! Can't go anywhere without hearing these chaps talking about it. Why are you asking? Going to take some of the stuff yourself, eh?

Want to get young again, is it?' he asked with a mischievous twinkle in his eye.

'Oh! Pish-posh, Vincentius,' protested Joolius, pretendingto be aghast at the thought, although secretly relishing the notion of becomingyoung again. 'Not me, my dear fellow. We old codgers don't want to be young again, do we? No. I'm just asking if it could help my goats, you see! I was thinking, why not make the poor fellows young all over again? I mean, if that sage fellow's story proves to be true, that is! What do you think, eh? Could it work?'

'Harrumph!' said Vincentius, scratching his woolly white head. 'Why, I never thought of that before! I suppose if that sage chap said that humans can take the stuff without getting sick or dying, then it must be safe for animals too! Stands to reason, doesn't it? Animals have almost the same anatomy as we humans, don't they?' He continued, slightly nonplussed as to why Joolius was so eager to make his goats young again. 'But do you really want to give them goats of yours the stuff? They're getting on, yes, but they're not *that* old, what? Why, they might get so young they may become small ones again, and you will have to wait years before they start giving you milk! Besides, you have four pukka youngsters waiting in the wings that will soon give you milk. Is that not so?'

'No, no, Vincentius, my dear fellow! That sly Catnips fellow, the same chap who went and put them dead crows at old Hazimudoo's meeting and all that, has proclaimed that it all boils down to the *dosage* one takes. I'm only thinking of giving them a weeny dose! This will make them only a wee bit younger, young enough to start their milk-producing cycle all over again from scratch, so to speak! Wouldn't that be wonderful?'

Vincentius was greatly impressed by his friend's brilliant reasoning and astute business sense. He invited Joolius into his kitchen to discuss it more over a cup of tea.

The duo discussed the matter long into the evening. By the time Joolius departed, both he and Vincentius had firmly decided they would definitely give their goats a small dose of serendib at the eclipse. Influenced by Joolius, Vincentius reasoned even his excellent billy could become young again and sire many more kids, increasing and prolonging his own income in the process – an admirable state of affairs. He had long wondered what he would do the day his old billy couldn't copulate anymore – or worse still, if the animal died of old age! How could he have been so blind not to have seen that the solution lay in this serendib thing? It had been staring him in the face all this while, and he didn't even see it! The reasonable thing to do was to make his old billy young again. And while he was at it, why not take some of the stuff himself? After all, what was the use of his goat's regaining his youth if *he* would remain old? Why, he could die before the goat! The horror of his probable demise and the goat's superseding him made him firmly make up his mind; both he and his beloved billy *were* going to drink serendib tea on the eclipse day! Completing his reverie, Vincentius put on his old coat over his baggy trousers, tucked his favourite black umbrella under one arm, and anxiously hightailed it to Galahad Street, where there were still a few small shops open selling Ayurveda medicines and ingredients. By jingo! He thought it was a blessing that old Joolius had come visiting that day.

At Grandmummy's, the predictions and expectations of events to come at the forthcoming eclipse had not gone unnoticed – far from it. The aunts and Rohan's mother discussed matters constantly and with a great deal of passion. Both Primrose and Celeste giggled often at how surprised Giles and Don would be to see their enhanced looks after they had drunk a portion of serendib. Even the normally composed and wise Rebecca put aside her sobriety temporarily, well and truly caught up in the madness that had taken such a firm hold on everyone else. 'They're saying now that even a small dose of serendib is not enough! There is a rumour going around that one has to increase the dosage for the *whole* body to change,' said an excited Rebecca.

'Yes, I heard that too. There is a girl at the office who says she is going to take three tablespoons. She is not only ugly, but fat too,' chipped in Primrose, glancing down appreciatively at her own streamlined figure.

Celeste was doubtful about the dosage theory. 'I heard the dosage thing was all started by Catnips, that horrible fellow who tried to hoodwink us into marrying him. That fellow cannot be trusted. Don told me the other day that a doctor friend of his said that even two tablespoons could be very dangerous, but I don't know whether to believe Don, either. I suspect he just wants to put me off the stuff. Anyway, whatever we do, I think we must agree not to tell Mother anything. She'll just blow her top and bring the whole bloody house down!'

The sisters made a pact. They would somehow buy the dangerous root, make a decoction, and drink a tablespoon or more apiece on eclipse day. Grandmummy was to be kept in the dark…

It wasn't all plain sailing for the sisters, though, as obtaining a small portion of serendib root proved to be a bit of a stumbling block. They were much too bashful to visit an Ayurveda shop on their own and buy the stuff over the counter. Luckily, the problem proved short-lived, thanks to the efforts of Primrose, who saved the day for them all. A most unlikely heroine, she came home one evening after work and announced breathlessly without much ado that all was well. 'Our office boy, Rupert, is getting the stuff for some of the staff, so I can get him to buy some of the root for us too,' she said conspiringly, well out of Grandmummy's hearing.

'Is it going to be expensive?' asked Rebecca, who was always walking a financial tightrope these days.

'Yes, but we need only a small quantity – and we must order now or Rupert says stocks will soon vanish completely. He said people are buying the stuff like madmen,' said Primrose airily, conveniently forgetting that she and her sisters were as mad as the rest.

'I'm in. Here, take this ten-rupee note and give me the balance after you pay the chap for my share,' said Celeste in a decidedly determined fashion.

Not to be outdone, Rebecca – hard-pressed as she was – produced a five-rupee note she had been holding onto for many weeks, and handed it over to Primrose. She looked long and wistfully at the note before handing it over. She had saved the money to go out with Uncle Pongo's wife, Bella, to see a much-hyped Clark Gable film and was much loath to let it go.

The very next day, Primrose placed her order with Rupert, triumphantly coming home the same evening with a small package of serendib root nestled safely inside her handbag.

Grandmummy was kept in the dark, but nothing bypassed the children, who soon became aware of what the sisters were planning. Rohan, who had recently seen a Zorro matinee featuring Errol Flynn, a popular Hollywood actor, fancied a teaspoonful or two of serendib tea himself. He had visions of his high person decked out as a handsome young Zorro copy, black cape flowing in the wind whilst he swung dashingly from a banister with a drawn sword in his free hand. Mahan had his own private visions – mainly showing off his newfound beauty to his wealthy Moor friends at school. Even the little girls caught onto the act, playing make-believe games of drinking serendib tea and becoming beautiful princesses. Only two persons in the household firmly put away all notions of consuming serendib or anything having to do with it all. One was, of course, Grandmummy, and the other was young Laura. Grandmummy firmly refused to be drawn into any conversation on the subject, totally forbidding the household to discuss the matter. Her objections stemmed mainly from religious grounds, influenced to an even higher degree by her friend Father Clement, whose many outspoken tirades denounced the sage and his prophecy as works of the Devil. As for young Laura, she was a true scholarly type, extremely rational in her way of thinking and thoroughly sceptical of superstitions of any sort. She was forever having her nose buried in some book or other, and completely pooh-poohed the supposed miracle that was expected to happen at the eclipse.

Celeste and Primrose, after making discrete inquiries at their workplaces, gradually obtained sufficient information for the best way to make the tea. Their joint research revealed that one had to crush the root into a small pulp and then strain it through a small cloth bag, adding boiling water to make a strong tea. The modus operandi settled, all that was left now was to await the date of the fateful eclipse – a thrilling wait of hopeful anticipation. They could hardly contain themselves...

Catnips, the recently elevated 'senior advisor' on serendib at the Nameless, was having a ball. He hadn't enjoyed himself this much since he nefariously and successfully sabotaged Hazimudoo's election meeting and further sullied the latter's reputation by filming the ex-politician having sex with prostitutes. Firmly adapting himself to the role of proclaimed and widely accepted 'guru' on all matters purporting to serendib, he went around the neighbourhood discussing the best way to drink a portion of serendib with anyone who cared to listen. Even Bellakay's friend Baking Jane did not escape Catnips's attentions. With his glib talk and mercurial powers of persuasion, he got Baking Jane firmly hooked on the idea of taking a strong portion. Not that Jane needed much persuasion. As with everyone else in the country, she had more or less committed herself to taking the poison. Catnips's silver tongue only served to strengthen her resolution into a roaring finality.

One morning during one of her chats with Bellakay in her kitchen, Baking Jane casually declared that she was going to take a dose of serendib. Bellakay was flabbergasted – aghast with horror. In love with Jane, he was distressed that she – as he envisioned – was going to harm or even kill herself through a foolish act dictated by a crackpot sage. He sternly warned her against consuming serendib, an act he considered out-and-out life-threatening. Usually laudatory whenever addressing Baking Jane, he burst out angrily this time around. 'Oh my God, woman! Do you want to kill yourself like a damn-blasted fool? Who's going to take care of your bloody children and grandchildren if anything happens to you, eh? That damn stuff is pure poison, don't you know that? Are you gone off your bloody head?'

Bellakay didn't care if he upset her – not now. All he wanted was to firmly drill into his mundane love's head the dangers of what she was contemplating. He hated her to get sick and suffer – or, worse still, die! Her demise would just be too horrendous to bear, especially now, after his election success, and when he was so close to making her an offer of marriage!

Baking Jane did not take offence at Bellakay's heavy-handed chiding. She replied in a low-key sort of voice, seemingly subdued, not at all in her normal chirpy manner. Bellakay had stood by her through thick and thin. Only a month ago he had used his newfound influence as an MP to get her a much sought-after loan from a cooperative bank – not an easy task – since she had no collateral. Secretly, she felt sorry for old Bellakay for missing out on such a golden opportunity to transform himself and become young and handsome.

'It's not going to be any trouble, Bellakay. All them astrologer fellows say the serendib poison will not have any effect at the time of the eclipse. Why, even the old monk at the Lord Nelson Street temple has said that there will be absolutely no harm in taking the stuff,' she protested gently whilst tending her small baking ovens. (The monk mentioned was the only religious cleric at Jellicoe Junction who openly encouraged people to drink the serendib.)

'Astrologers! Bah! What damn astrologers! A bunch of cursed conmen, that's what they are! Guttersnipes and blackguards, the lot of them! Full of bloody monkey tricks. As for that old monk fellow you're talking about, why, everyone knows the rascal's taking offering money from the till and using it to drink quality whisky and beer every bloody weekend! The fellow also orders big sirloin steaks from the De Luxe Hotel, when his religion says he should refrain from eating meat! How can you people rely on a scoundrel like that?'

Baking Jane kept silent. True, the old monk had an unsavoury, albeit unproven, reputation for leading a double life – sitting cross-legged solemnly in meditation during the mornings up to lunch, only to disappear into his private chambers for the rest of the day, allegedly to drink alcohol and eat like a glutton. Nothing could be proven, however, as nobody had ever caught him in the supposed surreptitious acts. The whistle-blower who made the allegations – a former young acolyte – had cut short his apprenticeship and run away after a dispute with the old monk. Anyway, monk or no monk, Baking Jane was totally aligned with her fellow citizens, adamantly and firmly believing that the poisonous properties of the root would be rendered innocuous on the auspicious day of the eclipse. She possessed – as did the breakfast-eaters at the Nameless and many others – a deep respect for Bellakay, but in this instance decided to ignore his advice. All those famous holy people could not be wrong, she reflected. Why, the whole country seemed determined to drink serendib in some form or other, so why listen to old Bellakay's spoiling ramblings? The man couldn't be right in *everything!*

Although middle-aged, Baking Jane still had a wonderfully curvy figure – a bit on the plump side perhaps – but many men turned around to take a second look at her. She would often sigh, reminiscing nostalgically the days when suitors fought over her like madmen. She was flattered then by the effect her great beauty had on men, but she had suffered silently at her appearance's steady decline these past few years. She was still attractive in a reduced sort of way, but she yearned for her former beauty. Her large breasts, projectiles that constantly enthralled many, were not the firm, well-shaped pair she possessed before. Of late, she noticed tiny wrinkles appearing close to her nipples. The growing grey in her hair was also disconcerting – showing out now and then amidst her otherwise coal-black plumage. She knew she still possessed an eye-catching figure, but was wary that it too would disintegrate as Father Time marched relentlessly on. A dose of serendib was her only way out, and nobody – *nobody,* not even wise old Bellakay – was going to stop her. Chuckling softly, she envisioned the look of surprise on Bellakay's face the next time they would meet up after the eclipse. Her beauty would be so alluring that even the old boy who was known never to be swayed by a woman's charms would fall for her newfound youth and rejuvenated beauty. Looking at the framed pictures of the seated Buddha and an imploring

Jesus above her baking ovens, she mumbled a few words of humble thanks. 'What a stroke of luck that you sent us that holy sage man, great lords. Truly, you are enlightened ones!'

Baking Jane's daughter-in-law was in the act too, Bellakay having successfully wormed this bit of information from his friend. He shuddered in utter hopelessness. There was nothing he could do. His mind drifted to the several half-naked little children who ran about Baking Jane's house, the daughter-in-law's offspring, and wondered what would become of them all if both Baking Jane *and* her daughter-in-law were to die. It would be the streets for them, he concluded sadly – the only orphanage at Portopo bursting to overcapacity.

Down at the Nameless, discussions continued daily. Much talk was centred on whether children and animals should also be administered a dose of serendib.

'I heard that old Joolius is thinking of giving them goats of his serendib,' said Catnips, whose knowledge of other people's affairs could put the best secret service organisations in the world to shame.

'What! What the hell for!' spluttered Trevor, almost choking on his tea. 'What does the old fool want to go and do such a thing for? Goats are goats! Them animals are neither ugly nor good-looking. Why make them beautiful?'

'Ah! But you see chaps, that's the beauty of it all! He's doing it all for the milk! I heard him say only the other day that if them goats of his drink a bit of serendib, they might get younger and live longer, maybe ten years more! And what happens then, eh, chaps? Why, his blooming goats are going to have a whole lot of extra milking years,' added Catnips, pleased as Punch to be able to reveal Joolius's genial intentions, which he had somehow learned of.

'Ahhhh, that cunning, cunning, shrewd old bugger! The fellow is always looking for new ways to make more and more money. If he gives them goats the stuff, they're sure like hell going to give him milk a longer time before he marches them off to Killing Fellow for slaughtering,' burst out Sonny in irritation, obviously jealous of the fact that another businessman was innovative and resourceful.

'Maybe you ought to give some of that serendib stuff to Strangefellow. He maybe needs to live longer too. I mean, who's going to protect your business place once the old chap's gone, eh?' said Karolis, whose soft spot for the unique incumbent dog was well known.

Sonny couldn't help but feel a surge of pride at Karolis's reference to his beloved eating house as a 'business place', especially now after he had become a legitimate owner of the property the Nameless stood upon and had rebuilt the structure. The temporary moment of self-felicitations passed quickly, though, as he refocused on the ongoing conversation. He said, 'No, that's not necessary. Strangefellow doesn't need to improve his looks. He's the best-looking damn dog in the area, and besides, he's sure to leave many fine-looking puppies after him.'

'Ha, no doubt about that! That's one hell of a dog you have there, Sonny! A real Don Juan. Why, that dog has penetrated almost every bitch in the marketplace. I'm telling you, he's a bloody sex maniac, that's what he is!' The proud tone in Karolis's voice was unmistakeable.

'Like owner, like dog,' smirked Catnips from the comparative safety of his favourite corner seat, where he usually sat next to Bellakay.

'What's that you said? What the devil do you mean by that?' thundered Sonny, a pretended dark scowl appearing on his face as he looked menacingly at Catnips.

The breakfast-eaters laughed heartily at Catnips's telling comments. Nobody needed reminding what an out-and-out philanderer Sonny was – how he was always involved in some affair or other with the opposite sex, even married women. Somehow, by a combination of guile and determination, he had always wriggled out of compromising situations and had managed to stay single through the years, preferring to keep it that way. He did not really take offence at Catnips's comment – secretly enjoying being likened to a local Casanova.

Catnips replied in mock reconciliation, 'Nothing! Nothing, my dear Sonny! I meant nothing at all – just a joke. No need to get all huffed up. Bad for your heart, you know!'

The object of their discussion – Strangefellow – nestled serenely on a trifurcate fork in the banyan tree, all the while keeping a watchful eye on the breakfast-eaters and his four-footed family below. He had sensed with his keen radar that something was afoot these days and kept his good ear cocked to 'alert' all the time so as not to miss out on anything important. 'You never know with the two-legs,' he reflected philosophically. 'They're a mighty strange bunch who could make all sorts of things happen when least expected. You can't be off guard for even one blooming minute with those chaps. What a troubling species God went and created!'

Musing on in this reflective mood, Strangefellow's thoughts drifted to Bellakay's recently concluded election campaign. He hadn't quite forgotten the rides in the mobile van, the ruckus created at nearly all the election meetings, and the unforgettable election 'wake' inside the marquee with all those vociferous supporters belonging to that very odd fellow Bellakay. Still, he didn't regret the chain of events the campaign brought in its aftermath. All things considered, it had given him a permanent partner and a son, although the young fellow was such a pest, always trying to lick his ears inside out and bite his tail whenever he got the chance. 'Thank God for the tree,' Strangefellow mused further. At least it offered him some quality time away from the missus and the young rascal.

Killing Fellow, the very same to whom Sonny had referred when talking of Joolius's intention to give his goats a dose of serendib, was contracted by the city's municipal council to run its slaughterhouse, doing all the butchering himself. Private slaughtering of larger livestock was forbidden by the council authorities, and anyone having larger livestock needing slaughtering *had* to go to him. Anything from poultry to rabbits was allowed, but cattle, pigs, and goats had to be slaughtered at the municipal council's slaughterhouse under strict sanitary conditions.

Physically, Killing Fellow was well endowed for his work. He was a well-set man with strong bulging muscles, but was ugly as an ogre. Rumour had it that he had amassed a small fortune by secretly purloining and selling off some of his clients' produce to eating houses and hotels for a lesser price than regular market-stall owners charged. No one could prove the allegations though – the stories in all likelihood completely untrue and fabricated by jealous green-eyed monsters. However, what he did do on the side, making a tidy sum of money besides, was to boil down all the completely uneatable parts of the carcasses he slaughtered to extract loads and loads of fat for making soap. He sold the fat to a local soap maker who added caustic soda and a few other things, turning out a rough soap widely used throughout Portopo for washing clothes.

The malicious rumour claiming Killing Fellow purloined his clients' meat was started by none other than Catnips – a result of a private grudge he held against the giant butcher. Both men had vied for the affections of an attractive, buxom young woman who used to sell vegetables at the local market – Killing Fellow emerging the ultimate victor mainly because of his status as official slaughterer for the municipal council, a job that brought a more than tidy sum in monthly wages plus the spin-off fat production. The woman in question made a wise choice, preferring a comfortable future rather than hot, passionate love. She took on Killing Fellow in spite of his immense ugliness, much to Catnips's maddening incredulity and disgust.

Catnips had a hard time letting go of this humiliating slight on his person. He had this thing going with Rooney, the Amazon prostitute turned spa owner, but always longed for true love and romance, which somehow or other had eluded him all these years. Catnips tried desperately to win back the woman, thinking she would get tired after a while living with such an ugly man like Killing Fellow and return to him, but his assumptions proved completely wrong. The young woman remained staunchly faithful to her husband, recoiling from Catnips and spurning his best efforts to woo her back.

One day, things came to a head. Killing Fellow, after many previous complaints from his new wife, finally lost his patience. In addition to his wife's complaints, he was deeply annoyed about a matter that troubled him even more. Catnips's persistent re-wooing attempts had caused a malicious rumour to circulate suggesting that the giant butcher was a cuckold. Having no desire to be made *that* kind of a fool, he confronted Catnips head-on and gave him a sound thrashing. Catnips was no physical match for the formidable mountain of a man that was Killing Fellow – black and blue afterwards and limping considerably for a week after the beating. He wisely stayed away from Killing Fellow's wife after that, although he suffered a great deal of mental anguish over the permanent loss of the woman he so much desired and over the humiliating thrashing he had received. On and off, he would lament loudly whenever he brought up the subject with Sonny at the Nameless, which was quite often. Only last week, after the serendib palavers had eased up a bit, he brought up the matter yet again. 'How can that damn woman live with such an ugly fellow, God in heaven knows! Maybe he has to put a jute bag on his head every time he bangs her.'

Sonny, who knew a thing or two about women, having run through a great many, would always have his standard answer ready and waiting. His favourite riposte came cracking through like a whip. 'All cats are black at night, Catnips. All cats are black at night,' he said, adding testily, 'and you're not getting anywhere with Rooney, you know! She may give you a romp now and then, but she's not interested in true love and all that sort of thing! Why the devil can't you go and find yourself some other woman instead of whingeing about Killing Fellow's wife? There are plenty of decent young women all over the place. This time, see that you have a proper damn job before you go around courting! No woman in her right mind is going to take you on when she knows you are just hanging around all over the place with no blooming steady income or a regular job to show!'

Catnips strongly objected to this insinuation. He especially resented Sonny's comments about the state of his employment, the bit about his 'hanging around all over the place with no steady income' a hard pill to swallow.

'How the devil can you say that I don't have a job? How can you say I'm just hanging around and have no income! You all know I have plenty, plenty of money. How the deuce otherwise can I afford to come here every day and pay for your blasted breakfasts and buy cigarettes and tea all morning, eh? Anyway, don't I also have a regular job at the school gate selling merchandise on certain days? Besides, all you fellows know what a clever fellow I am. Who fixed up old Bellakay's election, eh? Who came up with all the ideas, eh? Who made all them huge crowds come to his meetings, and who got that damn old goat elected, eh?'

Almost everyone, not only at Jellicoe Junction but even in the whole of Portopo, knew of Catnips's sinister role in getting Bellakay elected. Yet somehow, the subtleness and cunning of his doings had only enhanced his reputation for slyness and dishonesty, doing precious little for anything else.

'Yes, yes, we all know that! But, you see, Catnips, women care fiddlesticks about fixing elections, past reputations, or selling bloody junk at bloody school gates. What they *all* like is for men to have a solid job – going to work in the mornings and coming home in the evenings. The only thing that makes them look up to a man is if he has a nice, steady income. A *respectable* income, not the kind of thing you do. Look at Dona Serafina [Killing Fellow's wife]. Didn't she take on the ugliest blooming man in this country for her husband? Now why do you suppose she went and did that, eh?'

'Bah! If them women can't see that I am a man for the future, then let them all go to hell. Bloody wretches, the lot of them!' Catnips replied with feeling. He concluded with another well-known prediction he made every so often. 'One day, all the women who rejected me are going to regret very much they did not want me. One day, when I am an important man, all of them will come crawling to me on their bloody knees; just wait and see. They'll all be sorry, especially that stupid wretch Dona Serafina, sacrificing herself like that to that bloody ugly ogre when she could have had me! *Me! Me, Me!*'

Sonny didn't bother to reply. He just shrugged his shoulders in resignation and pretended to be absorbed in something else.

Dawn broke out on the day of the eclipse. Crowing roosters and the early morning cawing of the city's crow population heralded the start of the auspicious day. As the noon hour approached, most people throughout the country had their preparations of serendib ready, anxiously waiting in mounting suspense for the moment when the sun disappeared behind the moon and temporary darkness descended.

The eclipse, a total covering of the sun, was expected to last for four to five minutes – given that Victoria was not sitting plumb on the equator. People were warned in no uncertain terms not to look directly at the sun and the immediate enfolding events lest their eyesight be damaged. They were strictly instructed to watch the proceedings in a basin of water where all that transpired until the sun slowly disappeared would be reflected in the water, or alternatively watch proceedings through a pair of specially tempered dark glasses to block out ultraviolet rays. Very few amongst the onlookers possessed sunglasses, let alone the special type recommended, resulting in many opting for the water-basin method – a popular and pragmatic choice.

At last, the much-awaited moment arrived. Almost everyone had a basin of water ready as the disappearing sun became clearly visible. People anxiously gripped their cups of serendib tea in blind faith, swallowing the deadly brew (almost everyone had taken much more than two tablespoons of root mixed in the tea) as darkness fell and the eclipse reached its zenith. A slight burning sensation in their stomachs immediately after the brew was drunk did not deter or worry the beauty-seekers too much. They all thought the mild discomfort was a sure sign their bodies were going through an immediate state of metamorphism, as predicted and promised by their holy sage. They assumed they were being transformed into something fine and beautiful, gorgeous butterflies emerging from drab cocoons. What followed next made history in Victoria...

Catnips, the new favourite at the Nameless, was hurrying back home after a last-minute drink at Ali Baba's toddy tavern before it closed earlier than usual on account of the eclipse, needing the alcohol-rich toddy to fortify himself for the task ahead. He had already prepared and put aside five tablespoons of crushed serendib root juice, intending to drink it all mixed in hot water, which was in total contrast to what he had recommended others to consume. Five tablespoons was much in excess of the standard and now widely recommended dose of one or two tablespoons of crushed serendib root, but he was fast determined to drink an overdose even if it caused him some slight discomfort, to make doubly sure he would be transformed into an exceptionally fine figure of a man. He still pined after Dona Serafina and intended to take this heaven-sent opportunity to enhance his looks and make a fresh attempt at wooing her back. When his newfound looks and importance at the Nameless were established without a shadow of a doubt, he intended to casually walk over to Killing Fellow's house and sweep Dona Serafina off her feet, dazzling her with his beauty and fame. Surely, he thought, the damn woman couldn't refuse him then? If Killing Fellow tried to interfere, he would thrash his rival black and blue with his rejuvenated strength. Dona Serafina aside, he also had a keen eye trained on claiming Bellakay's throne as official sage at the Nameless, a position he expected to be his own very shortly.

On his way back from Ali Baba's tavern to his cottage near the city, Catnips had to bypass the municipal council's slaughterhouse. Rounding it on unsteady feet, he encountered a completely unexpected Doan Serafina outside the building in the act of combing her long hair after having taken a bath. She was clad in a loosely wrapped towel from her breasts to her knees. The sight of her curvaceous body aroused the intoxicated Catnips so much that he could not for the life of him resist making a pass, but not before looking around himself warily to make sure Killing Fellow wasn't hovering about close by.

'Ah, Dona Serafina, my dear, came to work with your husband, I shee! Want to make sure he closhes shop early and goesh home in time for the ishklipse, eh?' said Catnips, his speech slurred and his breath reeking of alcohol. 'Going to give the poor chap some serendib so he can look like a human being, eh? I mean, what with that bloody awful ugly face of his and all.'

'You mind your own business now, Catnips, or I'll go in and bring out my husband. Be careful he doesn't give you another good thrashing again!' said the agitated woman. She didn't really dislike Catnips but found it hard going that her former suitor wouldn't accept defeat like a man and retire gracefully. Besides, she hated and resented jibes about her husband's extreme ugliness.

'Tchah! That ugly hushband of yours jush got lucky lash time. He hit me when I washn't looking. Dona Serafina, why are you still with him, eh? Come back to me and I'll give you everyshing you want. I'm going to be even more handsome and famous after the ishklipse. People are talking good things about me now, you know!'

'Bah! What good things? I've heard nothing! Only how you put them dead crows all over Hazimudoo's election meeting place. I'm not coming back to you – ever! And by the way, I *was* never with you in the first place, so how the devil am I going to come *back*, eh?'

Here, Catnips lost all composure and grabbed Dona Serafina in a fit of amorous passion. The toddy he had drunk gave him a good dose of Dutch courage as he recklessly pounced upon his scantily clad victim. Dona Serafina screeched out in indignation and fear, the towel she wore loosening at its knot and falling apart to reveal her stark naked body. Her screams brought out an alarmed Killing Fellow, who had been closing for the day inside the butchery, putting the day's cash collection into his strong safe. He was amazed and shocked to see Catnips embracing his protesting and screaming naked wife, one hand firmly pressing her naked buttocks. Putting aside his momentary shock, he rushed to her aid and proceeded to give Catnips a second sound thrashing – much worse than the first he had dealt him. In the ensuing scuffle, Catnips was knocked off his feet, his wiry frame landing in the shallow ditch adjoining the butchery. He was momentarily winded and unable to find the strength to get up. He made an attempt to stand but wobbled and then fell down again into the shallow ditch, face upwards, which was lucky. That way, the water couldn't quite get at his nose and drown him.

Killing Fellow and his wife locked up the butchery and rushed off home in order to arrive in time for the eclipse leaving Catnips to lie where he was. After a few minutes, his senses somewhat returning, Catnips managed to get up and totter over to the grassy embankment on the side of the ditch, only to fall down again and doze off, the combined effects of the toddy and the thrashing he had received proving all too much for him. He woke up a good two hours later and, glancing at his waterproof wristwatch, found to his horror that the eclipse had come and gone. He had missed the big event and couldn't take his precious serendib tea now. The drink would be pure poison now that the healing power of the eclipse was past and was no more...

Sonny had locked the front door of the Nameless behind him and had gone home early that afternoon. The regulars too had long since vanished after breakfast, heading to their respective homes after muttering multiple excuses. Even the usual stragglers who showed up quite often were conspicuous with their absence. Everyone was getting ready to drink a dose of serendib.

The entire core gang at the Nameless, with the exception of Bellakay, Sadhu, and Adonis, took the ill-fated tea in the privacy of their homes. Sonny, wisely and fortunately (as it proved later) decided only to alter the contours of his face and had restricted his intake to two tablespoons of crushed root. He would take care of his protruding belly by some other means later on, after he had obtained a new and beautiful face, he reasoned. In spite of Karolis's suggestion, and luckily for the incumbent mongrel at the Nameless, nothing was given to Strangefellow.

Karolis, Uncle Pongo, Trevor, Benjy, Milkfellow, and most of the other regulars at the Nameless all drank similar portions as Sonny.

Killing Fellow took a small draught his faithful spouse had lovingly prepared in the hope her extremely ugly husband would be transformed into a handsome young prince. In the years since marrying Killing Fellow, Dona Serafina had grown to love her giant of a husband dearly, but had grown tired of hearing the incessant jibes about his ugliness. Although she didn't dwell too much on her husband's facial features, she longed for him (and her) to be out of reach of the many telling digs they had to endure. She did not take any of the fateful tea herself, prudently reasoning that she was beautiful enough and that enhancing her looks wasn't necessary. Besides, she reasoned even more prudently, if she *and* Killing Fellow both took the tea and, against all odds, something *did* go wrong, then neither of them would be in a normal condition to nurse the other back to good health – the notion of one of them dying never crossing her mind.

Joolius, the avaricious town farmer, in spite of his assurances to his friend Vincentius, took some of the portion himself and gave each and every one of his goats a dose cleverly diluted in the swirl mixture they so dearly loved to drink.

The various clergy, bus drivers, white-collar workers, policemen, labourers, street vendors, businessmen, and nearly all other adults in Victoria took the poisonous brew in varying doses. The more desperate and extremely ugly took larger doses just in case a smaller dose didn't do the trick.

At Grandmummy's, Celeste, Primrose, and Rebecca each took two tablespoons and a few drops more of crushed root juice in a tea. Rohan, Mahan, Laura, Sussie, and Maria were more interested in seeing the sun disappear into darkness, which they thrillingly observed in a basin of water, heeding the local newspapers' warning not to look directly at the naked sun. They were not too concerned about the serendib decoction the adults took, making light of it. It was just another grown-up 'thing' that really did not concern them. Even Rohan and Laura, for all their natural cleverness, failed to grasp the gravity of what their mother and aunts had just done. Grandmummy, blissfully unaware that her daughters had consumed a dangerous poison, was looking out of the veranda window at the darkening sky, absorbed by the spectacle of daylight turning into dusk and then darkness. She disliked the eclipse and everything connected to it, considering it all the work of the Devil – anxiously waiting for it to all to be over. It made her feel uneasy, full of foreboding.

Some of the teachers at Rohan's grand school had also taken the poison in spite of their erudite background. Even old Vosper, the rather overzealous guardian of the sports ground, had taken a dose of serendib. Vosper's intention of drinking serendib hinged solely on his wish to run as fast as he had in bygone days – yearning to outrun and capture the evildoers who trespassed across *his* precious sports ground.

Mr Cedric, Salgado's mortal enemy and the much-detested administrator of canings and other hateful corporal punishment, had, after serious consideration, decided to take the plunge. Mr Cedric was a very intelligent and well-educated man but sadly, like most Victorians, a highly superstitious one too – staunchly believing in what most local sages, astrologers, palmists, and the whole motley crew of occult dabblers proclaimed. Besides, he was also a keen amateur astrologer, often drawing up different horoscopes for himself from which he could pick and choose. He had no record of the exact time of his birth – a standard requirement to cast an accurate horoscope. Searching the signs in his star chart for the fateful eclipse day, he had noticed that something big was going to happen, although he couldn't quite put his finger on exactly what. He wasn't an ugly man but was completely bald and dreamed of having masses of dark flowing hair like in his youth. At the masters' room, however, he sang a completely different tune wavering from his staunch beliefs. It was like the day before the eclipse when the masters were jointly discussing the whole serendib affair...

The arithmetic master Mr Strool, or Mr Fool, as the boys gleefully nicknamed him behind his back, addressed his colleague. 'I just can't understand these damn fools, Cedric. Just look at the morning's newspaper! Why, it seems that all these chaps are determined to take this blasted serendib stuff tomorrow. Why the dickens can't they realise what they are about to do? They just as well could sign their own death warrants! Foxley [the science master] informed me yesterday the stuff is a terrible poison, and *he* ought to know! These poor people will all die like blasted flies!'

Mr Cedric, who by now had firmly decided to drink a portion of serendib, felt somewhat cornered into giving a reply. He lied through his teeth, pretending to be as horrified as his erstwhile colleague. 'Tchah! These fellows get sillier and sillier day by day, Strool. A gormless lot. I only hope they limit their consumption to a safe dose.'

'Bah! Knowing these chaps, I think they are more likely to do the opposite and take overdoses instead,' butted in old Mr Withers, the English master. 'Why, in the last English class I had with the boys in form 3, that fat fellow Salgado – you know, the one who is always in some devilish spot or another – was openly talking about some scoundrel who, it seems, is selling the root outside our very own school gate!'

Mr Withers's claim was met with indignation and shock by his fellows. They were genuinely upset that even the sacred sanctum of the school was violated, tainted, and unsafe. Mr Pontybum, the sports master, spoke for them all in an agitated fashion. 'What! What! At our very gate! Preposterous, I am telling you, preposterous! This must be stopped at once. I shall speak to rector about this and get him to bring in the police. Just imagine! The very audacity of the chap, selling the stuff at the gate of our very own school! I only hope the boys will stay clear of the scoundrel. What this country is coming to, I really don't know!'

Leaving his erstwhile colleagues behind at the masters' room, Mr Pontybum made a beeline in the direction of the rector's office whilst muttering fierce invectives.

Mr Cedric hurriedly made his exit on the pretence of having an urgent errand to run. He walked briskly in the direction of the school gate before the police, tipped off by the rector, could arrive. He had intended to buy a portion of the root at the market bazaar that evening, but that old fool Withers had just told him where he could more easily and conveniently purchase it!

The eclipse, a truly thrilling and awe-inspiring sight, didn't last long. Daylight faded slowly into total darkness as an eerie silence descended upon the city. Sparrows stopped chirping, and even the boisterous crows went silent, baffled by the early and sudden 'night'. After a short while – some minutes – the sun slowly reappeared from its hiding place behind the moon and daylight slowly emerged again. The serendib drinkers had swallowed their deadly portions, wiping their lips on the backs of their hands to get rid of the bitter aftertaste of the tea.

A good five minutes later, all hell broke loose. Slight stomach discomfort turned into acute pain, breathing problems, vomiting, and shivering. Almost everyone who had taken a portion of serendib tea was now acutely sick as pandemonium and terror broke out on an unprecedented scale. Faces were contorted in agony. Many screamed outright, unable to compose themselves any longer on account of the horrible pain and discomfort.

Nearly every family in the island had a victim. The general hospital at Jellicoe Junction experienced an abundance of incoming patients – unprecedented in its fifty-year history. The whole area in and around the hospital was akin a battlefield, overflowing with wobbling, groaning, and vomiting patients. Private clinics and private-practice doctors had their waiting rooms filled to bursting capacity. To make matters worse, hospitals were short-staffed because some of the employees, including doctors, had taken the dreaded poison and were sick like dogs or already dying or dead. Special news broadcasts were aired over the radio advising victims as to what should, and should not, be done. There was no real antidote for the effects of serendib poisoning. Hospitals admitted only the most severe cases, brusquely turning away others with instructions to drink plenty of water to ensure that dehydration was kept at bay. For very serious cases admitted to the hospital, their situations proved to be a cul-de-sac of sorts. They went in but didn't come out – at least not as living beings. Those more fortunate who had taken just a tablespoon or two of the root mixture fared better. They only vomited, shivered, and had severe abdominal pain in addition to relieving themselves repeatedly until the worst effects wore off in a day or two. Others who had taken larger doses were less fortunate. Many died like flies. The city morgue was overfilled, fulfilling Bellakay's morbid prophecy about the funeral undertakers having a field day, although even the undertaking profession was severely handicapped. Many disposers of the dead had also drunk serendib and were either very ill or lay in line to be buried themselves by someone else.

The British ambassador's efforts with his mobile treatment centres saved a good many tea-estate workers. His timely intervention restricted the death toll from being much higher. The tea industry suffered, but not as catastrophically as expected.

At Grandmummy's, Celeste, Primrose, and Rebecca were rushed to the general hospital and then admitted into the paying ward, where more detailed help and care was given to privileged patients who could afford the steep costs. When the women's condition and what they had done became known, the Dragon kept her head. Shouting out for Rohan and Mahan, she ordered the boys to take a taxi to her eldest son Robert's residence at the other end of town, giving an urgent and imperious command that he come over at once. Luckily for the boys and the sick women, the boys found an old taxi driver who had fortunately dismissed the notion of taking serendib and was much better off for it. The frightened boys gave the taxi driver directions to their uncle's house. Arriving, they politely asked the driver to wait outside, as they did not have money to pay for the ride. They hurriedly informed their uncle of the situation. Robert, shocked and gravely concerned for his sisters' welfare, promptly paid the taxi driver and then rushed over in the same taxi to aid the distressed family in the company of the alarmed boys. Robert took full control of the situation; these were deep waters, and he knew it. He promptly arranged for the women's admission to the paying ward of the government hospital, paying the juicy deposit fee that was demanded, himself.

The two tablespoons and a few drops more of serendib root the sisters had drunk caused their condition to be quite serious. They proved resilient, though... After going through a week of indignities and suffering, they were pronounced healthy and were subsequently discharged. Well back at home, they braced themselves to face the music. They knew what to expect from their enraged mother.

'Ungrateful wretches!' screamed the Dragon as soon as the sisters entered the house. 'Bloody ingrates! Vixens! Godless brood! Always causing some trouble or other in this household. Is there no end to what I have to put up with you bloody lot?'

Grandmummy's high-pitched screams were more a manifestation of relief than anything else. She had lived in utter fear the past week. Nothing usually jarred the Dragon, but the terrifying prospect of losing her offspring – especially Primrose and Celeste – had given her the fright of a lifetime, almost driving her out of her wits. She had, of course, made several trips to the hospital the past week to visit, staying long hours by their bedsides, especially that of Primrose, whom she loved more than anybody else in the world.

Rebecca, Primrose, and Celeste were far too weak and utterly exhausted after their ghastly ordeal to bandy words with their enraged mother. Even the normally outspoken Celeste kept her mouth firmly shut. Right now, all they wanted to do was to lie down on their beds, close their eyes, and just make the world around them disappear.

Grandmummy continued in the same accusing vein, her face contorted with rage. She was totally lacking in empathy, or so it appeared to the listening children and Robert, who had brought the women home in a taxi.

'How you wretches could take that bloody heathen poison, I don't know. Hasn't God given you enough beauty? Must you also now also turn to the Devil? Didn't Father Clement tell you fools and all those other fools in this damn-blasted, demon-riddled country at Sunday

Mass that it was sinful to take that ungodly bloody serendib? Didn't he say it was the work of the Devil? Didn't he? Didn't he?'

The women remained silent, remembering the parish priest's words of warning. Rohan and the children, witnesses to this severe admonishing, watched on in awe, amazed by the way their grandmother addressed the sisters. Rohan, who always laboured under the misapprehension that Grandmummy never spoke out in real anger at Primrose and Celeste, was jolted, but at the same time gleeful that the two aunts were subject to a verbal tirade of such magnitude. More often than not, it was his poor mother Rebecca, who was targeted amongst the grown-ups – constantly bearing the brunt of Grandmummy's vicious tongue-lashings.

Grandmummy turned her chidings from the foolish and sinful deeds of her daughters to the financial implications of their misadventures. 'Look at the expenses! You blooming wretches think money grows on trees? If not for Robert, I don't know what we would have done. Who's going to pay Robert back, eh? You wretches save any money? You, Celeste! With all your fine talk about your bloody useless damn bank book and all that! And you, Rebecca, who has nothing after that fine-feathered husband of yours left you high and dry! It's *me* who will have to pay back Robert. It's *me* who will have to take out money from my savings.'

Of course, Grandmummy never intended to, and never did, pay back Robert anything. She had promised Robert with tears in her eyes to reimburse him after he had admitted the women to the paying ward at the hospital, but during the next few weeks she conveniently forget the subject altogether. Robert, for his part, said nothing. He knew his mother's ways all too well and had already written off the money he had spent. The proprietor of an audit and accountancy company, he had a nose for these kinds of things. He sensed a bad debt when he saw one.

Grandmummy, never one to let a foolish deed go unforgotten, continued her mantra of scoldings for over a fortnight. Rebecca, Celeste, and Primrose had to put up with her seemingly never-ending chidings and insults. They bore it up patiently, reasoning quite rightfully that just this once, they fully deserved their mother's verbal bombardments. In retrospect, they found it hard to believe that they had actually drunk the fateful poison. For the life of them, they couldn't fathom out how *they* could have been so prosaic and naive.

Sonny and the gang at the Nameless all suffered indignities and discomfort after taking excessive doses in varying degrees. Luckily, no one took more than two tablespoons of crushed root. None of them were hospitalised but cured themselves at home, acting on medical advice blared out on the radio. Sonny was forced to close down for two weeks to recuperate, whilst Uncle Pongo, Karolis, Benjy, Milkfellow, and Trevor all had the fright of their lives after being sick like dogs. They stayed away from the Nameless as long as Sonny did.

The old monk at the Lord Nelson Street temple, the very same whom Bellakay had denounced as a charlatan, had also taken the poison and suffered immensely for his folly. His new acolyte, a sober young priest, had tended him for days. Convinced that his master would die and hoping for expert help, he had confided discreetly to a few senior temple worshippers that his superior had taken serendib and was lying very ill in his quarters. The result of all this was that the old monk had to conveniently 'disappear' to somewhere far away after he had, against all odds, made a full recovery. Everyone shunned him thereafter. Nobody wanted to have anything to do with an incumbent chief monk who yearned so badly to be young and beautiful again. It didn't seem right or religious somehow; nor was it in keeping with the teachings of the enlightened one whom he was supposed to follow. The earlier rumours of his epicurean lifestyle surfaced again and seemed to ring true this time around after the folly of his beauty-seeking deed was exposed. A new incumbent monk was inducted into service. It was none other than the young acolyte who had tended the old monk in his time of need. The first thing the new man did was to dispose of the old priest's cooking utensils which he had used to prepare his meat dishes; they seemed to taint the sanctity of the temple and its immediate surroundings somehow. Searching through the old monk's large larder, he also discovered huge portions of salted beef, cured pork, and many tins of corned beef, which he prudently distributed to the many beggars in the city. There were also bottles of opened and unopened whisky, which he diligently crushed in a nearby abandoned stone quarry.

Catnips never did divulge he had missed out on the eclipse on account of his altercation with Killing Fellow and Dona Serafina. All of his cronies at the Nameless assumed that he too was a victim of serendib poisoning. Secretly and to himself, Catnips thanked God for the good fortune that had made him indulge in toddy that fateful day, causing him to make quite a scene with Dona Serafina. The thrashing he had received at Killing Fellow's hands and his subsequent long nap by the side of the ditch had in all likelihood saved his life. No one in the country had survived after drinking more than three tablespoons of serendib root. Catnips's intention to drink the five he had planned would have definitely proved fateful. He shuddered at the thought that he might be lying on a cold mortuary slab this very moment, exactly as old Bellakay said would happen to most of the beauty-seekers.

Joolius, the avaricious livestock keeper, survived too, but his goats didn't. In monetary terms, he was the worst affected; all his goats died, causing the parsimonious old man untold misery and great financial loss.

'Lucky that bugger didn't give the stuff to his hens. They would sure as hell have all died like them damn goats,' said Catnips after a few weeks had passed, when the regulars were assembled again as usual at the Nameless for their morning breakfast. Catnips didn't quite seem to realise that the breakfast-eaters were no longer favourably inclined to listen to anything he said. His preposterous pre-eclipse lectures on 'correct measurements and doses' and the other 'expert' advice he had grandiosely offered his gullible listeners were not easily forgotten. In light of all that had transpired, his proclamations had proven to be complete balderdash, a pack of outrageous lies. To a man, they all felt extremely foolish for having listened to him and even more foolish for rejecting the advice of Bellakay, who was firmly reinstated as the one and only guru and wise man at the Nameless. The pretender's brief reign was over...

Catnips continued. 'You've got to be careful of eating eggs these days. If Joolius gave them hens of his the stuff and some of them survived, any eggs they laid afterwards are sure to be infected with serendib poison too. It's a terrible poison, you know – deadly!'

'I think you should keep your damn-blasted foul mouth shut, you bloody liar,' shouted out Uncle Pongo, the one most furious over Catnips's pre-eclipse falsehoods. He was itching to give Catnips a piece of his mind. 'You're the one, the bloody mighty big shot, the dang-blasted lying scoundrel, who pretended to be the expert on that buggering serendib, aren't you? You're the one who told us all those lies about what dose to take and what dose not to take and all that other poppycock. If it weren't for you, we would have escaped all this trouble. How the devil can you show your face around here after all your bloody lies? You dirty rascal!'

Catnips was taken aback by this very telling and most volatile accusation. Speechless for a brief moment, he recovered quickly enough to say heatedly, 'Bloody hell! Damn bloody hell! That's right, that's right, put the blame on me! Maybe I was wrong about them doses and things, but was that sage fellow and all those doctors and big shots who took the stuff any wiser? Just like you, Pongo, to go and blame me for everything! Who took the stuff, eh? I came to your houses and forced you, did I? Was it me who forcibly poured it down your blooming throats, eh? You fellows are all hypocrites, I'm telling you. Did you all not want to be handsome like those Hollywood actor chaps in the pictures? Did I come to your homes and *give* you the stuff to drink? Did I? Did I?' He asked again and again, looking around himself ferociously, daring anyone to contradict him.

Here, Uncle Pongo and the breakfast assembly went silent. Catnips's jibes about the sage, the doctors, and the Hollywood film stars went home – especially the 'wanting to be as handsome as Hollywood actors' quip. The favourite movies most folk at Jellicoe Junction loved to see apart from local Victorian reels were Hollywood box-office busters where female actors were very beautiful and their manly counterparts handsome hunks. True, they surmised in honest introspection over their recent actions, Catnips's talk and encouragement *had* influenced them a great deal, but even if Catnips hadn't trumpeted his expertise in his now defunct role as chief serendib expert, they knew secretly within themselves they would have taken the poison anyway. To a man, they had all yearned to be handsome. Catnips's propagandising and aggrandising of serendib was just the additional spur that tilted them over the edge. They knew within themselves they couldn't really blame him, although they yearned to give their fallen hero a jolly good kick up his backside.

In the silence that followed the acrimonious exchange between Catnips and Uncle Pongo, the former, for the first time, realised he had lost face – a great deal of face. In future, the breakfast-eaters would be extra-wary of whatever he professed. He could no longer have their partial, let alone absolute, trust. Bellakay, on the other hand, in light of his warnings against consuming serendib, had greatly enhanced his position as the only true 'guru' at the Nameless. Catnips could no longer challenge him for that title – not in the near future, anyway. He had mounted a few bombastic challenges even before the serendib matter surfaced but had always fallen flat on his face. This time, however, he appeared to have fallen flat on his sword. It would be a long while before he could have another crack at the title.

The notion of the eggs being infected took root and spread like wildfire. Nobody ate eggs at the Nameless for a week or two, in spite of Sonny's vehement insistence that the eggs in his possession were bought before eclipse day. Nobody even ate eggs at Jellicoe Junction for a few months after the incident, Catnips's hypothesis spreading even to the rest of the city and then to all parts of Victoria. Apart from eggs, even meat consumption dropped alarmingly. It seemed that

Joolius was not the only one to give his goats a portion of serendib. Many livestock owners at Portopo and the rest of the country had given their cattle the poison, and almost a third of the beasts had died. Beef became a rare commodity at butcher stalls, although it affected nobody. Meat was frowned upon, almost totally spurned. Nobody could tell for sure if meat sold at butcher shops hailed from cattle that had sickened and died after being given serendib. Most people turned to eating fish instead. Karolis, the fishmonger, made brisk sales of his wares, everybody clamouring to buy fish, crabs, and prawns these days. Down at the Nameless, the likeable fish vendor discussed his good fortune with Sonny.

'Never knew I could sell that amount of fish, Sonny! Why, only yesterday I sold my whole basket of fish by eleven o'clock and had to go back to the Central Fish Market to buy some more, and even that lot was finished by two o'clock in the afternoon. The fish market buggers charge me double now, but I'm selling for three and four times *their* price! Nobody is protesting. They are all clamouring for my wares like madmen.'

'Good for you, Karolis! Good show! I am happy for you,' replied Sonny, genuinely glad for his friend. 'Now maybe you can put down some money and buy that new sewing machine your wife has been hampering after. You said you went and asked old Joolius for a loan and he refused you – didn't he?' (In addition to his farming business, Joolius also lent out money, charging very high interest rates to people whom he knew could, and did, pay back.)

Karolis was a simple man who rarely raised his voice, but he couldn't help himself this time around. He said with great feeling, 'Bah! What a horrible man! See how God has punished the greedy pig! He was very sick, I hear. Lost all his goats and even his eggs don't sell. The niggardly old bugger has to start all over again. Like Sadhu says, it's all karma. Joolius refused me a loan, sold watered-down milk, and never helped anyone in his life. Now God has punished him and given *me* this golden chance to sell so much fish. Why, I don't need a damn loan from that old miser, or from anybody else, for that matter! You know, as things turned out, I might just be able to give that insufferable old wretch a loan instead! Just imagine that! *Me*, a moneylender!'

'Would you, really?' asked Sonny curiously.

'Would I what?'

'Give old Joolius a loan?'

'Naaah! Let the old bugger stew in his misery. He deserves it. It's karma, as I said, you know! One shouldn't interfere in karma when you see it happening before your very eyes. Let the gods handle it their way.'

Baking Jane and her eldest daughter had returned home from the non-paying ward at the general hospital. Miraculously, the duo had survived in spite of taking a larger dose of serendib. Baking Jane had lost a fortnight's business but was thankful for her escape. Bellakay had visited her in hospital. He knew she was remorseful, but, being a tactful man and not wanting to rub it in, he didn't speak much about his well-meant pre-emptive warnings she hadn't heeded. He was overjoyed that his friend had survived and although agnostic, silently gave thanks to whatever power that had spared her life.

Matters didn't go well for Lizard and Moon, either. They didn't turn up for school for over three weeks. The excuse notes their parents had written did not state the true nature of their absence. Both boys had drunk the now infamous serendib and were very ill for a long time. Their anxious parents had suffered agonies when their sons sickened and had wisely sent sick notes to the school rector to the effect that their beloved offspring had contracted a tropical fever and would not be attending school until further notice. Secrets were hard to keep at Jellicoe Junction, and somehow or other the boys in Rohan's close circle got to know the true cause of their young friends' absences. For a long time afterwards, both Lizard and Moon were the butt of many jokes. Salgado was in the thick of things – not that he was extensively cruel or heartless – but for the life of him, he couldn't allow such a wonderful opportunity to have fun go a-begging.

'Why, my dear Moon,' he said sarcastically when the sick boys had come back after recuperating. 'I heard you were sick from fever and were in bed during the eclipse. You sure missed out seeing Mr Moon in the daylight. Why, he looked so big that we even saw all them craters and things Mr Foxley told us about at science class. Very clear-like, them craters were. Poor old Mr Moon, he sure does have a bad case of pimples. I've not seen old Mr Moon for several days now in the sky! Perhaps he took some of that serendib stuff too and got sick.'

Moon, too disconsolate and weary after his recent horrendous ordeal, didn't offer a riposte, sick and tired of the whole subject of pimples. 'Let them bloody pimples sprout all over my face. Who the devil cares?' he murmured, resigning himself completely to his seemingly inevitable 'pimply' fate.

Lizard kept a very low profile too – serendib having no visible effect on his scaly lower legs. He had gone through a lot and, as with Moon, decided to accept his affliction without any further attempt to hide it. He stopped trying to camouflage his condition by wearing ankle-length socks.

'Let everyone see my blooming scales,' he thought gloomily, but then brightened up considerably as a sudden thought struck him. He wouldn't have to wear short trousers in a year or two. He would be a senior then, and all the senior boys wore long trousers. No one would be able to see his scales then, he mused with a comforting sigh of relief. Of course, he still wouldn't be able to swim in the school pool, but then, on the other hand, who the devil wanted to swim in that germ swirl? That fat fool Salgado boasted often how he urinated and farted in the pool quite close to the swimming coach, Mr Dolfin, who always joined the boys in the water to bark out coaching instructions. Salgado's urinating and farting stunts were pure revenge. Mr Dolfin wasn't over-fond of the fat one who often dived very clumsily into the pool from the highest board to deliberately splash water on the non-swimmers watching by the pool edge. Mr Dolfin couldn't punish him for his diving stunts – the boards were after all meant for diving – but he often made Salgado do several push-ups before the swimming lessons on the pretence that it would help reduce his excess weight – an action thoroughly detestable to young Salgado.

Mr Cedric suffered in silence. When he got sick, he dared not enter hospital as he did not want word to go around that a person of his high intellect and standing had committed such an obvious faux pas. Like Rebecca, Celeste, and Primrose, he asked himself constantly how he could have been so gullible and naive as the rest. It was one thing for the plebeian masses to be duped, but how on earth could *he* have gone along with the whole damn rigmarole? Surely he must have been in a state of temporary lunacy when he took the serendib poison? True, the horoscopes he cast had encouraged him into believing that a great change would come to most people, but he had erroneously assumed the change would be beneficial. It never crossed his mind that it would be the other way around and cause such widespread agony for him and everyone else. Mr Cedric knew something about medical matters and treated himself alone at home. He knew the vomiting would pass, and kept drinking water regularly to prevent his body from becoming acutely dehydrated. He was constantly on the lookout for a worsening of his condition and just to be on the safe side, was in regular telephone contact with his only brother, to whom he had confided his folly. The brother, an important bigwig in a private commercial company, could be trusted for absolute discretion. Mr Cedric telephoned the school rector and said that he would be away for two weeks to attend the funeral of a close relative who had died of serendib poisoning. The rector trusted the integrity of his senior master without reservation and didn't doubt that anything was contrary to what the latter purported. After all, so many people had died through the whole damn serendib folly!

The great sage who was responsible for the bizarre serendib proclamation, his henchmen, and the hordes of astrologers and the like who had propagated drinking serendib decoctions all went underground, not to be seen or heard from for many weeks. Finally, having to make some sort of explanation to save face for their ill-fated collected lunacy, they came out with a story that was more or less acceptable to their host of gullible followers. Even the great sage from whose lips the original prophecy fell went along with the explanation. Very briefly, it went like something like this: 'Things went wrong and people died because they did not take the serendib decoction at the *exact split second* the sun disappeared from view. The *exact split second* was the great secret to nullifying the venom in the serendib and bring about a successful metamorphosis from ugly to beautiful.' The masses hadn't followed their instructions clearly, they said; portions of serendib tea should have been drunk the very moment the moon completely covered the sun, and not a fraction of a second before or after. Of course, none of the motley crew had ever said that before, but so strong was their influence and sway over their trusting and gullible followers that this tenuous excuse was gradually accepted without reservation by all, including the surviving victims. In due course, after a long period of absence, the great sage and his followers crept forth from their hiding places and slowly wormed themselves back into people's trust. Life went on as before with a single exception – never again did anyone have the slightest desire to embellish his or her physical form by drinking poisonous portions on *any* day – eclipses especially...

The survivors went back to their normal lives after a month or so, except for Joolius, who lamented after his dead goats for a considerable period longer. His milk business suffered badly as he had to wait until the four remaining young goats attained the right age to be milked. Even his egg sales suffered for some time, no thanks to the rumour of contaminated eggs inadvertently started by that king of mischief-makers, Catnips. Joolius went about like a ghostly apparition. He wasn't a pretty sight, wild and unkempt, attired in unwashed clothes, lamenting out loud for all to hear at the main market square.

'Oh, my goats! Oh, my milk! My goats! My milk! Oh, my poor darling goats! My darling, darling goats!'

Bellakay, who had heard the lamentations whilst doing a marketing chore at the bazaar, likened Joolius's cries to those of Shylock in *The Merchant of Venice*. At the Nameless, when the subject of Joolius and his goats came up at one of the morning's breakfast discussions, he said with strong and marked alacrity, 'That fellow Joolius is going about crying like Shylock – the old miser in that *Merchant of Venice* play. You know, the chap who went about shouting, "My daughter, my ducats, my Christian ducats." That Shakespeare fellow was one hell of a writer! He always showed the follies of dishonour and greed.'

The breakfast-eaters had often heard of Shakespeare through Bellakay's incessant ramblings, but they hadn't the foggiest notion who the devil Shylock was. 'Ducats', on the other hand, sounded a bit familiar. Wasn't there this new imported motorcycle from Italy that was called a Ducat or something like that? But then what had motorcycles to do with it all? Surely stingy old Joolius couldn't have owned an Italian motorcycle? Still, they respectfully paused to listen to what Bellakay said – didn't understand much of it – and returned back to their previous discussions and trenching. They nearly always listened to what old Bellakay had to say, knowing what a clever sort of chap he was. Half the time, they didn't quite get the gist of anything he said or proclaimed, but they listened anyway, not wanting to miss out on anything important that might benefit them in some way. Besides, Bellakay had earned additional kudos for being the only one who had warned them all against taking serendib, and they were not likely to forget *that* in a hurry! In retrospect, they felt quite foolish for having listened to Catnips in the run-up to the eclipse, wondering how on earth they could have abandoned Bellakay's words of wisdom for their mercurial companion's frivolous lies.

Gradually, life returned to normal at Jellicoe Junction. The regulars at the Nameless recovered fully. Rohan's mother, Rebecca; his aunts, Celeste and Primrose; and his schoolmates Lizard and Moon showed no signs of permanent disability. Even Joolius, Vincentius, Mr Cedric, Killing Fellow, and the rest all returned to good health. Families who lost loved ones buried their dead and mourned awhile.

Surviving victims had their health restored, and life went on as before in the teeming, bustling community.

Catnips never bothered Dona Serafina again. He was not an exceptionally religious sort of man, but he recognised the hand of fate that had caused his ominous altercation with Dona Serafina on that fateful eclipse day. He could never quite forget Dona Serafina, but he left her alone immediately afterwards and never bothered her again. Nobody mentioned the word *serendib* at Jellicoe Junction for a very, very long time afterwards...

CHAPTER 8

Kismet

On the twelfth day of Christmas, my true love gave to me ...

EVERYBODY, NOT JUST THE JEUNESSE dorée, celebrated Christmas in a big way at Jellicoe Junction as well as everywhere else in Victoria. Even looking at it from a religious perspective, none of the Christians divisions, whether Catholic, Protestant, Anglican, or any other, could claim Christmas as their very own prerogative. The Yuletide season and all its trimmings belonged to just about everybody on the island. People of all faiths and even diehard agnostics joined forces with Christians in a burst of joyous revelling beginning a week before Christmas and lasting right up to twelfth day, or rather the Feast of Epiphany, when it all rather reluctantly fizzled to a stop. Apart from the religious significance of Christmas, everyone was most grateful for the Yuletide season, considering how much it helped to break the humdrums of day-to-day life and the grinding ennui it brought in its wake.

A genuine ambience of goodwill shone upon Victorians – most people forgetting past disputes and differences to show a much more amiable front to one another.

The Yuletide season was originally initiated and celebrated by the island's first European usurper, the Portuguese, in the early fifteenth century – well supported and nurtured by the Dutch, and finally solidly cemented into place during the British period of occupation, which lasted nigh on three hundred years. Even after the British left at the end of the Second World War and the country became independent again, Christmas celebrations remained an unshakable tradition, steadfastly strong, very much loved, and eagerly looked forward to by the islanders.

A few remnants of the Portuguese Christmas greeting 'Feliz Natal' remained and lived on in certain parts of the country, but the commonest Yuletide greeting in present times was undoubtedly the much-loved and very British-sounding 'Merry Christmas'.

Midnight Mass on Christmas Eve was a must, although nobody knew for certain if its current form and celebration had any connection to the Portugueses' 'Misa de Galo' or their late-supper 'Consoada', both events celebrated and revered on Christmas Eve in the fifteenth century. A large school of thought, however, insisted it was the British who first introduced the much-loved church service later on, in the eighteenth century. Nobody cared either way. Midnight Mass *was* the start of actual Christmas Day celebrations, an epitome of Nativity for all Victorians.

A month before Christmas, the window displays of the shops would dazzle with miniature winter-wonderland scenes or jolly-looking red-nosed Santa figures covered in silver tinsel powder, all glittering and winking like a million microscopic stars. Outside the shops, sturdy Christmas trees would be firmly mounted beside the sidewalks, alight with colourful intermittent electric lights, and complete with a brightly illuminated silver star mounted right on top.

Shortly prior to Christmas Day, Benjy was seen walking alongside Uncle Pongo, admiring the window displays at Sir Galahad Street near the marketplace. Stopping outside Bernard's Bookshop, they gazed at the paperbacks displayed.

'Just look at that damn foreign book they're advertising about them

Christmas ghosts and rubbish. Who ever heard of such nonsense! Christmas ghosts, indeed! All humbug, I'm telling you.'

'Can't be all humbug, Benjy. That book was written by that famous English chap Dickens, you know! The fellow lived a long time ago and wrote very many great books. Even Bellakay admires his writing!'

'Bah! Bellakay is a damn romantic dreamer, always going on and on about them foreign books and stuff. Look how the chap is trying to turn this country into Utopia after he won that damn election – typical! A dreamer, I'm telling you. Got himself elected by telling fairy stories to the people, that's what!'

'There are awful thingies that walk in the night, Benjy. Catnips claimed only last week to have seen headless ghosts at old Sonny's place. Said he saw them when visiting the outhouse.'

'Catnips, eh! That no-good liar and ganga smoker! What fools you all are for believing all his bloody cockeyed lies. Will you chaps never learn?'

Uncle Pongo let matters lie. He knew he couldn't rub old Benjy once the latter took a stand on anything. In any event, he wasn't over-fond of defending Catnips, secretly gloating whenever the mercurial mischief-maker was chastised in any way.

At Grandmummy's, everyone was looking forward to the coming season. The children had just received their school Christmas holidays – Rohan and Mahan cock-a-hoop over the five weeks they had received, and Laura equally happy for the four weeks from her girls' school.

Grandmummy set about enthusiastically to the task of making preparations for Christmas Day – a day where the extended family gathered together to partake in traditional Christmas lunch and merrymaking. Her son, Robert, was expected to be present, and so were Daisy and Oswald. Primrose had managed to persuade her rather testy young fiancée, Giles-Piles, to attend, whilst Celeste, not to be outdone, had invited the genial and affable Don. Rebecca and the children, as resident 'guests', needed no special invitation. In past

Christmases, prior to his downfall, Rainier would grace the occasion too, but not this year. He was still AWOL, nobody quite knowing his exact whereabouts. Grandmummy wasn't too upset about her son-in-law's absence, although this time around it was for selfish reasons rather than her usual and incessant castigation of his supposed criminal deeds. The times when Rainier was around for Christmas lunch, his eloquence and charm always won him centre stage, upstaging Grandmummy, who strived to play the role of benevolent host. On those past Christmases, the Dragon would watch on perplexedly, her brow furrowed in jealousy and frustration as Rainier stole the thunder she rightly considered hers and hers alone. In fairness to Rainier, he never meant to upstage his host. Quite often in social gatherings, and anywhere else, he would give the impression of being distinctly nondescript, chuckling and conversing in a low-key sort of fashion, but always ended up silkily dominating the company he found himself in. It all came naturally to him and never done on purpose. Everyone was drawn to Rainier. He had an undeniable, magnetic attraction – a trait young Rohan was also fast developing at his tender years and would reach its inevitable zenith in the near future...

Grandmummy always celebrated Christmas in a whopping-big way. From this she never wavered an inch. Whatever the cost and whatever it took, Christmas was always a feast at Grandmummy's. The Dragon transformed into a benevolent avatar during Christmas season, her old self lost in an unknown dimension. For once in the year, her antigregarious ways relaxed as she changed into a 'joie de vivre' personality, treating everyone alike and momentarily forgetting favourites, hierarchy, and past disputes. She treated just one person in her old scathing and haughty way: Uncle Pongo, her only brother.

Grandmummy's sudden behavioural hiatus during the festive season was metamorphic, albeit temporary. After the festivities were brought to a close, she closed shop and reverted to being her normal idiosyncratic and unfathomable self.

'Christmas is over,' she would say abruptly and rudely to the listening ménage. 'Put all them damn decorations and balloons away, and get rid of that blooming Christmas tree and those useless Christmas cards hanging near the radio.'

Rohan and Mahan weren't spared, either.

'You boys better start doing your breakfast rounds tomorrow. I'm not serving you lot any damn fancy breakfasts anymore. You can buy that damn eating-house muck once again.'

The household was ready for the Dragon's outburst. It was a process of reiteration, repeated at the end of Christmas season year after year.

A few weeks before Christmas Day, Grandmummy financed a thorough refurbishing of the old house including polishing and repairing furniture and fittings, whitewashing walls, painting doors, and buying other household trappings like curtains, carpets, and rugs to replace the old ones. On the culinary side, she bought meats, fowl, pickles, greens, sweet potatoes, stacks of vegetables, and the best available whisky, beer, and brandy.

Grandmummy did all the cooking too, ably assisted by the household in every possible way. She conjured up a most scrumptious Christmas lunch for everyone to enjoy – a true culinary aesthetic delight. Additionally, she baked large quantities of cakes and pastries intended to last many weeks. In the immediate weeks before Christmas, the household descended into a turmoil of activity, everybody propelling themselves eagerly into some task or other as ordered and supervised by Grandmummy. There was a marked difference in the Dragon's manner during the season. Whereas earlier she would command the ménage to do chores in an imperious manner, during Christmas she would ask politely, almost humbly, in a sweet and serene tone.

Down at the Nameless, the Christmas spirit was also conspicuous. Sonny had already hung up a few colourful paper streamers and Christmas wreaths inside and was regularly seen dusting and cleaning the little eating house spotlessly clean with Strangefellow trailing behind him sniffing curiously at the dust-free floor as though discovering strange and new aromas that had suddenly been unearthed.

However, despite Sonny's well-meaning efforts, a creeping sense of gloom put a severe strain on the usual high spirits expected around this time of the year at the eating house. Celebrations were put on hold somewhat and were considerably marred by the alleged appearance of headless ghosts, frightening and troubling almost all the ultra-superstitious breakfast-eaters no end. It was none other than Catnips who had started it all, setting the stage for a string of eerie weeks in the run-up to Christmas Day and for weeks afterwards.

It had been raining heavily a fortnight before Christmas, the showers cascading down in heavy torrents, making it difficult to get about even with the aid of an umbrella or a raincoat. It was clear enough in the mornings, but the skies turned dark soon after, ugly grey clouds gathering and expanding to such an extent that they blotted out the struggling sun. The skies got worse by ten o'clock. Previously looming grey clouds would become positively black, at which point the rain would come pouring down in long intervals. One never really knew when the next drenching shower would stop and a new one would begin. Even Strangefellow, his newfound partner, and his young son had long since abandoned the immediate area on and under the banyan tree for the comparative safety of the Nameless.

'Sit here beside my cash counter, dogs, and don't go around nosing and begging customers for food. You fellows get two big meals a day but are always looking to eat more and more. Sit quietly here and don't walk about or trip over anybody, and don't get mud all over your damn paws and mess up the floor.'

Of course, Strangefellow had no intention of sitting quietly beside the cash counter as Sonny advocated. He was soon seen mingling with the breakfast-eaters, his mate and young son trailing behind, the puppy enthusiastically trying to grab and bite his father's bushy tail.

One particular day, it rained hard and heavy immediately after breakfast, continuing right through the afternoon and well into the evening, trapping the breakfast-eaters inside the increasingly damp confines of the Nameless.

After Bellakay's success at the recently concluded parliamentary elections, Sonny had utilised his friend's newfound political influence to rush through an application to the municipal council to get an electricity connection for his newly renovated eating house. Bellakay was a fairly important man these days with powerful connections in politics – his influence extending even as high up to the incumbent prime minister. Usually, there was nearly a one-year waiting line for a connection, but Sonny got his in a matter of weeks. For the first time in its history, the Nameless had actual electric lighting. It was a step up for Sonny – a proud moment – given his aspirations to be a restaurant owner of repute at Jellicoe Junction, and it pleased him no end. He had, of course, long since renovated the ramshackle structure that was the Nameless, adding a brand-new kitchen with modern facilities, including an electric stove and a refrigerator. Sonny would have loved to build an even handsomer construction, but he lacked the money. The eating house eked out a fairly good income but never enough for savings of any kind, mostly because of Sonny's philandering lifestyle. It cost quite a lot to buy presents for his latest paramour (he always had a new lover lined up amongst a long list of discarded ones) and even more for discreet cash settlements to the various women he successfully wooed and then callously left in search of new pastures. Sonny's adventures weren't *affaires du coeur* in the least bit, rather pure wanton debauchery; a trait which many considered marred an otherwise excellent character. There was still some hope of putting up a really eye-catching structure, though. Bellakay had repeatedly hinted in recent times that a bank loan wasn't out of reach now that his friend had a legal lease for the land on and around the Nameless, including the area circling the huge banyan tree. It was excellent collateral, and the banks – formerly Sonny's staunch enemies – couldn't refuse, insisted Bellakay.

Evening turned to early nightfall that fateful day, but still the rains came cascading down in buckets, trapping Sonny and the others within the confines of the Nameless. The rain continued to fall, with no apparent end in sight. The much-used checkerboard was placed on the main table, and few patrons played a couple of games under the bright new electric lighting whilst the rest watched on, praising the players' gambits, deriding their follies, and giving advice on what the next moves ought to be – the last mentioned act quite annoying for the opposing player, who would often curtly ask the 'experts' to keep their 'damned mouths shut'. They soon tired of it all, though. Abandoning the checkerboard, they started to engage in the type of idle banter they were so fond of, huddling closer together to keep away the creeping cold and damp air.

Karolis, the fish vendor, started a conversation about how some of the local fishermen he often mingled with – a few his closest friends – had gone out to sea and hadn't returned for several days. The bad weather had even affected the seas around Jellicoe Junction. Rough waters along with giant waves and gale-like winds swept along the coast, causing a great deal of mayhem to the small fishing industry and real danger to life and limb for the few brave fishermen who dared to venture out in such atrocious conditions.

'My unfortunate friends are sure to be dead by now, poor buggers! Nobody has sighted their blooming boats for three days in a row,' lamented Karolis resignedly.

'Maybe the fellows are fishing in heaven now,' quipped young Adonis.

Sadhu, the octogenarian, normally a taciturn sort with a tendency for the elliptical, perked up considerably at Adonis's talk of the fishermen plying their trade in the afterlife. He wasn't known to practise any particular religion but was well versed in the theological nomenclature of every known faith. He spoke out in a sober fashion, as was his wont. 'Don't joke about them fellows going to fish in heaven, Adonis! If the poor chaps are really dead, then their ghostly spirits are still on this earth, where will they remain in limbo for some time until they go to heaven, to hell, or to their karmic rebirths. Nobody goes to heaven or hell or attains nirvana at once, you know, dear boy! Who knows where their spirits are right now, eh? They knew our dear friend Karolis very well, so maybe their ghosts are all here at Sonny's place, watching over their friend and listening to our conversations. It might make them angry if we joke about their deaths. It was their fate to die at sea. It's all fate or karma, you know. Even you, Adonis – you too are a child of karma. See how handsome you are! Why, in your earlier life you must have been a prince who offended the mighty lords with deeds of great evil and debauchery, and have been thus punished for your sins by being born beautiful again, but with no blooming money to scratch your backside with.'

Here the assembly went silent for a moment, reflecting upon young Adonis's fate, but what really had caught their attention was what Sadhu had said about the missing fishermen's being ghosts. His talk of the dead fishermen's spirits made them perk up something extra. Nothing captured the breakfast-eaters' imaginations more than a jolly good ghost story or doings of any sort purporting to come from the 'other side'.

It was nearly pitch-dark outside now. Karolis's account of the dead fishermen, Sadhu's talk of ghosts, and the storm's frequent flashes of lightning and rumbling thunder all contributed to an eerie sort of atmosphere. There was a dip in the banter as everyone gloomily looked outside at the pouring rain, wondering when, if at all, it ever would cease. Only Catnips aired his opinions, as usual talking nineteen to the dozen. He had received an upward boost in the eyes of the breakfast-eaters after the infamous rotting-crow heist he had pulled off to get Bellakay elected to Parliament, but then had fallen flat on his face after making an ass of himself over the serendib business. Weighing the two matters separately, his colleagues at the Nameless generously forgave his folly vis-à-vis the serendib matter. They continued to admire his avant-garde tendencies and chutzpah...

For all his flamboyant and mercurial ways, Catnips had a secret weakness – a colossal fear of spirits, ghosts, vampires, devils, or whatever ghoul purported to originate from the twilight zone. Even so, and for all his fear, Catnips still managed to put on a brave front.

He spoke out with a false sense of bravado, bottling his real feelings within himself as only he could. 'Bah! There're no such things as spirits or ghosts or vampires or any other blooming evil things – all damn bunkum, I'm telling you. How can them dead fishermen be here at Sonny's ? Dead people are dead people. If you didn't fear people when they were alive, why fear them when they have kicked the bucket? It's all poppycock, you know. Pish-posh, this ghost business! Nothing but bloody old wives' tales made up to frighten old people and small children.'

'What! Whaaaat?!' exclaimed Uncle Pongo indignantly. He was also one of the few trapped inside the Nameless that day and was absolutely outraged by this seemingly flippant afterlife denouncement. 'What the hell are you talking about, Catnips? No ghosts, you say? What about them stories about the demon woman who picks up men at the cemetery, eh? Or that horrible ghost fellow who followed them schoolboys on that fishing trip? All that's bunkum too, eh? Answer me that! And you!' He pointed a bony finger directly at Catnips. 'Aren't you a fine one to talk about there being no evil things and all that? Weren't you the one who went around with that big crucifix hanging from your blooming neck for several weeks after seeing that first *Dracula* picture at the Elphinstone Theatre? The one we all attended? Eh? Eh? *Eh?*'

Catnips was stumped and had no ready riposte. Inwardly, he was convinced that the ghostly incidents Uncle Pongo mentioned were true, but he didn't want to lose face and show fear or reveal his actual beliefs. True, he reflected in retrospect, he did wear that crucifix for nearly a month, but who the devil wouldn't after having seen that terrible bloodsucking vampire demon on the screen? Surely such horrors couldn't exist? Or could they? His mind whirled in a jumble of doubt and belief. He had never even come remotely close to actually seeing a ghost, a vampire, or any other demon, but it was hard to discard all the stories that made the rounds, especially those Uncle Pongo had touched upon.

Catnips didn't give Uncle Pongo a reply and, instead, looked away from the assembly sheepishly with downcast eyes. Nobody could accuse *him* of being elliptical, but right now he was at a loss for words. The others, expecting a riposte and not receiving one, turned their attentions away from him. The talk of vampires and ghosts was an excellent opportunity for the breakfast-eaters to reminisce and discuss popular 'other side' stories they loved dearly, those usually told and retold at Jellicoe Junction. The one Uncle Pongo referred to about the ghostly woman at the local cemetery who picked up young men was a clear and dear favourite.

It seemed that on the stroke of midnight, a beautiful buxom young woman would scale the surrounding Portopo cemetery wall from within, walk down the side of the pavement outside, and try to hail passing cars driven by young men, ostensibly to hitch-hike a lift somewhere. If she succeeded in hailing a car, she would engage the young man in sexually suggestive conversation for a few minutes and then get in the vehicle – but only if invited. She was so alluring beautiful that the would-be victim would be mesmerised, totally under her spell, well and truly smitten by her voluptuous bodily charms. The pair would drive off together and at a suitable moment, almost always coinciding with the unsuspecting victim making a move to fondle her, the woman would transform herself into a horrible demon with Medusa-like serpents wriggling in her hair. She gave forth peals and peals of demonic laughter, her outstretched, grabbing hands reaching for the unfortunate's throat. The young men subjected to the horrifying ordeal were reputed never to recover their reason after this incipient and last meeting with the demon. They were doomed to wander the streets as madmen for the rest of their lives.

The macabre stories continued, and so did the rain. Catnips remained uneasy throughout his companions' ghostly narrations, wishing to high heaven they would stop their eerie banter and change the subject. He had consumed a great many cups of tea and assorted food the whole day and felt a strong call of nature coming on that required immediate attention.

The outhouse at the Nameless wasn't as yet wired for electricity, prompting Sonny to keep a kerosene lantern handy for after-dark visits. The lighted lantern in his hand, Catnips reluctantly made his way to the outhouse, trembling like a leaf after hearing the ghost stories gleefully related by his cronies. He had put on a stoic face throughout the ghostly palavers to create an impression he didn't give a damn for any such nonsense but found it an altogether different matter to leave the present company for the isolated outhouse. Cursing the bad luck that had induced his treacherous stomach to betray him thus, he cautiously approached the outhouse adjoining the massive banyan tree, his heart pounding like a drum, his fears reaching fever pitch. For the life of him, he was unable to shut out the ghostly narrations related by his cronies. He tried hard to be rational, to obliterate the existence of demons and horrors as bunkum, but he didn't quite succeed. Well at the outhouse, he quickly finished what he had to do and then closed the door behind him with a shaky hand, carelessly dropping the lantern in his haste to get back. The globed chimney shattered as it hit the ground, and the rain did the rest, quickly snuffing out the lighted wick. Catnips was mortified. He froze in the pitch-blackness and looked around himself in terror, trying to focus on his surroundings and the footpath leading back to the Nameless. The long beards of the nearby banyan tree whistled and swayed around him in the wind and the rain. In the darkness, they *looked* like an army of ghostly spirits about to pounce upon him with their thin wiry arms. He screamed out loud and ran back in panic as fast as his two legs could carry him, back to the safety of the beckoning electric lighting at the Nameless. Once inside, he closed the door behind him and leant against it huffing and puffing, his body trembling like a leaf, his face contorted in fear. He struggled to speak, but only gobbledygook mutterings came forth from his mouth…

The clientele at the Nameless were dumbfounded. They had never seen Catnips in such a state before. Gone was the swaggering, provocative Catnips of old. His ashy face and shivering body told a tale of their own. This was a stranger, someone they hardly knew!

'Why were you screaming just now like a blooming madman?'

inquired Sonny gruffly, the same question on everyone's lips. 'And where the bloody hell is my lantern? What have you gone and done with my lantern, man? Where is it?'

Catnips answered shakily, his words barely coherent. 'Your lantern! Your dang-blasted bloody lantern! Is that all you care about? God! What horrors I've been through down at the outhouse! I'm telling you I saw them spirit fellows that Sadhu spoke of, and they chased me all the way from the outhouse to your front door, Sonny. Their horribly thin, long arms tried to grab me. I'm telling you, this place is one big dang-blasted haunted house. Maybe those fishermen chaps have come here to haunt us for good! You better get hold of old Fotheringill tomorrow and do a spirit-exorcist ceremony here, Sonny! It's not safe to stay in this place anymore!'

Apart from his rain spells, the warlock Fotheringill was even sought after by the good people of Jellicoe Junction whenever they found themselves bothered by apparitions of a supernatural kind. Sonny, though, wasn't having any of Catnips's insinuations about spirits or dead fishermen, nor was he anxious to solicit the services of Fotheringill. The last thing he wanted for his precious eating house was for it to earn a reputation for being haunted. It would only serve to drive away customers and bring a jinx and a curse on the place. He shouted out sternly, putting on his best Captain Haddock-like manner. 'You stop that foolish talk about ghosts hanging around this place at once, you hear me, Catnips! Did you or did you not tell us all only a short while ago before you started screaming like a little girl that there were no such things as spirits? Bunkum, you said, wasn't it? *Bunkum* was the very word you used; we all heard it from your lips. Well, why are you talking about spirits now, eh? There are no spirits living here! I've been here for ten years now and never seen no damn ghost, vampire, devil, or anything else! It's the most peaceful place to be in except when you lot start your bloody arguments and fighting!'

'Huh! I'm telling you, Sonny, old man, I'm telling you truly, I saw a whole bunch of ghosts and they all tried to grab me. Them chaps had no real faces, just swaying thin bodies and long, hanging arms,' said the frightened Catnips in an insistent tone, in all likelihood mistaking the hanging vines of the banyan tree for headless apparitions. In his present terror-affected condition, he actually believed every word he said.

'No faces, eh! No faces, you say, eh? Why then, man! That explains it! Them horrible fellows must be those headless ghost chaps – you know, like the ones in that English horror matinee we saw at the Elphinstone,' remarked Benjy in open-mouthed awe, his jaw dropping several notches.

The Elphinstone cinema hall had recently shown a horror film that attracted large crowds and was much talked about. Many of the breakfast-eaters had seen it. It was about a headless ghost that tormented a remote English village – riding around on a black horse with his head tucked under one arm whilst brandishing a sword with the other, which he callously wielded to behead anyone who came his way.

At this injunction, and as usual, a spirited discussion took place amongst the breakfast-eaters. They all believed that Catnips had indeed seen a headless ghost or ghosts – all, that is, except for Sonny, who was getting more and more irritated, even alarmed, at the turn the conversation was taking. He repeated incessantly, red-faced and flustered, that there were no ghosts living in or around the Nameless. Bellakay, who was also present that fateful day, joined Sonny in denouncing Catnips's story as utter rubbish. Faithful to his agnostic philosophy, the resident sage and MP didn't believe in anything supernatural, especially purported manifestations of any kind from the 'other side'. The duo's protests proved fruitless – totally futile. Nobody paid the least bit of attention to them. To a man, they all believed that Catnips had indeed experienced a rendezvous with spirits from the underworld and were thrilled to the core about it all. At long last, after seeing so many horror films and hearing so many ghost stories, they found themselves, right here and now, in the midst of a terrible visitation played out under their very noses. What a story they would have to tell people at Jellicoe Junction the next few days!

Raconteurs in the future would relate and re-relate the story about the headless horrors haunting Sonny's place. History was in the making, and they were sitting plumb in the middle of it all.

The days that followed were extremely displeasing to Sonny. Everyone was now starting to see strange figures and shapes as imaginations ran riot. Strangefellow, courtesy of his 'doggie' sixth sense, felt the special tenseness of his human friends and gave out a series of shrill barks, more in hysterical uncertainty about what was bothering his two-footed friends than anything else. Little did the resident mongrel know that he was unwittingly adding fuel to the ghostly fire Catnips had started. The breakfast-eaters, eager to drive a point home, took the dog's barking as a sure sign the headless ghosts were visible to Sonny's canine and not to them.

'Them dog chaps can see ghosts and spirits all the time,' said Trevor solemnly. Catnips, the former self-proclaimed unbeliever and now an absolute ghost convert, wasn't slow to pick up Trevor's theme and expand the canine phenomenon . 'Yes, yes, animals can sense ghosts, you know! That's why old Strangefellow is barking his bloody head off like that. He can see them ghost chaps around us, all right. Proves I was right all along about them ghosts. I'm telling you lot, this damn place has become haunted – that's for sure! The dog's barking settles it beyond a shadow of a doubt. What do you say, eh, Sonny? You damn well can't deny it now!'

'Bah!' snorted Sonny, a look of great cynicism written all over his face. He wanted to speak at length – hold a long tirade – but held back, extremely exasperated about reassuring everyone that there were no ghosts present at the Nameless. He kept his riposte short. 'Bloody foolish jackasses, the lot of you! Braying like damn donkeys about stupid and impossible things! For the hundredth dang-blasted time, I'm telling you there are no bloody ghosts here! The damn dog's just confused, that's what! He's barking because you fellows are creating such a blooming ruckus – nothing else! He can't see any damn ghosts because there are no bloody ghosts to see!'

Nobody paid any attention to Sonny, although Sadhu, who was

softly murmuring a mantra to himself, ceased his chants to intervene, not in a direct fashion, but in a novel sort of way. He addressed Strangefellow, looking him in the eye, as though the incumbent canine could understand every single word he said. 'Here, dog! My dear four-footed friend! Stop that barking, will you, dear?! It's only our departed dead friends who have come to visit us and see if all is well. Don't harass them, Strangefellow! Let them walk around this place in peace! They will soon leave to heaven, hell, or limbo, according to their predestined karma. Stop your barking now; there's a good dog!'

Strangefellow had no intention of letting anyone, 'dead friends' or otherwise, walk around in peace, as Sadhu advocated. He continued his shrill barks until Sonny lost his temper, grabbed his favourite stick from under his cash counter, and threatened the dog with bodily harm. He had fashioned the stick from a branch of the banyan tree that had fallen off after being hit by lightning; using it at times to chase away the bold crows that often sneaked off with a tidbit or two of his food. On a few occasions, he even used the stick to threaten and discipline Strangefellow, although he never ever actually struck the dog. He loved the canine far too much for that.

'You shut up now, Strangefellow. That's enough now, you hear me! One more bark from you and you'll feel the weight of my stick, you bloody big jackass!' Sonny hollered.

Strangefellow disliked the stick intensely. He had slyly made off with it a couple of times when Sonny wasn't looking and hidden it amongst the bushes beside the banyan tree, even partially burying it in the garden once, but Sonny always seemed to find it, much to the canine's disappointment. Strangefellow had seen what the stick could do whenever Sonny managed to connect a thieving crow with it and had a healthy respect for the weapon. He decided right then and there to keep quiet, letting out just a few small, defiant final barks before finally retiring to his corner behind the tea counter. His little 'doggie' family, the bitch and the pup, looked upon his antics in a puzzled fashion. They had behaved most decorously all through the rain and the breakfast-eaters' sudden surge of excitement and wondered why their hero kept up his implacable barking tirade when there was nothing really to bark at. His mate looked upon him most disapprovingly, whilst his son, the young pup, licked him around the ears to comfort his old dad from whatever demons that were bothering him.

At the Nameless, hardly anything changed, weather wise or 'ghost wise' in the subsequent days. Customers often found themselves trapped inside the little eating house, unable to leave, when the heavens opened up. One day it rained non-stop directly after everyone had finished breakfast, and it continued till nearly six o'clock in the evening, the all-drenching shower accompanied by unusual darkness and gale-like winds. Most of the hard-core gang, who just hung around after breakfast for want of something else to do, were glumly waiting for the rain to cease so they could go home. The partial absence of the sun for several days together with the incessant rain had caused a cold front to sweep across Jellicoe Junction. Everyone at the Nameless shivered – heating unheard of for any building construction in Portopo. It was only houses and buildings in the cold hill country that had water-borne and electrical heating.

Unexpectedly, and adding to the clientele's misery, the electric lights fused after a particular loud peal of thunder. It was pitch-dark now. Sonny fumbled around, groping and searching for his faithful lantern, the glass chimney of which he had replaced after Catnips's earlier mishap at the outhouse. The recent eerie palavers, a daily event since Catnips's alleged encounter with the headless ghosts, and the now well-accepted notion that the Nameless was haunted, made everybody uneasy – more than a tad frightened in the sudden darkness. They waited tensely for Sonny to find and light the kerosene lantern. Suddenly, the sound of footsteps walking down the stone pathway leading to the Nameless were heard, followed by a loud banging on the latched front door. Strangefellow gave out a long drawn wolfish howl of warning instead of his usual canine bark, as the petrified breakfast-eaters froze in terror and apprehension, fully believing that a phalanx of headless ghosts had arrived in the darkness to cut off their heads and drag them all to hell. The door opened and, horror of horrors, there in the faint light of the doorway did indeed stand a nebulous and chilling apparition of a headless man or something that looked almightily like one. To a man, they all screamed in terror as absolute mayhem broke loose, everyone scurrying and falling over one another in a mad panic to get as far away from the front door as possible. Only Sonny kept his head, screwing up enough courage to successfully find and light his faithful lantern with fumbling, frightened hands.

The light revealed the features of the new arrival. Much to everyone's great relief, the figure turned out to be just a tall, well-dressed man who held a large mackintosh well over his head, an act that had given the earlier impression he was headless...

'Who the devil are you, and what the bloody hell do you mean by banging on my door and frightening us all like that?' thundered Sonny, more in relief than in any real anger.

'My dear fellow,' replied the unknown guest, who paused to discard his heavy mackintosh and flick away a few raindrops from his person. Freed of the rain-protecting gear, he bore no resemblance to a ghost at all, nor did he appear to be anything remotely Mephistophelian. In fact, he looked quite fresh and dignified in spite of the bad weather and the verbal salvo he had just received from Sonny. Even Strangefellow seemed impressed, nosing and sniffing about the newcomer's feet and legs in a very fawning fashion. The stranger patted Strangefellow on the head and continued showing remarkable sangfroid.

'My dear fellow!' he repeated. 'My dear, dear fellow! I'm most sorry to disturb you like this, most sorry indeed. I beg a million pardons if I frightened you all. I'm looking for old Pongo, you see! He said he is usually here in the mornings and evenings. I drove over here in my car and parked it outside by the road. The damn rain was coming down in buckets, so I had to use my old army raincoat to walk down the footpath to your place. Good that the damn thing was in the car boot or I might have got soaking wet!'

From the corner where the rest were still huddled close together, Uncle Pongo arose with a great big smile on his face, surprised and delighted upon recognising the newcomer. 'Why, Rainier, my dear man, where on earth did you spring from?' Turning to Sonny, Pongo then explained. 'Old Rainier here is Rebecca's husband. Rainier is the chap the stupid police charged in that big case a few years back, and had to go away for a while. You know, the very same I have been telling you all about for some time now.'

'Oh,' said Sonny, somewhat subdued after learning the identity of the newcomer. He had heard a lot of good things about Rainier through Uncle Pongo over the years and was further impressed seeing him now in person, obliquely taking in the newcomer's impressive clothes, expensive leather shoes, and quiet air of dignified confidence. 'You're welcome here, Mr Rainier. My floor is in a bit of a mess because of the rain and mud brought in, but please stay and talk to Pongo as long as you want.'

That was exactly what Rainier wanted… He rummaged through his pockets and fished out an almost brand-new packet of cigarettes – a pack of twenty. After lighting one for himself, he offered the rest to Uncle Pongo and the present company. The cigarettes were an aesthetic treat, a more than welcome sustenance to compensate for the damp weather and the recent shock the breakfast-eaters had experienced. Sonny's own stocks of cigarettes had finished that very morning due to excessive demand from his clientele, who were trapped daily for hours inside the Nameless. He had intended to restock, but the rains made it impossible for him to close up for an hour or so and walk over to the tobacco company wholesaler's at the market square to buy fresh stocks, a chore he otherwise reiterated once a week.

Rainier quietly drew Uncle Pongo aside to the farthest end of the Nameless and spoke to him in hushed tones to keep the others from overhearing what he had to say.

As fate would have it, Rainier's unexpected appearance turned out to be a blessing in disguise for the much-suffering Sonny, who was now presented with a heaven-sent opportunity to put his foot down firmly and re-establish his absolute authority over the ghost enthusiasts. He wanted to stamp out and destroy once and for all the current consensus purporting that his beloved eating house was haunted. He spoke out sharply in his most belligerent voice and threatening manner. In the dim light of the lantern, he looked exactly like Captain Haddock screaming out a salvo of choice invectives at some unfortunate.

'Listen, you blasted birdbrained lot! Listen very carefully, for it's the last bloody time I'm going to tell you. I want you fellows to stop all this cock-and-bull talk of headless ghosts or any other damn ghosts haunting this place from this moment on. It's bad for my business! If any one of you fellows goes around and spreads fiddly-diddly stories about my place being haunted, I'm warning you. I'm warning you good and proper: I will not allow you rascals to set foot in here again. Banned for life – that's what will happen to any of you fellows who speak of ghosts inside my place. It's my last warning, and I swear to God I will kick out the very next person who persists in saying that my place is haunted. I'm sick and tired of it all! Sick and tired, I'm telling you! Sick and tired!'

The breakfast-eaters duly noted Sonny's imperative warning. Banishment wasn't an option that appealed to them. The Nameless was a second home, a haven, a sanctum. Here in the comfort of the humble microcosm, they all knew each other's rough and gruff ways, enjoying the daily banter that often resulted in hefty arguments: and in any case, as they reasoned quietly to themselves, where on earth were they going to get food and drink for such low prices Sonny charged?

To a man, they decided to heed Sonny's warning. None of them spoke of ghosts anymore or insisted the Nameless was haunted, although for the life of them they couldn't but help turn over and over in their minds Catnips's account of the headless ghosts he claimed to have seen. In spite of Sonny's insistence and assurance the eating house wasn't haunted, they staunchly believed that Catnips had in fact seen headless demons who tried to attack him that night at the outhouse. True, the former's sly and mischievous ways preceded him, and many were disinclined to believe half the things he said, but they couldn't help feeling that just in *this* case Catnips wasn't lying. They were an inflammable lot, the good breakfast-eaters, highly superstitious and easily influenced into believing anything that had to do with the 'other side'. They heeded Sonny's warning, but nothing could convince them that the little eating house wasn't haunted.

Catnips wisely decided to keep a low profile too. It was unlike him to be elliptical, even nondescript, but he knew Sonny's explosive temper could manifest itself in all manner of punishing forms. Like the rest, he prudently decided to stop all references to ghosts – headless or otherwise – considering it a sound policy, at least for the time being. In retrospect, he realised that he had come out rather ignominiously in the whole business. He was ashamed of his behaviour after his eventful visit to the outhouse and wasn't too keen to hear the matter being discussed over and over again. Reflecting more deeply, he considered his actions even cowardly for a man of his reputation and standing. Sonny's inference to his screaming 'like a little girl' still burned in his ears, and the obvious fright he showed after his visit to the outhouse embarrassed him a great deal. He knew he had a reputation for madcap exploits – good deal misfiring – but in no past exploit had he ever being accused of cowardice. One remembered especially his superb role in Bellakay's successful election campaign as one of his absolute highs, and the ignominious role he had played in the serendib business as one of his disgraceful lows. Catnips winced openly whenever he thought about the serendib business where he had gone and lost a lot of face through his lies about the serendib root's properties – additionally suffering the worst thrashing of his life at the hands of Killing Fellow, the formidable, super-ugly city butcher, for trying to seduce the latter's wife.

What transpired that fateful evening between Rainier and Uncle Pongo was sufficient for the latter to jump up and down in pure joy – joy unselfishly not so much for himself, but for Rebecca and her young family, who, it seemed, were soon to be liberated from Grandmummy's clutches. Rainier even hinted that he could be in a position quite soon to offer Uncle Pongo a job as a senior security guard at his new place of employment, a prospect that thrilled the dapper old man immeasurably. Uncle Pongo's finances had improved a great deal after Bellakay had made him his private secretary, but political work and filing dozens of documents and papers just wasn't his cup of tea. Finally, after a good half hour or so, Rainier wound up his little talk, trusting Uncle Pongo to pass on an important message to Rebecca after Christmas, but absolutely not before. He had his reasons for doing so, but he didn't divulge them to Uncle Pongo.

That night, Sonny, unable to control his erotic urges, defied the rain and cold to visit his latest paramour, a buxom young woman living alone.

'Ah, Leonora, my dear! I just dropped by to see if you were all right. What damn foul weather we're having, eh! A few houses had their roofing tiles blown away near my place. And there's flooding down at the market square, I've heard.'

'I'm all right, Sonny. I knew you couldn't come earlier because of the rain. Have some dinner with me and stay the night.'

'All right, but I have to get up early. Got to feed the dogs and then open the restaurant, you know.'

Sonny was most anxious these days to call his eating house a restaurant now that he had put up a decent structure and legally owned the premises and land around it.

That night, he didn't perform as well as he usually did when making love to Leonora, his mind very much focused on the alleged haunting of his eating house.

'You're getting old,' teased Leonora, looking on amusedly at Sonny's limp member.

'Bah! I'm not old. It's just that blooming Catnips and all that haunting talk of his that's eating me up from inside. We'll see next week. I'll ravish you so much you won't be able to walk for days, woman.'

Leonora giggled at this assumption. Sonny was indeed getting on, but she knew what he was capable of. He was the best lover she'd had for a long time.

At Grandmummy's, the matriarch was ready and well equipped financially to celebrate Christmas Day. She had received quite a lot of 'Christmas money' – a sort of extra allowance from her children – a process reiterated year after year. In the past, Robert and Rebecca were always the chief contributors. The former's contributions were unsurprising because he owned a lucrative accountancy and audit business, whilst Rebecca, of course, rolled in money in those splendid days of thunder. Daisy's contribution was sizeable too, and one that brought howls of protest from an angry Oswald. This year, even Primrose and Celeste had received yearly bonuses from their employers – Primrose giving her mother half of what she got whilst Celeste typically contributed a tiny sum – her parsimonious nature coming to the fore.

Rebecca too received a fairly large sum of cash – from Robert, who was a kind man and felt genuinely sorry for his sister's plight. It was the second Christmas Robert had helped her in this generous fashion. It was also the second Christmas she was spending at her mother's house, which, as events happily turned out later, was going to be her last in the Dragon's lair.

In addition to all the monies she received from her children, Grandmummy boosted her Christmas income after restarting her wine business, this time in the comparative safety of the back garden shed. As the pre-Christmas season progressed, she was coyly selling many bottles of wine in a brisk pace to her circle of regular customers, gleefully counting the smelly old currency notes that kept flowing into the money compartment of her ancient almirah. The total of her tangible assets saved up during the years, all in the form of currency notes, was considerable – a small fortune, some would say, or even a big one, depending on the beholder.

It was the custom for Grandmummy's sons and daughters, their wives, husbands, and children, and even a few selected friends to gather at the Dragon's lair for Christmas lunch. The tradition was started by Grandmummy many years ago, and nobody wavered from attending – ever! It wasn't as if anyone was *forced* to come or anything like that, but Grandmummy's Christmas lunch *was* genuinely loved and eagerly looked forward to by everyone with the exception of Oswald, who always grumbled about forfeiting Christmas lunch at *his* parents' home in lieu of the enemy's. He would have dearly loved to spend Christmas Day at his beloved parents' home, but Daisy always forced him to attend Grandmummy's lunch, shouting him into submission, and brooking no refusal. It was the same this year...

'It's always your mother's place, isn't it Daisy? Oswald protested. 'Why can't we spend Christmas at *my* mother's? The last four years, Ma has being pleading for us to have lunch with her and Pa, but you just have to creep into that wretched blooming house for lunch.'

'You stop your damn talk about my mother and her house, Oswald. And what the devil are you moaning about? We spend the whole damn year with your ma and pa, don't we? It's just one day I'm asking you to spend at my mother's.'

The argument wavered back and forth for several days before Christmas Day, Oswald indignantly giving up at the end. Daisy's tight leash on Oswald had tightened considerably more in the aftermath of the embarrassing affair at Meadows. Daisy watched Oswald like a hawk these days. In spite of her husband's shortcomings and wretchedness, she *did* genuinely love the man and didn't want to lose him.

Christmas lunch at Grandmummy's was the grandest of lunches imaginable, august and sumptuous. Gastronomically speaking, it left everyone satiated. Even Rebecca's little family had abundant quantities of the choicest of foods to eat, something quite alien ever since Rainier had fled, leaving the small family to suffer the ignominy of living under Grandmummy's idiosyncratic rule. Joints of wonderfully smelling roasts were prepared along with spicy curried chicken, fried fish, salted pork, fried sausages, spicy pickles, roasted potatoes, special flavoured rice, favourite vegetables, salads, and a host of other terrific delicacies, whilst cans of imported golden peas were opened in gay abundance. The whole kitchen area was a wild shemozzle of cooking pots, utensils, baking trays, joints of meats, spices, and everything else that went into preparing the magnificent feast that was to come. Everybody chipped in to help Grandmummy with the lunch. Preparations began on Christmas Eve, where a few preliminary things were done, and then continued in earnestness after Christmas morning's hearty breakfast was over.

There was also the famed Christmas cake, which Grandmummy made and baked at home a week before Christmas. It took almost a whole day to prepare. The children helped to cut the many ingredients, including raisins, plums, cashew nuts, almonds, preserved cherries, crystallised ginger, pumpkin preserves, and other mouth-watering stuff. Everybody pinched the ingredients regularly when they thought nobody was looking, slyly popping savouries into their mouths to discreetly munch their goodness. Even Poppsy joined in. The little dog loved sweets above anything else, and the children lovingly tossed him a tidbit now and then, sometimes holding it waist-high to make the canine do a series of pirouettes until he finally got at the treat. Grandmummy was aware that the helpers sampled the ingredients, but she did not mind. She was a different person at Christmas, amiable and kind, completely opposite the cantankerous, dominant figure she cut most of the year, except, of course, in the aftermaths of her visits to Mr Macmillan, when she would purr like a contented cat for a few days at least.

The cake was baked for an hour or so and, when taken out of the oven, gave off the most marvellous, mouth-watering aroma. The gigantic mixing bowl used to stir the cake's raw ingredients was given to Sussie and Maria, who licked it clean, using their fingers to scoop up the gooey cake mix. It was all good fun, and for once in the year, Grandmummy's ménage forgot about rankings, petty differences, and other negative matters, behaving like an equal and loving unit.

Two weeks before Christmas, Grandmummy arranged for a builder to do minor repairs to the old house. Together with an entourage consisting of two pimple-faced youths, he tended to the various leaks in the tiled roof, patched up cracked or broken walls, whitewashed the entire house, and did scores of other minor repairs and refurbishing. The whole house had a lingering smell of fresh paint a long time after the work was done, a smell that heralded Christmas at the Dragon's lair.

Back at the Nameless, despite Sonny's grave warnings and threats of expulsion, banter purporting that the eating house was haunted had grown almost out of control. Nobody spoke in Sonny's presence, slyly confining their palavers to moments when he was doing odd jobs outside in the clearing beside the banyan tree, or when he visited the outhouse. The breakfast-eaters, all flamboyant gossips, had spread the story of the headless ghosts all over Jellicoe Junction. Small crowds would gather each evening outside the Nameless, hoping to catch a glimpse of the terrible demons, much to Sonny's chagrin. Everyone came fully armed as only they knew how. They wore protective amulets cleverly worked into bracelets on their arms, small wooden crucifixes around their necks, or other miscellaneous paraphernalia on their persons intended to ward off the evil ones. The crowds made Sonny angry, very much so. He almost choked with apoplectic rage when he saw the ruckus and scenes enacted before his very eyes in front of his beloved eating house. However, as fate would have it, he soon changed his tune. Sonny was on course to do a flip-flop of gigantic proportions…

Whilst fuming at the eager crowd outside his premises, Sonny just couldn't refuse anyone who wanted to buy something or other. He was too astute a businessman for that. The somewhat unwelcome visitors quickly realised they just *had* to buy some food, or at least a cigarette or a cup of tea, if they were to stay as Sonny uncharitably drove them away if they didn't. Sonny's sales soared, the little cash register on his counter tinkling merrily like at no other time in the entire history of the Nameless. Gradually, his anger over the ghost-seekers' presence and the dismal fact that his eating house was fast earning a reputation for being haunted disappeared like magic. A look of serene satisfaction replaced his earlier scowls as he discovered the ghost business was truly a gold mine – a godsend. Sonny stopped all his grumblings, threats, and protests, no longer caring if his eating house had a spooky reputation or not, even encouraging Catnips to enhance and continue his ghostly narrations to keep up the unholy momentum. Sonny had never been on a 'best friends' level with the grand vizier of mischief, but he was now often seen putting an arm around Catnips's shoulders, greeting him lovingly like a long-lost son whenever the latter made his appearance at the Nameless. The new and welcoming front he showed Catnips didn't augur well for everybody, not in the least Strangefellow. The shaggy mongrel, always a more than keen observer of everything going on under his nose, watched on in horrified disgust as Sonny fawned all over the 'enemy'.

'What the bloody devil??? What's going on here? Has the master finally gone mad? Why is he embracing that sly cat creature like that? He's always kept the horrible fellow at a distance, but just look at him now embracing the sly pig! Master seems to have lost his bloody mind! Poor man! I always knew he would go bonkers someday from the way he gets so angry and shouts and thunders at people all the time, even at me! Dear God! What's going to become of us all? Will that damn cat creature take over the eating house? Oh! The horror! I'll have to find a new home for the missus and the boy. We won't be able to live here with that damn cat bugger in charge and the master gone off his blooming rocker and all that! What if the master never gets well again? Oh, my poor, poor master!'

In the days immediately afterwards, whenever Strangefellow saw Sonny hugging or patting Catnips on the back, he would let out a long, drawling howl of sorrow over the former's fate – a howl that sent shivers of fright down the breakfast-eaters' spines. The dog's unprovoked howls were now firmly confirmed as a sign that the Nameless was infested with ghosts. Not all were impressed by Strangefellow's howls, though. His canine partner and son, the young pup, found it most irritating. As in the earlier instance when Strangefellow had barked shrilly at the breakfast-eaters' excessive banter following Catnips's first 'headless' sighting, they still didn't know what the devil the old boy was creating such a ruckus for.

Catnips was in seventh heaven over all that was happening. His recent shaming after the outhouse incident was a thing of the past – a minor setback that had turned into triumph. What pleased him most was that for the first time in his life he had won over his partial nemesis, Sonny. They had begun a friendship – an embryonic one – but a friendship nevertheless. It was no mean feat, considering the numerous times he had tried to bond with the big, bustling eating-house owner over several years – unsuccessfully always, but never for want of trying.

Meanwhile, crowds assembling around the little eating house urged Catnips to relate over and over the tale of his encounter with the headless fishermen. On these occasions, Sonny would actually beam benevolently upon the mercurial mischief-maker, granting the latter a licence to speak as freely as he wanted – conveniently forgetting his previous threats of banishment. As his cash register jingled away merrily, Sonny seemed to care less and less for his eating house's mounting ghostly reputation. Only a day earlier he had bought five times the raw products than was usual to make his breakfasts and snacks, including dozens of packets of tea, even purchasing ten times the number of cigarettes he normally did.

'Let the damn morons talk about ghosts,' he mused, profound contentment written all over his bearded face. 'What the hell do I care as long as they buy my food and drink and smokes? That's all that matters!'

One evening soon after Sonny's abrupt change of mind, Catnips spoke to the assembled crowd (crowds now gathered daily outside the Nameless) in a more flamboyant fashion than usual. He had, the previous day, worked out a surreptitious scheme to make some money from the situation he had created and was eager to put his plan into action.

'You know, good people, dear friends, you know I'm not a man to be easily frightened of anybody, whether they be humans or ghosts or any other thing.' (Here, the regulars at the Nameless sniggered openly, remembering the precautions the 'fearless one' had taken against evil Count Dracula)

Catnips continued serenely, hardly giving his deriders a second glance. 'Those headless chaps I saw all wore suits of armour that glowed with a demon-like light, and their necks were all bloody stumps after having been chopped off and all that. They carried their chopped heads under their arms, and, believe me or not, it was indeed the heads of those poor fishermen chaps who were drowned at sea.' (He didn't know for sure that the lost fishermen had actually drowned, but he took for granted they had.) 'You know, chaps, I must sadly inform you all now that they *were* indeed those very same fishermen. How they lost their heads, I don't know, but I recognised at least three of them who worked at the fish market, and I am telling you, dear citizens, I'm telling you truly, as God is my witness, they all looked a terrible sight! The rotting and horrible heads under their arms were almost unrecognisable, black tongues sticking out and swollen eyes nearly popping from their sockets. They were very angry too and would have killed me on the spot if I hadn't muttered an instant mantra that old Sadhu once taught me. I bravely demanded they leave me alone. The ghost fellows all trembled before my holy mantra, and, although they groaned and screeched in anger, my holy utterances stayed their hands. The devils had no choice but to allow me to return back to the safety of our good friend Sonny's eating house.'

The crowd gasped in wonder at this harrowing tale, admiring the raconteur for his dashing bravery in the face of a sure death.

Catnips then made a startling offer to the ghost-seekers, an offer he knew quite well they wouldn't refuse, one they would eagerly pounce upon. 'You know, my dear, dear people, I have fashioned several crosses from a branch of the old banyan tree that fell down before my very feet the same night the headless horrors came visiting.' (A blatant lie; Catnips had cut and fashioned the crosses from a heap of firewood at home, tying two suitable pieces together in the centre with rough cord.) 'This fallen branch was a mystery, my dear people, completely unexplainable. It wasn't rotten, nor did lightning strike the tree that night to bring it down. I believe that the heavenly powers sent it to me for protection. It is holy wood, I'm telling you! These crosses I made have a special power, as I learnt just the other day. You see, I have taken to sitting up in the evenings and at nights under the banyan tree with a cross around my neck, trying to talk some sense into the headless horrors so that they leave old Sonny's place and go somewhere else. So far, they are stubborn and won't leave, but I am expecting success at any moment. The headless ones were frightened – terribly frightened – by my cross. They didn't dare attack me when I had it around my neck. For your own protection in any future encounter with a ghost or spirit or that terrible Dracula chap, I can offer you a cross each. I'd give it to you for free, but I promised the old priest at the temple at Lord Nelson Street that I would make a big contribution to the main worship room's fresco-restoration fund (a big whopping lie!). You fellows can pay me two rupees each for a cross. Don't think of the money, good people. It's for a good cause. And besides, the crosses will enable you to walk amongst ghosts, demons, or vampires without been frightened, gobbled up, or having your blooming blood all sucked up.'

Here a wild furore broke loose. There was a God-almighty rush to buy the 'holy' crosses. The listening audience, awed and utterly enthralled, didn't need persuading. Superstitious to the core, they all duly paid up and bought a cross each, some even clamouring for two or three. Catnips fashioned several new crosses over the next few days, but then he had to reluctantly inform his growing list of customers that the wood had been all used up. He silently cursed himself for saying that only a *small* branch had fallen by his feet, when he could have easily said a *huge* branch. He did, however, have another trick up his sleeve. He resorted to making use of Strangefellow, the apple of Sonny's eye and mongrel *exceptionnel,* in a new and even more dastardly scheme requiring monumental guile and cheating. Catnips explained his new plan in detail to Sonny that very night, the latter playing along although he had his reservations and was reluctant. The new scam was as deceitful as the 'holy crosses' one – even more deceitful – which was the chief reason for Sonny's reluctance. At the end, though, he acquiesced in the hope that the small crowds encroaching his eating house would continue for at least a few weeks more. Sonny was keen to milk the situation as much as he could. As a businessman, he wasn't averse to making a fast buck if it was there for the taking, but he disliked duping people, at least on the scale Catnips was proposing. At the end, though, he put away his bad conscience, reasoning philosophically that the actual cheating would be done by Catnips, not himself. As things stood, nobody suspected that Sonny was in cahoots with Catnips's ghostly affairs. *He* wouldn't, and couldn't, be accused of any wrongdoing if things went awry.

The two plotters – one enthusiastic and buoyant, the other wary and reluctant – sat up late that night and worked out the details of the new scheme before parting company.

For the second time since his painful separation from his beloved Ida, Rohan felt truly happy. The first, when he was selected to play for the junior cricket team at school, still took pride of place, but he was equally happy now. He was especially pleased for his little sister, Sussie. His aunt Daisy, perhaps less a tartar than Primrose and Celeste and definitely not possessing their parsimonious traits, had bought it upon herself to buy the little girl a new wardrobe of quality clothes, including decent nightwear and a pair of solid leather shoes. Sussie, not really understanding why her little cousin Maria had such pretty clothes and she hadn't, was overjoyed. Daisy often felt sorry for Rebecca's fate, trying conscientiously now and then to put right any injustice she considered ought to be righted. An avid reader in her free time, she had recently read a novel about a slave family in the deep South of the United States, which had spurred her on to do the deed she had just done. Daisy was like that, easily swayed by the doings of the heroes and heroines in her novels, often falling heavily for sentimental stories that brought a tear to the eye – stories that often centred on the injustices of life.

A few days before Christmas, Rebecca took the children Christmas shopping. She had managed to put together a fairly decent sum of money through her small bonus, Robert's contribution, and a more modest one from Daisy. With the money at her disposal, she bought the children a few new clothes and shoes, and also a few things for herself. It was a frugal shopping expedition, déjà-vu-like, since it was done in the same fashion last year, but it was going to be the last of its kind. A wonderful change was coming, looming delightfully around the corner ...

On Christmas Eve, Grandmummy's old artificial Christmas tree – in her possession a good many years – was pulled out of an old cupboard, given a thorough dusting, assembled, and then decorated by Primrose and Celeste. The aunts revelled in their monopolist task, putting on profound looks of know-how as though they possessed some superhuman acumen for decorating Christmas trees. Rohan wanted to help in the decorating but was shouted into submission by Primrose. 'You leave those decorations alone now, Rohan. What do you know about decorating Christmas trees, boy?'

'But, Aunty Primrose, Daddy and Mummy allowed us to help decorate the tree before! Daddy always said we could all join in.'

'Huh! You shouldn't talk back, you know, Rohan. Hasn't Mother told you always to listen to what we say? And kindly don't talk of you father. Isn't it enough he disgraced us all?'

Rohan, cowed by the insinuation that his absent father had disgraced them all, kept his mouth shut, leaving the two grand ladies to decorate the tree as they liked.

The young grasshoppers were compensated for being banned from the Christmas tree decorating by being given the honour of blowing up the balloons to be hung up in the four corners of the living room. A good many balloons burst whilst they were blowing, and there was much laughter and horsing around, especially given

Poppsy's antics. He would boldly nose around the blown-up balloons only to scoot off in alarm whenever a weak one in the bunch burst, or whenever Rohan and Mahan would hold the neck of a blown up ballon tightly across and then let out the air slowly, the resulting high-pitched squeak causing a frenzy of loud barking from the little dog.

A new linoleum, bought at the market bazaar, was then rolled out on the living room floor, whilst repolished and recushioned chairs together with the large couch were taken out of the dining room, where they were temporarily stored, and placed upon it. New curtains were hung, and all of this, together with the shiny and glittering Christmas tree, made the whole effect rather grand. It was a distinct improvement to the otherwise drab living room. Christmas at Grandmummy's was a wonderful setting for a Dickens novel. It was just old Scrooge, Christmas ghosts, Tiny Tim, and a big fat Christmas goose that was missing.

The children stayed up till late on Christmas Eve. Primrose, Celeste, and Rebecca ordered a taxi and, together with Grandmummy, departed to the nearby parish church to attend traditional midnight Mass. Rohan, Mahan, Laura, and the two little girls would attend the late morning Mass the following day. It was a long wait until the adults came back, but the children still managed somehow to stay awake, even young Sussie and Marie. They were listening to Christmas carols on the radio when the Midnight Mass party arrived back home. Grandmummy served wine and Christmas cake to everybody, graciously allowing even Rohan, Mahan, and Laura to drink a small glass of wine.

'Mummy, isn't it bad for Rohan and Mahan to drink wine when they are still so young?' bleated Primrose, resenting her mother's actions.

'Bah! What harm can it do! It's Christmas! The chaps will soon be men! A little drink on Christmas will do them good. Anyway, missy, you keep your comments to yourself. Don't question my actions.'

Primrose pouted at her mother's reply whilst Rohan gave her

a triumphant look of vindication, very much appreciative of his grandmother's special Christmas hiatus.

Grandmummy, who thought her actions liberal, was blissfully unaware that Rohan and Mahan were past masters at consuming the potent drink, their having purloined her fermenting young wine on many occasions before...

A toast was drunk for Christmas, everyone decorously lifting their glasses. The two little girls had fallen asleep by now, unable to keep up any longer, and would not awake until morning – Christmas morning.

The following morning, no breakfast was brought from the nearby eating houses or Baking Jane's. The entire household ate a breakfast of white bread with liberal coatings of butter together with cheese, imported sausages, and rashers of quality bacon. A special Christmas breakfast cake, or 'brooder', as it was popularly called – a relic from the country's Dutch usurpation – was also cut up and served. Everyone felt quite grand consuming Christmas breakfast, especially Rohan and his siblings. Poppsy too was having the time of his life. There were mounds to eat for the little dog, who appeared to have put his famous wandering traits on hold for the moment, showing remarkable pertinacity in not leaving the house the whole day. Spirits were high at the breakfast table, everyone feeling gay and buoyant.

After breakfast was over, Grandmummy waddled off to the kitchen to tend to Christmas lunch, which she had cautiously begun the day before – Rebecca and Laura trailing behind, ready to help. Celeste and Primrose, absolutely hopeless when it came to cooking, sauntered about the house rearranging the furniture, adjusting the new curtains, and sweeping and dusting the whole place spotlessly clean.

Apart from her children and their immediate families, the only close relative who did visit Grandmummy at Christmas was her brother, Uncle Pongo, Rebecca's great friend and protector. Grandmummy refused to speak to her brother even on these Christmas visits. Her siblings' feud with Uncle Pongo was as legendary as it was puzzling, nobody quite knowing what had caused the initial break-up in their relations, which resulted in their present coldness to each other. Uncle Pongo, to his credit, often made sporadic attempts to put things right, but Grandmummy was having none of it. She snubbed all his attempts, cutting them off in the bud with cruel and unfailing regularity.

During Christmas season, Uncle Pongo always managed to get himself into a carolling party. They would motor all around the city in a ramshackle old open-back lorry, warbling popular Christmas carols, hoping for small presents of cash or festive food and drink in return. He had no real singing voice, Uncle Pongo, barely able to hold a note, but he was grandiosely presented on the group's printed program card as 'Mr Adrian Pongo – Baritone'. The carolling group were enthusiastically welcomed wherever they went. Uncle Pongo had assured Rohan in advance that the carolling party would make a stop later on that evening outside Grandmummy's ancient house and warble off a few popular carols, something young Rohan eagerly looked forward to.

Grandmummy's excellent lunch was leisurely consumed and greatly complimented by everyone present. The Dragon smirked in satisfaction at the overwhelming avalanche of praise showered upon her magnificent culinary effort. It was her moment of crowning glory on Christmas Day, the one she was expecting and the one she always got, even when 'scene-stealer' Rainier was present.

As evening approached, Uncle Pongo and the mobile carolling party made their expected appearance. They stopped in front of Grandmummy's house and warbled off a few popular Christmas carols, surprisingly in tune and harmony this time around. Uncle Pongo's strange and gurgling 'baritone' did threaten to burst through and upset the harmony now and then, but, fortunately, the combined voices of the rest of the carolling party prevailed, drowning out Uncle Pongo's best efforts.

'Just look at the damn old goat,' spat out Grandmummy,

momentarily forgetting her newfound Christmas spirit. 'Look at him making an ass of himself. He couldn't sing for toffee when we were children, and now he goes around calling himself a bloody baritone! What a disgrace to the family.'

The rest of the family didn't agree, Robert expostulating for them all. 'I don't think Uncle is disgracing anybody, Mother. He's such a wonderful showman. Why don't you make up with him this Christmas, eh? How long are you going to carry on your silly feuding? Uncle is getting on in years, and it might be too late to leave it for later.'

'Bah! Me make up with him? You children don't know what happened so long ago. If you did, you wouldn't want me to make up with the old goat.'

'What did happen, Ma? Why don't you tell us?' asked Robert, the others listening to the conversation keenly. 'What exactly did he do that was so bad?'

The Dragon said nothing and retired into the bowels of the kitchen. Perchance she did have something disgraceful to say about her brother, but her Christmas metamorphosis shone through, preventing any ugliness.

Meanwhile, the run-up to Christmas Day at the Nameless was like no other. Despite Sonny's best efforts to induce a spirit of Christmas, the 'headless ghosts' Catnips claimed to have seen occupied everyone's thoughts. Christmas was almost forgotten. The small crowds that came every evening hoping for some sort of visitation from the headless ones didn't show signs of petering out. As word spread, even new faces from other parts of the city showed up, hoping to catch a glimpse or more of the much-talked-of ghosts. They were a morbid, superstitious bunch, the good people of Portopo, and although they feared ghosts and ghouls more than anything else in the world, they still didn't want to miss out on this 'once-in-a lifetime' opportunity of seeing real-life spectral beings from the twilight zone, or rather, in this instance, the purported headless horrors.

Everything had gone well for Catnips. He had won over Sonny – a minor miracle – and was additionally grateful that Bellakay was more or less rendered immobile and not in a position to enter into any discussions. The incumbent sage and member of Parliament hadn't made an appearance at the Nameless for more than a fortnight, nursing himself through the severe bout of influenza he had contracted a few weeks before Christmas. Sonny had gone to see his erudite friend and discovered poor Bellakay with a high fever, hardly able to speak on account of a hoarse and very painful throat condition. Sonny immediately went over to St John's Pharmacy a few yards away at the market square and bought some fever tablets, a tin of throat lozenges, a stick of Vicks VapoRub, and a few over-the-counter painkillers. Returning to Bellakay's new apartment, he handed over his purchases, giving strict instructions for how to use them.

'You take them fever tablets three times a day and suck on the lozenges whenever your throat aches. Take the pain tablets if your throat gets worse. You do as I say, you hear! I don't want to come back and find you half dead. You're a bloody MP now, for God's sake, and you have responsibilities. And the next time you get sick, go to Dr Nader immediately. You're not immortal, you know! Besides, you're quite well off now and don't need to hang on to every damn cent you earn!'

The next morning, Sonny casually informed Catnips and the breakfast-eaters of his visit to Bellakay. He described the sage's condition and wound up by saying that he wouldn't expect to see their man for a fortnight, possibly even more. Catnips was most relieved by the news. Bellakay, in his normal demagogue form, would have definitely scoffed at all of Catnips's 'ghostly' insinuations and torn them to shreds. Given the man's agnostic ways, he was sure to come up with some brilliant argument or other to pummel Catnip's claims and disprove the existence of the headless ones. Catnips prayed silently and fervently to all the deities he knew for Bellakay's continued absence, asking that the latter remain indisposed at least over Christmas and the New Year. Catnips, although mischievous, wasn't a cruel man, and his prayers were only meant to keep Bellakay away as long as possible so he could continue propagating the ghostly claims he had started. Unlike Sonny, it wasn't money that motivated him. He had plenty of that!... It was his old nemesis, his craving for fame and notoriety that spurred him on relentlessly.

Unable to sell any more crosses, Catnips cunningly set about implementing the plan he and Sonny had colluded together a few days ago – a plan that required Strangefellow's services to trick the mundane and highly gullible ghost-seekers.

Catnips's plan to use Strangefellow to fan the flames of his claim that the eating house was haunted wasn't going to be easy. The incumbent watchdog at the Nameless distrusted and disliked him immensely. Strangefellow wasn't an unfriendly dog – far from it – bonding well with the breakfast-eaters, who, in their turn, were quite fond of the unique mongrel. They would often toss him a piece of fried fish, which they knew he was immensely fond of, stroke his shaggy coat, and often throw small sticks for him to fetch – a game Strangefellow never grew tired of. Their love for the dog was reciprocated, with one exception – the canine drew the line with Catnips. He genuinely thought for some reason that the mercurial schemer was a cat in disguise, and would bark threateningly at a bemused Catnip on sight – a few disgruntled barks at first – and then a bark or two of extra disapproval before getting out of the way. Strangefellow never barked at the other regulars, reserving his ire for Catnips alone. After his obligatory barks of unwelcome, he would settle down by Sonny's cash counter or on his high perch in the banyan tree and reflect irritably over the object of his displeasure, his canine brain whirling around in distrust and contempt.

'Bloody two-footed devil! Sashaying about like he owns the place! Only a wretched cat walks like that! A filthy cat in disguise, that's what he is! Why else do the others call him Catnips? How I wish the master would get rid of the bloody wretch! Probably has a stupid cat tail inside those fancy trousers of his, the scoundrel! I'm jolly well going to continue barking at him whenever he comes, even though Master doesn't like it. If I catch the tiniest whiff of a cat smell on him,

I'll take a piece off his damn skinny backside, master or no master. Just wait and see!'

Catnips learned to ignore the dog's unwelcoming barks over the years. He knew he upset Strangefellow in some mysterious way and accepted his lot, often shrugging his shoulders resignedly in an apathetic sort of way. The others regularly laughed over the canine's ill treatment their colleague was subjected to, but there was nothing Catnips could do about it. As dogs went, it wasn't just Strangefellow who treated him thus. Even most of the other neighbourhood dogs would give out a small bark or two for no apparent reason whenever Catnips was in their sights, although none barked so loudly and aggressively at him as Strangefellow did. No one knew really why dogs didn't bond well with Catnips, for the man himself loved dogs. He yearned to have a dog of his own, but he discarded the idea, knowing deep within that he was a rolling stone, never in one place for a long time except for his occasional long stays at the Nameless.

Whenever Strangefellow was in a spot of trouble because of something he had done, Sonny punished him by chaining the mongrel to a tree stump close to the banyan tree. The dog's misdemeanours often coincided with Sonny's frying a fresh batch of fish in the outer garden, the canine looking on keenly. The alluring smell of freshly fried fish was almost unbearable to Strangefellow's canine nose – a pinnacle for all alluring smells. He would slyly take off with a whole fish in between his teeth whenever Sonny was momentarily distracted elsewhere, gobbling it up hastily behind the banyan tree. Sonny always knew even if a single fish was missing and who the culprit was, the telltale remains of fish bones Strangefellow spat out beside the tree being a dead giveaway. Whenever detected in his fishy felonies, Strangefellow was subjected to the 'chaining punishment', something he disliked intensely. Sonny never kept him chained for too long, though – a half hour at the most – but Strangefellow, an absolute free spirit, would make an almighty fuss over his temporary incarceration, letting out a series of long, drawled wolf howls until he was released. Catnips knew only too well of this, especially the wolf-like howls, and decided to use it to his advantage in his grandiose scheme to deceive the ghost-seekers. When he first laid out his plan to Sonny, the latter scratched his head a bit after hearing the details, not exactly overenthusiastic about it all. The plan involved mass cheating, something Sonny wasn't really comfortable with, but at the end he reluctantly agreed to go along, if only to keep the 'haunted' momentum going, the visiting crowds intact, and his recent sales bonanza continuing. If Catnips wanted to cheat, then let him, he mused silently to himself, washing his hands off the matter like Pontius Pilate of old.

Unlike Sonny, Catnips had no conscientious qualms about cheating anybody. Stopping short of murder, he was quite willing to do *anything* to make people admire him. His craving to be the centre of everyone's attraction was insatiable, as was his yearning to be recognised as a great thinker, an intellectual giant. Even his visitations at the school gate, where he sold strange merchandise to young schoolboys, was deemed completely unnecessary, the clientele at the Nameless and everyone else knowing perfectly well he did so only to impress the schoolboys with his very strange merchandise, although another school of thought declared he did so just to escape life's ennui. Completely unfettered by laws, rules, and morals, a more archetypal anarchist was hard to find at Jellicoe Junction – perhaps even in the whole of Victoria.

'People, people! My good people!' Catnips began affably, addressing the crowd that had collected one evening in the hope of catching a glimpse of the headless horrors. He paused deliberately after his initial remarks, ostensibly to clear his throat, but more for enhancing the theatrical effect of what he was about to say. 'Some poor souls don't believe in ghosts and demons and the like, but I for one am a firm believer and *always* have been.' (Loud sniggering was heard coming from the hard-core breakfast-eaters.) 'I would like to show you that headless ghosts, even bloodsucking vampire chaps and other horrors we have seen in the matinees and read about in books and newspapers, do really exist. Now just look at that innocent dog over there inside Sonny's place.' He pointed to Strangefellow, who, as usual, was vacuum-cleaning the floor of the Nameless with his large nose in his effort to find a tidbit or two of fried fish that might have inadvertently fallen on the floor. 'Look at that dear, dear dog. He guards old Sonny's place day in and day out, and nobody knows better than he if bad and nasty spirits are about – ghosts and thingies, you know! That animal, and all dogs, for that matter, can really see these awful ghost chaps, whilst most humans can't. It's a known fact! You can ask old Bellakay here or anybody else, and they will all agree with me on this point.' (He used Bellakay's name on purpose, knowing jolly well the latter was conveniently away at home nursing his influenza.) 'You all know them headless fishermen chaps are living on and near the banyan tree – it's proven beyond a doubt! They are hovering over the place and looking for an innocent human to frighten to death and turn the poor fellow into a ghost too. You lot can't see them, but I can! I am blessed or cursed like Strangefellow with the ability to see ghosts. You all know it was I who first saw the headless horrors that night I visited the outhouse, but our dear, *dear* old Strangefellow can see them too. If you doubt my word that I saw and still see them headless ghost chaps, then let our good friend Strangefellow convince you! Here, let me show you how with Sonny's help!'

As planned in detail by the two plotters, Sonny emerged from the Nameless, but not without first grabbing a surprised Strangefellow – putting a leash on him and half dragging the bewildered mongrel away to the tree stump, to which he proceeded to firmly chain him. Strangefellow protested twice as much as usual at this absolutely unwarranted punishment, whining at Sonny and pulling back on the chain in an effort to get back inside the Nameless and away from the detested tree stump, his mind whirling frantically, confused as to why he was being treated thus. He hadn't gone anywhere close to the dratted fried fish on the display counter this time around and just couldn't comprehend it all. Had Master finally lost his senses? It was always on the cards that he would!

'Bloody hell! What the devil did I do, Master?' Strangefellow whined in protest. 'I was just sniffing around the floor looking for something to eat, and here you are tying me to this accursed root again! I didn't make off with any of your blooming fried fish, did I? Why are you chaining me, then? What the devil's the matter with you, Master? Have you finally gone and gotten completely bonkers?' After a few more protesting whines, he looked up at his beloved vantage spot high up on the banyan tree and then back at the Nameless, letting out a series of heart-wrenching, wolfish howls that chilled the blood of the beguiled onlookers. It was a singular sight and sound. To a man, the assembled crowd concluded that the dog was howling at the headless fishermen's ghosts which only he and Catnips possessed the prerogative to see. Catnips then put on a great show of pretended bravado. He put his special cross around his neck in a dramatic gesture and sauntered over gingerly to the banyan tree, where he stopped and pretended to engage in conversation with the unholy terrors. The watching crowd, standing well behind, looked on in shivering rapture. Catnips struck up an imaginary conversation with the ghouls, gesturing pleadingly at the onset with his wiry arms outstretched, but then accelerated his actions, pretending to be in heated argument with the headless horrors. His 'conversation' was clearly heard by the awed onlookers.

'You demons! You headless fishermen devils! You bloody beasts! I'm ordering you to leave this place at once and never come back! Go away immediately before I cut down this banyan tree and make you all a homeless lot. Away with you, in the name of the Holy One! Go back to the fires of hell from where you lot came from. This eating house and the tree is no place for horrible demons like for you!'

The crowd, utterly convinced that Strangefellow had indeed seen the dead fishermen and that Catnips could see them too, were deeply impressed, full of admiration for the latter's splendid chutzpah. Catnips then cautiously untied Strangefellow, who immediately ran out into the pathway leading to the Nameless, where he stayed for a few minutes, sniffing about earnestly for a suitable spot to calm his nerves by urinating.

Back amongst the safety of the crowd after shaking his fist in defiance at the headless ghosts in a parting gesture, Catnips boldly declared in a pretended weary voice as though he had gone through a horrendous ordeal and was thoroughly drained from talking to the dead fishermen's spirits, 'Oh, the horror! The horror! I don't how much longer I will be able to talk to these terrible chaps or hold them back. They are a difficult bunch and are not easy to get rid of. Even old Fotheringill wouldn't be able to ward them off, so horrible and fierce these chaps are. To make matters worse, my friends, the holy crosses I made are now losing their power and may soon be unable able to protect me or you lot anymore. The headless ones are gaining the upper hand day by day, increasing their power, but do not fret, my friends! I spoke to Sonny last night, and he has agreed to sell you all a few hairs from the dog, which I have placed into small envelopes for you to buy. The money all goes to the temple restoration fund. You all saw clearly how the horrors could not harm the dog although he *didn't* wear a cross and was tied so close to the tree. That's because this dog – yes, our very own Strangefellow – has been given a divine power by the Holy One. His fur will protect you against any demon, goblin, headless ghost, vampire, or whatever foul creature that dares trouble you. You may buy the fur now, as I don't know how long I can keep cutting old Strangefellow's coat. He needs his fur, you know! It protects him from the cold monsoon weather! Can't have the old chap shivering and getting sick, can we?'

The small crowd, superstitious as only Victorians can be, rushed to buy the 'holy' fur. It was like the 'holy crosses'. Sales soared, and in a matter of minutes about twenty-five small paper envelopes containing Strangefellow's fur changed hands – enthusiastically gobbled up by the more than impressed and awestruck crowd.

Strangefellow, who had re-emerged from the pathway and had missed Catnips's talk of his protective fur, was flabbergasted at the scene playing out before his eyes. He had been a good deal puzzled as to why Sonny had given him a haircut the previous evening. His master had never shown such fastidious tendencies at any time in their long acquaintance. Apart from a weekly bath and a daily brushing, Sonny never bothered to trim Strangefellow's shaggy fur or groom him any further. He always thought the 'two-legs' a mighty strange bunch, but that they coveted his old fur for some reason really surprised him.

'What the hell! Look at the two-footed fools. What the devil do they want to buy my old fur for? Why, only last week after the boy [Rohan] had given me a bath and I had gone over to the marketplace, that blooming blind beggar Pinato accidentally threw his chamber pot of old urine at me. My bloody fur still smells of two-leg urine, yet here they are, the bloody jackasses, all clamouring to buy it!'

True enough, Strangefellow did give off a strong odour of urine a few days after the incident, but the acrid smell had worn off after a day or two – at least for the substandard noses of Sonny and the rest of the bipeds. The smell, although no longer detectable in the least by humans, was still very powerful for Strangefellow's supremely sensitive canine nose. In any event, Sonny was quite used to the dog's giving off odd smells now and then. Despite his weekly bath and a rigorous brushing from Sonny every night, Strangefellow always managed to get muck on his shaggy coat during his wanderings at the marketplace – muck that he would energetically roll all over the little grassy clearing by the banyan tree to get rid of. He couldn't quite get rid of old Pinato's urine smell though through his rolling antics – it definitely needed a soapy bath! He would just have to wait until the boy bathed him again on Saturday, he mused philosophically.

Catnips repeated his deceitful charade a few times more before the bubble finally burst, as it invariably did for Catnips's countless other schemes. Soon after the 'holy fur' sales cumulated (Sonny point-blank refused to trim an inch more of Strangefellow's coat), the now widely believed dead fishermen made a joyous reappearance – not a spectral appearance this time around – but a living, breathing one.

It appeared that they had indeed been lost at sea but had survived the ordeal after being washed ashore on a tiny island, which, luckily for them, had a few coconut trees growing on it. They survived for more than five weeks on coconut water, beach crabs, and a few dead fish washed ashore by the tide. The persistent Victorian rain had followed them even to the island, helping a great deal, but when it stopped after a few weeks, there was nothing to drink, the coconut trees long since stripped of their mature nuts. Finally, when almost at the point of dehydration and half-starved besides, a passing Coast Guard vessel espied the wreckage of the marooned fishermen's boat on the island's rocks, even spotting the hapless crew on the beach signalling weakly to be rescued. Needless to say, kith and kin of the presumed lost fishermen were overjoyed to see them again, especially since Catnips had so callously declared them dead and resurrected as headless demons with stumpy necks and rotting, bulging eyes. Filled with anger at Catnips's perfidy, and mortified besides to learn they were categorised as headless ghouls haunting the banyan tree, the rescued fishermen lost no time in making their way to the Nameless. Armed with clubs and canes, they were intent on seeking out and thrashing the living daylights out of the man who had so callously stamped them deceased and added insult to injury by even branding them horrible headless demons.

Catnips was in the midst of enacting his 'talking to the headless ghosts' act, his back to the assembled crowd and his front facing the banyan tree, when the supposedly deceased fishermen made their dramatic appearance. There were five in the motley crew, and they were, to a man, hell-bent on giving Catnips the worst thrashing of his deceitful young life.

The little crowd gaped in open-mouthed wonder as the fishermen made their way into the clearing by the banyan tree, where events were in full swing. Many recognised them – not least old Karolis, who knew them all only too well. Their appearance scared the wits out of the assembly at first – many believing they were actual ghosts – but then seeing they had their heads firmly screwed onto their necks, the onlookers soon realised that these were indeed living, breathing humans, not ghostly apparitions. Catnips turned around from his position facing the banyan tree after his 'chat' with the headless horrors to face the watching crowd, hoping for the usual accolades from what he imagined was his adoring, admiring public. He recoiled in fear and surprise. The very people he had declared dead and resurrected as demons were now in the front row of the watching crowd, to all purposes and appearances very much alive and well. He wasn't slow to notice their angry faces and the clubs and canes in their hands, either. Even the rest, his adored 'fan club', had immense looks of resentment imprinted on their faces after seeing the supposed dead fishermen alive and well – resentment directed entirely at Catnips. It took them just a few seconds to realise they had been almightily duped.

Staring at the sea of hostile, angry faces in front of him, Catnips realised the game was up. There was only one thing left to do. He turned and made a bolt for it. A noted slouch and never one to indulge in physical activity of any sort, Catnips still managed to put a good hundred yards between himself and his pursuers before the angry mob gave up, seeing it was futile to give chase anymore. Strangefellow, though, had the last laugh! Excited by the furore, he too had joined in the chase of the enemy, seeing that everybody else did. It was the opportunity he had long, long been waiting for. Payback time had finally arrived! Strangefellow easily outran the chasing mob and, catching up with the fleeing Catnips, actually managed to give the latter a jolly good bite up his backside, a treat he had been promising himself for ages. Catnips let out a yelp of agony, but he didn't dare stop despite the painful bite – fleeing on with a punctured backside and a deflated ego. He would deal with that damn-blasted mongrel later on, he mused fleetingly as he sped off on mercurial wings. Strangefellow retired from the chase instantly and trotted back to the Nameless a wonderfully satiated dog – a lifelong dream fulfilled. He proudly carried a small piece of Catnips's trousers in between his teeth which he later on buried very carefully in a secluded spot beside his beloved banyan tree amongst other odd treasures he coveted.

Catnips didn't show his face at the Nameless (or anywhere else at Jellicoe Junction, for that matter) for nearly six months afterwards, his position utterly untenable. Gradually, though, after matters had died down considerably, he crept back once more into the sanctuary of the eating house, although he did shun the fish market and its vicinity forever. Those amongst the breakfast-eaters who had bought his 'holy' merchandise demanded, and got their money back, as did many others whom Catnips did meet up with eventually. It wasn't a major debacle refunding the money. Catnips had plenty, but he had lost a lot of face. He airily dismissed his outrageous trickery to cronies at the Nameless, saying it was all an innovative scheme to make a spot of money. 'And what was wrong with that?' he asked boldly. It was a hard world, he insisted with a pretended knowing air, and one had to do whatever necessary to live in it. The breakfast-eaters listened to him, shaking their heads resignedly. Catnips was Catnips! There was just no end to his mischievous lies and incorrigibility; they knew this only too well. In retrospect, they found it hard to believe that they had been duped by their innovative, lying colleague *yet* again.

The breakfast-eaters never suspected Sonny of being in cahoots with Catnips over the selling of the holy fur or anything remotely connected to the scandalous affair. As expected, Catnips was roundly castigated for the whole charade, although his fellow breakfast eaters and the crowds that had come to see him in action 'talking' to the headless horrors weren't quite ready as yet to totally abandon their beliefs in ghosts and ghouls. Nobody could definitely say that Catnips *hadn't* seen headless ghosts that fateful night at the outhouse. Perhaps he *had* really seen ghosts – headless or otherwise – and it wasn't just the blowing wisps of the banyan tree's vines. Certain places are imbued with light and dark sides, and banyan trees were well documented in Victorian folklore for harbouring ghosts and other strange things.

Life went on as usual at Grandmummy's in the days immediately after Christmas Day, but not for the old Dragon, who hadn't quite finished her celebrations as yet. Grandmummy spent Boxing Day in the company or her secret friend and suspected paramour, old Mr

Macmillan, and was quite buoyant for at least a week thereafter, as was her wont after these very special annual visits.

'Look at the old sex goddess,' sniggered Celeste to Primrose and a listening Rebecca after Grandmummy had come back. 'Got her damn mojo running again, the horny old cow!'

'You stop that vulgar talk at once, you hear, Celeste! Mr Macmillan is Mummy's closest friend. She just visits him at Christmas to have a chat and lunch. What's wrong with that?'

'Huh! Christmas lunch and a chat, eh? You're a naive fool, Primrose. Hasn't that damn Giles of yours taught you anything yet? The woman's going over to that old Englishman's place to have her old "thingie" serviced, that's what!'

'Shut up, Celeste,' butted in Rebecca, incensed by her sister's insinuations. She had grown to dislike her mother immensely these past two years, but she wasn't prepared to hear her slandered so atrociously. 'One word more and I'll tell Mother myself what you have been saying.'

Celeste backed off, but not without giving Rebecca and Primrose a withering look of disdain.

Alone, to herself, Rebecca pondered gloomily. She was getting increasingly desperate over the fact that Rainier hadn't contacted her for so long. After all, the man had been gone for two years now – a really long two years. Rebecca doubted her ability to continue leading the kind of life she led. Her patience with Grandmummy, her sisters, and her demanding supervisor at work had almost run out, contributing enormously to her unhappiness, which grew in leaps and bounds with each passing day. The children's health and well-being also constantly worried her, as did the nagging prospect of a fast-approaching mental breakdown.

All through the two years Rebecca was left high and dry, there was no word forthcoming from Rainier. Nobody seemed to know his exact whereabouts, although he was rumoured now and then in recent times to have been spotted in the vicinity of the large commercial business houses at Coronation Park. Although the embezzlement case against him was thrown out of court for lack of proper evidence, he had quite a fight on his hands to make any sort of comeback in another establishment, courtesy of his former employer's vicious colluding tactics. Annoyed over Rainier's acquittal, they cruelly and collectively schemed to persuade other major commercial establishments in Portopo to refuse Rainier a new billing. He was effectively and conclusively blackballed.

At last, one day, Rainier's run of bad luck finally changed for the better. Matters took on a new and unexpected twist. Through the diligent and astute detective work of an ambitious new inspector at Portopo's criminal investigation department, the police were able to prove beyond any shadow of doubt that it was one of Rainier's superiors in the firm he had been employed at who had done the actual embezzling *Rainier* was accused and tried for at the Portopo assizes. At long last, Rainier's torturous exile had come to an end. The industrial courts, armed with the new evidence in hand, castigated Rainier's former employers in no uncertain terms, further manifesting their displeasure by effectively ordering the latter to pay Rainier a substantial sum of money in compensation. None of this state of affairs reached the ears of Rebecca, though. The original furore and interest in the case had long since cooled, and the press had lost interest – although later on, when the story did break, Rainier's triumph did made the headlines. Despite his sudden change of fortune, Rainier did not make any move to get his family back and his life on track again – at least not as yet. Knowing that his compensation money wouldn't last forever, he concentrated his efforts instead on first and foremost finding a solid position in another commercial company before buying or renting a decent house and reuniting with his little family. Rainier's former employers, the very same who brought on the hastily trumped-up charges against him in the first instance, pompously offered him reinstatement, but he was having none of it, scorning their offer in no uncertain terms. Rainier wanted revenge – to hurt his former employers as much as they callously hurt and disgraced him – and revenge was what he eventually got, at least partially. He succeeded in wounding them where it hurt most. Contacting an international motor company chain recently established at Portopo, he presented the board of directors with a brilliant and brand-new revolutionary business concept at a special meeting. Rainier was a past master in business methods. He could sell sand to an Arab. So good was his presentation and so brilliant was his new concept that he was immediately employed – on the spot – as working director with a salary almost double that he earned earlier. His new idea was so effective that it 'stole' more than half the clients away from his former employers, almost obliterating their business in the process and expunging them from their position as top dogs in the motor industry.

Sadhu wasn't slow to comment on it all when the story of Rainier's success reached the ears of the breakfast-eaters. 'It's all karma, my dears. Everything is written, you know! You can't escape karma! See how the false accusers became the victims! See how the wheel of life whirls out its eventual justice! There is no place to hide from karma, my friends. Karma will always get you!'

When Rainier met Uncle Pongo at the Nameless that famous rainy and 'ghostly' night, he was a fully rejuvenated man, once again in full possession of his sharp mental faculties and in perfect harmony with life. All throughout the humiliating and tenebrous two years he was down and out, he had maintained regular contact with Uncle Pongo, swearing the old man to secrecy as to his whereabouts. It was through Uncle Pongo that he got regular reports of Rebecca and the children's situation at Grandmummy's. There were dark moments when Rainier would actually cry upon hearing a particular bad account from Uncle Pongo, the helplessness of his situation engulfing him, although his spirit could never be broken.

Some time after Rainier had so dramatically appeared at the Nameless; Uncle Pongo burst into Grandmummy's house and excitedly pulled a surprised Rebecca into a corner, indicating he wanted to speak in private. Grandmummy, as usual, ignored his arrival, not bothering to greet him, inquire why he had come, or ask whom he wanted to see. Strangely enough, for all the animosity the Dragon showed Uncle Pongo, she still allowed him a free run of the house, but that was as far as she would go, never condescending even once to speak to him. She ignored her only brother at all times as though he was evil personified. The cruel ostracising was bizarre, something that raised many an eyebrow but never got an explanation.

The very sight of Uncle Pongo – the only person known to have any contact with Rainier after his disappearance – always raised a glimmer of hope in Rebecca's heart. Uncle Pongo cautioned Rebecca into silence by putting a finger over his lips, all the while keeping a wary eye out for Grandmummy – even peering around inquiringly to see if Celeste and Primrose were close at hand. Satisfied that no one was within earshot to eavesdrop, he said excitedly, 'Rebecca! Rebecca, my dear, I have some information for you from Rainier.'

Rebecca's heart skipped a beat. She said breathlessly with a sharp recoil, 'Rainier? What! What! Where is he? Is he all right? Has anything happened to him? Why has he contacted you and not me? What information? What did he say?' The words gushed out in a torrent from the fully roused and anxious Rebecca.

Uncle Pongo stuttered and stammered a few times before breaking out clearly. 'Oh! Old Rainier's all right. Nothing bad has happened to him. I met him at the Nameless recently, and he told me he has got himself a top job at that large car import and engineering place they opened after Christmas near the sports stadium. He's the big-shot working director and all that at the new place, and them foreign owner chaps have given him a new car for free and a large house at King George's Avenue. Old Rainier's even given *me* a new job there as chief security officer.' He bridled with pride at the last part of his revelations, immensely happy about his new employment and title.

Rebecca gasped in open-mouth wonder. King George's Avenue was the most exclusive living area at Jellicoe Junction, and the new company Uncle Pongo mentioned was much talked about in Portopo circles. She knew her husband was a clever man and always felt deep within that he would somehow, someday, arise like an avenging phoenix and recover his former position and glory, but this bit of news surpassed even her wildest dreams and hopes.

Uncle Pongo continued. 'Old Rainier told me to tell you to pack your things and be ready tomorrow evening, when he will drive over here and take you all to the new house. He also said that you need not bother to go to that blooming job of yours anymore, so you can stay at home all day tomorrow. The children are still at home for the Christmas holidays, so they can help you. He said that you are not to tell Clotilde anything, as he will speak with her himself.' (Clotilde was Grandmummy's first name. Very few besides Uncle Pongo referred to her thus.)

Rebecca could scarcely contain herself. It was like a dream come true. Faith in her husband had kept her going these past two years enduring every insult that Grandmummy and her haughty younger sisters had thrown at her, fiercely determined that all would be well someday soon. Here at last was redemption for all the tribulation she had gone through, and what redemption it was! A new job! Working director! A new car! And a house at the grandest address at Jellicoe Junction! She hugged Uncle Pongo and sobbed in his arms, tears streaming down her cheeks – tears of joy more than anything else.

Rebecca broke the news to the children that very same day after dinner. Rohan jumped for joy and hugged his mother – Laura following suit. Little Sussie did not understand much of what was going on, but knowing her little family had a good thing going, joined in the celebrations. The only person having misgivings about the impending reunion was Mahan, who realised that his superstar status at Grandmummy's was doomed and would now clearly come to an end. He had enjoyed being lionised by Grandmummy and the young aunts these past two years and couldn't help being torn between two loyalties. Although he loved his father very much and, like the others, secretly hoped for his return, he would sorely miss the very special attention he had become accustomed to. It was a no-win situation – a catch-22 moment of his very own...

After dinner, the family started packing amidst loud laughter and a general feeling of carefree happiness. For Rebecca, Rohan, and Laura, it was more a state of ecstasy rather than happiness. Grandmummy, who had only now observed what they were engaged in, was startled, to say the least. It was rarely the Dragon was taken off guard. She was such a busybody that nothing going on in the lives of her minions usually bypassed her astute observations.

'What are you lot all packing for? You going somewhere? Was that why that damn useless bloody Pongo was here this morning? Is it one of that fool's eternal church feasts in some godforsaken village parish again? What village and what church is it this time?'

Uncle Pongo was addicted to attending church feats and celebrations all over the country. He loved to camp in the open, to live life in the rough at religious festivities, often inviting Rebecca and the children to come along. While the others accepted, Mahan, Grandmummy's biggest supporter, always staunchly declined. Like Grandmummy and the aunts, he did not approve of Uncle Pongo, although he had no earthly reason to. He just followed his favourite adults' example like the true little sycophant he was.

Grandmummy's inquiring words bored a hole into Rebecca's head. Right now, even at this exalted moment, she couldn't help but remember the ignominious treatment she had suffered at the hands of her mother the past two years, deciding to be hard as nails in her moment of triumph. Payback time was long overdue... She knew nothing angered her mother more than being ignored when asked a direct question, so she intentionally declined to answer, continuing her packing as though she didn't care an iota for her mother's query.

Grandmummy, used to instant obeisance, was thoroughly vexed by Rebecca's seemingly lack of response. However, thinking perhaps that Rebecca hadn't really heard her the first time, she demanded to know once more – in a harsh voice now – why they were packing. This time around, Rebecca shifted her attention from what she was doing and answered, a sweet and serene look upon her face. She yearned to annoy and surprise her mother, to hurt her as much as she herself had been hurt many countless times before.

'Why are we packing, eh? Why are we packing? Why, Mother dearest! We are packing because we are leaving this damn-blasted hole of yours tomorrow! My beloved Rainier is coming to take us all away from this wretched, stinking place!'

Grandmummy's jaw dropped at this phenomenally surprising bit of news and her daughter's sudden rudeness. She had gotten quite used to Rebecca and the children living with her, especially Mahan and Rohan, the latter doing numerous marketing and other chores for her. In her twisted way, she would miss Rebecca too, whom she had increasingly persecuted in the latter's helpless position, a kind of warped persecution – cruel and bizarre. Apart from timid Primrose, Rebecca and the children were the only persons she could totally roll over and treat as she pleased. True, she dominated almost everyone else as well, but they didn't live under her roof and weren't at her beck and call as Rebecca and the children were. As for Primrose, Grandmummy knew the girl would get married to Giles soon and move out – one less person to dominate. Celeste might just go and do the same with Don, and even if she didn't, there was no way that Grandmummy could dominate *that* young firebrand! There would be nobody left to boss around, to totally submit to her will, if even Rebecca and the children left! Slightly shell-shocked and dumbfounded, Grandmummy spoke up, her lips quivering uneasily in harmony with her shaking double chin.

'Rainier's coming back? Why? For what? That damn fellow doesn't even have a job now. He hasn't a bean! How on earth is he going to support you people? Where are you all going to live? Do you have any idea how expensive it is to pay rent for a decent house these days? How are you lot going to manage without my help?'

Rebecca had finally manoeuvred herself into a position where she could say all the things bottled within herself – things she could not say before for fear of being thrown out together with the children, or perhaps with just Rohan, Laura, and little Sussie. She was angry now and lashed out with feeling. 'Listen, Mother. Listen very carefully. Rainier's got a very good job again. He has a new car, a big house at King George's Avenue, and everything else now. We no longer need to stay in your damn-blasted house and be treated like servants and slaves. Yes, you took us in, all right, and gave us shelter, but I'm never going to forget how you ill-treated me, little Sussie, Laura, and Rohan. I'm never going to forget how you kept telling me over and over that Rainier was a no-good rogue and that he was never going to come back. I won't forget how my children were given just ten cents a day to buy tiny breakfasts while you ate your nice things from your food safe and Celeste and Primrose flaunted their heavy breakfasts right under our noses. I'm never going to forget how you frequently scolded me in front of my younger sisters, my children, and everybody else. I am going to tell Rainier that we never again shall step into your bloody house – never darken your damn doorstep. Never, never, never!'

Grandmummy was flabbergasted by this mega-onslaught. Never before, not even in her wildest dreams, had the otherwise docile Rebecca spoken to her with so much venom and spirit. She squirmed at the telling accusations, feeling profoundly guilty over the veritable darts that had gone home with such unerring accuracy.

'Bah!' she said after being dumbstruck a full minute, haughtily mustering whatever dignity she had left. 'Go, then! Go and live with that useless husband of yours again, but don't you come running back if anything happens! Go and live with that damn rascal! What do I care?'

Rebecca answered coolly, without rancour or anger this time around. She was once again the serene Rebecca of old. There was confidence in her tone, a new zest in her body language. 'Not a chance of us coming back here again, Mother. Not a blooming chance! We are never going to come to this awful damn hellhole again – never!'

'Tchah!' exclaimed Grandmummy. 'Do what you damn well like. See if I care! I still say that husband of yours is no good. Mark my words – the fellow will do something criminal again. Once a criminal, always a criminal!' She found some solace in the words she uttered and didn't say anything more to Rebecca, waddling off to the kitchen to make herself a cup of Ovaltine before retiring for the night. She was very much shaken by the jarring news she had just heard and also by Rebecca's rightful accusations – not knowing quite how to relate or what to make of it all...

Celeste and Primrose, who had listened to all that had transpired, went about their business sheepishly, avoiding looking directly at Rebecca. Unlike the Dragon, who was more angry at Rebecca's harsh words than remorseful, they felt guilty and very *much* remorseful over the atrocious treatment they had meted out to their sister these past two years. The sisters had never expected Rainier to come back – not even in their wildest dreams. They had a cruel streak in them, did Primrose and Celeste, something definitely inherited from their idiosyncratic old mother and not innate.

Rebecca's two-year torturous tenure at Grandmummy's was definitely a sort of Cinderella saga, with Primrose and Celeste ideally the two very cruel stepsisters and Grandmummy the scheming and cruel stepmother. It was hard to find a fairy godmother in the story, but perhaps Uncle Pongo fitted the bill best, even though his gender was wrong. He had all along supported and comforted Rebecca. Even now, in the final throes of the saga, he was a bearer of good tidings.

The next day, the exact twelfth day of Christmas, Rainier arrived as promised, looking sleek and spruce dressed in an immaculate suit of light flannel. He shone with elegance, his neat moustache trimmed, his hair well groomed and glossy. He arrived in a brand-new Mercedes station wagon, an eloquent, impressive machine that both thrilled and impressed young Rohan and Mahan immensely. Bouncing buoyantly up the steps leading to the crooked old house, he nodded briefly at Grandmummy, who was sitting on an armchair at her favourite vantage point in the front veranda, before walking up directly to Rebecca, whom he hugged with a great deal of feeling. There was much embracing and kissing between Rainier, Rebecca, and the children, even little Sussie seemingly remembering her long-lost father. Rohan pasted himself onto Rainier, looking on in utter adulation at his adored parent. He couldn't bear to tear himself away from his father, clinging to the latter's waist and leg like a leech, not letting go.

Meanwhile, Grandmummy, fuming at Rainier's all-too-brief nod of acknowledgement, felt slighted and sidetracked. She decided to have a regal go at the 'enemy' she had so often derided in the past.

'Huh!' she spat out. 'Here you come marching in like a damn big shot without even speaking two words to me! *Me,* who took good care of your bloody family these past two years whilst you went gallivanting to God knows where! If it were not for me, them children and that wife of yours would have all starved to death or had no place to live, yet you come strolling in here without having the bloody decency to greet me or even thank me for taking care of them.'

Rainier wasn't taken aback an iota by this harsh and volatile salvo. He knew perfectly well how his wife and family were treated at Grandmummy's; Uncle Pongo's accurate reports the past two years had revealed all. He answered calmly, a wry expression lighting up his otherwise debonair countenance. 'Yes, yes, Clotilde. You gave them shelter, all right, but don't talk of anything else. I know all what happened here. Old Pongo told me what I needed to know. You gave my growing young boys and Laura a miserable ten cents each day to buy breakfast – that's all you did. You, with all that bloody income of yours through your pension, your wine, and the monies you get from your son and daughters. You even made those young boys do all the marketing, carrying heavy bags of groceries all the way from the marketplace and back, and you frequently even struck my boy Rohan. How *dare* you strike him! How dare you! I have never even once laid a hand on my children all the years we lived together, but to you it came very easily, didn't it? And tell me – why did you stop old Sakkala's services when the boys came to stay with you, eh? Why? Let me tell you why! It was because you wanted to save a few measly rupees, wasn't it? You humiliated the boys! Rohan's just twelve! Pongo told me how the lad often staggered under the damn weight of that bloody marketing bag laden with your precious mangoes and things. *Your* damn marketing list was twice as long as my dear Rebecca's.'

Rainier paused dramatically to light a cigarette and then went on. 'My poor innocent little Sussie was never given any of your fine fancy food which you keep hidden away in that damn food cupboard of yours, while Celeste's child got everything. You realise how that would feel to a four-year-old girl? You also always nagged Rebecca at every little chance you got and forced her to cook separate pathetic meals for her and the children, besides bad-mouthing me to her face at every damn opportunity you got.'

Grandmummy's mouth opened and closed under this bombardment like a goldfish's, totally unable to produce a sentence in her defence – struck dumb yet again.

'Here,' said Rainier, continuing in the same scathing fashion whilst pulling out his wallet from his inner coat pocket. 'Here, take this two thousand rupees. It will cover Rebecca's rent for these past two years, your pathetic damn ten cents for the children's breakfast, and much, much more. Have yourself a ball. Knock your damn self out, you horrid woman!' He tossed a wad of currency notes onto his surprised mother-in-law's lap. It was a small fortune, and Grandmummy instantly knew it. She decided to swallow her pride and accept the money.

'Let them all go,' she thought resignedly. 'Who needs them?' The wad of currency notes felt good to touch. It had been ages since she had seen this much money on a single occasion.

Rebecca and Rainier did not say anything more to Grandmummy, even curtly brushing aside all attempts by Celeste and Primrose to say goodbye, snubbing the duo openly. Rohan, who detested his two aunts more than anyone else, could not curb his instincts. He stuck out his tongue at the sisters and stuck it extra longer at Primrose, whom he detested the most. Mahan, in contrast, was all over his aunts and Grandmummy, almost smothering them with warm parting hugs, which were more than generously reciprocated.

Their bags safely deposited in the spacious boot of the new car, the family drove off to their new home and new life. They took Poppsy along with them, the little dog wagging his tail madly in gratitude and excitement.

The smell of new leather upholstery in the car and the lavishness of its interior thrilled Rohan and Mahan. Laura, for her part, cared nought about the car, being more relieved instead about the prospect of having her very own room once again – something she sorely lacked whilst staying at Grandmummy's.

Rainier took some time to get his parked car going because of the excessive evening traffic. After he had started the engine and the car stood immobile a few minutes, Rohan looked back through the cars rear windscreen at the old house that had so many strange and even downright bad memories for him. Bongo, the fruit seller, had just arrived and was already cringing and lamenting over Grandmummy's haggling for a scandalous price reduction, as was her wont. The gormless street vendor had a morbid fascination for Grandmummy. Although he knew stopping over at the Dragon's lair meant a dent in his profits, he couldn't help doing so, secretly addicted to the regular showdowns with his nemesis. In a twisted, perverted sort of way, he even enjoyed the almost one-sided banter they engaged in. It was as though the old lady had a hypnotic effect on him. Haranguing now as she did with Bongo and doing the thing she loved best, Grandmummy had already put away some of her disappointment over Rebecca and the children's abrupt departure.

Rohan sighed to himself as Rainier finally got going and Grandmummy and Bongo slowly disappeared from view. He felt a bit like Alice in Wonderland waking up from her dream to see the playing cards and other characters fading away in the distance: the queen, the king, the Cheshire cat, the hookah-smoking caterpillar, the Mad Hatter, and everyone and everything else disappearing into oblivion – a dream – a nonentity. His truncated two-year stay at Grandmummy's seemed like a mad tea party of its own, surreal yet an actual part of his life – a part he would never forget, for all the wrong reasons. In spite of everything, he would still miss his fierce old grandmother's eccentric ways, Baking Jane's friendly banter, the crude old eating houses, the breakfast-buying expeditions, and not least Strangefellow and the rough-and-tough clientele at the Nameless. As the car sped on past the marketplace and a bit beyond, the little eating house came into view. Rohan had a parting glimpse of an irritated Sonny shaking his fist and rebuking Strangefellow, who was reposing high up in his favourite vantage point on the banyan tree, safely away from Sonny's verbal bombardments. In all likelihood, Strangefellow had stolen a whole fried fish and gobbled it up, scrambling up the tree to avoid punishment. A few of the breakfast-eaters also came into view seated on the long bench outside the Nameless, seemingly engaged in one of their never-ending feisty palavers. Parting company with Strangefellow especially caused an immense pang of sadness in young Rohan's heart. He loved the funny old mongrel and was determined to ask his father's permission to continue his dog-bathing chores at the Nameless, where he could bond with his canine charge again. He had no doubt in his mind that Rainier would say yes. Perhaps he could even take Poppsy along too, seeing how the two dogs bonded so well together. It would be a treat for both dogs; he knew that instinctively.

The headless ghosts hovering over the ancient banyan tree that Catnips, to his dying day, claimed to have seen, approved benignantly as Rainier's brand-new car sped by. High above in the bright blue sky, a cloud in the form of a grinning Cheshire cat looked down in devilish amusement upon the magical little clearing around the banyan tree, the colourful breakfast-eaters, and Strangefellow, the undisputed king of all mongrels.